After an eventful career as a spin doctor to the powerful, rich and notorious, Quintin Jardine found that his talents were equally well fitted to the world of crime fiction. He is the author of the Oz Blackstone mysteries in addition to the Bob Skinner crime novels.

His interests are playing football, watching football, talking about football and watching golf. He lives, as quietly as his nature will allow, in Scotland and in Spain.

DEAD AND BURIED

Murder usually follows its own unique, twisted logic. Deputy Chief Constable Bob Skinner has a failed marriage and a death on his conscience. However, he faces the biggest challenge of his career within the secret corridors where dark power is wielded. As his hunt develops, he goes to the top — the Prime Minister — lest he himself becomes collateral damage. Meanwhile, in Edinburgh, Skinner's daughter is being stalked. Can he protect her? A bookmaker taking one gamble too many has paid his debt in a gruesome fashion. Is it an underworld vendetta, or something more sinister? Then, Skinner believes he's discovered a bigamist at work — or is it something worse? Four crimes, four crises: can Skinner and his people solve them? Indeed, can they survive them?

Books by Quintin Jardine
Published by The House of Ulverscroft:

THE BOB SKINNER SERIES:
SKINNER'S ORDEAL
SKINNER'S MISSION
SKINNER'S GHOSTS
MURMURING THE JUDGES
GALLERY WHISPERS
THURSDAY LEGENDS
AUTOGRAPHS IN THE RAIN
HEAD SHOT
STAY OF EXECUTION
LETHAL INTENT

THE OZ BLACKSTONE SERIES:
A COFFIN FOR TWO
WEARING PURPLE
SCREEN SAVERS
POISONED CHERRIES
UNNATURAL JUSTICE
ALARM CALL
FOR THE DEATH OF ME

QUINTIN JARDINE

DEAD AND BURIED

Complete and Unabridged

CHARNWOOD
Leicester

First published in Great Britain in 2006 by
Headline Book Publishing
London

First Charnwood Edition
published 2007
by arrangement with
Headline Book Publishing
a division of Hodder Headline
London

British Library CIP Data

Jardine, Quintin
    Dead and buried.—Large print ed.—
Charnwood library series
    1. Skinner, Bob (Fictitious character)—Fiction
    2. Police—Scotland—Edinburgh—Fiction
    3. Detective and mystery stories
    4. Large type books
    I. Title
    823.9'14 [F]

    ISBN 978–1–84617–615–9

Published by
F. A. Thorpe (Publishing)
Anstey, Leicestershire

Set by Words & Graphics Ltd.
Anstey, Leicestershire
Printed and bound in Great Britain by
T. J. International Ltd., Padstow, Cornwall
This book is printed on acid-free paper

Once again, this is for my lady, my gem, my lovely wife, the impeccable Eileen, who never did anything remotely bad enough to warrant ending up with me, but who tolerates me nonetheless.
Thank you now and always, honey.

1

'Where did we get to?'

Bob Skinner blinked as he spoke. 'I'm sorry, Kevin, what was that? I let myself drift away there. It must be too damned warm in here. Is that one of your head-shrinker's tricks?'

The man opposite gazed back at him, a half-smile flicking a corner of his mouth. He made a faint sound that might have been a sigh; but then again, probably not, more likely only a simple drawing of breath. Kevin O'Malley was famous for his patience, that unshakeable, remorseless patience which made it virtually impossible to evade his questions, or to answer them in anything other than direct terms.

The deputy chief constable envied him: his own interrogation technique, successful as it had proved over the years, was based on relentless psychological pressure, rather than compassion. He guessed that in the weeks to come, he might find himself trying to adopt some of the consultant psychiatrist's methods.

'I asked you to think back to the other times you've had to use a firearm on duty.'

'Times?'

'We've had this conversation before, remember.'

'Sure, I remember.' Skinner scowled at him. 'They say I'm smart, Kevin, but when I drafted the standing order that requires all officers to

1

have counselling whenever they've been involved in a shooting incident, I didn't have the bloody wit to add, 'apart from me'!'

'What have you got against counselling, Bob?'

'You know bloody well, for I've told you often enough. I don't like anyone rummaging inside my head.'

'Maybe not, but . . . '

'But nothing . . . '

O'Malley's smile seemed slightly at odds with the look in his eye. 'But plenty: you've had a crisis with buried secrets in the past. There were things in there that you weren't admitting, even to yourself.'

'That's in the past. There's nothing I can't cope with, not any more.'

'So answer my last question.'

'It wasn't a question. You asked me to think back.'

'So do it.'

'I'm doing it.'

O'Malley waited.

'There was the time when we had the Syrian president in Edinburgh and some people had a go at him.'

'Yes. And you shot one of them.'

'I did. Not long after that there was an incident in the castle. I was there and armed, and I had to fire again. I hit him too.'

'Both these people died?'

'The first one died at the scene; the second was only wounded, but he died later in hospital, not directly of his wounds, something to do with the treatment . . . something about an embolism, as I recall.'

'But were you trying to kill him?'

'I was trying to render him harmless. Since he was pointing a fucking Uzi at me at the time, that did call for something pretty terminal.'

'And this most recent episode?'

'There was a situation; I had no choice but to fire.'

'Were you in mortal danger yourself?'

'No, but someone else was. I fired, I hit, the captive got away.'

'The person you shot this time, did he die?'

'Yes, but I'm not sure whether I killed him or not. His group escaped in a boat, which was later taken out by RAF action. They found three bodies, but it was a Humpty Dumpty situation.'

'What do you mean?'

'I mean that putting all the pieces back together was an impossible job.'

'I see.'

Uncharacteristically, O'Malley frowned, as if the words had conjured up a vision that he would rather not have seen. He took a sip from the coffee cup on his table as he looked at his patient.

'What are you thinking, Kevin?' Skinner asked him.

'You tell me.'

'You're thinking that for someone who's admitting to having shot three human beings, I'm remarkably self-possessed. You're thinking that you've examined psychopaths who reacted to their actions much as I have.'

3

'Crimes.'

'What?'

'Who reacted to their crimes: you avoided the use of the word.'

'So?'

'Do you feel remorse for these three deaths? Do you ever have nightmares?'

'Do their faces come back to haunt me, d'you mean?'

'Something like that.'

'In truth, Kevin, I don't remember what any of them even looked like. The last one I never saw, other than through a night-sight . . . and then only the back of him.' The DCC paused. 'Look, I have the odd bad dream, but they're not like I'm haunted. My nightmares are usually about what would have happened if things had gone the other way, if my gun had jammed, or if I'd missed my shot.'

'Doesn't that make you worry that you might be a psychopathic personality?'

A ball of almost tangible tension seemed to hang in the air as Skinner stared at his inquisitor . . . Then it vanished, as he laughed.

'Bollocks, man, I'm no such thing. I react to situations in the way I'm trained to; that doesn't make me a psycho. And you know why it doesn't just as well as I do . . . at least I hope you do. It's because I care, Kevin. I care about society, I love my family, and I fear the impact on them if anything happened to me. That's what gives me the strength to deal with these things, not some inner voice that says, 'Hey, I've got a gun and a licence to shoot that bastard!'

4

Don't be fucking crazy, man.'

'I'm a psychiatrist,' O'Malley retorted. 'Of course I'm crazy, we all get that way in the end. Don't worry, Bob, your self-analysis is spot on. If it wasn't, I'd be in a difficult position, for when I report to the chief constable I'd have to recommend that you never had a firearm placed in your hand again, and maybe even that you were compulsorily retired.'

'Some might thank you for that, but Sir James Proud wouldn't . . . I hope.'

'It's not long to his own retirement, so I guess that losing you is the last thing he'd want.' The psychiatrist paused. 'Getting back on topic, Bob, we've dealt with the effect this and other incidents have had on you, but what about your family? How has your wife dealt with them, and Alex, your daughter?'

Skinner's eyes narrowed. 'I'm not sure that it is 'on topic'. Why do you ask?'

Again, O'Malley seemed to lose a little of his self-possession; he shifted in his chair. 'Come on, Bob,' he protested. 'My concern is with your total welfare, and your ability to function in a very responsible job. If people close to you are damaged by what's happening to you, it's relevant.'

'Like hell it is. My family life is my own business, for better or worse. Did you ask Neil McIlhenney or Bandit Mackenzie that same question when you interviewed them?'

'Yes, I did, and they both gave me straight answers, unlike you.'

'What did they say?'

5

'Don't try to shift the ground. That'll be included in my reports to you, as far as it's relevant. It's you I want to talk about.'

'Why?' Skinner demanded again. 'Have you been hearing things?' From nowhere, there was suspicion in his voice. 'Has Jimmy been talking to you?'

'Bob, I haven't a clue what you mean by that.' O'Malley seemed genuinely surprised. 'Maybe we should move on from psychopathology and consider paranoia.'

'No, let's not do that. You just touched on a sensitive area in my private life, that's all.'

'Do you want to talk about it? Indeed, can you talk about it?'

'Ah, you know both of us, so I don't see why not. The fact is, Kevin, that Sarah and I are splitting up; she's leaving me and going to set up a medical practice in New York. Mind you,' he rushed to add, 'her decision has nothing to do with the stuff you're talking about. This is something that's been brewing for a while.'

'What about your children? I assume they'll be going with their mother.'

'Then you're assuming wrong. We're sharing custody; Mark, James Andrew, and Seonaid will live with me during the school term and spend their holidays with Sarah.'

'How do you feel about this?'

Skinner shrugged his shoulders, an awkward movement since he was seated. 'I feel as well as can be expected: that would sum it up. I hate failure in any form, but failing at marriage is just about the worst. We're both being very civilised

6

about it, though. A confrontational divorce wouldn't help anyone.'

'You mean it wouldn't help your career?'

'Do me a favour, mate! That hasn't occurred to me at all. Since you ask, I don't think it would harm it, but that's not an issue. Neither is the fact that Sarah's a hell of a lot wealthier than I am since her parents died. If we do a conventional property split, I'd be the winner, but we won't. No, the kids come first and that's it.'

'You're quite sure this has nothing to do with the areas we've been discussing?'

'I said so, didn't I?' the DCC snapped irritably. 'Things have happened between us.'

'There's been a third party?'

'Over the years? Third parties, on both sides, to be honest: mine even made the lower end of the tabloid market, remember.'

'I was trying not to. Okay, you haven't been a paragon. Is that why Sarah's going?'

The big man shook his grey-maned head. 'No, she's much better at forgiving than I am. I suppose that's it. She had an affair in the States a while back. I've had trouble dealing with that.'

'Why?'

'Why have I had trouble?' Skinner's voice had an air of incredulity.

'No, no. That's a male ego thing, typical behaviour, nothing unusual about that. Why did Sarah have an affair?'

'Ask her. Ask her about the other times as well.'

'How many?'

7

'Okay, just one other . . . that I know of. It happened that first time we were separated, and I was, I was . . . Let's just say I don't blame her too much for that. This one? Why? I don't know why. She found the other fellow attractive, and they were far from strangers to each other. They'd been close at college, then gone their separate ways. Maybe she'd been carrying an Ever Ready for him all along. Or maybe it was just like she said, that I'd left her out there on her own when she needed me.'

'Or maybe she just found him safe,' said O'Malley, quietly.

'Safe?'

'Yes, Bob, safe. I've interviewed more than a few police officers' wives in my time. Their stories all have the same thread running through them. 'When he goes out the door in the morning in that uniform, I can never be one hundred per cent sure that he's coming back.' That's what they all wind up saying, one way or another. Okay, there may be little or no statistical basis for their anxiety, but that doesn't make it any the less real.'

'If she was after safety, she got it wrong, big-time. He's dead.'

'That's too bad, but it doesn't affect what I'm saying.' He paused again. 'Bob, the women I'm talking about, they're the wives of ordinary officers, people on the beat, in office jobs, even. You are not one of those people. Look at the things that have happened to you; man, you're a lightning rod for trouble, and still you go charging out into the worst thunderstorms. But

8

the irony of it is that you don't have to. You're a deputy chief constable, for God's sake. You're in the Command Corridor; you have a desk job, yet you still go out there, whenever you can from what I gather, into the line of fire. You go on about how much you care for your family, and I believe you, but did you ever stop to consider how much the professional choices you've been taking might be harming Sarah?' The psychiatrist let out a long sigh. 'I wasn't going to bring this up, but you did. She left you once before, as you've just said. Didn't you get the message then? Not at all?'

Skinner started out of his chair. For a moment, it seemed that he would explode in anger, but he settled back down, with a calm, sad look in his eyes.

'If not me, who?' he asked.

'Pardon?'

'Don't go dumb on me, Kevin. The operation I've just been on: how much do you know about it?'

'I know as much as was in my brief for these interviews, and what I've read in the papers. Why? Was there more to it than that?'

'That's irrelevant. My question is, if I hadn't been there to lead it, who else could have done it and seen it through to success?'

'The army?'

'No time: it all happened too fast.'

'Andy Martin?'

'He wasn't there.'

'McIlhenney?'

'Close, but no; there was only me, Kevin. And

if I hadn't stood up, then and on all those other times you mentioned, what would the consequences have been? Innocent lives would have been lost for a start, lives that I've sworn an oath to protect. You're telling me that's had an effect on my wife? Of course it bloody has: it's had an effect on me too. But it's my job. Yes, I do it my way, but it's the only way I know how to, and I cannot run away from it before my time is up. As I said, if I do have a nightmare, it's about not living to see my kids grow up. But if I turn my back on my duty . . . that's what it is, Kevin, my duty, not just another job . . . who's going to protect them, and others like them?'

'Come on, man, you're part of a team.'

'No, I'm the leader of a team, a very special team, and I do my best to lead by example; always have, always will.'

'You're addicted to it, to the danger.'

'Maybe I am, but if so, that's what makes me so fucking good at it.'

The unexpected grin made O'Malley blink. 'Maybe you're thinking,' Skinner chuckled, 'that you could save my marriage by declaring me off the wall, by giving me a psychological red card. If so, forget it; if Sarah can't live with me in the job, then without it I couldn't live with her, for a bit of me . . . no, all of me . . . would always blame her for forcing me out of it while there was still work for me to do. Anyway, she doesn't love me any more.'

'You're not the man she married, you mean?'

'Ah, but I am, that's the problem.'

'Do you love her?'

'No, not the way I should. Kevin, we've had this discussion, Sarah and me; we know where each other stands, and we're content with that and with what we've agreed. I understand your professional interest, and I appreciate your concern as a friend, but there'll be no going back.'

'Okay,' O'Malley conceded. 'If that's the way it is, so be it, and good luck to you both.' He frowned again. 'This session is over, but there is one other thing. Earlier you asked me about my interviews with McIlhenney and Mackenzie.'

'Yes.'

'I'll let you have my reports on them, which are fine, but you won't find what I'm going to say in McIlhenney's. You're very close to the man, Bob, I know that, almost as close as you are to Andy Martin. Just don't try to mould him in your image, that's all.'

'Who says I am? Neil?'

'No, I do. That's how it seems to me, and I'm usually right about these things. He's an exceptional officer, and a strong man, but there's something in him that isn't in you, and vice versa. You have a quality he hasn't.'

'What's that?'

'To boil it all down, he won't always pull the trigger in time.'

It was Skinner's turn to frown.

'I believe that you're going to London soon, on special assignment, and you're taking him with you.'

'Yes, but it's very far from common knowledge. Did Neil tell you that?'

11

'It came up during our discussion. Of course, that makes it a privileged communication, so you don't have to worry about confidentiality. Bob, he will never tell you this himself, but he doesn't want to go.'

'Why not?'

'Jesus, man, you can't guess? Because his wife is pregnant and because she was scared to death by his involvement in what just happened.'

Skinner whistled. 'Bloody hell! I should have considered that.' He leaned back and stared at the ceiling for a few seconds. 'My problem is,' he said, 'that I'm taking Neil because he's in the loop, so to speak.'

'Do you have another option?'

'No, but it looks as if I'll have to find one. Thanks for marking my card, though. And thanks for our chat. It's always good to talk to you.'

'Indeed? Why?'

Skinner winked. 'It reminds me how sane I really am.'

2

There were days when Sir James Proud could not help but agree, reluctantly though it may have been, with his wife. He could retire at any time he chose, with a pension that would fund a lifestyle that would be the envy of most, and with the certainty that he would be able to top it up by accepting one or two of the offers of directorships that would be bound to come his way.

He could have gone, honourably, after the warning shot of his coronary incident. Instead he had lost weight, taken sensible exercise, and resumed his duties.

Proud Jimmy had been a police officer for all of his adult life, and had been the chief constable of Scotland's capital city, of which his father had been Lord Provost, and of the green lands around it for far longer than any of his predecessors. Indeed, only one of them was still alive, and he was in his mid-eighties.

In his heart of hearts, he had never expected to make it to the highest rank in the service, and certainly not to the command of Scotland's second largest force. When he was appointed there had been whispers that his elevation owed much to his connections to people of influence, but he had ignored them. He knew his strengths: he was a good administrator, a first-class personnel manager, and he had an authoritative appearance, with bearing to match, that made him stand out in a crowd. Strangely, the virtue which he valued least, the natural diplomacy he had inherited from his father, was the one that had been crucial in taking him to the top. Never, at any time in his service, had he ever been known to upset anyone, other than certain members of the police advisory board, and even then, only when it had been absolutely necessary.

On the other hand he was aware of his weaknesses: he was oldfashioned in his attitudes, almost his entire career, after four years of beat-pounding, had been spent behind a desk, and he had no background in detective work. He had spent his early years protecting public order and preventing crime, usually from a distance, but he had never been a thief-catcher and, in truth, had never really understood what made a good one stand out, not, at least, until he had met Bob Skinner.

He had understood from the outset that there was something exceptional about the young man, whose very early promotion to detective sergeant had been sent to his office for approval. He had seen it first in his personnel file. Graduate officers were unusual in those days, but one who came from an affluent professional family was unique in Proud's experience. And then, of course, there was his father. The young Skinner's promotion would be likely to take him into sensitive areas, and so, without his knowledge, he had been vetted. The screening had revealed that William Skinner was far more than an ordinary Scottish solicitor. During the

Second World War he had been a member of the Special Operations Executive, and although the Ministry of Defence had refused to divulge any details of his service, they did reveal that he had been decorated three times, the last being the award of the George Cross. Because of the nature of the SOE's work, none of the citations had been made public, and there had been no mention of them on the younger Skinner's original application to join the police service. At the time, Proud had found this slightly strange: it was some years later that he discovered that Skinner himself had been unaware of his father's distinctions until after his death.

His imposing deputy was on the chief constable's mind as he sat at his desk that Friday morning, staring at Kevin O'Malley's 'Eyes Only' report. The psychiatrist was not one to mince his words.

Deputy Chief Constable Skinner [Proud read] *has come through another testing operational situation with flying colours. He shows no sign of emotional or psychological damage; indeed, the calmness and detachment which he showed in discussing the events which led to his discharging his weapon mark him out once more as an exceptional person.*

In my years in practice, during which I have counselled many officers following potentially traumatic experiences, I have never encountered an individual, not one as rational as he is, at any rate, with such self-control. And yet, that in itself gives me cause for concern. Every person has an emotional breaking point. With most, it is easy to predict when this is likely to occur. With someone who is as tightly wrapped as DCC Skinner it is virtually impossible.

I am aware, since he was willing to discuss it during our session, that he is facing the imminent, and apparently irreversible, break-up of his marriage. I have to say that he appears to be handling this with the same calmness that he shows in professional situations. He and his wife seem to have reached an amicable parting of the ways in which the interests of their children will be paramount, and this is to be welcomed. Nevertheless, the arrangements which he described mean that he is about to become, for the second time in his life, a single parent, throughout the school term at least. Even with domestic assistance, this will impose a further burden upon him.

Mr Skinner has done a great deal in his career, for his force and indeed for his country. He is at an age and in a position of seniority where any other individual would be content to stand back entirely from any operational role that might place him at risk. Yet he is unwilling to do this, arguing that if a situation similar to that with which he has just dealt were to arise again, it would be his duty to assume field command in the absence of anyone with equal experience and skill. It would be easy to say that it is

16

unlikely that such a crisis will occur again in this area, but given the times in which we live such a prediction would be foolish.

I have known Mr Skinner for many years. I would not like to be in a position of having to counsel or, worse, treat him, after he has found where his breaking point lies. I believe that it is in his interests for him to be taken away for a period from any chance that he might have to lead another active operation. I understand from our discussion that he is about to go, for a short period, on special assignment to London. This is timely, and may serve the purpose, but from what I gather it is not likely to be enough. Short of a complete reorganisation of your command structure, and reallocation of responsibilities, I recommend that DCC Skinner, on his return to Edinburgh, be given sabbatical leave for a period of six months.

Proud Jimmy sighed as he finished the report and tossed it into his pending tray. 'Certainly, Kevin.' He groaned. 'Maybe you'd like to try telling him.'

Yes, this was a Chrissie moment, all right, one of those times when his wife's wish, unspoken but crystal clear nonetheless, seemed very attractive. He enjoyed gardening. His golf clubs were gathering dust in his locker at the Royal Burgess . . . not that they had ever seen much use, but he had always promised himself that there would be a time when they did. There was the book that he wanted to write, the one about the history of policing in the city of Edinburgh. And there was Lady Proud herself, above all, and the time that he knew he owed her.

The moment when he would have no choice but to retire would come soon enough, in a little more than a year, in fact. Christmas was on the way: he would have, potentially, one more of them in post, but by the Easter after that, he would have to be gone. What more could he achieve, he asked himself, between now and then?

Nothing, he answered.

Nothing, other than his most cherished wish: to see Bob Skinner appointed his successor. Normally a deputy would never succeed in his own force, but Proud's diplomacy had overcome that hurdle years before, by having Skinner's spell as security adviser to the Secretary of State recognised officially as outside experience.

So what had kept him in the job? Paradoxically, it was Skinner himself, and his ambivalence, his refusal to commit himself to applying for the position. For a while it seemed that he had decided firmly against it, but a wise counsellor had persuaded him to consider where his duty really lay. But still, Proud could not be sure whether, when he did give up the baton, his anointed successor would pick it up.

And now here was Kevin O'Malley, throwing a spanner into the works. Sabbatical leave, indeed; he respected O'Malley, and he saw the merit in his proposal, but the timing was just plain wrong. It was an open secret that the name of

Willie Haggerty, his assistant chief constable, was pencilled in for the newly announced vacancy in Dumfries. When that happened a successor would have to be appointed, and he would want to consult his deputy about the candidates. Then there was the unexpected vacancy in the head of CID's office, brought about by Dan Pringle's retirement. That would accelerate an intended shake-up of the divisional CID commanders, and Bob would want to be around for that. Indeed, he had already mentioned turning down the London assignment, but Proud had been able to persuade him that it was too important.

He looked at Chrissie's photograph on his desk. 'Sorry, love,' he whispered.

He had just turned back to his morning's workload when Gerry Crossley, his secretary, buzzed him. 'Sorry to interrupt, Sir James,' the young man began. 'I have a caller on the line who's asking if she can speak to you, personally.'

'Police or civilian?'

'Civilian, sir. She says her name is Trudi Friend, and that it's a highly sensitive personal matter.'

The chief constable gasped. 'I've never heard of the woman. She's asking for me personally, you say?'

'Yes, sir. I asked her if she could give me a little more detail, but she declined. She says that because of the nature of her request she can only explain it to you.'

'Tell her to explain it in writing, in that case: if it's a complaint against one of my officers it has to be handled formally.'

19

'I've told her that already. She assures me that it isn't; she says that the matter is private and not professional.'

'How does she sound? Is she hysterical in any way?'

'Not at all: she's perfectly calm, and perfectly polite.'

Proud sighed, then looked at the pile of work before him. What was getting him down, if not the routine? 'In that case, Gerry,' he said, 'I'd better be the same. Put her through.'

As he waited, he realised that he was curious. It was an unusual feeling for him. He spent his life being bombarded by briefings, reports, committee minutes, and assorted other facts. Most of the time, people told him things that he already knew. He was protected, expertly, by his secretary and others, from callers outside his circle. He tried to remember the last question he had needed to ask at work, before the three that he had just put to Gerry, and failed.

'Mrs Friend,' Crossley announced. He heard the usual click on the line.

'Sir James?' The woman's voice sounded fresh and vigorous.

'It is. How can I help you?'

'It's very complicated, but what it boils down to is this: I'm trying to find my mother.'

The chief constable felt a bristle of indignation, but he controlled it. 'Mrs Friend,' he said, 'there are routine channels for reporting missing persons. You can approach them directly, and save yourself quite a bit of time.'

'It's not like that, I assure you; it's not that

simple. I've come to you because I believe that you are the person best placed to help me.'

'How long has your mother been missing?'

'Forty-one years.'

'Forty-one . . . '

Trudi Friend cut across his exclamation. 'I know it sounds ridiculous, but there are circumstances. Sir James, does the name Annabelle Gentle mean anything to you?'

The chief constable frowned as his mind travelled back to his teenage years. 'Annabelle Gentle? No, I'm afraid that it doesn't.

'How about Claude Bothwell?'

Claude Bothwell? he thought, and as he did, a face appeared before his mind's eye. *Claude? No, but Adolf, that's another matter.*

'Where are you calling from, Mrs Friend?' he asked.

'I'm in Peebles.'

'Can you get to Edinburgh easily?'

'Yes. I can come up tomorrow, if necessary. Why?'

'Because I think we should meet. I'd like to hear your story in person.'

3

Inspector Dorothy Shannon enjoyed being based in Leith, for all its exotic reputation. Most of that came from times past: the eighteen years of her police service had seen considerable change, with bonded warehouses being turned into designer apartments, and new homes going up on demolished factory and warehouse sites, and in the dockland areas.

She had experienced a few misgivings when she was posted there, on promotion, but she had found it a pleasant place to work after years in those parts of Edinburgh that do not figure on the tour-bus routes.

She liked her job, too, most of the time. That morning was one of the exceptions. She was standing in a bookmaker's office, in Evesham Street, not far from Great Junction Street: the proprietor, whose name was Gareth Starr, was facing her across the counter. She had answered a call-out to an attempted robbery. It had not gone well for the thief; indeed, he had suffered a net loss in the transaction.

Dottie Shannon glared at the little, grinning man. 'Do you find this funny?' she asked.

Starr's shoulders shook with suppressed laughter as he looked at the object on the counter. 'Fuckin' hilarious, doll,' he replied.

'That may change soon,' said Detective Sergeant Sammy Pye, from the doorway. 'Tell me what happened here.'

The man pointed to the uniformed inspector. 'I just told her.'

'Fine, now tell me again.'

'If you insist. I'd just opened up when this bloke comes in.'

'You were alone?'

'Aye. I'm not usually, but Big Ming, ma board man, was down at the corner shop getting coffee and bacon rolls for us. Anyway, this idiot comes crashin' through the door, youngish fella, but no' that young, late twenties, maybe. He looks around and then he pulls out a gun and waves it at me. 'Ah'm armed,' he shouts. I told him that I could see that, then I asked what he wanted. I took a look at his eyes: they were all over the place. He was drugged up, for sure.'

'Did he offer any other violence?'

'Nah, he just pointed the gun at me and told me to hand over all the cash I had in the place. I told him that I don't have a lot of cash at the start of business, just my float. I expect the punters to give me theirs as the day goes on. He told me to shut the fuck up and gi'e him what I had. I took another look at his eyes, then at the gun . . . he was waving it all over the place . . . and I opened the safe. He couldn't see in, so I only took some of what was in there, about a grand, and put it on the counter.'

'So far so good,' said Pye. 'And then what?'

'Then the stupid bastard,' Starr beamed at the memory, 'tucks the gun under his left oxter, and goes to pick it up with his right hand. And that's when . . . '

'That's when he whacked him with the bayonet.' Dottie Shannon's lip seemed to curl with distaste.

'Where did it come from?' asked the detective sergeant.

'It was in the safe,' Starr told him. 'I palmed it when I took the cash out.'

Pye leaned over and looked at the great blade. It was embedded in the wooden counter, nailing down a pile of cash, on top of which lay a severed finger. There was blood all around, and in a trail to the door. 'Where did you get it?' he asked.

'It was ma father's. He brought it back from Korea: he said it had seen the insides of a right few Chinese.'

'You keep it sharp, don't you?'

'It's no use if it's blunt, is it?'

'Do you have any other weapons here?'

'What do you mean, weapons? I'm entitled to defend maself, am I no'?'

'I'm going to leave that for the procurator fiscal to decide,' Pye told him. He crouched, took out a handkerchief, and very carefully picked up a Luger pistol, which lay on the floor. 'Have you touched this since the intruder dropped it?'

'No, I left it for you people.' The bookie's ebullience seemed to be fading away.

'Come on, Mr Starr, did you really think this was a firearm?'

'How can you say it's not?'

'By the weight, for a start: this is plastic. And by the size: a real Luger would be bigger than this.' He glanced at it. 'Finally by the fact that it's got 'Made in China' stamped on the butt.'

'How was I to know that?' Starr protested.

'I'm not sure you cared.'

'The bastard was trying to rob me. Why should Ah care?'

'Like I said, that's not a question I'm going to deal with at the moment. The man you mentioned, Big Ming? Where is he?'

'He's in the back shop.'

'Is that Ming as in Menzies?' asked Shannon.

'Nah, his name's Jim Smith. We call him that because he smells a bit.'

'Did he see any of this?'

'The boy bumped into him when he ran for it, but that was all.' Starr scowled. 'Knocked the coffees and the bacon rolls all over the fuckin' place.'

'Had you ever seen the thief before?'

'Not that I remember; he's not one of my regulars, that's for sure.'

'Description?'

'Maybe six feet, skinny, needed a shave. He wore a green jacket and a grey woolly hat: at least I think it was grey. The thing was filthy.'

Pye turned to Shannon. 'We'd better find this bloke quick, Dottie. Could you arrange for uniformed officers to check with the Western General and the Royal for anyone who's wandered in minus a right index finger?' He took an evidence bag from his pocket, picked up the detached digit and, very carefully, placed it inside. 'I'll take care of the forensic side. At least we won't have any trouble getting a print. Mr Starr, I want you to come with me: we'll need a formal statement from you. Meantime, you'd better hope that this man hasn't bled to death. In fact, I'll let you call your lawyer right now. You might want him to meet you at my office.'

The bookmaker's smiles were long gone as he walked over to a phone in the far corner of the betting office. Shannon felt a glow of satisfaction as she reached for her radio, but before she could hit the transmit switch, her mobile sounded.

She fished it from the right-hand pocket of her uniform trousers and hit the OK button. 'Shannon,' she replied, tersely.

'Dottie.' She knew the voice, but at that moment was unable to put a face or a name to it. 'Neil McIlhenney.' Mentally, she kicked herself: she had been with the Special Branch head only a few days before. 'Are you able to talk to me?' he asked.

She glanced around: Starr was dialling a number and Pye was bagging the toy Luger. 'Yes.'

'I'll be brief. You're wanted up at headquarters this afternoon: DCC Skinner's office, three thirty.'

'What's it about?'

'I don't know for sure.'

'Am I on the carpet?'

'No, because you don't need to wear uniform. Anyway, if you were, he'd be phoning you himself. Don't be anxious, just be on time.'

4

'Will it always be like this?' Aileen de Marco asked the question without looking directly at him.

He waited until he had caught her gaze. 'A few hours together here and there, do you mean? Quick lunches like this one, in quiet restaurants where we can trust their discretion?'

She laughed lightly. 'Make that rhyme and you've got a big country-and-western hit on your hands.'

'That's the west of Scotland gene pool: deep down we've all got a touch of the maudlin in us.' He grinned back at her. 'You'll never get me to sing it, though.'

'I'll bet you've got a great singing voice.'

'You'll never know. I don't plan ever to get that drunk again.' He took her hand in his. 'To answer you, no, Aileen, it won't always be like this: that's a promise. Why do you ask, though? Are you having second thoughts about the two of us? Do you want to stop this thing before it goes any further?'

'No, I don't. Forget I said that, Bob; it was stupid. I know it's got to be this way for a while, given your position, and mine. 'Deputy Chief Constable and Justice Minister in Glasgow Love Tryst': God, the headlines were swimming before my eyes last night, in the dark.'

'You're selling yourself short.' He chuckled.

'When I saw them, they read, 'First Minister de Marco and Top Cop Skinner: the secret uncovered' . . . or words to that effect.'

'There's no certainty I'll be First Minister.'

'Are you going to run for the leadership of your party?'

'Yes,' she conceded.

'Is there any sign of anyone running against you?'

'No.'

'In that case it's an absolute certainty.'

'I wish I had your confidence. The electoral process can drag on a bit: there's always the chance of someone else throwing their hat in the ring.'

'The voters will chuck it back out again. But until that happens, and until Sarah and I have ironed out all the details of our split, you and I should avoid being seen together, other than in professional circumstances. Agreed?'

'Agreed. I'm sorry I had my wee wobble there. It's just that being with you makes me feel . . . '

'Yes?'

'It makes me feel content: I don't know how else to put it. Somehow, I just feel like I'm at home, in a way I haven't since I was a kid. Does that make sense?'

'It does to me,' Bob replied.

'How does it make you feel, then?' she teased.

'I have trouble describing that too,' he admitted. 'The best I can say is that I don't feel alone any more.'

'Alone? You've got four kids: how can you feel alone?'

'See? I told you I have trouble describing it.' He looked down at the table for a moment, at the remains of their meal, then back at Aileen. 'It's this way, love. Ever since Myra, my first wife, died, there's been a part of me that's never healed up. I'll tell you a truth: in the years I was on my own, bringing up Alex, I dreamed of Myra all the time; in those dreams she wasn't dead, only away visiting her mother, or a friend, and then she'd come back, and it would be all right. But every morning after, I'd wake up and she was still dead, and inside I was as lost and alone as I felt on the day of her funeral. When Sarah came along, and we got together, I hoped that I could put all the hurt, all the loneliness behind me, but I never did, not quite. I still dreamed of Myra, never Sarah, always her, and she still wasn't dead, only gone for a while. The dreams grew more frequent, until I'd see her almost every night, full of life, but every morning my mind's eye would see her dead once more.'

'Did you ever tell Sarah this?'

'How could I?'

'Didn't you tell anyone, not even your friend Kevin, the psychiatrist you saw?'

'I only tell Kevin what he needs to know; some stuff I can't share with him.'

'You carried all that inside you, for all those years?'

'Yup.'

'So what's happened?'

'You have. They've stopped. I don't dream of Myra any more. When I do, it's you I see.'

Her eyebrows came together, slightly. 'Are you

telling me that I'm a substitute for your dead wife?'

He squeezed her hand, firmly, but not hard enough to hurt. 'Not for a moment. You're nothing like her, nothing at all. She and I had little in common, other than the fact that we were crazy about each other. You and I, we've been drawn together by qualities we share. No, Aileen, what I'm telling you is that I believe, I honestly do, that Myra's finally satisfied that I've found the person I should be with.'

Her eyes glistened. 'Won't you miss her, if she never comes back at night?'

'No, for all I have to do to see her is look at my older daughter. She's as like her mother as two people can be,' he smiled again, 'although she's a little less wild, I'm glad to say.' He drank the last of his bottled water. 'So here I am, saved at last. Yes, my marriage is over, and that pains me, because however well Sarah and I manage it, the kids will not have the upbringing that we had planned. Despite that, when I look into the future, although I don't have a clue what it holds, I see you in it, and that makes me . . . I'll use your word. It makes me content. No, I'll go further: it makes me feel happy in a way I haven't for the last twenty years.'

'Would you like me to chuck it?'

'Chuck what?'

'Politics. I wouldn't be the first just to up and walk away from it.'

Bob leaned back, his scepticism written all over his face. 'Sure, you do that,' he said slowly, 'and I'll give up my job as well and we'll do what

30

with our time? I'm sure I could lecture in criminology. You could go back to civil engineering. We'd live happily ever after, except we'd both be bored stiff during the day, and we'd both regret what might have been. No, my dear, you stay the course: you've got your destiny to fulfil.'

'What's that?'

'To be First Minister of Scotland. What else?'

'You really believe I can do the job?'

'For the next ten years, given the strength of your party, and as long as you want to after that: I know it, and so do you; don't try to kid either of us.'

'Now there's a word: kid. What if I want one?'

'Then have one: we'll need to wait until my divorce is through, if I'm to honour part of my agreement with Sarah. But if that's what you want and we can make it happen, why not? Ministers have had paternity leave before now. Where's the difference?'

'None, I'll grant you. Can you picture me breast-feeding in the parliament chamber?'

'Don't start me picturing your breasts at all,' Bob murmured. 'I have a busy afternoon: I have things to tie up before I leave for London.'

'Will I see you before you go?'

'I don't know for sure. Sarah and I are seeing our lawyer at five this evening to look at a draft separation agreement, then tomorrow I'll have to spend time with Mark, the Jazzer, and Seonaid . . . '

'The Jazzer?'

'James Andrew, my younger son: we used to

call him Jazz before we started using his given names.'

'What's he like?'

'Rough and tumble, bright.'

'Like you?'

'He's showing all the signs, I fear. Anyway, I need to give them some spoiling before I'm off, then on Saturday night I'm having dinner with number-one daughter, Alex. Sunday morning, I've got a golf tie that I can't postpone, because it involves other people. How about late Sunday afternoon, at your Edinburgh place?'

'What if the press are staking it out?'

'They won't be.'

'How can you be so sure?'

'Because Special Branch are keeping an eye on you when you're in Edinburgh. They'll move them on.'

She gasped. 'Did you think of asking me before you did that?'

'Yes, and then I decided not to. You're First Minister in waiting: I'd do the same for anyone. It's not just about privacy; there's the security aspect as well.'

'Is that something I'll have to live with, if I get this job?'

'You'll be entitled to it, but it won't be forced on you. It won't be obtrusive, I promise, and when we're able to come absolutely clean about our relationship, there'll be less call for it.'

'You mean you'll be all the protection I need?'

'Something like that.' He caught the waiter's eye and signalled for the bill. 'Sunday it is then, around five?'

'Okay. I'll cook something: that'll probably finish us.' She fell silent, as the bill arrived: Bob paid in cash. 'This London trip,' she continued, after the waiter had gone to fetch their coats, 'you can't tell me what it's about?'

'It's sensitive.'

'My security clearance is pretty high, you know.'

He laughed. 'You're right, it is: I'd forgotten that. Okay, between us, there's a situation in the security services. The directors want someone from outside to run an inquiry, and I'm the man.'

Aileen whistled. 'Must be serious for them to bring in an outsider.'

'How does the word 'treason' sit with you? I've investigated everything else in my time, but this is a first.'

'My God, that serious? It'll take a couple of weeks, you reckon?'

'That's what I've allowed, but to be honest, I haven't a clue.'

'Where are you staying?'

'They've booked us into a hotel called the Royal Horseguards. Why do you ask?'

'There's a meeting at the Home Office next Wednesday,' she said, 'to discuss progress on the new casinos. Next day, there's a session on immigration. The Home Secretary's chairing the first one, so I have to go. In that event, I might as well stay and do the second meeting. Lena hasn't booked the accommodation yet. Wouldn't it be a coincidence if we wound up in the same hotel?'

'It would,' Bob agreed. 'It would also be fairly

embarrassing for the officer who'll be accompanying me on the trip. I could rely on that person's discretion, I'm sure, but I'd rather not have to, if you see what I mean; personal and professional overlapping, and all that.'

'True. I hadn't thought about that.'

'On the other hand, if you found that you were booked into, say, the Charing Cross Hotel . . . When I'm away, I always go for a walk before I turn in. Sometimes I stay out for hours.'

5

Dottie Shannon lived in a flat in Elbe Street, so close to the police station in Queen Charlotte Street that she always came to work in uniform. She was about to go home to change for her appointment with the deputy chief constable when DS Pye appeared in the open doorway of her office.

'Got a minute?' he asked.

'Just one, Sammy, literally. I have a meeting out of the office this afternoon.'

'That's funny, so has my boss.'

The inspector's curiosity was triggered. 'Indeed? Where's Mr McGuire's, did he say?'

'Fettes, half three. I won't keep you, if you're in a rush. I just wanted to know whether you'd had any reports back from the hospitals about our failed armed robber.'

Shannon took longer than normal to reply: she was still pondering the fact that she and Detective Superintendent Mario McGuire had appointments in the same place, at the same time. Fettes was a big building, and there was always plenty going on there, but still . . . To a good copper there was no such thing as coincidence. 'No,' she said finally. 'No, I haven't. Nothing positive at any rate. Our lad hasn't turned up at the Eastern, the Royal or the Western General looking for treatment. I widened the search as far as Livingston, but no joy there either. If he does arrive anywhere we'll hear about it . . . or you will at least. I told my colleagues to pass any information to you.'

'Thanks.'

'Anything else we can do?'

Pye scratched his head. 'If we don't get anything from the hospitals soon, we might have to start asking around the city GPs, but I'm holding off on that. The scene-of-crime woman took a print from the finger, and I'm waiting to hear if Criminal Intelligence has it on file.'

'Fine, but in the meantime, could this bloke have bled to death?'

'From the amount of blood in the betting shop, and in the street outside, I'm advised by the SOCO that it's unlikely. He'll need medical attention at some point, sure, but if he's a junkie, like Starr said, there's a good chance he's gone home and shot up again, to kill the pain.'

'What about Starr? What's the CID view on him?'

'He's a shit. Would the uniform branch disagree?'

Shannon grinned, showing the gold filling in one of her teeth. 'We'd concur, but, as you know damn well, I meant, do you see him as offender as well as victim?'

'Difficult. I've talked to Superintendent McGuire about that: his instinct is that the fiscal's office would be reluctant to lay a charge. What would it be? Assault, probably. He'd go to trial, and his defence would be pretty obvious. Odds in favour of conviction? Probably against, even money at most, but suppose he was found

36

guilty, you can be sure it would go to appeal. It could become a test case, a *cause célèbre*, and maybe it could set the sort of legal precedent we don't want.'

'So you've let him go without caution or charge?'

'No, I cautioned him formally before he made his statement. His lawyer was there, I had to.'

'How did he take that?'

'Oliver Poole, the solicitor, told him that it was normal procedure and that he shouldn't worry about it. He was right, too. So I took his statement, and turned him loose. I told him that the SOCOs would have to hold on to the cash for a while, in case we need more prints. That annoyed him a bit, I'm glad to say.'

'Does that mean you've hit the buffers already?'

'Almost. I've got his board man, James Smith, in the interview room now. Starr was right: he does hum a bit. I'd better get shot of him, and let you go to your meeting, too.'

Pye closed the door as he left. His mind was on Shannon and her appointment as he walked back to the interview room where Big Ming was waiting. He liked the inspector: she was something of a fixture in the Leith office, popular with the officers under her command, but not too much, always careful to maintain a proper balance between familiarity and authority. She reminded him a lot of Karen Neville, his DS friend from his uniform days in the Haddington office, as she had been before she stunned the force by marrying Andy Martin, then the head of CID, and settling down to a life of blissful domesticity. He found himself wondering if Dottie's private life was as interesting as Karen's had been. She was pushing forty, he knew, and single. He had heard a hint in the locker room of a relationship that had ended badly, but when he had asked about it, the whisperer had clammed up, so he had let it go.

Big Ming was unhappy when Pye rejoined him. His body odour was more rank too, as if it was an inbuilt gauge of his mood. 'How long is this goin' tae take?' he asked.

'Got anything better to do?' the detective shot back. 'Your boss knows where you are.'

'It's lunch-time,' Smith grumbled.

'Oh, yes, I forgot,' said Pye, as he switched on the tape-recorder on the desk. 'And you never had your bacon rolls and coffee, did you, thanks to our friend knocking them all over the street?'

'The bacon rolls were okay. Ah picked them up.'

'Are you telling me that you and Starr stood there munching bacon rolls with an amputated finger lying on the counter?'

'They'd hae got cold.'

'Jesus, I don't believe it. If you'd been really hungry would you have eaten the finger as well?'

Smith looked wounded. 'Dae you think Ah'm a fuckin' cannibal?'

'Nothing I learn about you is going to surprise me, pal. But for now let's just stick to what happened this morning. What time did you leave the office?'

The witness rearranged his eyebrows as if it was part of his thought process. 'It wid hae been about five tae eleven, Ah suppose. But whit's that got tae dae wi' it? The boy wisnae there then.'

The detective sergeant grimaced. 'Listen. This isn't a formal interview, and you're not under suspicion. All I'm doing here is getting your version of this morning's events. But we'll be done much quicker if you let me ask the questions.' He ground out the last four words.

'Aye, okay. Get on wi' it then.'

'Very good, sir. When you left, were you aware of anyone hanging around? Think about it, please; give yourself time to search your memory.'

Smith's face twisted again, indicating intense thought. Suddenly a light seemed to go on in his eyes: it took Pye by surprise. 'Aye, now ye mention it. There was somebody standin', lookin' in the windae of the shop two doors doon. Ah think it wis the boy. It struck me as strange at the time.'

'Why was that?'

'Because the shop two doors doon belongs tae a plumber. He uses it as an office an' a store, ken, but just for a laugh he has a lavvy in the windae, wi' a cistern, seat and everything.'

'Okay, that's good. You said you think it was the robber: without putting any pressure on you, is that as positive as you can be?'

'Naw. Naw. Naw, naw, naw. It wis him a' right. Same jacket, same hat, same height. Big skinny cunt.'

'Fine. Now, let's move forward. How long were you away?'

'Just a few minutes, like. The corner shop's just a wee bit up the road. Ah went in, picked up the rolls and the coffee, got ma fags, had a wee chat wi' Vijay, and that was it.'

'Cold bacon rolls?'

Smith gave a small shudder at the thought. 'Fuck no. Hot. Wi' brown sauce.'

'Didn't you have to wait for the bacon to be cooked?'

'Usually Ah dae, but today Vijay was off his mark right early. He had them waitin' for me, right on eleven.'

'You and Starr have bacon rolls every morning?'

'Aye. He pays, like.'

'Top-class employer.'

'Aye, he's no' bad.'

'Okay, let's say you were gone ten minutes. Would that be about right?'

'Just aboot.'

'Tell me what happened when you got back.'

'Ye know a'ready. Mr Starr telt ye.'

'Yes, and now I want to hear it from you,' said Pye, patiently.

'It wis just like he said. Ah'd got tae the door o' the shop when it opened and the boy came chargin' out like one o' thon Pamplona bulls.'

The sergeant was struck dumb. Experience had taught him that every so often a nugget of pure gold would be found in the most barren seam, but it could never prepare him for such a discovery.

'And you collided?' he asked, after a few seconds, resisting the urge to ask Big Ming whether he had run the bulls in his time.

'Naw, Ah was just standing there, gettin' ready tae open the door, when he crashed intae me.'

'Let's call that a collision.'

'Call it a waste o' two coffees.'

'Be that as it may, how did you react?'

'Ah didnae have time tae react, otherwise Ah'd have banjoed him. He never even looked at me, just turned and legged it doon the street and round the first corner.'

'You got a good look at him this time, though?'

'Oh, aye.'

'Was he bleeding badly?'

'Ah didnae notice him bleedin' at a', tae tell ye the truth. He was haudin' one hand tight with the other.'

'Did you see his eyes?'

'Aye.'

'Describe them.'

'Whit . . . colour, like?'

'No, just their expression.'

'He looked like a fuckin' Martian, like he wis frae another planet. Ken what Ah mean?'

'Maybe, but explain.'

'They were standing oot frae his heid like big pickled onions. But Ah suppose that's no' surprisin' gi'en that he'd jist had a finger whacked aff.'

'And had you ever seen him before?'

'Naw, Ah don't think so.'

'There we go with that 'think' again. Had you

41

seen him before or had you not?'

'Ah . . . Ah'm just no' sure. There wis somethin' about him that rang a bell, sort o', but Ah'm buggered if Ah can remember, like Ah've seen the boy somewhere, but no' there. D'ye ken?'

'Sure, I know what you mean. One more thing and then we're done. All the way through you've called him 'the boy'. How old did you think he was?'

'Early twenties.'

'Are you certain?'

'Oh, aye, Ah'm sure of that. Ah've got a brither that's twenty-four, and this lad's younger than him.'

Interesting, thought Pye. 'Okay, Mr Smith, that's us done.' He switched off the tape. 'I'll have this typed up as a formal statement. You can either wait to sign it, or I'll have an officer bring it to your home address or to your work.'

'Ah'll wait. Dinna want the polis at ma door, and Mr Starr'll no thank me if yis come tae the shop for me.'

'As you wish. Since you've missed your lunch, I'll have somebody bring you a coffee and a sandwich while you wait. Want a paper as well?'

'The *News*, if ye've got it. Ah'll try and remember where Ah've seen the boy, honest.'

'You do that,' said Pye as he opened the door. 'Maybe you bumped into him running the bulls in Pamplona.'

42

6

'My apologies, Neil,' said Skinner, glancing at his watch as McIlhenney came in. 'I said three o'clock, and I hate being late for a meeting I've called myself, especially when it's in my own office.'

'No worries, boss. I've been pretty busy clearing my desk anyway.'

'Did you contact Inspector Shannon?'

'Yes, I got hold of her. She'll be here, three thirty on the dot, along with Mario.'

'Fine, that gives us fifteen minutes. Coffee?'

'I'll pass: I'll have some water from your fridge, though.'

The deputy chief constable frowned. 'Of course you will. Christ alone knows why they want me on this London operation: I'm so bloody efficient I forgot you've chucked caffeine.' He took a bottle of water from the small cooler beside his desk, and tossed it to McIlhenney, then poured himself a mug of coffee from his filter.

The chief inspector moved to take the chair that faced across the DCC's desk, but Skinner motioned him towards his informal seating. 'So,' he asked, as he settled into the soft leather upholstery, 'why did you want to see me first, before the other two get here? Is it to talk over the London job?'

'In a way, a negative sort of way: it's to tell you

43

that you're not going.'

McIlhenney's face was impassive. 'I see. And are you going to tell me why, sir?'

'Look, stop the 'sir' stuff: there's no one else here and it makes you sound like you're in the huff. You've no need to be, I promise you.'

'Okay, but why the change of mind? Has that man O'Malley been saying things he shouldn't?'

'No, he hasn't. Kevin's report on your counselling session was very positive, not that I ever had any doubt that it would be. I'm not taking you with me because I've got more need of you here; it's as simple as that.'

'But Special Branch is quiet, now that the last crisis is over and done with.'

Skinner laughed. 'You can predict when the bird's going to hit the windmill, can you, Neil? That makes you a better copper than me. No, it's got nothing to do with SB. It has to do with you and your career. There are two appointments I need to make. Greg Jay's sudden vanishing trick has left me needing someone to take over command of CID in East and Midlothian.'

'Yes, so what's the other?'

'It's in Leith.'

'Leith?'

Skinner nodded. 'Yes, and don't act so surprised. You know there's a head of CID vacancy as well, now that Dan Pringle's gone, and you know who the grapevine says is favourite for it.'

'The grapevine gives Maggie Rose a chance, and Brian Mackie, and Alastair Grant too.'

'Maybe, but it doesn't know that Maggie's

ruled herself out of consideration.'

'Has she?' said McIlhenney, surprised.

'Yes. I saw her the other day, just to sound her out, mind, not to offer her the job. She told me that she's happy in uniform, and that if she moved back to CID it would be awkward, now that she's living with a detective inspector. As for Brian, he's doing a great job commanding the city division, plus he's first in line for ACC if Haggerty goes. Alastair? Between ourselves, he's reached his ceiling.'

'Which leaves . . . '

'Your boyhood mate, Mario McGuire. He's our choice, the chief's and mine, effective immediately.'

'Which leads to the vacancy in Leith?'

'Yes, but . . . '

'There always is a 'but', isn't there?'

'It's one of life's immutable laws. In this case it comes about because I'm making some changes in the CID structure. I need more foot-soldiers out there, but there are budget constraints as always. To fund them, I need to cut down on the number of chiefs. That means that there are going to be fewer detective-superintendent posts. Obviously I can't demote people who are already *in situ*, so the phasing in's going to take some time.'

'And Leith's where it begins?'

'Exactly.'

'So?'

'So I'm putting Bandit Mackenzie in there. He's fitted into the Drugs Squad well, but with the Scottish Drugs Enforcement Agency making more and more progress, I can get by with a detective inspector in that post.'

McIlhenney scratched his chin. 'I see. Does that mean you're working up to telling me that I'm going to Jay's old job on a level transfer?'

'Do you want it?'

'Honestly? I'd rather stay where I am.'

'That's not an option: you've done your stint in Special Branch. But don't worry: I was taking the piss about moving you to Dalkeith. Jay's deputy will step up there. I owe you more than that, for all you've done for this force, and for me. I've got something in mind for you, but I'll tell you about it when the others arrive. I wanted you in here first, not just to break it to you that you're not coming to London with me, but to ask you about Shannon's vetting.'

'It's done, boss, as you asked. You gave us short notice, but Alice Cowan, my assistant, briefed me an hour ago. She's clean as a whistle, an exemplary officer with nothing in her background that need worry you. She's firearms qualified and a bloody good shot too, according to the range supervisor.'

'And the personal thing that we'd heard about?'

'She's over that: she has a steady relationship with a man who works in the Bank of Scotland computer department. They've been seeing each other for three years.'

'She's not likely to get pregnant on me as well, is she?'

'Not a prayer. She was involved in a road accident when she was fourteen: a drunk driver hit her father's car. He, the dad, was killed, and she suffered severe abdominal injuries. She recovered, but minus her uterus.' McIlhenney looked at his friend. 'What did you mean by 'as well', by the way?'

Skinner blinked. 'Your wife's pregnant, isn't she?'

'Ah, so that has had something to do with me not going to London?'

'Of course not, Neil; you're imagining things.'

'If you say so, boss. But Lou'll be pleased, and I'm not imagining that.'

'I'm glad to hear it. You just tell her that her influence over me had nothing to do with my decision. It was made on purely operational grounds. How are the kids, by the way?'

'They're fine. Spence is looking forward to his next adventure, and Lauren's looking forward to being eighteen, so she can go to university and get out of doing the ironing. Only five more years to go: she'll be thirteen next week.'

'Are they pleased about the new baby?'

'God, yes. Lauren's funny. She's about two-thirds woman now, trying to be very mature about it, but the other third kicks in every so often, and the excitement just bursts out of her.'

'You're lucky, in that way. My Alex is twenty years older than her blood siblings. She still worships them, mind.'

All at once, McIlhenney's face grew solemn. 'Yes, your Alex; and your own bereavement. You know, Bob, I don't think I've ever thanked you properly for the way you supported me when Olive died.'

'You supported yourself, man. Your friends were just around to help, that's all. And you have thanked me, by the way you've got on with your life. You've set an example that I couldn't live up to.'

'But you tried your best, and so did Sarah, I'm sure. But if it's really bust . . . '

'It's really bust.'

'Then Lou and I will be there to support you, whenever you need it.'

'Cheers, mate.' Skinner finished his coffee. 'Better get the other two in: they should be here by now.' He rose, walked across to his desk, picked up a phone and called Detective Sergeant McGurk, his assistant. 'Jack, I'm ready for my three-thirty meeting.' He poured more coffee as he waited. He had barely finished stirring in the milk before the door opened.

Mario McGuire stood aside to usher Dottie Shannon in before him. The inspector looked as if she was doing her best to hide her nerves, and almost succeeded. She wore little makeup, but her short blonde hair was expertly cut. She had replaced her duty uniform with a grey trouser suit and a white shirt. McGuire wore a brown suede bomber jacket and blue denims.

'Welcome, both of you,' Skinner greeted them. 'Comfy seating today,' he said, ushering them towards McIlhenney. 'Coffee?'

'Yes, please, sir,' Shannon replied, a little nervously.

'Fine. Mario, pour them, will you? Did you bring what I asked?'

The dark-haired superintendent nodded as he

picked up the coffee jug. He waved a brown-paper bag in the air with his left hand. 'One bag of doughnuts from the Viareggio deli: the finest in town, guaranteed.'

The DCC sat on the sofa beside McIlhenney, positioning himself so that he was facing the newcomers. 'It's good to see you up here, Dottie,' he said. 'I've been keeping my eye on your career for a while.'

'Thank you, sir,' the inspector replied, caution still in her tone as McGuire took his place beside her, handing her a mug and laying a plate bearing half a dozen sugar-coated doughnuts on the coffee-table.

'There's only four of us,' Skinner pointed out.

McGuire displayed his most Italian grin. 'Maybe, but two of them are for me: the rest of you can fight over the one that's left . . . unless someone here pulls rank, or unless Neil decides to stick to his diet, in which case there's two each.'

'You wish,' McIlhenney growled, reaching across the table and taking the top doughnut from the pile.

Skinner followed suit, then waited until he judged that everyone was comfortable and settled. 'I want you all to know,' he began, 'that contrary to the occasional rumour you may hear, I am not a one-man army. I do not run this force, Sir James Proud does. The powers that I exercise are delegated by him, and the policies I put in place are approved by him, and where necessary by the police advisory board. So, what I'm telling you now has his blessing.'

He paused until he was sure that each listener appreciated what he had said. 'I've asked you three here to give you what I hope will be good news, so I'll get right into it. Mario, you are promoted detective chief superintendent and head of CID with immediate effect. Congratulations: it's a year or so earlier than we'd expected, but it's one of the easiest appointments we've ever had to make.'

McGuire's Irish side seemed to take over: for once he looked diffident, and lost for words. 'Thank you very much, sir,' he said, at last. 'It's an honour.'

'One that's been well earned.'

'Can I take Sammy Pye with me as my assistant? I've got nothing against Ray Wilding, but I know Sammy better.'

'I thought you'd ask that; of course you can. Wilding's ready for a move anyway, so he and Pye can do a straight swap. You'll need a sure-footed back-up, one with Pye's tact: one of your tasks will be to oversee a gradual restructuring in CID, one that'll have to be explained to quite a few people. As a first step, a detective superintendent will be appointed and given responsibility for all of the City of Edinburgh. The three divisional commander posts will be down-sized to chief inspector as time goes on, but those who are there at the moment will continue. That's where the need for diplomacy might come in, for two of them are superintendents, and they'll be reporting to the new appointee, Detective Superintendent Neil McIlhenney.'

'You . . . ' McIlhenney spluttered, spraying doughnut crumbs across the table.

Skinner laughed at his reaction. 'Well earned too, and I'm glad I kept you guessing till the end.'

He turned to Shannon. 'Inspector, Neil's move leaves a vacancy at the head of Special Branch. I don't need to tell you that, with the new parliament, the supreme courts, an international airport, and the main royal residence in Scotland all within our area, it's the most responsible post of its type this side of the border. It's not a task that should be forced on anyone, so we're only offering it to you, with nothing being held against you if you turn it down. It's got its up-sides, though. It's a hell of a good career move, plus it'll take you out of uniform and into this building.' He paused. 'Would you like some time to think about it?'

The woman's eyes widened. 'Do you mean it, sir?' She gulped, and her cheeks flushed. 'I'm sorry, that was a silly thing to say. But can I be bold and ask, why me?'

'That's not bold, that's sensible. It's because I believe that you're the best person for the job, simple as that. I've been taking soundings among senior officers for some time now; your name was put into the hat by Chief Superintendent Mackie, and by Detective Superintendent McGuire. Those two aren't famous for agreeing with each other, so that swung it for me. If I back their judgement, why shouldn't you?'

'Put like that, sir, there's no way I can argue. Thank you very much: yes, I'd like the job.'

'Very good, Detective Inspector, I'm pleased to hear it. Now, tell me what you have in your diary for the next fortnight or so.'

Shannon thought for two seconds. 'Nothing I can't cancel, sir.'

'Good. Cancel the lot then, for you're coming to London with me, to play with the big boys. If today's been a surprise to you, Dottie, you have no idea what next week's going to be like.'

7

'It's been a funny old Friday,' Sammy Pye mused.

'Maybe so,' Detective Sergeant Ray Wilding said, 'but it's been on the cards. Your gaffer was always going to take over from Dan Pringle: it was only a matter of when.'

'What about you, Ray? Are you not pissed off at being moved out?'

'Not a bit. I don't know Mr McGuire and he doesn't know me, so I didn't expect to stay on when he was appointed. Actually I'm pleased to be back on the operational side: being the head of CID's assistant might look good on your record, but it gets boring after a while . . . at least it did with Dan Pringle.'

'I wonder what he'll do now.'

'He might drink himself to death, I fear. He's got no interests outside the job, as far as I could see, other than the Masons.'

'Have you seen him since he chucked it?'

'No. He didn't even come in to clear his desk: he just called and asked me to have all his stuff sent to the house. The DCC told me to organise a whip-round, and I've done that. You'll find the money locked in the filing cabinet in your office.' Wilding handed Pye an envelope. 'These are the keys. There'll be some more dough to come in from Borders and West Lothian. Mr Skinner said that once it's all gathered, you should touch base with big Jack McGurk, in his office, to organise a farewell do and presentation.' Wilding looked around the office. 'So this is Leith, eh? You know what? I've been in the job for nine years, and I've never been in here before. Do you know anything about my new boss?'

'DCI Mackenzie? Only that he's got a reputation for being a bit flash, and for sailing a bit close to the wind at times.'

'How will that go down with your man?'

'Fine,' said Pye, 'as long as he stays off the rocks and gets results. But we won't see much of him: he reports to Neil McIlhenney, remember, not Mr McGuire.'

'Of course. It's funny,' Wilding mused. 'When I joined the force those two were a bit of a legend, great mates, liked a pint, wild boys. Now here they are, running CID and pillars of the force establishment. Your boss might not have changed that much, but you'd barely recognise McIlhenney from what he was then.'

'A lot of people have underestimated big Neil in their time. Many of them are still locked up. Mind you, from the hints I've picked up, he underestimated himself too. Not any more, though.'

'Should I watch out for him?'

'No, he's a good bloke. You watch out for Mackenzie, that's all.'

'I'll bear that in mind. Now, what about this hand-over we're supposed to be doing? I hear a story about a body being found in a van in Newcraighall the other day. Is that one of yours?'

'This office attended, but Dottie Shannon told

me it was a suicide, so you won't find a file on that.'

Wilding scratched his chin. 'Dottie Shannon. I'm sorry she's going; I've fancied her since she was a probationer. Of course, back then she was going with . . . '

'Don't have any wet dreams over Dottie: she's paired off. Besides, she's too old for you.' Pye picked up the top folder from the small pile on his in-tray. 'She and I were out on an investigation this morning. The story's all in here.' He described the attempted robbery at the Evesham Street bookmaker's, and its grisly outcome.

'Did you get a match on the print?'

'No, God damn it, we did not. They're working on DNA comparisons, but I don't see us doing any better there: if they don't have fingerprints on file, they're unlikely to have that either. That means that the robber is a first offender, not known to the police. He hasn't shown up at any hospital as yet, and our telephone trawl of health centres has come up with nothing. My next step was going to be to ask all officers to keep an eye open, on and off duty, for a tall young man with a bandaged hand, but that's as far as I can take it.'

'So, putting it as delicately as I can, Sammy,' Wilding grinned, 'you're leaving me fuck all to go on.'

'Not quite. You've got the weird Mr Smith's vague recollection of having seen the suspect before. Against that, you've got a conflict between him and Starr over his age. I haven't made up my mind how reliable either of them are.'

'Is it worth much more effort, do you think? I mean, the robbery failed and the perpetrator's been punished pretty effectively. What would you do if you were staying here?'

'I'd probably dump it in my boss's lap,' Pye answered, 'and tell him to decide. You're right, Ray: there's been justice done, of a sort. My only niggle is a personal one. I really don't like that bastard Starr. I've had this mad scenario in my head, where we arrest the robber, he gets a soft judge to give him probation, and he gets legal aid to sue Starr in the civil court.'

'And probably gets one pound compensation from the jury for the loss of his finger.'

'Sure.' Pye sighed. 'I told you it was a mad idea. Ah, you know what really bugs me, Ray? It's the idea of my last investigation in this place being written off as unsolved.'

Wilding patted him on the shoulder. 'Take it on the chin, Sammy. When you're head of CID in ten years' time, nobody will remember a thing about it.'

'The man with the missing finger will. And that little bastard Starr will probably still be telling the story at dinner parties!'

8

'Are you sure about this?'

'Funny,' said Sarah Grace Skinner to her husband. 'I was going to ask you exactly the same thing.'

'You first.'

'Yes, I am. I've spent a lot of time lately asking myself why we got married in the first place, and I haven't come up with the answer.'

'We thought we were in love.'

'I reckon it was more a case of us hoping that we were.'

'Maybe we should have thought more about the age difference.'

'That's never been a factor, not as far as I'm concerned at any rate. No, Bob, we both brought baggage with us. You were still fixated with your dead wife; I was trying to forget Ron Neidholm. I'd tried in vain to forget him with a few men in New York before I came to Scotland. With you, I thought I'd succeeded. I suppose that was it; that was why I said 'yes' when you asked me.'

'When did the memory come back?'

'The first time I fell pregnant. I found myself thinking, *This could have been Ron and me, if I hadn't dug my heels in over the conflict between my career and his.* Don't get me wrong. I don't regret having your kids, that's not what I'm saying. It's just that the yearning was still there. Our marriage was over the moment that I met

Ron again in Buffalo. I know that now. The fact that he died, that's changed nothing. It could never be the same between us. That's why I'm sure. How about you?'

'You've said it all, really. Baggage, mine just as much as yours.'

'Suppose I did change my mind, and said I wanted us to carry on?'

'I think you know I'd never leave you and the kids.'

'Yes, I do. That's why I have to go.'

'Okay, let's call Mitch Laidlaw back in and sign this thing.'

Bob rose and left the meeting room, returning a few minutes later with a fresh-faced, heavily built man, and a woman in her thirties. 'I'm glad you could do this for us, Mitchell,' said Sarah, as the solicitor took a seat opposite her at the oak table.

'Not at all. It's the least I could do for friends in these circumstances: even though your divorce will be on grounds of irretrievable breakdown, the court must still be satisfied that the children's interests are being looked after, and it's required to approve the custody arrangements. The fact that I'm acting for both of you in drafting this agreement will impress them. If you're ready to sign, please do so where indicated. My secretary will witness both signatures.' He watched as both Skinners put their names to the document, which set out the division of their property, and the arrangements for the care and upbringing of their children.

When it was done, Bob pushed the paper

across to the secretary, who added her name. 'What about the divorce?' he asked.

Laidlaw waited until his secretary had left the room. 'Once you've been separated for two years, you can apply for divorce in Scotland. I'm not an expert in US law, but I believe that the situation would be the same in New York State, as Sarah, even though she's an American citizen, would have to establish a period of residency there before she could file.'

'What if the ground was adultery?' The question made Bob turn almost involuntarily and look at his wife.

'If it was, you could proceed straight away,' the solicitor replied. 'Are you saying that is a possibility?'

'Yes. I'd be prepared to admit to it.'

'Wait a minute, Sarah,' Bob exclaimed. 'That isn't necessary. I'm not pushing for a quick divorce.'

'Maybe I am, though,' she countered. 'In a few weeks I'm going to be living in New York, alone. I want to put this marriage to bed so I can be free, completely free, as soon as I can. Do you have anything against that?'

'No, but . . . Mitch, could there be publicity? Wouldn't it have to go to court?'

'If it's uncontested, it would be done by affidavit. Nobody would have to give evidence under oath or anything like that.'

'See?' Sarah said. 'In that case, Mitch, we'll take that option. I'll give you all the information you need. Let's get it over with as soon as we can.'

9

In the rooftop restaurant, Paula Viareggio gazed across the table at the two men opposite. 'When I look back at you characters fifteen years ago,' she said, 'I see the two widest wide boys I'll ever see in my life. Honest to God, Lou, they were known in every bar and disco in Edinburgh.'

'Known and loved,' Neil McIlhenney interjected. 'The owners smiled when we went in their places, and the bouncers breathed that bit easier, because they knew there wouldn't be any trouble that night.'

'Yes,' Mario McGuire added, 'and how do you come to remember all that way back? Let me remind you: it's because you were tagging along with us, more often than not, playing the little Italian princess with her two minders.'

'I was not!' Paula protested. 'My heart used to sink every time I was in a place and you came in. The number of times you ruined my chances of getting off with someone . . . '

'Rubbish! The number of times you ruined mine by turning up at my elbow just as I was about to score.'

She grinned, her silver hair shimmering in the candlelight. 'I only ever did that when I thought you were about to make a serious mistake. I knew who the slags were, you didn't: I saved you from countless erotic diseases.'

'Don't you mean exotic diseases?'

'Same thing, I guess.'

'Remember that night with the Spanish girl, in that pub in Rose Street?' Neil chuckled.

'What was that?' Louise McIlhenney asked.

'Mario was doing really well with this lass, a real wee stunner, she was, and Paula moved in to do her thing. She thought that she was being real clever, speaking Italian as she tells Mario what a slag the girl was. But Italian and Spanish aren't all that far apart as languages, so she understood most of it. She went ballistic, and Mario had to separate the two of them. The lass threw her drink over him, kicked him in the shins, and stormed out into the night. It took us months to live that down.'

'Why did you catch the flak for it? You weren't involved.'

'If someone threw paint at either of us, the other one got splashed too. That's the way it was. Paula was something else, though. She was there the night I met Olive: I was dead scared she'd come over and do her trick with me. She did once or twice, you know.'

'What trick?'

Mario looked at his friend's wife. 'The same as she did with the Spanish girl. She'd walk up to me, just as I was about to seal the deal, and speak to me in Italian. If it was Neil, she'd take him aside and whisper in his ear in English. Everywhere we went, she claimed to know the personal history of just about every woman in the place, and she'd relate it in some detail. I always tried to ignore her, but she was really good at it: she always said

61

enough to put me off the woman.'

'She was only looking out for you, Mario.'

'No, I wasn't, Lou,' said Paula, 'not entirely. I have to confess that I fancied him myself, even then, but I was too wrapped up in my shawl of Italian guilt about kissing cousins and all that to come out and tell him. When I did get round to it, I found that he had the same hangups. Then he went and married someone else. It's taken us half a lifetime to get together.'

'And now you are, you're happy.'

'Blissfully. We will never marry, we will never have children, we will carry on as we are for the rest of our lives. That's how we see it,' she winked at Mario, 'isn't it?'

He smiled back at her and nodded his head.

'Will you live together?'

'We'll always have two homes,' Mario replied. 'But in the future one might be in Edinburgh and another somewhere else.'

'Like Bob and Sarah,' said Louise. 'They have property all over the place, between them. I was going to call Sarah to invite them to join us tonight . . . Bob's the man who gave us the reason for this promotion celebration, after all . . . but Oloroso only had a table for four left at this notice.' She saw a change in her husband's expression. 'No? Why not?'

Neil said nothing, but drew his right index finger across his throat.

'You mean they're . . . ?' she whispered.

'Yes, they are, but I don't want to talk about it here.'

'Does it have anything to do with . . . ?'

62

'It has nothing to do with anyone else: it's been brewing for a while. I'm sure he'll tell you about it himself when he's ready, after he gets back from London.'

'What a shame.' Louise sighed. 'London,' she said. 'That's something else I have to thank him for: the fact that you don't have to go there.'

'Me too, I suppose. Although when he told me, I thought that O'Malley had advised him to bench me.'

'He did,' said Mario. 'The boss told me that after you and Dottie Shannon had left this afternoon. He was right, too. When you're involved in something like you were, you need a recovery period, whoever you are . . . even Bob Skinner, although there's nobody brave enough to tell him that, now that Andy Martin's gone. There's Alex, maybe, but she thinks he's immortal.'

'Sarah tried.'

'Then she should have known better. This London job: what's it all about anyway?'

'I can't talk about it.'

'You're right: this isn't the place.'

'No, I can't talk about it at all, even though you are my new gaffer.'

Mario picked the last *petit four* from its paper casing. 'I see,' he murmured. 'That, by itself, probably tells me all I need to know.'

10

For all his years in office, Sir James Proud still found a way to travel around his city relatively incognito. He was seen so often in uniform that when he discarded it in favour of grey trousers and a Daks sports jacket, with a grey fedora in place of his silver-braided cap, he could have been any middle-aged man on a Saturday shopping expedition.

In fact, he was: Lady Proud's birthday was only a week away, with Christmas not long after that. He was pleased with the cashmere stole and leather handbag that he had found in Jenners, so pleased that he was still smiling as he walked towards the Balmoral Hotel, on the stroke of midday.

The doorman was one of the few who would recognise him in any guise, but he was also discreet and confined his greeting to a murmured 'Good morning, sir,' as he ushered him into the foyer.

The chief constable nodded acknowledgement and strode through the Victorian hallway to the Palm Court, which lay beyond. Not unexpectedly on a Saturday, it was full: equally predictably, almost all of the customers were ladies, many of them with Jenners bags like his own.

'Mrs Friend's table, please,' he asked the young waitress, who approached him as he stood in the doorway.

'Certainly, sir. She's over there in the corner.'

As Proud followed her pointing finger, he saw that he had been spotted. Trudi Friend was on her feet, looking towards him, smiling, a little uncertainly. He judged her to be around fifty; she was tall, tanned and attractive, if a little busty, in her close-fitting jacket. He thanked the girl and made his way across between the busy tables, hardly drawing a glance.

'Sir James?'

'Yes, sit down, please, Mrs Friend.' A lock of lustrous brown hair fell across her forehead as they shook hands. She smoothed it carefully back into place as she resumed her seat. As he looked at her, he realised that her skin tone was natural, rather than acquired on a Caribbean holiday or on a sunbed. The waitress had followed him over. 'Have you ordered?' he asked.

'No, but I was only going to have coffee.'

He tried to pinpoint her accent, but failed. 'That will be fine for me too,' he told the server, 'and some shortbread as well, I think.'

'That's automatic, sir,' she replied, then turned and headed for the kitchen doorway, next to the bar.

'It's very good of you to see me,' said Trudi Friend.

'I'm intrigued,' he told her. 'You've pushed a curiosity button that I'd forgotten I had. People who phone me normally want me to approve things. They rarely ask me things, and they never bring me mysteries.'

She frowned. 'It's just that, I'm afraid . . . a bit of a mystery.'

'You haven't seen your mother for forty-one years, you told me.'

'Longer than that, I'm afraid; I've never seen her, not that I could possibly remember, at any rate. I was a Barnardo's baby, Sir James. My mother had me when she was nineteen, and she christened me Gertrude. She was unmarried, and my father's name doesn't appear on my birth certificate. The only thing I know about him is that he was Mauritian. That's what she told the Barnardo's people, when she gave me up for adoption.'

'What do you know about her?'

'I know that her name was Annabelle Gentle; she'll be seventy years old now.'

'If she's still alive,' said Proud, softly.

'I believe that she is. I've done some genealogical research; that is I paid someone to do it for me. She was born in Inverurie. My grandfather, John Gentle, was a railwayman and my grandmother, Rosina Bell, was a seamstress. They're both dead, as you'd probably expect.'

The chief constable waited while the fresh-faced young waitress placed their coffee and shortbread biscuits on the table. 'When was this research done?' he asked.

'Within the last month.'

'Then the obvious question is why have you waited so long to go searching for your mother?'

'For a number of reasons. I've been away from Scotland for some time. When I was five years old, I was adopted by a couple from Peebles,

George and Mary Strait. When I was little, I was darker than I am now, and, people being what they are, or rather, what they were in the 1950s, it took that length of time to place me. My mum and dad are saints, they really are. They're still both hale and hearty: I'm staying at their place while I'm in Scotland. Dad was a librarian until he retired, and Mum worked for one of the local law practices. I had the loveliest upbringing any child could have been given, and during all that time, I never thought of my natural mother. I did well at school, and when I left, I went to teacher training college in Edinburgh. I qualified when I was twenty-two, and got a job back in Peeblesshire. It was round about that time that the law was changed, and adopted children were given the right to know who their natural parents were. I suppose I might have done something about it then: I thought about it, I admit, but somehow I felt that it would seem disloyal to Mum and Dad. Then I met a man.' She smiled shyly, and sipped her coffee as if to cover her embarrassment.

'His name was Felix Friend,' she continued. 'I was at an end-of-term night out in Peebles Hydro with the school staff, and he was there. We got talking. He told me that he was from Kuala Lumpur, that he worked for an oil company, that he was in Scotland for a conference, and that he was taking some holiday time once his business was over. I thought he was charming, so when he asked me out I accepted without a second thought. Two weeks later, when he asked me to marry him, I accepted just as quickly. That's where I've been for the second half of my life, living in Malaysia.'

'So what brought you back to Scotland?'

'Felix died last year.'

'Ah, I'm sorry to hear that. He couldn't have been very old.'

'He was twelve years older than me, but you're right, it was most unexpected. He was a very neat, trim man; he was never overweight, played golf, and swam a lot, yet it didn't stop him having an aneurism and dropping in his tracks.' A look of pain came into her eyes, and stayed there. 'But I'm sorry,' she continued, 'I'm distracting you. Now Felix isn't . . . isn't there any more, I can come back to Scotland for longer periods. Up till now, a month's the longest I've managed. I'm here now because of Zandra, my daughter: she's the reason I'm looking for my mother.'

'How old is she?'

'Twenty-two. I have two children, Zandra and Felix junior; they're twins.'

'And she's decided that she needs to know who she is? Is that what you're saying?'

'Yes, but it's more than a whim. She's just become engaged to an American she met at university in Utah, in the United States. He's a Mormon, and they, apparently, are very big on ancestry.'

'They're also fairly big on polygamy, are they not?'

'Hah! Not any more, I'm glad to say. But she is serious about her need to know who her natural grandparents are.'

'That's understandable, I suppose,' said Proud. 'What progress have you made? And where does Adolf Bothwell come into this?'

'Adolf?'

'Don't worry, I'll get to that. Go on, please.' He picked up a biscuit. *Full of butter and sugar,* he thought. *Bad for me, but what the hell?*

'Okay, I began by going to Barnardo's and asking them what material they held on me. They told me that my file still existed, but that, believe it or not, the law required me to have counselling before they could let me see it. I know that Britain's become a nanny state, but that's ridiculous.'

'There are reasons. It can be very traumatic for some people.'

'Lowest common denominator, you mean?'

'No, I mean for the natural parents. Your mother, for example, may believe that you have no means of tracing her, for that was the case when you were adopted. Many people in her situation still don't appreciate that the law has been changed. Think of the shock for them when a middle-aged person arrives on their doorstep.'

'And says, 'Hello, Mum'? I suppose so. I hadn't thought of it from that angle. How very self-centred I've become. In any case, I had the counselling, and I got to see my file, which included my birth certificate. That's when I hired the genealogist.'

'What did that turn up, apart from your grandparents?'

'I found that I have an aunt: her name is Magdalene, and she's three years older than my

69

mother. She lives in Forres, she's married to a man named Sandy Gates, and she has two sons, a granddaughter and two grandsons. There was a third grandson, but he was killed in Iraq a couple of years ago.'

'Did your search reveal all this?'

'Not all of it: my budget ran out before he got to the grandchildren, but what he gave me was enough. I checked the local telephone directory against the address shown on the report, and found that they still live there. So I phoned them: Sandy answered. I didn't tell him who I was straight away. I asked if I could speak to his wife, and I asked whether she was in good health, as what I had to tell her would come as a big surprise. He laughed and said that she was out getting coal for the fire, and that she'd speak to me when she'd washed her hands. Now I've met her, I don't think he was joking. She came on the line: I told her what my birth name was, and that I thought she was my aunt.'

'How did she react?' asked Proud, intrigued.

'There was nothing for a second or two. At first I thought she'd hung up, until she said, 'My, my; you're Annabelle's wee girl. I've always fretted about what happened to you.' I asked her if she knew where my mother was. She told me that as far as she knew she was dead, but that she couldn't swear to it. Then she invited me to visit her. I wasn't really expecting that; the fact is, I wasn't sure she'd speak to me at all. I drove up next day, in my dad's car. It was much further than I thought, away up in Morayshire. I left early, but didn't get there until about four in the afternoon.'

'You must have felt very strange, seeing her.'

'Did I ever! It was like looking at a little old version of myself, paler-skinned, perhaps, although Aunt Magda is nut-brown from the sun. I was determined to be completely composed when I saw her, but I couldn't manage it. I cried a little and so did she. Poor Sandy didn't know where to look.'

'I know the feeling,' Proud murmured sincerely.

'Once we'd composed ourselves, she sat me down and gave me a cup of tea. Then I told her my story, all about my life, and how it had turned out. Finally I told her why I needed to find my mother. 'I see,' she said, and then she added what struck me at the time as the strangest thing. 'Do you want to know about your birth, and why you were adopted?' I realised at that moment that such a thought had never entered my head. I had come to Scotland for my daughter's sake, not for my own: I had long since stopped thinking about how I had come to be in Barnardo's.' Her hand shook slightly as she picked up her coffee. 'But I said, 'Yes,' all the same. It's a sad story, but far from unique. Genes must mean something, for my mother, like me, was a teacher. She did her training in Aberdeen, but she had a different approach to the social side. Aunt Magda described her as 'a bit of a girl', with that knowing smile people of her age are so good at. She must have been indeed, for in the summer

71

she completed her training course, she came back home to Fochabers looking, as my aunt put it, 'rather out of shape'.'

'Pregnant?'

'About five months, to judge from the date on my birth certificate. Now remember, Sir James, this was back in the fifties, a few years before the permissive society. My grandparents went ballistic. They threw her out, and told her that if she ever wanted to set foot in their house again, it would be without me. Aunt Magda wasn't long married herself, and she was pregnant too, but still she took her in. When I was born . . . in those days, with no job, and no money, my mother simply couldn't afford to keep me. Poor Magda, she said that she and Sandy wanted to bring me up as their own, but they were young and they just couldn't afford it. On top of that, there was the question of my colour. They weren't worried for themselves, you understand, but for me. They were afraid I'd face a lifetime of sniggering and finger-pointing. It was bad enough being illegitimate in those days, even without . . . '

'I imagine so.'

'And that was that. The decision was made, and Sandy got in touch with Barnardo's: when I was less than three months old I was taken in. I was looked after in a place in North Berwick, called Glasclune. I can still remember it, just little bits: it overlooked the sea, and we could see the ships go by from our dormitories, and the lighthouses, on the Bass Rock and all along the coast. The other kids were all right: we were really well taken care of, but we all knew we were different, and that made us all a bit sad.'

'Your mother never came to see you?' asked Proud.

'No. I grew up thinking that my parents were dead. Mum and Dad knew differently: they were told my background when they adopted me, but they didn't tell me until they thought I was old enough to handle it emotionally.'

'How old was that?'

'Eighteen. I handled it fine: I didn't feel rejected, I felt lucky to have such a great mum and dad.'

'And your natural mother?'

'She seems to have handled it as well. She went south to find work.' Trudi Friend smiled. 'In those days 'south' in Forres meant Aberdeen, but she went much further than that. She went to Edinburgh, where jobs were plentiful. She found one in the Academy, in the junior school.'

'Ah,' the chief constable exclaimed. 'I thought we'd wind up there.'

'Yes. My mother settled in well: she got herself a room in a house and she made friends. At least that's what she told Aunt Magda, for although she went back to her and Sandy for holidays, they never visited her. It was on her last visit that she told them about her new man. His name was Claude Bothwell, and he was on the staff of the senior school. She said that he was very handsome, very eligible and that they were engaged. This was at Easter. The way it was left, she was going to bring him up to meet them

73

during the summer holidays. Only they never turned up. They were expecting a letter or a postcard from my mother to say when they'd be arriving . . . they didn't have a phone then . . . but nothing came. They waited until the holidays were over, but still nothing. Eventually, Aunt Magda wrote to the address they had for Mother: after a few weeks the letter was returned, marked 'gone away'. That worried them enough for Sandy to go to the public phone box and call the school. The secretary told him that neither Mr Bothwell nor my mother had returned after the break, and that as far as the headmaster was concerned, they no longer worked there. From that time on, until I got in touch with them, they heard no more of my mother. When my grandparents died, they even put death notices in the Edinburgh papers in the hope that she would see them and get in touch, but she never did.'

Proud scratched his chin. 'That's what happened, was it? Very interesting.'

'So you knew Claude Bothwell?'

'Yes, but first, can you tell me how you came to contact me?'

'I went to the school, and I looked up the record, back to the year of their disappearance. I assumed that most, if not all, the staff would be dead or retired by now, so I looked through the senior pupils. Yours was the only name I recognised.'

'If you'd done a little digging you'd have found a few High Court judges, but they're all called Lord Something-or-other now, so it's understandable that you wouldn't have known them.'

'What can you tell me about Bothwell?' she asked him.

'Not very much, I'm afraid. He taught French and German, and was unwise enough to wear a small moustache, so inevitably we all called him Adolf. I don't remember him being especially handsome, but we tended not to think of our teachers in that way ... at least we didn't in those days. As for being eligible,' he hesitated, 'I'm afraid the same applies. I'm sorry I don't remember your mother at all, but I'd have been long gone from the junior school by the time she arrived.'

'Do you remember anything about their disappearance, or his, at least?'

'A little. I was head boy when it happened; I was also doing a crash course in German in my final year. Our first class was on the opening day of term and we were supposed to have Adolf, but one of the other teachers turned up instead. Afterwards, the rector called me in and told me, as a courtesy, that he wouldn't be coming back. But that's all he told me, I'm afraid.'

Trudi Friend could not keep the disappointment from her face, although he could see that she was trying. 'Thank you, Sir James,' she said, with a sigh. 'I should have known that it was too much to expect any more than that, given all the time that's passed.'

'You have no other leads?'

'None. I'm afraid I've hit the wall. My daughter will be disappointed, but that's too

75

bad. There's no more I can do.'

'Let's not be so hasty,' said Proud. 'Now I know more about the situation, I may be able to do some digging. Most of my classmates are still around. Let me make a few enquiries and see how far I can get. I'm not proposing an official investigation, you understand, but I am a policeman, after all. Can you give me your date of birth, and your mother's?'

'Yes. I have a folder with all the information in it, including the genealogist's report, and copies of my birth certificate and hers. I brought it with me today, just in case you wanted to see it.'

'Excellent. I know the general manager of the Balmoral well enough to borrow his photocopier. Let me make duplicates of your material, and we'll see how far I can run with it.'

'Are you sure? It's really very good of you. I didn't expect anything more than . . . '

'Of course I'm sure. I'm quite looking forward to it, in fact. It'll be just like being back in action.'

11

By any measurement, James Andrew Skinner was a handful. He was also a very perceptive little boy. It was not lost on him that he never did things with both his mum and dad together any more. His older brother Mark was less observant: he was a child of the Internet generation, and he had to be persuaded to leave his computer for an afternoon, even to see a special pre-Christmas morning showing of the newest *Shrek* movie. Happily, he was also a child of the pizza generation, and the mention of lunch afterwards at Benny and Jerry's swung the issue.

'It's too bad Seonaid couldn't come,' James Andrew said, as he picked up a wedge of his mozzarella, tomato and pepperoni selection.

'She's too young, Jazzer,' his father replied, 'you know that.'

'She watches *Shrek* on the DVD at home.'

'Yes, but that's different. She never sits still all the way through, plus she gives us a running commentary. You can't do that in a cinema.'

'When will she be old enough?' he said, as he took a bite.

'In a couple of years I guess. How old were you when we took you to your first movie?'

'Four,' the boy mumbled, through a mouthful.

'There's your answer.'

'Why didn't Mum come with us?'

Bob shot a glance at his son. 'She's looking after Seonaid,' he replied.

'Trish could have done that.'

'Mum doesn't like *Shrek*,' Mark pointed out. 'She thinks Mike Myers's accent is silly and she can't stand the man who does the donkey voice.'

'Dad can. Dad likes him, don't you, Dad? You like Eddie Murphy, you laughed all the way through.'

Bob wound the last of his spaghetti round his fork. 'I like what he does in *Shrek*, and I like some of his early stuff, like *Forty-eight Hours*.'

'And you like Mike Myers?'

'Only when he's a green ogre.'

'So you like him.'

'In that part, yes.'

'So why don't you and Mum like the same things?'

'Jazz, shut up!'

Bob's fork had stopped halfway to his mouth at the question: when his older son spoke, he laid it back down on his plate. He had never heard Mark raise his voice to his brother, or to anyone else for that matter. James Andrew's fists bunched, and for a moment it seemed that he was going to use them, until he caught his father's eye and subsided back into his chair, his expression sullen, but not cowed. 'I'll ask what I want,' he muttered.

'No, you won't,' his brother shot back at him. 'It's a silly question, it's none of your business, and it's upsetting Dad. Married people don't have to like the same things all the time. Isn't that right, Dad?'

'That's true,' Bob replied gratefully. 'We're all different, boys; every one of us is a unique individual, with our own likes and dislikes. It would be virtually impossible for two people, even people who are married to each other, to have exactly the same tastes.'

'Tastes?'

'Likes and dislikes, Jazz. Life isn't like that. What if everyone liked the same football team?'

The youngster grinned, his irrepressible humour surfacing once again. 'It would be all right if it was Motherwell.'

'I didn't know you were a Motherwell supporter.'

'You are, so I must be too.'

'What have I just said? You're a person in your own right. You don't have to support the same team as me.'

'But I want to.'

Relieved that the conversation had moved away from the difficult direction in which it appeared to be heading, Bob gave in. 'Have it your own way, then, be a 'Well fan . . . but don't say I didn't warn you. Come on now, finish up that pizza. There might just be ice-cream after it if you do.'

The bribe worked: the boys concentrated on lunch and on talking about the movie. When they were finished he took them round to Borders, where he bought a video game for the boys, a tactile story book for Seonaid, a golf magazine for himself, and . . . he made a show of choosing it . . . a style glossy for Sarah. Harmony was restored completely, on the outside, yet as they drove home, after feeding the evergrowing colony of swans in Holyrood Park, Bob found himself glancing at Mark in the rear-view mirror, and wondering. The boy's outburst in the restaurant had been astonishing, and completely out of character.

Sarah was in the sun-room when they got back home to Gullane; when he glanced in, Bob saw her there with Seonaid sitting at her feet. The child was concentrating hard on screwing one of the legs off a Barbie doll. He unwrapped the video game in the kitchen and sent the boys upstairs to the playroom to plumb its mysteries, then went through to join them. When she saw him in the doorway, his daughter squealed, pushed herself to her feet and ran towards him. He swept her up in his arms, just as her balance became unsteady. 'Daddy!' she yelled, and kissed him, square on the nose.

'Hey, baby, have you been a good girl?'

'No,' she replied firmly.

'That's true enough,' said Sarah. 'She's made me watch *Shrek II*, and *Finding Nemo*. Not that she understands either of them.'

'It's the colours.' He sat on the sofa, placing Seonaid between them and fishing inside his jacket for her present. 'There,' he said. 'Play with that just now, and I'll read it for you later.' The toddler took the book with only moderate interest, slid back down to the floor, and resumed her attack on Barbie.

Bob reached into the other pocket of his jacket and handed Sarah her magazine. 'That's for you,' he said.

She looked at it. 'Mmm, interiors: that'll come in handy.' She picked a sheaf of papers from her lap and held them up. 'The agent I commissioned to find me a place on Manhattan emailed me these this morning.'

'Anything interesting?'

'One or two. I'm not going to rush into anything, though. I'm quite prepared to rent, until I find the right place. I can afford to now. I've had an offer on my parents' place that's way above what we expected. It opens up the possibility of a smaller place in New York and a weekend house in Connecticut, somewhere more suitable for the kids when I have them. I'm not going to work when they're with me: I'm going to be a full-time mother then.'

'I like the sound of that,' he told her. 'Listen, Sarah, we have to tell them what's happening. I'm quite certain that Mark's guessing already, and even the bruiser knows that something's different. I know we'd wanted to put it off till after Christmas, but that's not going to work.'

She drew a deep breath. 'You sure you're not imagining things?' He described the flare-up in the restaurant. 'I see,' she said. 'Yes, it sounds like you're right. Okay, let them enjoy the rest of the day, then we'll change their little lives tomorrow.'

'Don't put it that way, please.'

'Sorry. Look, Bob, I wasn't implying anything: no fault, no blame, that's what we agreed, and I'm happy with it.' She paused. 'Are you still seeing Alex this evening, to tell her?'

'Yes. Want to come?'

81

'No: it's better that she hears it from you alone. If I'm there it could be awkward: she's bound to take sides.'

'As you wish, but you're misjudging her.'

'No, I'm not. She's your daughter: it's only natural she's going to resent me for what's happened.'

'She won't, but never mind.' He picked up Sarah's emails and began to look through them.

'I almost forgot,' she said. 'There was a call for you while you were out.'

'Who was it?'

'He didn't give me his name. He said he was calling from London, and he left a number you could call him back on. He said it was a secure line.' She reached into the pocket of her shirt, took out a slip of paper, and handed it to him. 'One of your spook friends, I suppose.'

'Not just any old spook, I think. Thanks.'

He went upstairs, to what was now his bedroom, and his alone, picked up the phone and dialled. He heard the ring tone twice, and then a click as it was answered. 'Yesss?' The enquiring voice was as dry as a skeleton.

'Sir Evelyn?'

'Yes.' The tone changed with recognition. 'Bob, thank you for calling. You left a message with my PA yesterday about a personnel change.'

'That's right. DCI McIlhenney's no longer accompanying me: instead I'll be assisted by Detective Inspector Dorothy Shannon.'

'Is she up to the task?'

'Of course she is, Evelyn. I wouldn't be bloody bringing her otherwise.'

'I'm sure that's so, but some of my colleagues are worried that you're entrusting the task to someone with so little experience of our . . . how to put it . . . environment.'

'Which colleagues, exactly?'

'You know, I'm sure; people from across the river.'

Skinner almost growled: 'This may be a daring thing for a simple Scots copper to say to the director general of the Security Service, but given the monumental catastrophe which your fucking environment almost brought about, it's essential that the subsequent investigation is run by people from outside. You can tell your friends from the place across the river that Dorothy Shannon is my choice. She's had positive vetting, and she's been security cleared by me, personally. If she's vetoed, then I'm not coming either. You know me well enough to understand that's not a bluff. You also know, I reckon, that if it came to that, you'd be shat on from a great political height. My appointment was recommended by you, but, as you assured me, approved by the Prime Minister. If I'm forced out of this investigation, I will make certain that he knows how it came about.'

'Don't get excited, Bob,' said the DG. 'I'm not trying to force you out; as you say, you're my personal choice for this assignment. If you're happy with Inspector Shannon, that is good enough for me, and I'll override any objections. I'm looking forward to seeing you on Monday. Is there anything I can do to help you when you get here?'

'I'll need a runner from within your organisation, and maybe someone from that other place, someone who can ensure that whatever I ask for, I get in full, and quickly.'

'You'll have my personal authority.'

'So did Sean Green, and look where that got him.'

'*Touché*. How have you dealt with that, by the way?'

'The Fiscal's Office has stamped the file as a suicide and closed it.'

'Discreet, and effective. I'll take your request on board. You'll have your runners.'

'Thanks. See you next week.'

12

Detective Chief Inspector David 'Bandit' Mackenzie loved his family. He enjoyed all the free time he spent with Cheryl and the kids, but this weekend, well, it was something special: it was one that might never have been. A few days before, he had been involved in a shootout: he had escaped with his life, but still he felt as if he had left something behind him.

He hugged his beer to his chest as he looked out of the window of his new home. It was not his first of the day. Three Miller Draft empties were sitting in a line in the kitchen, waiting for their friend to join them. He was unaware of his wife's presence behind him, until she slipped her arms round his waist.

'Hey, big boy,' she whispered in his ear, 'are you all right?'

He jumped involuntarily at her touch. 'I'm fine,' he said, tipping his head back with the bottle. 'Why do you ask that?' He tried to sound casual, but it came out as defensive.

'Because it's not even five o'clock yet, and you're halfway through a six-pack. Because the football results are on telly and you're not paying the slightest attention.'

'I'm fine,' he repeated. 'It's been a hard week, that's all.'

'It finished all right, though: a nice transfer to a CID section, away from all the druggies and the pushers. It's what you wanted, isn't it?'

'Sure, you're right, it is.' He turned in her arms to face her, switching on the old Bandit smile as he did so. 'Okay, how do you want to spend this promising Saturday night? Will we get a baby-sitter and go paint the town? Or will we get a takeaway and settle for a night of passion?'

'One more beer and that's off the agenda for sure. As it happens, the baby-sitter's booked, and we've got a table for two at the Spanish restaurant near the parliament building.'

'*Olé!* Will there be dancing? Do they have flamenco?'

'I don't imagine so.' Cheryl Mackenzie laughed. She plucked the unfinished bottle from her husband's hand, and headed towards the kitchen. She was passing the phone when it rang. She answered the call, listened, then turned, her hand cupping the mouthpiece. 'It's someone called DS Wilding. He says he needs to speak to you.'

Bandit scowled. 'He's one of the people at Leith,' he explained. 'We met very briefly yesterday. Sorry, love; if this is his way of impressing the new boss he's got it badly wrong.' He took the handset from her. 'Ray, what's the panic?'

'No panic, sir,' Wilding replied calmly, 'but something you need to know. I'm at a crime scene.'

'Where?'

'A house in Trinity: twenty-two Swansea Street.'

'Where's that? I'm new to this patch, remember.'

'Up from the waterfront, near the Starbank pub.'

'What is it? A break-in?' asked Mackenzie, irritably.

'Do me a favour, sir. I wouldn't have called you on your day off about a simple house-breaking. This is a homicide.'

'Shit. Who's the victim?'

'His name's Gareth Starr: he has to be the unluckiest man in town. Yesterday someone tried to rob him, but failed. Today somebody's tried to bump him off, and succeeded.'

'Definitely a homicide? Not just a suspicious death?'

The chief inspector thought he heard his sergeant chuckle. 'Oh, no, sir; all the suspicions are confirmed on this one.'

'I suppose I'd better turn out. I'll be there as soon as I can.' As he spoke, he saw Cheryl, standing in the kitchen, waving the beer bottle. 'Tell you what, Ray,' he added quickly, 'have a car pick me up, so I don't waste any time finding the place.'

13

Lady Proud smiled as she gazed at her husband, settled in his armchair, his face slightly flushed. Normally such a coloration would have worried her, but he had come back from his mysterious meeting in the Balmoral Hotel looking like his grandson always did after a trip to Toys R Us. She never asked him about his business, and normally he did not volunteer information, but on this occasion he had blurted out the whole story as soon as he had hidden his Jenners bags in the cupboard under the stair. 'She must be quite a woman, this Trudi,' she said. 'It's a long time since I put a look like that in your eye.'

Sir James blinked. 'Really, Chrissie, I don't know what you mean by that. She's attractive, certainly, with her Mauritian blood, but she's not, well, she's not like you at all.'

'Keep digging, Jimmy, keep digging.'

'What? Och! It's got nothing to do with her. It's her story that's got me interested: her missing mother, the involvement with Adolf Bothwell. It's a proper mystery when you think about it. This young woman, she has her illegitimate child with the help and advice of her sister and her husband, who also oversee its transfer into the care of Barnardo's. After it's all behind her, she goes off to make a new life for herself, but she still comes back to them for her holidays, the last time all excited about this man she's met, and is going to marry. And then she disappears, from their lives, from the school, from everything, without leaving any trace. Yes, a real puzzle.'

'And you're going to solve it, are you, Sherlock?'

'I'm damn well going to try.'

'It's what you've always wanted, Jimmy, isn't it?'

'What?'

'To be a detective, like Bob Skinner, that man McGuire and all the rest.'

'I'm quite happy with the way my career's turned out,' he said defensively.

'Of course you are, but still, don't tell me you've never envied Bob his skills.'

He frowned. 'Some of them, I admit; others, no. For example, I think I've proved myself rather better at marriage than him.'

Chrissie Proud laughed. 'You've had expert help.'

He almost asked, 'From whom?' but realised, just in time.

'So now you're going to prove that you can find things out too.'

'I think I can help the woman, if that's what you mean.'

'But you have a couple of thousand people at your disposal who could help as well.'

'No, no, that would never do. This situation doesn't warrant police time being spent on it. This is something I have to handle myself. Who better than me anyway? I was there at the time all this happened. So were quite a few other people: I know who they are, and where they are today, as you'll find out if you sit down and listen. Just wait for a moment until I get my book.' He rose from his chair and left the room, returning a minute later, empty-handed. 'Do you know where it is?' he exclaimed. 'It's not where it should be. Have you been tidying up again?'

Lady Proud rose, walked over to the television cabinet, opened it and took from its shelves a loose-leaf notebook, bound in heavy brown leather. 'You used it on Tuesday,' she reminded him pointedly. 'When you were finished, you put it in there.'

'Sorry,' he muttered sheepishly, avoiding her gaze as he took it from her and resumed his seat. He unclipped it, opened it, and flicked through the thick directory section until he found the number he sought, and dialled it. 'Bertie,' he said, as his call was answered. 'Glad I caught you; I thought you might be at Muirfield. It's Jimmy Proud here.' He laughed. 'I'm doing fine, and you're not in trouble, if a Court of Session judge can ever get into trouble, that is. I want to pick what's left of your brain about our schooldays.' Pause. 'Of course you can go that far back, it's only forty-five years or so. Remember Adolf Bothwell?' Pause. 'That's right: taught French and German. More than a bit full of himself, we all thought. Do you remember any whispers about him being involved with a junior school teacher called Annabelle Gentle?' A longer pause. 'No? Do you remember her?' Pause. 'No? Pity. Do you remember anything about his leaving the school?' Pause. 'Yes, that was my recollection too. There was no warning, his timetable was fixed, and he just didn't turn up for the new term. Your brother, the Solicitor General: would he have been in the junior school then?' Pause. 'Upper primary, you reckon? Maybe I'll have a word with him. There's just one other thing. Remember when we were in our fourth year and we won the relay trophy at the school sports? Who presented it?' Longer pause. 'Yes, that matches my recollection. I was sure it was Adolf's wife.'

14

There was a full scene-of-crime team in attendance when Bandit Mackenzie's Traffic car taxi dropped him at the stone-built terraced villa, its gateway marked with coloured tape. Ray Wilding was waiting for him in the doorway, clad in a disposable white tunic. He waited as the chief inspector struggled into an identical garment.

'When did we get the call?' Mackenzie asked.

'About two hours ago, sir. The victim's a bookmaker: he didn't show up to open his shop this morning. That's not unprecedented, apparently. The board man has keys, so he let himself in, and he and the clerk got on with business. It was pretty brisk, this being a Saturday and all, but eventually the clerk found time to call Mr Starr. When he got no reply, he tried his mobile. When he got no answer there either, he left a message. After an hour, he called again, and still got no reply. They were having a bad day and the accountant was afraid that the float was going to run out, so he sent Smith, the board man, up here to find out what was up, and if possible get some more cash. When there was no answer to the front-door bell, Smith went round to the lane that runs behind these houses and let himself into the back garden. The door was locked, but he could see through the kitchen window well enough. When he'd stopped yelling, he called the police.'

'What did he see that made him yell?'

'Come on through and see for yourself.' Wilding led the way into the house and through the hallway, until he reached the big kitchen.

It took all Mackenzie's willpower, and possibly the fact that his senses were dulled by four bottles of strong lager, to keep from screaming himself. Gary Starr was sitting at an oak table in the middle of the room, his back to the doorway. His head was angled back, his eyes were staring, sightless, and his mouth gaped wide open. His legs and torso were bound to his chair by thick brown tape, which had been used also to secure his arms to the table top.

It was covered in blood. Mackenzie had never seen so much, but he knew that when an artery is severed, the heart, until it stops, keeps pumping it out. Both of the bookmaker's hands had been severed at the wrist, cleanly. They lay on the table in front of him, palms upward. 'Jesus Christ,' the chief inspector whispered. As he did so, his stomach sent him a warning of imminent activity: he rushed over to the kitchen sink and vomited, retching until there was nothing left to come up, then turned on both taps to wash it away.

'Magic,' said a voice from behind him. 'Now that's what I call contaminating a crime scene!'

He turned to see a man glaring at him, red hair sprouting from beneath the cap of his tunic. 'Who are you?' asked Mackenzie.

'DI Dorward, head of the crime-scene unit. You just beat me to the same question.'

'This is DCI Mackenzie, Arthur,' said Wilding, 'from Queen Charlotte Street. He's my new boss, as of yesterday.'

'I don't care if he's the chief constable, Ray: that was as bloody stupid a thing as I've ever seen.'

'Wind it in, Inspector,' Mackenzie growled. 'We're all human, so I'll have a wee bit less of the chat.'

'No, you bloody won't. I'm in charge of this crime scene, not you: it's my responsibility to keep it sterile. Could you not have thrown up in the garden, man? There's every chance that whoever did this washed the blood off his hands in that sink, and that he left traces of himself behind. There's also every chance that they're not there any more. Now please, don't touch anything else.'

'You don't want to make an enemy of me, Dorward,' the chief inspector warned.

'Frankly, I don't care whether I make an enemy of you. On the other hand, if my report is less than complete because of you, you've made one of me. Maybe you want to think about that. Now, are you the senior investigating officer?'

'Yes,' Mackenzie snapped, then paused. 'At least I assume I am.'

'This set-up's all very new, Arthur,' Wilding explained. 'Maybe Mr McIlhenney will want to run this one, or maybe even Mr McGuire.'

'Well, find out, please. I need to know who's to get my team's results.' He turned and left the kitchen.

'Some start, eh?' Mackenzie murmured.

'Don't worry about it,' said his sergeant. 'It's your call whether you pass this one up the line.'

'I suppose I'd better. Do you have a mobile? I came away in such a rush I've left mine in the house.'

'I've got a mobile, and I've even got Neil McIlhenney's number. DCS Pringle made me keep it close when I was his assistant as head of CID.'

'Good, but before I call him, bring me up to speed. Has the doctor been?'

'Been and gone. His provisional view is that the man's been dead since last night.'

'Come on into the garden,' said Mackenzie, 'before that man gets his Carmen rollers in an even bigger twist.' He led the way: floodlights had been set up outside, and officers were working in their glow going over every inch of ground. 'Any thoughts?'

'There must have been at least two of them,' Wilding replied. 'One bloke on his own couldn't have subdued the victim and trussed him up like that.'

'Agreed. He was a bookie, you say? That can be a rough business; from the looks of it, he's really upset someone.'

'That's a thought,' the sergeant conceded. 'But I can't imagine who it could have been. I know Edinburgh, and I know the gambling scene around here. There's nobody I can think of would do something like that, so if your theory's right, I reckon we're looking for someone from out of town.'

'Was the victim in business in a big way?'

95

'That's another thing: he wasn't. He had the one shop and that's all. Looking at this house, it did well enough: property up here's not cheap. Yet he wasn't a high roller; no way was he that.'

'So why would a business rival hit on him? Is that what you're saying?'

'Yes.'

'Maybe somebody's trying to take over all the small bookies. Could be they made Starr an offer and he refused it so they . . . '

'Lashed him to the kitchen table and chopped his hands off? That's a bit extreme.'

'Sending a message to everyone in town, maybe.'

'Maybe, but there's something else. Remember I said that Starr was the victim of an attempted robbery yesterday?'

'Yes.'

'It was unsuccessful because Starr whacked off the thief's right index finger with a bayonet. That's one I was going to brief you about on Monday.'

'Have we made an arrest?'

'No. He hasn't shown up anywhere in our area for treatment, plus he's not known to us: his print isn't on record.'

'You don't think . . . '

'Hardly. Even if he was treated somewhere that we haven't found yet, he couldn't have been in shape to do that on the same day, even with a helper.'

'So maybe he had two helpers. Maybe there were three of them, maybe four.'

'In that case, why did he try to stick up Starr's

shop on his own? And how did a team of three or four get in here? From what I hear, that character in there wasn't the most sociable man in town, and there are absolutely no signs of forced entry anywhere.'

'Maybe not, but it's the best lead we've got, and that's what I'm going to tell Neil McIlhenney. Did anyone see this robber yesterday morning?'

'Smith, the board man, he did.'

'Get him back in, pronto. Have him do an E-fit for us, and get it out to the media. And when you do, don't forget to mention the missing finger.'

15

Bob Skinner took in the view from the balcony of his daughter's new apartment. 'You've done all right here, kid,' he called across to her. A few feet below the Water of Leith flowed past, reflecting the lights from the properties on the bank opposite.

'Haven't I just,' Alex replied, coming towards him with a flute of cava in either hand, holding one out to him. 'It helps being a lawyer: you get whispers of things that are coming on the market, and of people who might be looking to buy in a specific area. I've always fancied living in Stockbridge, and now, here I am. I've even got a spare room, so that my old man can crash out when he comes for dinner.'

He stepped into the living area, closing the door behind him to shut out the winter chill. 'I'm impressed that you can afford it, at your age,' he told her, as he took the glass.

'I thought it was a gamble when I signed up,' she admitted, 'but I've had a nice rise since then. I can handle it.'

'Are you going to stay with Curle Anthony and Jarvis?' he asked, as they settled into armchairs. 'I seem to remember that when you started your law degree, you were full of talk about going to the Bar.'

'I know, and it's still a thought at the back of my mind, but the longer I stay with the firm, the more opportunities keep opening up. I'm an associate already, and that means that a partnership could be on the distant horizon.'

'At your age most things seem distant, but they're not. They have a habit of zooming up on you.' He glanced at the table, set for two. 'What's for dinner?' he asked suddenly.

'Reindeer carpaccio as a starter . . . '

'Reindeer?'

'Trust me, it's terrific.'

'Reindeer? You mean we'll be eating Rudolph?'

'I prefer to think of it as one of the others. What's your problem anyway? You like venison: that's like eating Bambi's mum.'

'Is she the main course?'

'No, I'm doing seared tuna steaks.'

'Damn, I should have brought white wine, rather than red.'

'Not at all, that Montecillo Reserva will go very well with it.'

'I wish you'd let me take you out, you know.'

'Not a chance. I've never cooked dinner for you before, not in my place. This is the first chance I've had since I moved and I'm not going to let it pass me by. Besides, I thought that you might prefer total privacy for what you've got to tell me.'

'What do you mean?'

'Don't play games with me, Dad. When you call me to say that you want to take me to dinner, you on your own, without Sarah, I'm going to start to think. When I hear that you two had a meeting last night in my firm's offices,

99

after closing time, I'm going to start forming conclusions.'

Bob rose from his chair, walked through to the kitchen and returned with the cava bottle. 'I'm sorry, babe,' he said, as he topped up both glasses. 'I was trying to be delicate about it.'

She laughed, a little sadly. 'Dad, you can't do delicate. What's the point anyway? I know that you and Sarah have been having troubles. The fact that she's not here tells me that you're not going to say that you've kissed and made up. You've come to the end of the road: yes or no?'

'Yes. Sarah's going back to the US.'

'With the kids?'

'I'll have them during term-time, and they'll spend their holidays with her.'

'The nanny's staying on?'

'Of course.' He looked her in the eye. 'Well, what do you have to say?'

'Good luck.'

'That's all?'

'What do you want me to say? 'Please don't, Dad! Think again, for your children's sake!' Sorry, that's not going to happen. Your marriage has run out of steam; you've both been playing away games. It's time to move on.'

'Even for you, that's a pretty calm reaction. I'd expected more . . . '

'Sympathy? Is that what you came for? Dad, you've already got Sarah's replacement lined up.'

'Aileen is not Sarah's replacement: she's a friend.'

'Pull the other one: if she's just a friend then she won't be for long. I know you. I've seen the woman; she came to lunch in our office a few weeks ago. She's your type, Dad, more . . . and I am sorry to say this . . . than Sarah ever was.'

'What do you mean, my type?'

'Work it out for yourself.'

'No, come on, tell me what you mean.'

'When I saw her she reminded me of Mum. Okay?'

'Well, she's not. There may be something in the way she looks, the way she carries herself, but she's different. Okay?'

'Okay, if you say so.'

'You're your mother's double, and she's not a bit like you.'

'Okay, Dad, okay. That's fine: but she's still your type.'

'Well, that's good, for she's going to be around for a while. Now, sympathy: I did not come here for sympathy. I came to break some bad news to you and that's all. Except you seem to be treating it as if it was good news.'

'No, I'm not, really. If I'm not upset enough for you, it's because I think you're right. You're forgetting one thing, Pops.'

'Thank God, you called me Pops at last.'

'What do you mean?'

'When you call me Dad, it's usually because you're lecturing me about something or other. So what am I forgetting?'

'You're forgetting that I've been there myself. Okay, we weren't married, but Andy and I were living together. The same thing happened to us. We weren't right for each other, we got together when both of us were on the rebound from bad

101

experiences, and eventually our relationship ran out of legs. If I hadn't had my termination, and we had married, then it's better than even money that you and I would be still sitting here right now, only both of us would be crying into our cava for the very same reason.'

'Do you really think that Sarah and I got together on the rebound?'

'Yes, I do. You might have rebounded further than Andy and me, but the principle was the same.'

'Yes.' Bob sighed. 'I suppose it was. So you're fine about it, really?'

'As long as my brothers and sister are looked after as well as both of you possibly can, I am. If I ever doubt it, I will come down like a ton of legal bricks on each of you, but I'm confident it won't come to that.'

'Fair enough. Now, let's change the subject. How's your love life?'

'Low level is probably the best way to describe it. I don't have a steady, but I don't go short of dinner dates, and if there's a function where I need a partner, I have a list to choose from. I plan to enjoy this place on my own for a while; filling my wash basket with some man's smelly socks is not on my agenda, I promise you.'

'How about the accountant bloke you mentioned to me a few months back? The fellow from London.'

'Guy? He's still around, but only in the background, and only when I go down there. Nothing will come of that; he's nice enough, but he's just a bit too up himself, as they say in the City.'

'You sound like you've got it taped, kid,' he said, with a touch of admiration.

'I like to think so.'

'No black clouds . . . apart from me, that is?'

'You're not a black cloud; you're a constant beam of sunshine in my life.' She shot him a quick glance. 'Everything's fine, Pops, honest.'

Bob's eyebrows twitched. 'That's another giveaway. Whenever you say 'honest', it means there's something you're not telling me. What is it?'

'Nothing, honest.'

'See? Come on, what is it?'

'Oh, it's just that I've had a couple of phone calls.'

'What sort of phone calls?'

'The silent kind.'

'Breathers? How many?'

'Three within the last week; Tuesday, Thursday and last night.'

'Describe them.'

'What's to describe? The phone rang, I picked it up: there was someone on the line, no doubt about that, but nothing said. No, that's not quite right: last night I thought he said, 'Alex,' in a whisper, a sort of hoarse, croaky whisper.'

'He?'

'Yes, it was a male voice, I'm sure of that.'

Bob was perched on the edge of his chair. 'How did you respond?'

'The first time, I just kept on asking, 'Who's there?' until the line went dead. The second time

I said nothing. The third time, after I thought he whispered my name, I said, 'Fuck off,' and slammed the phone down.'

'Did you try 1471?'

'Of course I did, Pops, but even the dumbest pervert these days knows how to withhold his number.'

'You'd be surprised. Right, what are we going to do about this? I'm off to London on Monday, but you'd better come to stay with us for a few days.'

'Bollocks, I'm not doing that!'

'Why the hell not?'

She gasped. 'You're really asking me that? For a start, in the circumstances I don't want to share space with Sarah: it wouldn't do either of us any good. But most of all, this is my home, and I'm damned if I'll let some creep think he can scare me out of it.'

'Let's change your phone numbers, then; make them ex-directory.'

'That's impossible, for business reasons.'

'Rubbish. If I tell Mitch Laidlaw why it's necessary, he'll make sure that all your colleagues and clients are advised of the changes within the day.'

'And all my friends? Will he tell them too? Pops, I'm not bowing down to this.'

'Maybe not, but I'm not having anyone stalking my daughter either. I'm going to find this person, and I'm going to give him a piece of my mind, and maybe a right good tanking as well. I'm going to have someone camp on your line, and monitor your mobile. Next time you get one of these calls, keep him on the line for as long as you can, however you can. Talk dirty, whatever.'

'Pops!'

'Humour me, love, please. You know I'll do it anyway.'

She shrugged her shoulders. 'If you must. Meantime, I must get dinner under way.' She poured the last of the *cava* into the flutes, picked up her own and headed for the kitchen.

As soon as she was gone, Bob took out his mobile and called a programmed number. 'Neil,' he said, as the call was answered. 'Glad you're in. I've got something that needs taking care of now. I'm at Alex's new pad. She's been having breather calls. You've got her numbers, haven't you?'

'Yes,' McIlhenney confirmed. 'I'll get people sitting on both of them. She'll be aware of it, yes?'

'Yes, she's okayed it. Make sure Mario's up to speed on this, please.'

'Will do.'

'And when you find him . . . '

'He'll be interviewed, by Mario and me, and if that doesn't scare the living shite out of him, he'll be reported for prosecution. Never in this century will he be allowed in the same room as you.'

Skinner laughed. 'This new rank of yours is going to your head. Just find him, Neil, and kick his arse as hard as you have to.'

'Consider it kicked.'

'Good. Anything happened since we spoke last

that I need to know about?'

'Motherwell won two — nil, but I guess you've heard that already. Apart from that, Bandit Mackenzie called me from a very bloody crime scene in Trinity. The victim's a small-time bookie called Gareth Starr.'

'I know that name: a seedy wee chap, from what I remember. Did he welch on the wrong man?'

'That's one of the possibilities Bandit will be pursuing. He called me to ask whether I wanted to take over the inquiry.'

'Hah! That's more tact than I expected from him. What did you tell him?'

'I told him that if I was going to be senior investigating officer on every serious crime in Edinburgh, I'd hardly need him.'

'Spot on. What happened to the victim?'

'Have you eaten yet?'

'No, my lovely daughter is being creative in the kitchen.'

'In that case, I'd best keep the detail to myself. You don't want to be doing what Mackenzie did.'

'What was that?'

'He barfed in the victim's kitchen sink, in front of a house full of SOCOs. Arthur Dorward went ballistic, apparently.'

'How did you hear about it?'

'Like I said, there were witnesses: you know the force gossip mill. Once it starts . . . '

' . . . there ain't no stopping it. Keep an eye on him, Neil. That's not the way you want to start a new job.'

16

'Have we got that E-fit yet?' asked Bandit Mackenzie, scowling irritably at Ray Wilding across the mobile crime-scene headquarters that had been parked in the lane behind Starr's house.

'Not yet, sir. Big Ming is not the easiest man to deal with: he lives on his own wee planet. I'm not sure we're going to get anything meaningful. Maybe we should just put out a statement saying that we're looking for a number of people, one of whom has a bad hand injury.'

'We'll do that, Sergeant, but I want that image to go with it. Not tomorrow, not the day after, but now, within the hour. Get on to the office and bloody tell them that, will you!'

'Will do, sir.' He made to pick up the phone, then stopped. 'I'm still not happy, though, that we're going about this the right way.'

'Oh, yes? What would you do differently?'

'I'd look into the victim a bit more deeply than we're doing just now. The way things stand at the moment we know sod all about him, other than that he was a bookie, and now he's dead. Whoever did that to him was very angry with him. Maybe your assumption is right, but maybe it wasn't Frodo fucking Baggins and some mates, come back to take revenge.'

'Who? Christ, you told me we didn't have an ID on this bloke.'

'That was a joke, sir. *Lord of the Rings*: remember the end?' Mackenzie looked blank but angry. 'Sorry, you don't. Anyway, what if it wasn't them? Shouldn't we be trying to explore every line of enquiry we can find, and doesn't that begin by trying to find out everything we can about Gary Starr's life, business and private?'

'Now you listen to me, Ray,' the chief inspector hissed. 'Gwennie Dell, my old sergeant through in Strathclyde, has put in for a move, and she could be on her way through here. I could have her in your chair on Monday just by asking. So don't you try to tell me how to do my fucking job, okay!'

Wilding stood his ground, glaring back at him. 'First of all, sir, you couldn't do that. DS Dell is coming through here, but she's been approved for a posting to the Drugs Squad, working with the new commander. That was one of the last pieces of business across my desk yesterday afternoon, when I was in the head of CID's office. You may have got to work with her if you were still there, but not now. Second of all, I'm not trying to tell you how to do your job, I'm asking you to let me do mine the way I think it should be done.'

'You are? Well, get fucking on with it, Ray.' Mackenzie snatched up his coat from the back of his chair and headed for the door. 'I'm off to rescue what I can of my Saturday night.'

17

Sir James Proud picked up the newspapers from the doorstep of the little house in Anglesey Drive. The *Sunday Post* was wrapped round a copy of the *Sunday Mail*: he guessed that the old man had read these all his life. He rang the bell and waited, glancing at the front page of the *Post* as he did so. The banner headline told of an atrocity in the Middle East, but below and to the left, a face stared out at him, one of those staring-eyed E-fit things that, it seemed to him, hardly ever produced a positive identification. He read the story below, and realised that it had been issued by his own force, in connection with a murder the day before.

'We are pursuing several lines of enquiry,' said Detective Sergeant Ray Wilding, 'but we are particularly keen to trace this man, last seen yesterday morning in the vicinity of Evesham Street and Great Junction Street. He is known to have sustained a bad injury to his right hand, which would certainly require medical treatment. We are appealing to him to contact the police so that he can be eliminated from our investigation. If you know this man, please contact our hotline.'

'Never seen him before in my life,' the chief constable muttered, as he looked at the gaunt,

109

ageless face and the grey wool hat. 'But I'll bet we've had a few calls by now.' He knew also that most of them would be wild geese thrown up by well-meaning citizens, that a few would come from pranksters, and that others would be malicious. There was someone out there, undoubtedly, with a grey woolly hat and a badly injured hand, but he was unlikely to be traced by an approximate likeness in a newspaper.

He was still looking at the page when the big green door creaked open. 'Good morning, young Proud,' the old man greeted him. He was dressed from another era, but immaculately, in grey flannels and a smoking jacket, and he had carpet slippers on his feet. His thick white hair had a Brylcreem shine and he was freshly shaved. Proud wondered if he had made a special effort for him, then thought back to his school days and recalled that the rector was always turned out like a new pin.

'Good morning to you, Mr Goddard.' He held out the newspapers.

'Ah, they've arrived at last,' the throw-back said, checking his watch as he took them. 'Eleven thirty: not good enough. I must have a word with the newsagent.' He stood aside. 'Come in, come in. It's too cold a morning to be standing out there.'

Proud allowed himself to be ushered into a well-lit hallway, then through a living room into a sun-bathed conservatory. The previous week-end's snow had cleared, but a crisp frost sat on the grass outside like a lambskin carpet.

'Were you reading about our local sensation?'

110

Goddard asked, waving the *Post* in the air before tossing it, and the *Mail*, on to a table on which a pot of tea and two cups sat waiting.

'The murder? Did that happen near here?'

'Swansea Street runs parallel to this one. If you go to the end of the garden and look along the vennel you'll see one of your caravan things. Damn nuisance, actually; it prevented me from getting my bicycle out this morning. Have them move it, will you, James?' He smiled, revealing teeth that were too white to be anything but false. 'Sorry, I'm forgetting myself: that should have been Sir James.'

'Only my wife and my secretary call me that, Mr Goddard. It's James, as always.'

'Now that you're no longer a pupil, you'd better call me Russell.'

'It wouldn't sound right, sir. You're still the rector to me, and to everyone else who was at Edinburgh Academy in your time.'

'In that case, you'd better pour the tea, like you used to in my study when we had our regular chats in your year as head boy. Did you know that there were people who said that I appointed you because you were the Lord Provost's son?'

'I heard the whispers, yes,' Proud admitted, as he picked up the teapot.

'All rubbish: I couldn't stand your father. No, I chose you in spite of that fact, because you were good at everything you did, if excellent at nothing, and because you commanded the confidence of every pupil in the school and most of the masters. Time proved me right too. You're still head boy, aren't you?'

'I suppose I am in a way. My present establishment is co-educational, though. I expect that there will be a head girl one of these days.'

The old rector looked genuinely shocked. 'Surely not! I know we live in an age of change, but that would be taking political correctness just a little too far.' His voice dropped to a conspiratorial whisper. 'My late wife would have crucified me, had she heard me saying something like that. She'd be happy otherwise, though; it looks as if we're going to have a woman as First Minister.'

'There are precedents for that too.'

'Thirty-three of them to be exact, starting with Mrs Bandaranaike in Ceylon. Did you know that when she assumed office for the third time she was appointed by her daughter, Mrs Kumara-tunga, who was president at the time?'

'No, I did not.'

Mr Goddard's eyes twinkled. 'In that case you won't know either that both Mr Bandaranaike and Mr Kumaratunga were assassinated: risky business, being married to a female politician. This de Marco woman doesn't have a husband, does she?'

'I don't believe so. I've met her on several occasions and I've never heard her speak of one.'

'In that case, aspiring suitors should bear the Bandaranaike women in mind.' The old man sipped his tea. 'Sorry: you probably don't remember this, but history was my main subject.

112

However, James, you haven't come here for a lesson, have you?'

'I'm always willing to learn, sir, but no, I haven't.'

'Have you come to ask me what I knew of the murder victim, then?'

'Did you know him?'

'I have made his acquaintance on a few occasions over the years. I found him to be an unpleasant man, surly, no manners at all. I canvassed him for the Conservatives at the last general election. He was abusive. Quite unnecessary: there's no reason at all why politics can't be conducted in a civilised manner. Indeed, they must be. The world in which we live now is full of examples of the evil that can come about when that principle is forgotten.'

'Did he have a wife?'

'He did when he moved here twenty years ago, but she left him as soon as their son had finished school. Heriot's,' he added.

'Did he upset anyone else around here?'

'He was the sort of man who would upset anyone, but mostly he ignored his neighbours and we ignored him.'

'Have you been interviewed by my officers, Mr Goddard?'

'No, I haven't, although I did see some of them in the street this morning.'

Proud looked at his old headmaster. 'I should know this, but how long have you been retired?'

'Thirty-three years, James.'

'Which makes you?'

'Ninety-three.'

'My goodness. How's your memory?'

'What did I just tell you about woman Prime Ministers?'

Proud laughed. 'Point taken: in that case, here's the real reason for my visit. I want to ask you about Claude Bothwell.'

'You mean Adolf?'

'The staff called him Adolf too?'

'What else would you call a German teacher with such a damn silly wee moustache? What do you want to know about him?'

'As much as you can tell me. It's not him I'm trying to trace, but a woman with whom he was said to be carrying on, a teacher in the junior school, Miss Annabelle Gentle.'

The old man's thin eyebrows rose. 'He was, was he?' he murmured. 'There was conjecture about that at the time, after they both left.'

'You didn't know about it?'

'Not for a fact. How did this come to your attention?'

'Through Miss Gentle's daughter; she's trying to trace her.'

'I don't know if I'll be much help to the woman.'

'I don't know either, but you're the best lead I have. Can you tell me about the circumstances of their leaving?'

'It was abrupt; that's the best I can say about it. You'll remember yourself, I'm sure, that Bothwell was supposed to be taking your German class that year. Well, he didn't turn up, damn him. There was no formal resignation, no notice was given or served.'

114

'Did you contact him?'

'I tried to. The school secretary phoned his house to see what was up, but she got no reply. She called several times, with the same result. Eventually I went to see him. The place was deserted: he and his wife had gone. One of the neighbours saw me on the doorstep and told me that they'd left a few weeks before. He'd seen Bothwell loading suitcases into his car, and assumed that they were off on holiday, but they never came back.'

'They left their house, and all their belongings?'

'They didn't have any. The house was rented: I found that out when the landlord's solicitor rang me at the school looking for him.'

'What about Miss Gentle?'

'I didn't have much to do with that. I left it in the hands of Bessie Stone, head of the junior school. I barely remember the girl, to tell you the truth. I had very little contact with her. She absented herself in the same way that Bothwell did, on the same day.'

'Did you call on her, or did Miss Stone?'

'No, Bessie phoned her on the morning she failed to appear, thinking she was sick. As I recall, one of her housemates answered. Apparently Miss Gentle had gone up north on holiday at the beginning of July, or so she'd led them to believe, but hadn't come back. She hadn't given up her room, but they were thinking about letting it.'

'How did you deal with the matter?'

'Peremptorily: Bessie gave her until the end of

the week to return, then sent her notice of dismissal by recorded delivery.'

'Where?'

'At her flat,' said Mr Goddard. 'That was the only address we had for her. I gave Claude an extra week's grace, and then I did the same with him.'

'Did you ever hear from either of them again?'

'There was a phone call, I believe, from the girl's family, looking for her. The secretary told them that she was no longer with us.'

'What about Bothwell?'

'Nothing. I thought that someone might get in touch if he applied for a job somewhere else, but nobody ever did.'

'And you didn't link the two departures?'

'Not really. As I said there was conjecture, but it was staff-room talk, that was all, laughter about our Adolf being a bit of a wide boy. There had been no talk about them at all when they were both on the staff, no rumours. These things happen; people behave badly. To me, it was an unfortunate coincidence, but now you tell me they were carrying on after all. Where does that information come from, young James?'

'From Miss Gentle's sister. She says that Annabelle told them, the Easter before all this happened, that she and Bothwell were engaged.'

'Indeed? Mrs Bothwell would have had something to say about that, I'd have thought.'

'Did you ever meet her?'

'Of course, and so did you. She gave you a pot at the school sports, as I recall.'

'Thank you, I thought that's who she was.'

'What do you remember about her?'

Proud's smile had an edge of guilt about it. 'Quite a bit, actually: I was sixteen then and beginning to notice such things. Tall, dark hair, striking, well-built. 'Tits like racing airships' was Bertie Stenton's description, as I recall. We were more impressed by Adolf after we saw her.'

'Young Stenton always had a way with words,' the old rector remarked. 'He still does now he's on the Bench, from what I read in the *Scotsman* whenever he sentences some poor miscreant. Mrs Bothwell was Spanish. Her name was Montserrat, like the soprano; Montserrat Rivera Jiminez, the daughter of an hotelier. I know all that because I asked her to send me her *curriculum vitae*: she'd been a teacher too, of English. I thought about employing her in the modern-languages department but she'd have had to upgrade her qualification. She told me that she and Bothwell met in Girona, when he was on holiday one summer, trying to learn Catalan.'

'Was that her home town?'

'No, she told me that she was from a place called Torroella de Montgri.'

'I know it. My deputy has a property not far away. My wife and I go there quite regularly.'

'The place was very different in those days, though; it was Franco's time. Mrs Bothwell told me that she was happy to leave Spain because of him. Perhaps they're still there.'

'What age would they be now?'

'The Bothwells? Mid-seventies; he was thirty-six when he left, and she was a couple of years

117

younger. Miss Gentle? I can't say for sure.'

'She'd be seventy.'

Mr Goddard refilled his cup and topped up Proud's. 'What's the daughter's story?' he asked.

'Adopted.'

'I hope she knows what she's letting herself in for, assuming that you find Miss Gentle, which I doubt you will.'

'Is there nothing else you can recall about Bothwell? Did he have any particular friends on the staff?'

'He didn't have any particular friends at all, from what I could see. That said, I can think of two places you might ask. There's the pensions people: if he's still alive he may be claiming one. Then there's the SSTA.'

'What?'

'The Scottish Secondary Teachers' Association: Adolf was a staunch member. That did nothing to enhance his popularity in the Academy, I can tell you. Other than that, young James, I can't be of any more help to you.'

18

'I'm glad you could make it, Dottie,' said Neil McIlhenney. 'This is no sort of a hand-over, and we'll have a longer chat once you get back from London, but the boss and I thought it was important that I should talk you through things before you went away.' He nodded towards a blonde-tinted woman seated at a desk in the Special Branch outer office. 'It's good that you're having a chance to meet Alice Cowan too: she's been my eyes and ears in this job. She's the best back-watcher in the business.' The young detective constable smiled at the compliment.

'I'll need one, that's for sure,' Shannon admitted. 'This is all going to be very new to me: it'll take some getting used to. Working here at Fettes was just a dream for me a couple of days ago: now I find I'm right in at the deep end.'

'You'll be fine. The time you spend in London with the DCC will be all the learning curve you need.'

'Mmm. I'm more nervous about that than anything else. What can you tell me about it? What will we be doing?'

'I'm not telling you anything about it. Mr Skinner will brief you himself once you get to London.'

'He said we'd be 'playing with the big boys'. What did he mean by that?'

'Wait and see. This is the only advice I'll give

you: when you get where you're going, keep your face straight, your mouth shut and follow his lead.'

'Sounds heavy.'

'Don't worry, you're on the right side. You couldn't be with anyone better than him.' McIlhenney pushed himself up from the desk on which he was perched. 'Now, if you'll excuse me, I saw a familiar car outside when I arrived. I must go and see what its owner's up to. You two get acquainted.'

He left the suite and walked along the corridor, making a right turn at the end. When he reached the head of CID's office, he saw that the door was ajar. He walked in, through the outer area to the room beyond. Mario McGuire was leaning back in the swivel chair, his feet on the desk, reading a copy of *Scotland on Sunday*. He glanced across at McIlhenney as he entered. 'Where's the coffee, then?' he asked.

'Fuck off.'

'That's insubordination, Superintendent. Is that how it's going to be from now on?'

'More or less.'

'Been clearing your desk?'

'That and introducing Dottie to Alice. Been filling yours up?'

'I've brought nothing to put in it: I don't go for too much personal stuff in the office.'

McIlhenney pointed towards the newspaper. 'What do you think of that?'

'The E-fit? Tell me it's the Ghost of Christmas Yet to Come and I'll believe you. It looks just like a hundred others we've seen: PR to make the punters think we're on the case. I wonder how many calls they've had.'

'There's one good way to find out.'

'Surprise visit to the investigation?'

McIlhenney grinned. 'Exactly.'

'Just what I was thinking. Come on: we'll take my car.' McGuire folded the newspaper and stood up. 'Did you read the story?' he asked, as he closed the outer office door behind him.

'I read the *Sunday Herald* version, but I guess it's much the same.'

'Did anything strike you about it?'

'The quote was from Ray Wilding, not Mackenzie; that's unusually self-effacing for the Bandit.'

'Yeah, that's what I thought. He's just moved into a new patch: he should be taking every chance he gets to make his name.'

'I'll have a word with him.'

'Do that: you know him better than I do. Plus, you're his line manager.'

'True, and you're mine, so there's something I'd better tell you about. I had big Bob on the blower last night with steam coming out his ears. Alex has been having funny phone calls at her new flat. He wants us to find out who it is, and tell him not to do it again.'

'Too right we will,' McGuire exclaimed. 'Alex works for Paula and me at the Viareggio Trust, soon to be Viareggio plc. I'm not having some hooligan mess her about. What have you done so far?'

'I've got campers on her phone line and on her mobile: so far the bastard's withheld his number, but if he calls again she'll try to keep him on long enough for us to get a fix.'

'Are you watching her as well?'

'Discreetly, but we are. She doesn't know it, though. I'm not too worried. Alex is a strong girl and she can handle herself up to black-belt standard . . . the boss made sure of that when she was growing up . . . but it's not going to come to that. We'll pick the caller up, sooner or later.'

'When you do, don't interview him without me being there.'

'Don't worry, that's part of the plan. It'll be just you and me.'

The drive to the crime scene from the police headquarters building took less than five minutes. Swansea Street was lined with cars, apart from an area in front of the victim's house that had been blocked off by police parking cones. McGuire could have stopped there, but instead he drove round the corner to Anglesey Drive.

As he climbed out of the passenger seat, McIlhenney turned to stare at a car that had just passed them. 'Hey, Mario, that was the chief,' he exclaimed.

'No, surely not. He doesn't live anywhere near here.'

'I'm telling you, it was him. He was on his own too; his wife wasn't with him.'

'What the hell would Proud Jimmy be doing in Trinity on a Sunday afternoon?'

'How about checking up on CID?'

'The big man would just love that, wouldn't he? If he was, we'll find out directly.'

The two detectives walked the few yards to the mobile investigation centre. 'Jesus,' said McIlhenney, when he saw the big white vehicle. 'The residents must love this. It's practically blocking the bloody lane: there's hardly room for the door to open.' He trotted up the half-dozen steps with McGuire at his heels and stepped inside.

Detective Sergeant Ray Wilding was at a desk in the middle of the van, with a pile of papers in front of him. He jumped to his feet as the newcomers entered. 'Sit down, man,' said McGuire. 'This isn't a formal visit.'

'You haven't just had the chief constable here, have you?' asked McIlhenney. The sergeant gazed at him, taken aback by the question, and shook his head. 'Secret assignation, then.' The big superintendent chuckled. 'Where's DCI Mackenzie?'

'Not here, sir. He called around ten.'

'You mean called in?'

'No, sir, he phoned. He said he was sick and told me to get on with the investigation in his absence.'

'Are you comfortable with that? You're just back on the active side after your spell in Dan Pringle's front office. Have you got enough support here?'

'I'm all right just now, sir. I've got plenty of uniforms to do what needs to be done at this stage, canvassing neighbours for possible sightings and fielding calls about the E-fit as they come in through the hotline.'

'Have you had many?'

'A few, but nothing that's got me excited. There was one bloke called in and said it looks like his window-cleaner, but he doesn't know what his name is or where he lives. A woman contact said it looked like her daughter's boyfriend, but when questioned she said that she saw him last night and he had all ten fingers. A pathetic old lady said it reminded her of her grandson: it turned out that he was killed in a motor-bike accident ten years ago. Oh, aye, and a drunk phoned and said it looked like Osama bin Laden. That's the closest thing to an identification we've had, actually. But it can't be him: he was last seen driving a taxi in New York.'

'Just about what you'd expect, in other words.'

'Exactly.'

'Have you found the murder weapon yet?'

'We don't know, sir. There are a few things in the kitchen that look as if they might have done the job, but they're all clean, or rather Starr's are the only fingerprints on them. There is one odd thing, though. There's a full set of kitchen knives in a wooden block, only one of them's missing; a big one, from the size of the empty slot. But we'll need to wait for Professor Hutchinson's post-mortem report before we can take that any further.'

'Old Joe may need to bring someone in for that. Identifying a weapon from the marks left on a body can be a specialist task.'

'What about the neighbours?' asked McGuire.

'No more productive than the E-fit, I'm afraid. This is a quiet neighbourhood: you don't find people walking back from the pub at midnight.

We've had no sightings of anyone entering or leaving the victim's house.'

'Okay, Ray, where do you go from here? If it seems that I'm pushing this, it's because in a way it started on my watch. I was still in Leith when the attempted robbery at Starr's took place. It's also because I don't plan to have any unsolved homicides on my record as head of CID.'

'Understood, sir. Tomorrow morning I plan to re-interview Big Ming . . . that's Smith, the board man. I'm also going to talk to his clerk, and his ex-wife. I want to find out everything there is to know about Gary Starr.'

'Do I take it you're not keen on the idea that the boy with the missing finger came back with friends?'

'If he had friends, sir, why did he try to stick up Starr's place on his own with a plastic gun? There is no commonality between the two events other than amputation. I find it hard to accept that someone who was such a disastrous, half-hearted failure as an armed robber could be involved in something as fucking hard-core brutal as this.'

'I think I agree with you. Don't stop with the ex-wife, Ray. Talk to his bank manager; look into his accounts for money flowing in. Take his house apart, take his shop apart; find out who his associates were, look for cash piles, go through all his books and pin down every penny he had. If you want assistance from specialist officers, you've got it.'

'What about Mr Mackenzie, sir? He's the senior investigating officer.'

'He's not here, Ray,' McIlhenney intervened. 'He can't run a high-profile murder investigation from his sick-bed. Until he's back, you report to me directly, and when he is back, the inquiry is to be run exactly as we've discussed here.'

'And something else,' McGuire added. 'This is just a wild idea,' he grinned, 'but since it's my wild idea, I expect you to bear it in mind. When you're building up your list of his contacts and associates, keep an eye out for Muslims. Look at what was done to this man: he had both of his hands cut off. What's the punishment for theft under Sharia law? Amputation.'

'But not death,' McIlhenney pointed out.

The new head of CID smiled, wickedly. 'Maybe they weren't trying to kill him. Maybe they just didn't care.'

19

'Where's Lena? She hasn't made herself scarce to give us a clear field, has she?'

Aileen laughed. 'No, I wouldn't ask her to do that. She's visiting her parents, as it happens: she'll be back around eight, in time for *Monarch of the Glen*.'

'Will she cough loudly and rattle her keys before she comes in?'

'I'm sure she will, but there won't be any need, will there?'

'No, there won't. Your place is one thing, but here I wouldn't feel comfortable . . . and at my age, honey, that's a must. There's something else too,' Bob admitted. 'As long as Sarah's still here, well, call me inhibited if you will, but it wouldn't feel right.'

'I know. If we're truth-telling, I'm sort of glad that the opportunity's never presented itself. Call me old-fashioned if you will, but I've never slept with a man who's gone home to his wife afterwards, even if they are estranged, and even if they will be divorced in a couple of months.'

He stepped up behind her and slid his arms round her waist, holding her lightly as she cored and sliced peppers. 'I'm glad to hear it,' he whispered in her ear. 'I'll make you a promise. Next Easter, the kids should be with Sarah in America, as long as she has somewhere for them to stay by then. I assume that the parliament will

127

be in recess too. If that's the case, you and I will fly out to my place in Spain, where we will be completely and utterly alone.'

'A promise, you said? Just the two of us?'

'Well, apart from your protection officers . . . '

She turned in his embrace, her eyes widening. 'You're joking. I won't have . . . '

He grinned. 'Not in Spain. I'll be all the protection you need there.'

'And here, I hope.'

'No. We've discussed this already: once you're confirmed in office you should have personal security on an official basis.'

'Can't you just do it yourself, when we're together at least?'

'I'm talking twenty-four hours a day here. It's a professional job. Would you want me looking over your shoulder all the time, and never directly at you? Would you feel comfortable, bumping into my Glock in its holster?'

'You mean they'll be armed?'

'We don't give them catapults, babe. It comes with the territory you'll be taking over.'

She raised herself up on her toes, kissed him lightly and turned back to the peppers. 'If it'll keep you happy,' she said, 'I'll put up with it.'

'Thanks, it will.'

'In which case, there's the matter of keeping me happy in return. Now that you've engineered that horrible man Jay's resignation as the First Minister's security adviser, there's a vacancy to be filled. If, and I'll keep saying 'if' till it happens, I do get the leadership, I'd like you to take it on. I don't mean I want you to give up your present job: it would be part-time, on a consultancy basis.'

'God, no, love! Please don't ask me. I've done that job already, before the parliament was set up and when the Secretary of State for Scotland was the main man. It didn't work out well: in fact it ended with me telling him to shove it. What if I gave you some advice that turned out to be wrong? What if I gave you some advice, you didn't take it, and the situation went sour?'

'You'd forgive me and I'd forgive you, because we'd each of us know that the other was doing their level best.'

'Aileen, it's too close, too personal.'

'That's exactly why it's got to be you.' She slid the sliced vegetables into a colander, picked up two chicken breasts and laid them on the chopping board. 'There is nobody in this land that I trust more than you. You agreed to be my counsellor on police matters when I became justice minister, didn't you?'

'But this would be different.'

'No, it wouldn't. Look at it this way: let's say that in six months' time I'm First Minister, you're divorced, and if we're not living together, we're at the very least spending as much time as we can with each other. Suppose I appoint someone else? The first time he gives me advice, I come home and tell you about it and you disagree, bang goes my confidence in that person.'

'So don't tell me about it.'

'Do you mean that? Do you really want me keeping secrets from you?'

He smiled wryly. 'No, I don't suppose that's the ideal basis for any relationship. In that case, appoint Andy Martin, the DCC in Tayside.'

'You mean the same Andy Martin that was your right-hand man until he moved? And what would he do if I appointed him? Every time something big came up, he'd call you to ask what you thought before he advised me.'

'Andy's his own man, I promise you.'

'He's also a human being. Look, I wouldn't be against him touching base with a trusted colleague. My point is that if that trusted colleague is you, you might as well be doing the job yourself, and calling on DCC Martin when you think it necessary. Go on, my darling, do it for me. After all, it's not as if we're talking about an appointment that's going to be public property.'

Bob picked a wok from a hook on the kitchen wall, then poured olive oil, soy sauce and a little balsamic vinegar into it, running them around the surface of the wide pan before putting it on a gas burner. 'If it's what you want,' he said, 'I'll do it. But there will be no formal appointment, no consultancy, and absolutely no remuneration: that would be hugely improper, and could bring you down. I'll be your security adviser, but it'll be strictly between you and me.'

She kissed him again, for longer this time. 'Thanks, Bob,' she murmured. 'I promise it won't be a burden to you. As far as privacy is concerned, our friendship is a matter of record, so once people find out, as they will eventually, how close we really are, they'll assume you're doing the job anyway.'

20

Bandit Mackenzie had been expecting a phone call from Ray Wilding, updating him on the investigation. What he had not expected was a heavy knock on his front door. He had no doubt that the caller was a police officer, since a civilian would have rung the bell; from the weight of the thump, it was a man.

Cheryl looked at him. 'Are you not going to answer it?' she asked.

'You get it.'

She tutted, but did as he asked: as she left the room he found himself hoping that it was not Mario McGuire who was standing on his doorstep. Neil McIlhenney, he could handle: he was an amiable big bloke, easy to kid, but the new chief superintendent had a touch of the evil about him. He tried not to let his relief show when his wife ushered McIlhenney into the room.

'How are you feeling, Bandit?' the superintendent asked, as he took a seat facing him, hearing the door close as Cheryl headed for the kitchen.

'A bit better now, thanks. I've felt the flu coming on for a couple of days: it just seemed to come to a head this morning.'

'You do look a bit puffy about the eyes, I have to say. I know the feeling.'

'Yeah. That was probably why I threw up yesterday.'

'It happens.'

'You heard about it? Did that bastard Dorward complain? If he did I'll have him.'

'No, he didn't, so forget it. Arthur's well out of your reach anyway. There were other people there, including uniforms: that's probably how the tale got passed on.'

'As long as it was none of my people. Anyway, after that, the way I felt when I woke up I thought I'd be more use to the investigation advising from a distance than cooped up in the van infecting everyone else.'

'That's your call to make. However,' McIlhenney paused, 'it's for me to decide whether the investigation can handle your absence, or whether I need to draft in someone else, or even take over myself. So in the unlikely event of you ever needing another sickie at the start of a major inquiry, I'd be grateful if your first phone call is to me. Fair enough?'

Mackenzie nodded. 'Point taken: sorry, sir.'

'Are you taking the piss, Bandit? What's with the 'sir'? I was Neil a week ago and I still am.'

'That's good to hear. You can never be sure how a friend's going to handle promotion: I've seen some let it go right to their head. So, have you drafted someone in?'

'Not yet. Will you be fit tomorrow?'

'I reckon so.'

'Then I won't; Ray Wilding's handled things fine today in your absence. We're no nearer a solution, but Ray's got a plan for taking things forward, and I want you to run with it. He's a good cop. I'm sure the two of you are going to get along.'

'I'm sure we are,' said Mackenzie, in not quite the correct tone.

McIlhenney looked at him. 'Bandit, are you all right? I don't mean the flu, I mean are you all right about the job just now?'

'Why shouldn't I be?'

'Could you still be thinking about that thing you and I were involved in? I know you've had counselling from O'Malley, same as I have, and I know that he gave you a clean bill of psychological health, but that was a pretty hairy night.'

'And I didn't cover myself with glory?' Instantly, Mackenzie seemed to switch into defensive mode. 'Is that what you're suggesting?'

'No, I'm bloody not. If I had to do that again, I'd be just as happy to have you alongside me. But people died there: that can affect the strongest among us, after the event, when we expect it least.'

'I'm fine, Neil. I've had no aftershocks.'

'There's something, though.'

The chief inspector shifted in his chair. 'Okay, if you insist. Maybe I didn't like being booted off the Drugs Squad.'

'What makes you think you were booted off? The boss told you what's happening. There's a restructuring in CID: we're trying to create more jobs by reallocating resources; to put it bluntly we're trying to swap chiefs for Indians. As part of that, the Drugs Squad will now be run by an inspector, and CID offices will be headed by chief inspectors. There's no slight on you: part of the reason the DCC's been able to do this is because you've done such a good job on drugs in the city.'

'Thanks, but it hasn't been good enough. There are still suppliers out there that I don't know about.'

'There are always one or two that we don't know about,' McIlhenney pointed out. 'You sent the Irish teams packing when they tried to get in. There were big Brownie points in that.'

'Yes, but there was one operation that I was trying to pin down. Now . . . '

'Now Mavis McDougall will handle it. She's capable, and with your pal Gwen Dell to help her, your excellent work will be carried on.'

'They're both good officers, I grant you.'

'Exactly. Your old unit's in good hands, and so is your new one, CID in Leith. Get yourself settled in there. Get to know the patch, and your team. You're a man light at the moment, but that'll be rectified. I'm thinking about shifting DC Tarvil Singh from Torphichen to your office, as soon as George Regan gets back from compassionate leave. He's a bright young lad, plus he's as big as a house. Even today that can come in handy in Leith.'

21

Alex Skinner had spent much of her life worrying about her father, but she had never admitted it, not, at least, to a living soul. She never discussed him with anyone outside the family. Indeed, since his estrangement from Sarah had become obvious, the number of people to whom she could speak freely about him had dwindled to just one.

Her mother had been killed when she was a child, but she remained a constant presence in Alex's life. Her grave was in a small cemetery a mile or two outside Gullane. It was neatly tended: daffodils flowered upon it in the spring, and the granite memorial was flanked by heather. When she was younger, still at school, she would go there often, sometimes on her bike, sometimes on foot. She was still a regular visitor even though she lived in the city: a wreath at Christmas, a bouquet on Myra's birthday, in remembrance, one on her own, with love, another on the day she died, out of grief. On four or five milestone dates every year she would make the pilgrimage to Dirleton Toll, to the lair against the eastern wall; there she would stand, or sit on the grass if it was dry enough, and there she would tell her mum of the events in her life, the good, the bad and, on a couple of occasions, the downright ugly. But her talk would not be of herself alone, for she knew that Myra would want to know of Bob, and of the way his life was developing. As she had grown, she had told her of his years alone, 'in exile from life', as she had overheard him say to a friend at her grandfather's funeral. Occasionally, she had told of female companions, but those had been very short stories, until finally she had been able to describe the arrival of Sarah in his life, the growth of their relationship and its flowering into marriage and new family. As she spoke Alex felt that there was a place inside her head that told her how her mother would have reacted to each new development. She knew that she would have loved the children, as Alex did, although she would have been ambivalent about Sarah from the start as Alex . . . it was the only secret she had ever kept from her father . . . had always been. And she would be worried about Bob now, she told herself.

She had gone to the grave that afternoon. Alone in the cemetery, wrapped in a parka against the winter cold, she had told Myra of the final split, of how he seemed to be taking it, and of the guilt that was lurking just beneath the surface. She had told her of the counter-balance of his friendship with Aileen de Marco; as she did so, she had felt a sudden wave of relief flow through her as if it had come from the ground on which she stood.

But there was something else, she knew it, something lying underneath it all, gnawing at him, something that had happened to him or was going to happen. She had seen it in his eyes the night before as they had dined: he had drunk more than usual; the bottle he had brought had gone quickly, and he had opened another. He had been restless, fidgety: the meal was barely over before he had insisted on taking her to a pub that he knew in Stockbridge, then to another. They had returned to the flat just before twelve and he had gone to bed, but she had heard him through the night, in the bathroom then in the kitchen. And yet, in the morning, he had been clear-eyed and clean-shaven. He had brought her cereal, orange juice and coffee on a tray, as she lay in bed struggling to focus from her disturbed night and the onset of what she had hoped was not a hangover. He had kissed her on the forehead, as he had always done, and he had left, for a golf tie at Gullane.

'What is it, Mum?' she found herself whispering, as she looked out at the night, as he had done twenty-four hours earlier.

'Pardon?' said her friend Gina, from the chair in which he had sat.

Alex had forgotten her presence. She had forgotten that it was Sunday, their girls' night. 'Sorry,' she exclaimed. 'I was miles away there.'

'I'll say you were. You've been staring straight ahead for about five minutes now. Have you got a work problem?'

'No.'

Gina's face creased into a knowing grin. 'Ah, a man problem, then?'

'No.' Alex hesitated. 'Not in the sense you mean at any rate. It's my dad. I'm a bit worried about him, that's all.'

'I'm not surprised, after all that happened to him last week.'

'What?'

'Are you kidding me? That stuff he was involved in, with those gunmen, the soldiers and everything. Like Nicolas Cage did in that movie, he saved the fucking day, but there were people killed there. If it was my dad I'd be more than a bit worried, I'd be pissing myself.'

Alex looked down at her, as the obvious hit her between the eyes. Of course, that had to be it. But why had she not realised from the start? She knew the answer at once. Her father had been involved in dangerous situations before: he had emerged more or less unscathed but not always. There had been that time, that awful time, when he had been stabbed and had almost died. She had seen him in the aftermath of all those things, but she had never seen him like that. Everyone has a best-before date: she had said that often enough herself. She identified her fear: it was that his might be behind him.

'I suppose you're right, G,' she said. 'It's just that . . . I've never had to worry about him before. Poor old bear: he has to face all that, plus, he's getting divorced.'

Her friend gasped. 'He's not! You never told me that was happening.'

'I didn't know myself until last night, not for sure at any rate.'

'Poor guy. No wonder you're worried about him, you daft cow. But it's down to you to help him out of it. He's done the same for you in the past, when you and Mr Perfect split up.'

'Don't call Andy that: he wasn't like that, not really.'

'He expected you to be, though. Goose, gander, sauce, et cetera; he didn't deserve you, girl.'

'Well, he's happy with what he's got now, so that's okay.'

'I hope your dad will be too, one day.'

'He will. I'm sure about that.' She reached over and took an almost empty glass from her friend's hand. 'Come on, let's go along to Comely Bank and get those pizzas.'

She had her keys in her hand, one foot in the entrance hallway, one in the flat, when the phone rang. 'Bugger,' she muttered. 'Hell, it can ring.'

'No,' said Gina. 'Answer it: it might be your dad.'

'True,' she agreed, and ran back indoors, snatching the nearest phone, from the kitchen wall. 'Alex,' she announced brightly, hoping it would be him, calling to apologise for worrying her with his restlessness.

'I know.' The voice was a whisper, hoarse and faint, almost as if its owner was trying not to be overheard.

'Oh, shit.' She groaned. 'Not you again. Listen, who are you and what do you want? Do I know you? Should I know you? Or are you just some fucking greasy pervert who gets his rocks off by phoning women?'

Silence, other than background noise on the line.

Alex was aware of Gina staring at her, but she remembered her father's instruction to keep him

139

on the line as long as she could. 'Did I hit a raw nerve there?' she challenged. 'Are you standing there with the phone in one hand and your dick in the other?'

'Not right now.' The voice was clearer this time. It sounded accentfree; she tried to place it, but failed.

'Ah, you need both hands for that, do you? Listen, fruit cup. You know my first name, do you know my surname?'

'Ssskinner.' The word sounded like a hiss.

'Genius. In that case, I'll assume you know who my father is. Let me ask you something: do you have a death wish? Or a high pain threshold?'

Silence.

'Because if you have either, you're hassling the right girl. Weirdo, I want you to think of me as a health and safety adviser: if you value either of those, don't phone me any more. Well, do you get the message?'

'Sure.' The whisper again. 'I like your friend.' The words took her by surprise: she was still struggling for a reply, when there was a click and the line went dead.

22

'He was calling from a pay-phone, in a pub called the Amphora,' said McIlhenney.

'The Amphora?' Skinner exclaimed. 'Alex and I were there last night. It's just round the corner from her flat.'

'I know: Stevie Steele told me. Alex kept the creep on long enough for the boys to identify the number. Stevie had a car there inside five minutes, and he and big Singh were there inside ten. It was a Sunday night, so the place wasn't packed, but there were quite a few punters in nonetheless. The barman said that nobody had come in or left in twenty minutes, so they thought they were on a winner. The trouble was that everybody denied using the phone, and they were all in groups, so they each had someone to vouch for them.'

'At least two people were lying, then. I hope Steele got the name and address of everyone there. I want them re-interviewed, individually.'

'Of course he did, but they could all have been telling the truth. You've been there, and so have I. Can you remember where the pay-phone is in the place?'

At once, Skinner knew what he meant. 'It's just inside the door, isn't it?'

'That's right, and there's a big partition between it and the bar. It's quite possible for somebody to step in off the street and make a

141

phone call without anyone in the pub knowing he was there.'

'Yes, damn it, you're right.' McIlhenney heard a breath being taken, and knew what was coming next. 'But that doesn't mean that's what happened: I still want all those people seen again. I'm not saying haul them in or anything like that, but talk to them. You never know, someone might have gone to the toilet and seen someone on the phone.'

'It'll happen, don't worry.'

'Of course I'll fucking worry, Neil; he told her that he liked her friend. I take that to mean that he was watching her this evening, looking right inside her flat. You can do that, you know, and she never closes the bloody curtains.'

'She'll know to do that from now on.'

'Yes, but there's more to it than that. She's in the telephone directory, so getting hold of her number's no problem, but she's just moved house and she transferred it. This fucker knows about it: he knows where she lives. This isn't a random thing, man: he knows her or he's picked her out.'

'I'll have her watched round the clock. She won't come to any harm.'

'Use the best available.'

'That should have gone without saying.'

'You're right: I'm sorry. Now, there's another thought that's occurred to me. These things; quite often they start in the workplace, and Curle Anthony and Jarvis is a big firm.'

'You want me to . . . ?'

'Hell, no! We can't go crashing in there asking

questions: Alex would go bat-shit if we did that. No, I've taken care of that already. I've spoken to Mitch Laidlaw and I've told him what's happening; he got my drift straight away. First thing tomorrow he's going to speak to a few people in the office, those he can trust, and ask them to keep their ears to the ground, listening for hints about anyone who might have a crush on my kid. If he comes up with anything, he'll bring it to you, nobody else, and I'd like you to handle it in person.'

'Will do. Have you asked Alex about this idea?'

'Yes. She told me she can't think of anyone. But she wouldn't necessarily know, would she?'

'No, that's true. Are you going to check in with me while you're away, or do you want me to give you regular feedback?'

Skinner considered the question for a few moments. 'It's best if I call you, I think. My mobile may well be switched off quite often on this posting.'

'In that case, there's something I'd like to ask you before you disappear.'

'Fire away.'

'It's about Bandit Mackenzie. I know that Kevin O'Malley's report was confidential to you and the chief, but I'd like to know what was in it.'

'Why?'

'He's been a bit funny, a shade paranoid. He thinks he's been bumped off the Drugs Squad.'

'Did you put him right on that?'

'Of course, but I'm not sure the message got through.'

'Kevin says that he's guilt-ridden. He feels that he bottled it up there, when the bullets started flying.'

'But he didn't: he was okay.'

'Not by his standards. Self-belief is very important to the Bandit. He'd never been in a situation like that before, but he always imagined that if he was, he'd be out front charging the barricades. He found out that night that he doesn't have what it takes to do that. How he'll handle that knowledge in the short term, remains to be seen. He's going to need good management. He knows you, and he likes you; that's why I put him in your team. Maybe I should have spelled it out. Sorry, mate; my eye hasn't been one hundred per cent on the ball for the last few days.'

'No problem. I understand. This Alex thing can't be helping either. We'll get it sorted, I promise.'

'Do you want me to put Bandit somewhere else?'

'No, he'll be fine. I'm going to give him Tarvil Singh for a bit of extra support when George Regan gets back.'

'Mmm.'

'No?'

'It's your call, but maybe you should think about moving Stevie there.'

'A detective inspector?'

'You've got the whole city to watch now, Neil. You can't keep an eye on Leith all the time.'

23

'Who did you say is calling?' asked the telephone receptionist.

'The chief constable, Sir James Proud.'

'And why do you want to speak with the chief executive?'

'That is something I'd rather discuss with him.'

'We don't handle police pensions.'

'That's not what I want to talk to him about.'

'If you'll tell me what sort of pension you are asking about I can put you straight through to the appropriate section.'

'I give up!' Proud barked. He slammed the phone back into its cradle, picked it up again, and buzzed his secretary. 'Gerry, please get the chief executive of the Scottish Public Pensions Agency, down in Galashiels, on the line for me. Don't be fobbed off with anyone else.'

'Yes, sir.'

As he waited, the chief constable picked up Monday morning's *Scotsman* from a corner of his desk and glanced at the front page. The main headline concerned the Middle East, as was almost the norm; another covered an account of a fatal accident on a railway line in England, while a third seemed to confirm that there would only be one runner for the leadership of the Labour Party in Scotland, and with it, the post of First Minister. A day into the investigation, the Gareth Starr murder had been relegated to the inside pages: a bad sign, he knew from experience.

The phone rang. He tossed the newspaper aside and picked it up. 'I have Mr Manners for you, sir,' Gerry Crossley told him.

'Sir James: it's Simon Manners here.' The voice on the line was youthful and friendly, not Scottish, but the chief found nothing surprising about that. 'This is a surprise. Should I be worried?'

He gave the standard answer to the standard question. 'You tell me, Mr Manners. Actually, this is an informal approach: I'm looking for some assistance. I'm trying to trace a couple of people for a friend. They were both teachers, at Edinburgh Academy for a while, but they seem to have disappeared off the face of the earth. They'd be of retirement age by now, so I was wondering whether you could tell me if either or both are currently receiving a pension from you.'

'I see,' said Manners. 'This isn't an uncommon approach, Sir James. Normally they come from ex-wives or even ex-husbands looking out for their rights, and normally we'd ask them to contact us formally. However, in your case, I'll see if I can cut some corners.'

'That's very good of you. Do you have our number, so you can call back?'

'I won't need it for now. Just give me the names of your targets and I'll look them up on our system. I may have more than one hit initially, you understand, but your mention of Edinburgh Academy should help me be precise.'

'Let's see how you do, then. The names are Claude Bothwell and Annabelle Gentle.'

'Gentle as in meek and mild, or Gentile as in not Jewish?'

'The former.'

'Okay, here we go. It's just a matter of keying them into my terminal.'

Proud leaned back in his chair and waited, leaving the *Scotsman* undisturbed as he held the phone to his ear. Manners was back in seconds. 'It was definitely Claude Bothwell?' he asked.

'Yes.'

'No joy, I'm afraid. There are contributions credited to someone of that name, but they stopped over forty years ago. He has pension rights accrued, but he's never claimed them, nor has an executor. He must have left the profession and forgotten to reclaim his contributions.'

'How about Miss Gentle?'

'Annabelle, you said?'

'Yes.'

'Give me a second.' Again Proud waited. 'No, but here's a coincidence. There are contributions credited to her as well, and they ceased in the same month as Mr Bothwell's. They haven't been claimed either. Were you expecting this, Sir James?'

'Let's just say it doesn't take me by surprise. Thanks, Mr Manners. I owe you a favour: don't hesitate to take me up on it.'

'That's easy. If you find these people, let me know. I don't like untidiness in my records.'

The chief hung up. What he had said was true: Bothwell and Annabelle Gentle had disappeared in mid-career, so abruptly that he had found it hard to imagine that there would be an easy way back into the profession for either of them.

He reached for the phone once more. 'Gerry, I want you to get me another chief executive: the Scottish Secondary Teachers' Association.'

He returned to the *Scotsman* as he waited. He found only a few paragraphs on the Gareth Starr homicide, most of them quotes attributed to Detective Sergeant Wilding. 'We are pleased with the response to the E-fit image,' he had said. 'The response from the public has been gratifying and has given us a number of leads to follow.

'We are also appealing for anyone who knew the victim to come forward. We are trying to establish what he did in the last few hours of his life, and any information to this end will be helpful to us.'

'In other words you've got nothing,' he murmured. He found himself wondering why a DS was taking such a high profile in the investigation, but before he could consider the matter too deeply, the phone rang.

'General secretary, sir,' said Gerry Crossley, 'not chief executive. Her name is Miss Cotter.'

'Christian name?'

'Not volunteered. I don't think it's used much around the office.'

'I'll be on my best behaviour then; put her through.'

He waited until the connection was made. 'Miss Cotter,' he began. 'James Proud, police headquarters at Fettes.'

'How can I help you?'

There was something about her tone that made the chief constable conclude that he would be wise to let her believe that his call was official. 'I'm trying to trace someone, a member of yours, almost certainly a former member now. His name is Claude Bothwell. When he was last heard of, he was on the staff of Edinburgh Academy.'

'And when was he last heard of?'

'Forty-one years ago.'

Something close to a snort sounded in Proud's ear. 'Forty-one years ago! Why don't you ask Russell Goddard, the rector back in those days? He's still alive, and from what I hear as sharp as a tack.'

'I've spoken to Mr Goddard. He gave me all the help he could, but he also suggested that since Mr Bothwell was an active member of your association, you might have a more recent record of his whereabouts than he had.'

'Mr Proud, we have our hands full keeping track of our current members.'

'This is quite important, Miss Cotter. How far back do your records go?'

'They go back sixty years, to our foundation, but even if I found this man Bothwell, they wouldn't tell me much about him, other than where he taught, and you know that already, you say.'

'I know that he taught at the Academy, but that's all. I have no other information about his career.'

'And Mr Goddard said that he was an active member?'

'Yes.'

'That probably meant he was our representative there. However, in an independent school in those days, it's quite likely that he was our only member.'

'Is it possible that your predecessor might have heard of him?'

'Officer,' said Miss Cotter, heavily, 'I have been general secretary of this association for twenty-eight years. My predecessor was a contemporary of Mr Goddard, but wasn't nearly as long lived. If you give me some time, I may be able to find a record of his membership with details of other places he taught, but I'm not promising anything.'

24

He was unaware of it, but Bob Skinner smiled as the train emerged into the daylight. He had never suffered from claustrophobia to his knowledge, but he never felt comfortable in railway tunnels. Whenever he was in London, and he had the option, he chose bus or taxi over Underground.

The deputy chief constable was casually dressed, in jeans, a heavy cotton shirt and a lined cow-hide jacket that he had bought in America on one of his visits there with Sarah. He had packed a medium-sized suitcase for the trip: it held, among other things, an overcoat, a suit, several shirts, a pair of black shoes and, still in their wrapping, two packs each of new socks and underwear from Marks & Spencer. On extended trips away from home he regarded such items as disposable. It was easier to replace them as necessary than to have them pile up in his room, or hand wash them and dry them on radiators.

Dottie Shannon sat opposite him, engrossed in a Sheila O'Flanagan novel that she had bought at the airport. She was dressed more formally than the DCC, in a charcoal grey suit and white shirt. It had concerned her at first, but he had put her at her ease. 'You're fine; it's no problem. You'll make a good impression. I've been there before, so I can dress like a slob, as most of the people who work there do.'

'Where are we going?' she had asked.

When he told her that they were bound for the headquarters of the Security Service, she had gone instantly pale.

'Don't worry, Dottie. It's just another office, and the people we'll be interviewing will be subjects, that's all, just like any others.'

'But why, sir?' she had asked anxiously.

'Because they need their problem signed off by someone from outside.'

'Why us?'

'Because my signature counts for something, and because I'm privy to the nature of the problem and its aftermath. It isn't the sort of aftermath where you can stick a retired judge in a room for a month, let him hold public hearings and then write a whitewash report. But that's enough for now: I'll give you a full briefing when we're there.'

He glanced down at his own reading choice, a golf autobiography . . . he had never been able to concentrate on fiction when he had things on his mind . . . and was about to reopen it when his mobile sounded, deep within his jacket. He took it out and glanced at the screen identification. 'Hello, Jimmy, how're you doing?' he asked.

'Where are you?' the chief constable asked.

'On the Heathrow Express, heading to Paddington.'

'Can you speak?'

'Within reason. Why?'

'I'd like some advice, that's all.'

'Sure, if I can.'

'If you were looking for a missing person,

152

where would you start?'

'At the place where he was seen last, or in the mortuary: one or the other. How long's he been missing?'

'Forty-one years.'

'Bloody hell.' Skinner chuckled. 'Forget the morgue, then. Their fridges aren't that good. In that case I'd be checking with the people at the General Records Office to see if his death's been registered.'

'I'm told it hasn't.'

'Do you have a birth certificate for him?'

'No.'

'Then get one. What age is this absconder?'

'Mid-seventies.'

'Then try the Department of Work and Pensions. Give them all the details from the birth certificate, and as much employment history as you can, and see where they're paying his pension.'

'What if I do that and find he isn't claiming one?'

'Then you'll need to go back to his friends and family from forty years ago. You'll need to go back to my starting-off point, the place where he was seen last. Jimmy, fill me in on this.'

He listened as Proud described his meeting with Trudi Friend, and about her search for her mother.

'So what you're telling me,' he said, when the story was over, 'is that this married man, with a cracking-looking wife, bewitched a naïve, if not innocent, girl from up north, and told her he was going to marry her, then they both disappear

153

from jobs, home and everything else on the same day. Question: did Annabelle know he was married? Answer: assume that she did. They worked in the same school; he couldn't chance her finding out in casual conversation, especially if Señora Bothwell was known there and gave you your running cup . . . congratulations, by the way. Question: he vanished, she vanished, so what about the wife? She seems to have been a confident woman, by your account and by Mr Goddard's. So what did she do when the pair did their runner? If their house was empty when Goddard went looking for Adolf, where the hell was she?'

'I don't have answers for any of these.'

'Then find them. But if I was in your shoes, right now I'd be trying to find out everything there is to know about your old teacher.'

'But who's going to tell me?'

'There's always somebody. You don't live for thirty-six years in a modern, developed country without leaving a pretty big trail behind you. While you're waiting for your SSTA lady to get back to you, look for his social-security number and his NHS number. Do his health records still exist somewhere? Could he have paid social security after the day of his disappearance? Most of all, when you go to GRO, find out about every public record on which his name appears.'

'Such as?'

'There's his own marriage certificate for a start. Then, maybe he was a witness to someone else's. It's a long shot, but if that's the case and those people are still alive, they could be of assistance. Last but not least, and this is where my detective's nose starts twitching, was he married before Montserrat? If he proposed to commit bigamy with Annabelle, was he a first offender?'

'Bob, that's great. That's a big help.'

'Thanks, but, Jimmy, you're going to need more help than that.'

'Not at all. It's a private matter, my own initiative, something any citizen's entitled to do off his own bat. What's wrong with that?'

'Nothing, if you weren't the chief constable. This woman's reported her mother missing. Okay, she's forty years late, but she still deserves to have her complaint handled officially.'

'Bob, I'm not passing this down the line, and that's final.'

'You're the boss, but you still have to open a file on it. Once that's done, it has to be followed through. You have other duties, Jimmy, and you owe it to the public not to be diverted from them by something not worthy of an officer of your rank. Supervise the search by all means, but use a leg man at least. Take big Jack McGurk, my assistant. He'll have time on his hands till I get back.'

The chief constable considered Skinner's advice. 'Very well,' he said at last. 'I'll do that. But bloody hell, you're some man to be giving me lectures about delegating.'

25

Ray Wilding looked at the name on the brass plate on the railing, with the blue Legal Aid logo alongside. 'Oliver Poole WS,' he read aloud. 'You know, sir,' he said, 'it amazes me why allegedly smart people use lawyers like this one. Whenever they or their assistants turn up to represent someone in custody, it's as if they scream 'guilty by association' at us.'

'There are plenty of them in Glasgow too,' Bandit Mackenzie told him. 'But you shouldn't read anything sinister into it. There are big corporate law firms who make most of their money out of business clients, and there are those like this one who look to the criminal legal-aid system for their turnover. They all provide a service, that's all, so don't go putting them in the same box as their clients.'

'I'm not. What I'm saying is that when a straight citizen retains a firm like this, he doesn't know the signal he's sending out.'

'Maybe he doesn't. But Poole and guys like him advertise in the press and on telly, so maybe he's the only lawyer your Mr Straight knows by name. Let's find out.' He led the way up the three steps to the front door.

Although the solicitor's plate was the only one showing on the street, he shared the Haymarket office building with several other firms, including a secretarial agency, and an accountancy

156

practice. Each had its own entry buzzer: the chief inspector pressed and waited for an answer. 'Oliver Poole WS.' Even through the tinny intercom the woman's voice sounded nasal.

'DCI Mackenzie and DS Wilding for Mr Poole.'

'Do you have an appointment?'

'We're the polis, dear; we don't make appointments. We called to tell him we were coming.'

'Just a minute.' Mackenzie heard something unintelligible, shouted across an office, then, 'Open the door when you hear the buzzer, and come down to the basement.'

They followed the directions, pausing only to ensure that the door had closed properly behind them. The building was modest, but appeared to have been refurbished in the recent past. The paint on the walls was fresh and the carpets felt soft underfoot, as if the underlay was relatively new. The door to Oliver Poole's office faced the foot of the stairs. It was held open by a small, tubby, middle-aged man, his sparse hair swept back from his forehead as he peered at the detectives over half-moon spectacles.

'DS Wilding,' he said, as they stepped inside, 'good to see you again. The last time was in the Sheriff Court I believe: Her Majesty's Advocate versus McCafferty.'

'That's right, Mr Poole: he was sent to the High Court for sentence at the end of the day, as I remember.'

'We can't win them all, Sergeant. You were a pretty good witness.'

'Thanks for that; you didn't give me an easy time.'

'It's my job to give you a hard time.'

Wilding grinned. 'I know. That's why I don't hold it against you. Mr Poole, this is my new boss, DCI Mackenzie.'

'Ah,' the solicitor exclaimed. 'You're the man, are you? From what I hear, you've been causing a lot of fear and despondency among the under-classes since you came here from Strathclyde. So, you've moved on from drugs, have you?'

The two men shook hands. 'As of last week,' said Mackenzie. 'I'm back in the mainstream now.'

'You'll be relieved, I'm sure. Dirty business: if I'm allowed to class my clients in order of preference, the dealers are absolutely my least favourite.'

'So why do you represent them?'

'I don't believe I have the right to turn them away: our constitution, such as it is, says that they're entitled to the best defence available. My profession requires me to provide it. Yours requires you to prepare a case so formidable that I can't find any holes through which my client can wriggle. You might see us as adversaries, Mr Mackenzie, but I don't. We're both in the public service, the twin pillars of the justice system. Enough of the philosophy, though. Come through to my office.' He led the way across an open area big enough for five desks: two were occupied by young women, and the others were empty. 'I have three assistant solicitors,' he

158

explained. 'They're all in court just now. You know what Monday mornings are like.'

'We do our best to keep you busy,' said Mackenzie, as they took seats in the small private room. 'All our mornings can be like that, and the middle of some of our nights too.'

'I'm sure. So, gentlemen, what can I do for you? Which of my clients is in such deep shit that you come to me, rather than the other way round?'

'We believe that you represent Gareth Starr,' the chief inspector began.

Poole held up a hand. 'Wrong.'

'You accompanied him when he was interviewed in the Queen Charlotte Street police office last week.'

'Yes, but I'm being legally exact: I now represent his estate. I'm named as executor in his will. To be honest, I've been expecting your visit.'

'How long have you known Mr Starr?'

Poole ran his fingers through his hair. 'Gary? Let's see: I've been in independent practice for eighteen years, and he came to me not long after . . . Yes, I acted for him for sixteen years.'

'How did your relationship begin?'

'I was recommended by a partner in the firm where I had been an assistant.'

'What was the nature of the service you provided?'

'General. I handled all his legal requirements: my practice is mainly criminal but not exclusively so. I made sure his licence was always up to date, I handled his conveyancing, when he bought his house and his shop, and I acted

159

for him in his divorce.'

'What were the grounds?'

'Irretrievable breakdown; Kitty left him, simple as that. Her main complaint was that he was a skinflint.'

'Was she right?'

'I don't believe so. The truth was that his business made him a living and that was all. Kitty thought that all bookies own Rollers, not Ford Sierras and the like. If she had the idea that she'd walk away from the marriage with a lot of money, she was wrong, way off beam.'

'Do you know where she is now?'

'Yes. She's remarried and living in Gilmerton. She rang me first thing this morning: she wanted to know whether Gary's original will was still valid, or if he'd changed it.'

'And had he?'

'Happily, yes. His mother is still alive; she's in a nursing home in Joppa, and the new will leaves everything to her.'

'How did she sound when you told her?' asked Wilding.

'As you'd expect: a little disappointed.' Poole chuckled. 'I imagine you'll want to speak to her. I'll let you have her address. Her name is Philips now.'

'What do you know about Mr Philips?'

'Nothing. I've never met him.'

'Mr Starr's business associates,' said Mackenzie. 'What do you know about them?'

'What business associates? There was the clerk, Eddie Charnwood, and the board man-cum-gofer, the smelly bloke, but that was it.

Gary was a small independent bookmaker, Chief Inspector. The only other people in his life you could call associates were his punters.'

'Are you a punter yourself?'

'Very occasionally; but I'm what Gary would have called a big-event player. I'll have a bet on the Grand National and the Derby, and sometimes on the Open Championship. Naturally, when I did that I'd bet with him. He used to smile every time I came into the shop.'

'Did he have any awkward customers that you knew of? For example, were there any disputes over pay-outs? Have there been any threats of legal action, since the new legislation was floated allowing people to sue over gambling matters?'

'None. A bookmaker of Gary Starr's size can't afford to alienate customers. Word would get out and he'd find his shop empty.'

'Was he a violent man, Mr Poole? Was that incident last week typical of him?'

'If he was, he never showed it to me. We weren't close friends, Mr Mackenzie; we had a normal business relationship, but it had become established to the point of cordiality. I found him quiet, occasionally short-tempered, but nothing more than that. I know what you're leading up to. He contacted me on Friday afternoon and told me what had happened. He asked if I thought there was any chance of him being prosecuted.'

'What did you tell him?'

'I told him that I'd bet against it, but that I'd accompany him to the interview for safety's sake.

161

He asked me what odds he should give me, and I repeated what he'd often said to me, that the odds don't matter when you're going to lose, as he would have if he'd taken my bet.'

'There's no chance of him being prosecuted now, that's for sure.'

'There never was. You know that as well as I do.'

'Probably not,' Mackenzie conceded. 'Mr Poole, since you are the executor, you're in a position to help our investigation. We have an open mind on Mr Starr's murder.'

'What happened to him?'

'You don't want to know.'

'I am a criminal lawyer, Chief Inspector. I have seen things.'

'You haven't seen this, I promise you. Take it from us that it was brutal and leave it at that. The only thing we do know for sure is that there was nothing random about it; it wasn't a housebreaking gone wrong, or anything like that. We're going to need access to everything about his life, business and personal. It'll save us a hell of a lot of time if you can give us a written authority to access his papers, bank accounts, shop records, all that stuff.'

'You need it in writing?' asked Poole. 'Yes, I suppose you do: bankers can be very stuffy if they put their minds to it. Okay, that's easily done.' He opened a drawer of his desk, took out a sheet of headed notepaper, picked up a pen and began to write. When he was finished, he folded it, placed it in an envelope and slid it across to Mackenzie. 'There you are: that's all

162

you require. If anyone questions it, put them on to me.'

'There are safes in his office and house. There'll be no comeback if we have to force them, will there?'

'None: that note lets you go everywhere and do anything in pursuit of your investigation. Good luck, gentlemen. When you find the bastard who did this, I can promise you I won't be defending him. I don't have all that many straight clients, so I don't like losing any of them.'

26

'That was quick, Jack,' said Proud. 'I wasn't expecting to hear anything from you today.'

'I'm afraid it's nothing positive, sir,' the towering McGurk replied, filling the door-frame as he looked into the chief's office. 'I thought I should tell you straight away, though. The DSS check shows no social-security payments by either Bothwell or Gentle since the time of their disappearance. It's the same with the NHS: they were each registered to different Edinburgh practices, but nothing's been added to their records since then.'

'Mmm. It was too much to hope for, I suppose. In truth, I'm surprised that the health records are still accessible after all this time.'

'There is one thing that might interest you, though. Gentle's records show that on her last visit to her GP, she was prescribed the contraceptive pill.'

'Was she, by God? It was only just becoming available back then. When did they put her on it?'

'The February before she vanished.'

'That was the first time she took it?'

'Yes, sir; her only other visit to the surgery was for laryngitis, a year before that.'

'That ties in, Jack. Annabelle told her sister at Easter that she'd met Bothwell and she was going to marry him. Going on the pill indicates

164

that she became sexually active again, or at least she made plans to, just before that. I assume that having got herself pregnant once before, she'd learned her lesson.'

'There's something else, sir. I ran a check on Montserrat Bothwell too.'

'Would she be an NHS patient, if she was a foreign national?'

'She would as the wife of a UK subject, sir, and she was. She only used the service once, in the middle of June in that same year, when she had treatment for a broken nose. There was a note on the record that said she'd fallen at home.'

'And you think?'

'I wonder, sir, that's all, whether she might have found out about Bothwell and Gentle, confronted him, and got a thumping for her trouble.'

'You're making me wonder the same thing, Jack. Well done, Sergeant. Off you go to the General Register Office and see what you can dig up there.'

27

At one point in her career, Dottie Shannon had been a Police Federation representative: in that role she had been a member of a delegation that had gathered in London to lobby Members of Parliament, canvassing their support for improvements in police working conditions.

She had been impressed, but not overawed: thus, when Skinner had told her at the airport where they were going, after the initial shock had worn off, she had been sure she would take it in her stride.

Dottie had seen government offices before. She was a police officer and so she was used to crowd screening, and to being a part of it. But when a uniformed officer held the door of Thames House open for her, and she could see inside, she felt her legs turn to jelly. There was nothing special about it, nothing of the television version: the foyer could have been any one of dozens along Whitehall, but it had an aura, something that said, 'Be careful here.'

Skinner walked straight to the reception desk. 'We're from Scotland,' he announced. 'The DG's expecting us. Let his office know that we've arrived, please.'

The clerk picked up a telephone: there was a brief, quiet conversation. 'Very good, sir,' he said. 'If you go through the barrier you'll be met on the other side.'

'Show Security your warrant card,' the DCC told Shannon. 'It's like a boarding pass.'

Indeed the screening was almost identical to that which they had gone through earlier that morning. Just as their jackets were returned and as they were putting them on, a lift door opened and a figure emerged. Shannon could see the surprise in Skinner's eyes as the slightly built, sober-suited man approached.

'Bob,' the man exclaimed, extending his hand. 'Welcome to Thames House. It's good to see you again, and to meet you, Inspector Shannon.' He looked as dry as his voice; the skin was drawn so tightly across his lean features that it seemed about to crack. 'Come with me. There are a couple of people waiting to meet you, and in view of the hour I've laid on a working lunch.' He led the way into the lift, then, rather than press a button, entered a code into a pad in the instrument panel.

'This is something of an honour, Evelyn,' said Skinner, as the doors closed. 'I didn't expect to be welcomed by the director general himself.' He turned to Shannon. 'Inspector, this is Sir Evelyn Grey. He runs this place.'

'It wasn't just my usual excessive courtesy, Bob,' the DG replied. 'I was making a point to everyone on my floor, and to everyone who happened to be downstairs when you arrived.'

'Your point being?'

'That you are to be treated as a very important person while you are with us, and that your authority here comes directly from me.'

167

Skinner grinned. 'Shucks, you're embarrassing me,' he joked.

'I've never seen you embarrassed, Bob. I don't think it's possible.'

The lift came to a halt; the doors opened out on to a marble reception area, with a desk staffed by a dark-skinned woman. 'We'll be in conference room one, Jamelia,' Grey told her. 'Advise the other parties that we're ready.' He led the way along a corridor to the left until he reached a heavy panelled door: he opened it and led the way inside.

The working lunch lay on the conference table; it comprised croissants, filled with ham and cheese, on a large salver, and fruit, in a crystal bowl. Beside them sat a Thermos jug, on a tray, and five cups and saucers.

They had been in the room for less than a minute before the door opened again, and a man and a woman entered. He was lean, in his mid-thirties, and looked very fit, while she might have been ten years older. She was dressed in black, her face was pale and there were puffy bags under her eyes. 'Hello, Amanda,' said Skinner. 'How are you?'

'I've been better,' she answered sharply. 'I've just been to a cremation.'

The DCC knew without asking whose funeral it had been. 'I'm sorry,' he told her. 'I wish it had turned out differently.'

'Do you?' she asked. 'The information that was found on Sean's body was crucial. If it hadn't been, and the plot had succeeded, would you still be wishing that? There are casualties in

168

our business, Bob. We all have to live with that.'

'You two know each other, obviously,' said Sir Evelyn, 'but let me get the formalities over with. Inspector, you won't have met Amanda Dennis, who is the head of our Serious Crime section, and neither of you will have met Piers Frame, the deputy DG of the Secret Intelligence Service.'

'MI6?' Shannon exclaimed. It was the first time she had spoken since she set foot in the building: Skinner's sudden glare made her wish that she had kept her silence.

Frame gave her an urbane, indulgent smile. 'That's not our official title any longer, and this lot aren't officially called MI5 either. But the media and the public ignore statute and continue to call us by our old names, so we go along with it . . . now that we're out of the closet, so to speak.'

'Perhaps we should not pursue that analogy, Piers,' Grey murmured. 'It has more than one connotation.' He looked at Shannon, as if he was taking pity on her and trying to welcome her into the fold. 'The fact is, Inspector, the existence of the security and intelligence services is now publicly acknowledged, and even the locations of our headquarters are generally known, but much of the work we do remains covert for very obvious reasons.'

'As does some of ours,' Skinner pointed out. 'But it's better that people know where you are.'

'Do you really think so?' Frame's tone made his disagreement plain.

The DCC stared back at him. 'I don't say

169

things I don't mean. Let's say that a terrorist organisation had the resources to strike against your HQ building, but maybe not the wit to plan it too well. Would you rather that they went to the wrong place, one that wasn't prepared for such an event, as Vauxhall Cross and Thames House are, and blew up hundreds of innocents?'

'I don't like our people being in the front line,' said the man from across the river, frostily.

'Or you don't like being in the front line yourself? Actually, you're not. Sir Evelyn's identity might be known, and that of your boss, but the rest of you are still as anonymous as you ever were. You can go home at night to Bromley, or Wimbledon, or wherever the hell you live, to a street where not one of your neighbours, not even the bloke next door, the chap you share the odd amontillado with, has the faintest idea what your day job is. Not very long ago I shot a man, one of a bunch of very nasty people. In the country where he comes from, they live by vendetta. The media didn't say that I pulled the trigger, but I was identified, thanks to a well-meaning idiot of a police colleague, as the leader of the operation. I'm not anonymous, mate: I'm a public figure and everybody knows where I live and where my kids live. My house has got geophones round it, put there to let me know as soon as an intruder sets foot in my garden. It has movement-activated floodlights and shatterproof film on all the windows. Right now, up in Edinburgh, my daughter is having malicious telephone calls and I cannot be one hundred per cent certain that they are not related to the operation I've just mentioned. I can't dismiss that idea from my mind. What if that cell had a member we didn't know about and didn't catch? Try stepping into the real world, Mr Frame. Go public and share the paranoia with the rest of us.'

'Bob, I didn't know that,' Grey exclaimed. 'Can we do anything to help?'

'I didn't know myself until Alex told me on Saturday. It's long odds against the two events being connected, but I have the matter in hand just in case.' He smiled, then nodded towards the salver on the table. 'Are those things just for show?' he asked.

'Far from it. Help yourself, sit down and let's get started.'

The five each chose from the croissants and fruit, poured coffee, and took seats round the table, the police officers on Grey's right, and his colleagues on his left. When they were all ready he looked at Skinner and Shannon. 'Let me begin by summarising why we are here. A week ago, a group of what at first we thought were terrorists attempted an outrage in Scotland. It may have been dressed up as a kidnap for ransom, but within this room we are aware that it was an assassination attempt. Happily it was prevented, thanks to some very good work by your force, Bob, and by Amanda's section, one of whom was killed, while working undercover during the operation.'

Skinner leaned towards Shannon. 'The body in the van, Inspector,' he said. 'The supposed suicide.' He looked at Grey. 'Dottie doesn't know

171

all of this,' he told him. 'I thought it best not to brief her until we got here.'

'I understand, and I agree with that decision. To continue, one thing that the media do not and must never know is that it was, for want of a better term, an inside job, an operation set up by individuals working within the intelligence community, with the idea that what they were proposing was in the national interest. One of them, a senior military intelligence officer, was shot dead at the scene. A second, the man who ran the operation on the ground, was killed by subsequent military action. Two others have been detained: Rudolph Sewell, my own deputy, and Miles Hassett, an SIS operative. Bob, you are here to determine, as far as you can, whether the conspiracy runs any deeper, and to root out anyone else who might be involved. You will then prepare a personal report to be submitted to the Prime Minister, through me, on your findings. When we spoke at the weekend, you asked for the assistance of one of my officers in helping you to open doors, as it were, within this building and as necessary within MI6. Amanda, who has been cleared of any complicity in the plot, is the obvious person to take on that role. Piers is here to . . . ' He glanced to his left.

'To tell you,' Frame continued, 'that whatever you need from my department you will get. Any requests for assistance or information should be channelled directly to me, through Mrs Dennis.'

'That's fine by me,' said Skinner. 'Now let's get down to it. Where are Sewell and Hassett being detained? In this building, or across the river?'

The director general gave a tiny shudder. 'Good heavens, no. Even here, there would be whispers. They're being kept in a safe-house we maintain out in Surrey.'

'Have you picked up anyone else since last week?'

'No.'

'What pressure has been applied to them?'

'You asked that we didn't apply any.'

Skinner raised an eyebrow. 'I know I did, Evelyn, but I don't imagine you've been feeding them full English breakfasts, and châteaubriand and claret for dinner.'

Grey smiled drily. 'No, they've been on rather shorter rations than that. They haven't been sleeping much either; life in general hasn't been much to their taste. For example, Rudy Sewell is a devotee of chamber music, and absolutely hates modern stuff. I gather they've been playing him Status Quo at full volume for the last week.'

'That's cruel and unusual punishment in itself. But you can assure me, can you, that there's been nothing physical? Because if I find that there has, I will withdraw on the spot.'

'From what I've heard of you,' Frame chuckled, 'I didn't think you'd be so squeamish, Mr Skinner.'

'In that case it sounds as if you've been talking to the wrong people. I'm only interested in information which I know to be correct beyond the reasonable doubt required by the courts. Information gained through torture, or even the threat of torture, is unreliable, simply because when you pass an electric current through someone's genitals he's liable to tell you whatever he thinks you'd like to hear. There's nothing new about that either. Look at Galileo: he announced that the world revolved around the sun, not vice versa, those in power explained to him how the rack worked and what it did to you, and suddenly the sun started revolving again. They didn't have to torture him: we know that because he was able to write his recantation himself.'

'You have my word on it, Bob,' said Grey. 'Nobody's laid a finger on either of them . . . or plugged them into the national grid.'

'Good. When can we see them?'

'As soon as you're ready: Amanda will drive you there.'

'Tell me one thing, Mr Skinner,' asked Frame. 'Since you're dead against physical persuasion, what makes you think you'll be able to get anything out of Sewell or Hassett?'

'I'll ask them, simple as that. They may not break down and tell me everything, but if this thing does go further than them, I'll know. Save me some time here, both of you. I know that both your departments will have been going through both these men's contacts and movements as carefully as you can. Do you suspect any more of your colleagues of involvement, and if so, who are they? If I can throw specific names at them, it'll help.'

'None on my side, Bob,' Grey told him. 'We've unearthed Sewell's contacts with the dead military intelligence officer, and with Hassett, but there are no other threads.'

'Are the three of them linked in any way? One of the things I have to establish is what brought them together to discuss and plan this conspiracy in the first place. Someone triggered it: someone voiced it, someone started the ball rolling.'

'Northern Ireland: that's all I can tell you. The military intelligence man and Sewell were together over there. Rudy was in charge of Five activity and he was SAS.'

'And Hassett?'

'He and Sewell are old Harrovians.'

'Pardon?' said Shannon.

'They were both at Harrow School. Hassett is three years younger, but he had an older brother in Sewell's year. They didn't have any official contact, so we're assuming that's how they met.'

'What do we know about the brother?' asked Skinner.

'He died of MS five years ago.'

'Other family members of both men: what do we know of them?

'Rudy is single: he has an older sister; she lives in Perth, Western Australia. His mother's still alive, but she has Alzheimer's.' He glanced at Frame. 'Piers?'

'Hassett has no other siblings. He is homosexual, but currently unattached. His parents are both still alive. The mother's pharmacist, and the father . . . there's a slight awkwardness there. He's a Conservative MP.'

'First name?'

'Ormond.'

'I've heard of him. Isn't he on the Tory front bench?'

'Yes, he's an agriculture spokesman: the family business is grain merchanting. Ormond is the chairman, his brother Harold is managing director.'

'And does Ormond MP have any idea of his son's profession?'

'To the best of my knowledge he does not. He believes that he is a Foreign Office civil servant currently on secondment to the Commonwealth secretariat in Pall Mall.'

'Is he currently wondering why he hasn't heard from his son for a week?'

'The two are not close.'

'Ormond doesn't like having a gay son?'

'Correct.'

'Doesn't his sexuality make him a risk?' asked Shannon.

'On the contrary, Inspector. In certain operational situations it can make him an asset.'

'So Hassett's a field officer,' said Skinner.

'Oh, yes. That's why the Commonwealth cover story is such a good one. It deals handily with extended absences.'

'I'd like a list of his most recent assignments.'

Frame's mouth seemed to tighten. 'There are some things, Mr Skinner,' he murmured, 'that must be off limits to you.'

The Scot turned to the director general. 'Evelyn,' he said, 'my wife is getting ready to leave me and go back to America. My daughter has a stalker. We can still make the four o'clock flight back to Edinburgh, and I'll be happy to do that, unless the ground rules are spelled out again for your colleague.'

'No, that can't be,' Frame protested.

'It must be, Piers,' said Grey. 'Number Ten has decreed it. I appreciate your concern and so, I am sure, does Mr Skinner, so let's look for a way of keeping you as happy as possible. Would it be acceptable to you if Bob alone had access to that information, and that you showed it to him in Vauxhall Cross, without copies being made or handed over?'

The spy frowned. 'I suppose so,' he conceded.

'Bob?'

'I'll live with that.'

'Very good. That's settled.'

Skinner looked at Frame once more. 'I guess that Hassett's absence is being explained away as an operation.'

'Yes.'

'And Sewell's?' he asked Grey.

'He's in Brussels, officially.'

'Okay.' The big Scot reached out and took an apple from the fruit bowl. 'There will be other things I need to ask, but that's fine for now. We should go down to Surrey.'

The director general rose from the table. 'Yes,' he agreed, 'but first, a word in private. Excuse us, please, ladies, Piers.'

He led Skinner from the room and along the corridor until they reached another panelled door, with a key-pad. He hit four buttons in quick succession and turned the handle, then led the way into his office.

'I sensed that there are things that you didn't want to talk about in there,' he said.

'Yes. There's something I want Frame to do for me while we're heading down to Surrey. It may have been covered already, but if not it needs to be.' He explained his requirement.

'No problem,' Grey assured him. 'Let's get back . . . unless there's something else you want to discuss in private.'

'Actually,' said Skinner, 'there is one thing. Sewell and Hassett: what does the future hold for them? They're traitors, but you can't put them on trial: imagine the public reaction if the truth ever came out. Your service would be taken apart: God, the government could fall. For the same reason, you can hardly turn them loose either. It's not like the old days, when you could quietly swap them for a couple of our people in Soviet hands. So what happens to them?'

'You don't really want a straight answer, do you?' Grey replied.

'Not if it's too distasteful for you, Evelyn. What I was getting round to asking is what incentive these men have to co-operate with me? Why should they tell me a single bloody thing when they know that their futures are strictly limited?'

'There's no good reason I can see, I admit. Are you saying that there's no point in your interviewing them?'

'No, I'm saying I'd like to be able to incentivise them.'

'In what way?'

'I'd like to let them see a glimmer of hope:

nothing glamorous, you understand, but an alternative, at least, to a faked kidnapping in the Middle East and footage on a website of them having their heads sliced off with a knife.'

Grey's laugh was like a rattle in his throat. 'A posting as a librarian to the consulate in Uzbekistan, for example?'

'Something like that. A shitty existence but at least a continuing existence.'

'Offer it by all means, but whether they'll believe you, that's another matter. You realise, too, that I can't guarantee that anything you may promise will happen.'

'Yes, but they will believe it. What else do they have to hold on to?' Skinner headed for the door.

28

'Mr Charnwood,' Bandit Mackenzie asked, 'how long had you worked for Gareth Starr?'

The wiry clerk looked at him across the café table. 'Seven years,' he said. 'Seven years and six months.'

'Were you friendly, or was it just a boss-employer relationship?'

'We didn't visit each other's houses, if that's what you mean, but we'd have a pint together after work now and again.'

'Did anyone else ever join you? Did he have any other associates that you were aware of?'

'No; as far as I know, after his wife left him his circle took in me, Big Ming, and occasionally Oliver Poole, the lawyer. In the pub, it was often just the two of us.'

'So you got on.'

'Sure. Gary valued me, and he let me know it. I'm good at what I do, better than most.'

'What was your job?'

'I took the bets, and I kept an eye on how things were going on each race, looking out for fluctuations.'

'What do you mean?'

'Heavy betting on a particular horse or dog: outsiders usually. In the business you get a lot of rumours, alleged whispers out of stables and the like, about specific runners. Tips that they've been run down the park in their last couple of races . . . '

'What do you mean by that?'

'The jockey doesn't try too hard. As a result, the horse doesn't get a lot of weight lumped on it by the handicapper; when they reckon it's peaked in training and it's nicely off on the weights, they turn it loose.'

'That's illegal, isn't it?'

'It's well against the rules, that's for sure,' Eddie Charnwood conceded.

'Does it happen a lot?'

'I doubt whether it actually does, but the whispers are enough. When they start in your shop and you see money being piled on an outsider, you can't afford to ignore it, especially if you're a small operator like Gary. It's not just punters that get taken to the cleaners.'

'If you see it happening, is there anything you can do about it?'

'Sure. We can lay it off: spread the action out to bigger bookies to limit our risk.'

'I see.' Mackenzie smiled awkwardly. 'I'm an innocent when it comes to gambling, I'm afraid. My grandfather, on my mother's side, was a big punter, bigger than he could afford, and not very good at it. It caused a lot of problems: my mum never forgot it, and she made bloody sure I didn't inherit the habit.'

'Good for her.'

'How are you for coffee?' the detective asked. 'Want another?'

Charnwood glanced at his mug. 'No, I'm fine, thanks.' He had suggested the meeting place, just off Bonnington Road, as it was close to his home at Powderhall and to the late Gary Starr's shop.

'Have you had any whispers recently, any runs on outsiders?'

'No. There's been a lot of publicity about race-fixing in the last couple of years and a lot of people have been done, so the rumour mill's been quiet lately.'

'Any big losers?'

'Not as far as I know. Where we are we tend not to get big bets. To tell you the truth we don't encourage them either. We're a local bookie's, Mr Mackenzie: our customers are people of modest means.'

'So you have plenty of them?'

'Enough.'

'You must have. Gary Starr made a good living, enough for a nice house up in Trinity.'

'I suppose. Gary did the totals at the end of the day: I can't tell you for sure how much he was clearing.'

'What happens now?'

'What?' The detective's question seemed to take Charnwood by surprise.

'Well, you're out of a job as far as I can see. There's nobody to carry on the shop, unless you and Smith can take it over yourselves.'

Charnwood laughed softly. 'Big Ming may be a closet philosopher, but there's no way I'd go into business with him. I won't deny that since Saturday the thought's gone through my mind of getting in touch with Mr Poole and asking him if he'd consider renting the shop to me for six months, to see how I managed on my own, but I don't think I'm going to do that.'

'Why not?'

'It'd be a gamble, that's why not. I'm like you, Mr Mackenzie: I see the other side of betting. Sure there are the bright eyes of the winners, but there are far more of the others, the ones with hurt and disappointment written all over their faces. That's why I don't bet myself, not any more at any rate. If I took on the shop, it would be the biggest punt I ever had, and if I was laying odds, they'd have to be against my succeeding. Five years ago, I might have thought differently, but today . . . there's competition that we never had before, with Internet bookies and now super-casinos on the horizon. Gary managed to hold on because the shop's well sited, and because around here there are still people who like to come out for the afternoon and put their bets on over the counter. But they're dying out. I don't think he could have held on here for ever, and I don't think I'd last either. I could be wrong, but I have a wife and a wee boy, and I can't put them at risk by trying it. So I'll get a job somewhere else, with one of the bigger bookies, probably.'

'Are you fairly sure of that?'

'Yes. I made a few phone calls this morning: I've got an interview already. Gary was known about town, and so am I.'

'Good luck to you, then.' Mackenzie stood. 'Come on, let's walk round to the shop and you can open that safe for me.'

Charnwood nodded. The two left the café and turned into Bonnington Road, then round the gentle curve until the Evesham Street junction

183

came into sight. 'I know that Starr's marriage was behind him,' said the detective, as they walked, 'but did he have a girlfriend? There were no signs of a female presence in the house.'

'Nor would there be; there was a girlfriend, somebody he met in the shop, but he kept her at arm's length. Her name's Mina Clarkson and she lives in Saughtonhall. Gary was pretty bitter about marriage. Truth be told, Gary was pretty bitter about most things. He wasn't the sort to take much pleasure out of life.'

'From what my colleagues tell me he took pleasure out of whacking that boy's finger off last Friday.'

'Yes, that was well out of character; he could be abrupt, but never aggressive. I can only think that he panicked.'

'Panicked? He hacked him with a fucking bayonet!'

'He must have felt really threatened, in that case.'

'He saw the threat off, then. Did you know that he had the bayonet?'

'Yes, but I thought nothing of it. That and the toy gun, they were just for show.'

Mackenzie stopped dead. 'What toy gun?'

'He had a replica Luger: looked real, but it was plastic. He used to keep it and the bayonet under the counter.'

'You're not kidding me, are you?'

Charnwood looked astonished. 'Why would I do that? What's the fuss about anyway?'

'Starr told my colleagues, at the shop and in his interview, that the robber had brought the

184

gun into the shop and threatened him with it. Eddie, I'm going to need a formal statement from you after all.'

'No problem: I'm doing nothing else today.'

They walked on until they reached the shop. Padlocked steel shutters covered the windows and door, but Charnwood produced a bunch of keys from his pocket, and within a minute they were standing inside. It was gloomy, but the clerk found a switch, flooding the room with white neon light. 'The safe's in the back office,' he said.

It faced them as they opened the door, built into the wall: there was no lock, only a dial mechanism. Charnwood moved round behind Starr's desk and spun the wheel four times. After the fourth, it opened with a click and he eased it open.

'Jesus Christ,' he gasped.

The detective stepped alongside him, and took an involuntary breath himself. The strongbox was packed with money, wads of used notes held together with broad elastic bands, and with packs of white powder, wrapped in plastic. He took a pair of clear plastic gloves from his pocket, slipped them on and eased one of the packages out.

'What is it?' Charnwood asked.

'It's not fucking talcum,' said Mackenzie, 'that's for sure. Eddie, I'm afraid we're going to need to have a much longer talk than I'd reckoned with you and with Big Ming. You say that Starr didn't have any associates other than you two and Poole. In that case, who put this lot there?'

185

29

For all that there was a December chill in the air, and Princes Street was damp and grey, Detective Sergeant Jack McGurk was appreciating his day out. He would never have said that he found his job boring . . . being executive assistant to Bob Skinner could never be dull . . . and after a difficult beginning he and his boss had developed a good working relationship, but it did tie him to the office. McGurk had always been an outdoors copper: he had enjoyed his days on the beat, and the brief spell he had spent with Dan Pringle in the Borders on CID duty had been among the highlights of his career, despite the crisis it had caused in his marriage. That had all been sorted out when he had been offered the post with the DCC: he was grateful to Skinner for that, and yet it was good to be seeing the heart of Edinburgh again, rather than just the view from his window at Fettes.

He turned off the great thoroughfare, glancing to his right at Wellington's equestrian statue, as he always did when he passed it, and walked up the slight incline that led to New Register House.

He identified himself to a receptionist at the desk in the entrance hall. 'Ah, yes, Sergeant, I was told you'd be arriving. If you'd just go up one floor,' the man pointed to a staircase behind him, 'turn left and take the second door, someone will be along to see you.'

McGurk followed the directions, and found himself in a small meeting room, with a window that looked down on to the Café Royal, and the Guildford Bar next door. His dad had worked in the post office, when it had been in the big building across the road, and the Guildford had been his favourite hang-out.

He had been thinking of the past for five minutes when the door opened and a woman entered. She wore a high-necked sweater and black slacks, and she held a yellow folder in her right hand. 'Good afternoon, Sergeant,' she said. 'I'm Sylvia Thorpe; we spoke on the phone earlier. I hope I haven't kept you waiting.'

'Not at all. I was enjoying the view.'

'The view?' Her eyebrows rose and then she laughed. 'Ah, across the way, you mean: yes, there's always plenty going on over there.' She sat at the small round table in the centre of the room: McGurk joined her, settling his long body awkwardly into the standard civil-service-issue chair. 'It's been a while since we had a call from the police,' she said. 'In fact, I don't think we've had one since my old boss Jim Glossop retired.'

The detective glanced at her ringless fingers. 'I hope it isn't an inconvenience, Ms Thorpe.'

'Not a bit. 'Miss' will do perfectly well, by the way: the political correctness of the eighties and nineties passed me by. But 'Sylvia' will do even better.'

'Okay, Sylvia: do you have something for me? I'm sorry I didn't have anything more than the name and year of birth for you to go on.'

'That was quite enough. There weren't a hell of a lot of 'Claude' registrations in Scotland, not even back at the end of the twenties, when the man you're after was born. I have to say, I can see why you're asking about him, even if it is a right few years too late.'

'Why's that?'

'He's had a very interesting life, so far.'

'So he's still alive.'

'Let me put it this way: we have no record of him being dead. He could be six feet under in some foreign land, but if he is, word hasn't filtered back to us.'

'And would it?'

'That would depend on where and how he died.'

'So what records do you have?'

'I have his birth certificate: registration took place in Perth.' She opened the folder, took it from the pile of documents it contained then placed it to one side. 'And,' she said, 'I have his marriage certificates.'

'Certificates?' McGurk exclaimed.

'Oh, yes, Mr Bothwell was a serial husband.' She spread the rest of the documents out on the desk in a fan shape. 'He married three times. The first marriage was to Ethel Margaret Ward, in Wishaw, when he was twenty-three. The second took place four years later, in Glasgow: the bride's name was Primrose Jardine. And the third was four years after that, in Edinburgh, to Montserrat Rivera Jiminez of Torroella de Montgri, Spain.'

'Regular as clockwork, eh? Our Mr Bothwell

188

must be a meticulous man.'

'In all but one respect.'

'What would that be?'

'Before his second and third marriages he neglected to get divorced. I've checked with the courts: he didn't, and that's certain.'

'Maybe he was unlucky; maybe he was widowed twice.'

'By the time he was thirty-two? No, Sergeant: according to our records, all three Mrs Bothwells are still alive, and the second and third have some bad news coming to them.'

So Bob Skinner's tip to the chief had been spot-on. McGurk chuckled. 'Not nearly as bad as the news that's coming to him, once I catch up with the polygamous old sod, wherever he is.'

30

There had been little or no conversation as they left London and none on the drive down the A3: Skinner had been locked away with his thoughts, Shannon had been looking at the view from the back seat, as a means of keeping her nerves under control, and Amanda Dennis had been concentrating on the road, her knuckles white as she gripped the wheel.

They had turned off the main road, heading for a place called Churt, and had just driven past an inn called the Pride of the Valley when the inspector broke the silence. 'Wasn't that Lloyd George on that hotel sign?' she remarked.

'He lived in Churt,' said Dennis, 'towards the end of his life. I believe that when he finally married his secretary, Frances Stevenson, it was here they settled.'

'That sounds like a happy ending.'

'Yes. I wish there were more of them.' Her voice was so sad that Skinner reached across and put a hand on her shoulder. She gave it a quick squeeze of acknowledgement and, he supposed, thanks, then focused on the tree-lined road once again. The entrance came almost immediately: she indicated, then swung the car sharply to the left, halfway round a long bend. There had been no signpost, just a gap in the trees.

She drove for half a mile up a narrow avenue, until she came to a barrier. Before it, on the

190

right, was a metal post, with a keypad mounted on it. Dennis stopped, rolled down her window and punched in a code, then drove slowly through the gate as it opened. 'They'll know in the house that we're on the way. There are cameras that will track us all the way to the door.'

The roadway started to climb steeply: after a couple of hundred yards the forest came to an abrupt end, and they found themselves in open country. On the top of the hill that they were climbing, Skinner saw a two-storey house, in Tudor style complete with thatched roof. 'I take it that there's a fence,' he said. 'I looked at the gate, but couldn't see it.'

'It's not easy to spot,' Dennis told him, 'but it's there.'

'Electrified, I take it.'

'Yes. The first time you touch it, you won't get much more than a tickle, but if that and the razor wire don't put you off and you try to climb it, the charge gets stronger, until it's approaching lethal. Every so often we go round and clear away the dead cats and foxes.'

'How long has it belonged to the service?'

'It was acquired about fifty years ago, at the height of the Cold War. Officially, it was purchased as a staff college; occasionally the DG and department heads do use it for away-day meetings, but most of the time you wouldn't want to come to the kind of course that's held here. The trees around it were all cleared away long ago, so that all the approaches are clear. It's as secure as we can make it: there's even a bunker deep underneath, although we don't use it now.'

They wound round the long driveway until finally they reached the crest of the hill. Dennis parked the car at the side of the house, then led the two visitors round to the front.

The entrance door was open when they reached it. A bulky, dark-skinned man stood, waiting to greet them: his jacket hung loose, exposing a pistol in a shoulder holster. 'Hello, Big W,' said Dennis. 'This is Winston Chalmers,' she told Skinner and Shannon. 'He's the housemaster here. Winston, these are the visitors you were told about.'

'How many staff do you have here?' Skinner asked.

The minder looked at Dennis. She nodded. 'There are six of us,' he replied, 'working twelve-hour shifts, three at a time.'

'Where are they?'

'There's a basement level at the back of the house. The hospitality suite is down there.'

The sound of rock music forced its way through from another part of the house. Skinner thought he recognised the Pat Travers Band. He smiled at Winston. 'Have you run out of Status Quo?'

The 'housemaster' laughed. 'There is such a thing as a balanced diet. Do you want to see them both together?'

'Hell, no, one at a time. Who would you say is the stronger of the two?'

'Rudy Sewell, no doubt about that. He used to be my boss: I know how hard a bastard he is.'

'Is that right? You're making him sound like something of a challenge. Let's warm up on Hassett, in that case. What's he been on?'

'What do you mean, sir?'

'Has he been drugged?'

'No, sir. He hasn't had any more than two hours' sleep at a stretch since he's been here. That's as effective as any sedative for keeping people under control.'

'He's been given a normal diet?'

'He's been eating the same as us.'

'Clothing?'

Chalmers smiled. 'We don't want him to feel special, sir. He's still wearing the clothes he arrived with, and he hasn't washed since then.'

'It's time he did. Get him showered, shaved and into some fresh clothes, then we'll talk to him.'

'Will do.' He picked up a phone from a hall table, pushed a button and spoke quietly into it.

'I take it that Hassett and Sewell aren't able to communicate.'

'No, they can't.'

'Are they close enough together to hear activity around the other's room?'

'Yes, I think so.'

'Do they have windows?'

'Shatterproof mirror glass: it doesn't admit any light.'

'In that case, tell your people to switch off the music and make plenty of noise moving Hassett, but not to tell him where he's going. Once he's out of there, stay silent. Go on, catch them before they start.'

He waited while Chalmers phoned again. When he was finished, he said, 'Come on, big fella, let's go for a stroll.' He turned to Shannon. 'Dottie, come with us; learn some more.'

Leaving Dennis in the hallway, the trio walked out of the front door. 'How do we get down to the lower level?' asked Skinner.

'Over here.' Chalmers led them along a path and down a flight of stone steps, which opened out into a sunken garden area, enclosed by a six-foot-high stone wall.

The DCC looked around and nodded. 'Which is Sewell's room?'

The big man pointed to a double window about twenty feet away.

'Fine,' he murmured. 'Dottie, don't ask questions, and don't say anything.' He took her by the arm and rushed her along the gravel that led past the cell, Winston following, heavy-footed, behind them as they turned into the garden, then stopped. 'Okay, this'll do,' he said, slightly louder than was necessary. 'Gun,' he whispered to Chalmers, holding out his hand.

The other man grinned, as he understood what was happening. He took out his pistol and handed it to Skinner. 'Kneel!' he barked. Shannon stared at him, then jumped as the DCC fired two shots into the grass, by their feet. The two men retraced their steps along the gravel, past Sewell's window: Shannon walked beside them but silently, on the grass, as Skinner directed.

It was only when they were back on the upper level that Skinner realised she was trembling.

'Welcome to the dark side, Dottie,' he said. 'I don't care how hard Sewell is, that'll have got him thinking. With any luck Hassett heard as well: we'll find out when they've got him ready to talk to us, although it may take them a bit longer after that.'

Dennis was waiting for them inside, not in the hall but in a big lounge that looked out on to the upper garden. 'He won't fall for it, you know,' she said.

'Oh, no?' Skinner replied. 'The seed's been planted. Winston, when we've finished with Hassett, make sure that he doesn't get anywhere near Sewell. I want to keep that one isolated until I'm ready to talk to him. I may even delay it till tomorrow, to let him live with the uncertainty overnight.' He saw the frown on Shannon's face. 'What is it, Dottie?' he asked.

'Well, sir, it's just,' she began hesitantly, 'what you said in London about physical persuasion, and what you've just done . . . '

'Remember what I said about Galileo,' he told her. 'They only had to show him the rack. Sewell's been trained to withstand this sort of stuff, but every little helps.'

31

'How long did you work for Starr, Mr Smith?' asked Ray Wilding. 'Ten years, did you say? And in all that time you saw nothing happening there that wasn't related to the bookmaking business. Is that what you're saying?'

'Aye,' Big Ming replied, 'that's whit Ah'm telling yis.'

'So is Eddie Charnwood.'

'So why do yis believe him and no' me?'

'I'm not saying that's the case, but you worked longer hours than Mr Charnwood. He had keys, but so have you. In your earlier statement you told us that you opened the shop in the morning to pin up the day's race cards, and you locked up at night after you cleaned up.'

'Most nights. Sometimes Gary wid stay on late and Ah'd tidy up the next morning.'

'So you're changing your statement?' Mackenzie snapped.

'Ah'm telling yis what happened.'

'And how often did it happen? How often did Mr Starr let you go early?'

'Ah don't know, maybe once or twice a month.'

'Every two weeks or every four weeks? That's quite a significant difference. Come on, Mr Smith, stretch your big brain, how often was it?'

The witness glared across the interview-room table at the chief inspector. 'All right, it was every other week, sometimes more than that.'

'Very good; that's us gone from once a month to once a week. Listen, chum, you'll be out of here a lot sooner if you give us precise answers, not guesses and approximations.'

Wilding picked up a sheet of paper from the table. 'You're a man of hidden depths, James, aren't you?'

'Ah dinna ken whit yis mean.'

'When you were interviewed by my colleague DS Pye, after the incident in the shop on Friday, you came out with something about Pamplona bulls. He told me you almost took his breath away. When the hell did you hear about them?'

Big Ming shifted in his chair, as if something sharp had dug into him. 'Ah dinna ken,' he mumbled.

'Look at me,' said Wilding. He waited until the man caught his gaze. 'You, with your overpowering intellect, tell me that you don't know when you first heard of the Pamplona bull run, and you expect me to believe you. As my colleague said, don't piss us about. The rules here are simple: we ask questions, you give us honest answers. Come on, now, try again: how did you first hear of the Pamplona bull run?'

'Ah've seen it,' Big Ming replied, grudgingly, yet with a touch of pride. 'Ah've been there.'

'Do you go to Spain often?'

'Who, me?'

'There you go again. Answers only, please.'

'Naw,' Smith mumbled. 'Ah've only been there a couple o' times.'

'How many?'

197

'Two or three.'

'Which?'

'Three.'

'And which parts of Spain did you visit? Remember,' Wilding added, 'we can check.'

Big Ming swallowed the enormous lie, hook, line and sinker. 'Pamplona,' he murmured, 'just Pamplona.'

'When?'

'The last three years, in July, when they wis runnin' the bulls.'

'Bullshit!' Mackenzie exclaimed.

'Naw, it's no',' the witness protested. 'It's true.'

'And why, with respect,' asked Wilding, 'would a Leither like you develop a sudden love for Fiesta da San Fermín and for the capital of Navarre? It's not your usual holiday. It's hardly the Costa Brava, Mr Smith, is it?'

'It's good there.'

'Maybe, but it's about a hundred kilometres away from the nearest beach, and I'll bet you can't get Belhaven Best. Why did you go there?'

Big Ming sighed: the extravagant gesture seemed to make his body odour even more intense. 'Ah went because Gary asked me tae,' he said wearily.

'Mr Starr asked you to go there,' Wilding repeated.

'Aye.'

'Why?'

'He never said.'

'Come on, Mr Smith. We've been doing so well up to now.'

198

'He jist asked me to go, honest.'

'How?'

'Ah told yis, Ah dinna ken how.'

'No, Mr Smith, that's 'how' as in by what means, not 'how' as in why.'

'He lent me his car.'

'He did what? That was bloody generous of him, wasn't it?'

'Ah suppose it wis: Ah never thought of it that way, but.'

'What kind of car was it?'

'A Mercedes: one o' they wee ones. It wis a diesel: went for ever on a tankful.'

'How did you get to Spain?'

'Ah drove it down tae Portsmouth and got the ferry tae Bilbao.'

'Just you? Nobody else?'

Big Ming gave the detective a look that spoke for itself: he had nobody else.

'When you got to Pamplona, what did you do?'

'Ah checked intae a hotel and parked the car in a garage.'

'You mean a covered park?'

'Naw, it was a proper garage. Gary telt me tae go there; he said Ah could leave the car there, and pick it up when Ah wis ready tae go back.'

'How long did you stay there?'

'Four days, then Ah got the ferry back.'

'Who did you meet when you were there?'

'Naebody.'

'Where did you stay?'

'In a hotel. It was called the Three Kings: that isnae its Spanish name, like, but that's whit it means in English.'

'Los Tres Reyes,' Wilding murmured.

'Aye, that wis it. It wis a barry hotel like.'

'A what?' asked Mackenzie.'

'Barry means 'good' in Edinburgh-speak, sir,' the sergeant explained.

'Aye, good,' Big Ming concurred. 'Fuck knows whit it cost: Gary paid for it wi' his card, and he gi'ed me money for petrol an' ma drink.'

'But you met nobody when you stayed there?' Wilding asked again.

'Naebody.'

'Didn't the whole arrangement strike you as odd? A free trip to Spain three years on the trot?'

'Gary said it was a bonus, like; tax-free, like.' His face fell as a thought struck him. 'Yis'll no' tell the Inland Revenue, will yis?'

'If I find out that you've been making all this up, Mr Smith, the Inland Revenue is going to be the least of your worries. If I find out that you've missed out the smallest detail, likewise. What was the name of the garage?'

'Ah cannae remember. It was in a place called Carrer . . . that's whit they ca' streets there . . . Ortiz, that's all Ah ken.'

'What happened when you dropped the car off?'

'Nothin'. Ah just said tae the bloke there that Ah wis frae Edinburgh, and he took the keys aff me. When Ah went back, he gave me them back; Ah never had tae pay nothin', like.'

'Did you notice anything about the car when you picked it up?'

Big Ming looked puzzled. 'Naw. Naebody had

been usin' it if that's whit yis mean. Ah'd have kent frae the petrol tank. Naebody had been smokin' in it either, and a' thae Spanish folk smoke. Gary would have gone mental if any cunt hid been smokin' in his motor.'

Wilding glanced sideways at Mackenzie. 'A minute outside, sir.'

'Yes. I think so. We'll be back in a minute, Mr Smith.' The two detectives rose and left the room. 'That was a very nice kite, Ray,' said the chief inspector, as the door closed. There was more than a trace of sarcasm in his voice. 'It would have been nice to know in advance that you were going to fly it, though. We're a team and we should operate that way. I don't like surprises from my own side of the table in mid-interview.'

'I'm sorry you feel that way, boss. I didn't pre-plan anything: the idea just came to me as we spoke. I had no idea where it was going to take us.'

'So what are you thinking?'

'That we should get hold of Starr's car and take it apart: see what traces we find in it.'

'Do you think Big Ming's as dumb as he's letting on?'

'I couldn't say, sir, but if he was doing what we think he was, he's hardly going to come right out and tell us about it, is he?'

'He didn't strike me as that quick on his feet, I admit. Can you remember if there's a garage at Starr's house?'

'Yes, there is. The door opens on to the lane behind.'

'Then let's see if the car's there: if it is we'll have it taken up to the park behind Fettes.'

'I'll alert DI Dorward. His people will have to strip it.'

'They'll need help: I'll phone the local Mercedes dealership and see if they'll lend us a mechanic. We'll need a specialist for this job.'

'You're sure about this? I don't want to handle the flak on my own if we spend all this time and money and the thing comes up clean.'

Mackenzie's eyes narrowed. 'Don't you trust me, Wilding?' he asked.

'It's an old principle, sir, called covering my arse.'

'Thanks for the vote of confidence! Don't worry, I'll sign off on it. Gary Starr wasn't the sort of man to hand out free holidays, least of all in his car. Besides, I've got my own reasons for following this through. Ray, when I was on the Drugs Squad I reckoned I knew all the sources and all the suppliers, except one. I've never been able to pin him down, until now.'

'Should we inform the Drugs Squad, and the SDEA for that matter?'

'No, we'll run with it for now. I'm not letting them in on it until I have to.'

'Are you not going to tell Mr McIlhenney?'

'No, I'm fucking not! Are you suggesting I don't have authority here?'

'No, sir, it's your shout.'

'Thank you for that,' said the chief inspector, sarcastically. 'Now, before we go up to Starr's place, make that call to Dorward. I'm going back in to see Smith.'

Mackenzie stepped back into the interview room with a grin on his face. Big Ming saw it and looked even more nervous. 'Did you really never ask any questions about these free holidays, Mr Smith?'

The man shifted in his seat once more, sending another stale blast across the table. 'Listen, mister, you didnae know Gary. He was a'right, but he didnae like being asked questions. If Ah had, then Eddie Charnwood would have got the freebies.'

'I doubt that, Mr Smith: Mr Charnwood would certainly have asked what it was all about.' To his surprise, Mackenzie felt a sudden wave of sympathy for the hapless witness before him. 'Ming,' he found himself saying, 'I've got some bad news for you. Starr had another business interest apart from book-making. He was a cocaine dealer, and it looks as if he set you up to import the stuff for him.'

The last vestige of colour drained from the big man's face. 'Naw,' he whimpered.

'I'm afraid so: we still have some checks to do, and we'll need to keep you here while we make them. If it's confirmed, you'll be asked to remember every last detail of those trips to Spain, and to help us identify everyone you spoke to or saw at that garage. It'll be your way out of the situation. Do you understand me?'

The man nodded his greasy head. 'Aye.'

'Good man.' Mackenzie rose to leave, then stopped. 'You know, there's one thing about all this that still puzzles me. We know that Starr lied about the incident in the shop on Friday. There was no attempted armed robbery: he mutilated that lad, deliberately. So why the hell did he call the police afterwards?'

'He didnae,' Big Ming muttered.

The detective stared at him. 'What did you say?'

'It wis me that got the polis. When Ah went in the shop, after the boy bumped intae me, and saw that finger lyin' on the counter, Ah got such a fricht Ah ran back oot again. Ah saw a panda car turning intae Evesham Street, and Ah flagged it doon. Gary wisnae pleased: Ah could hear him in the shop cryin', 'What the fuck are ye daein'?' but it wis too late by then.' He stopped and shook his head. 'An' ye ken whit? Ah still ken that boy frae somewhere.'

'In that case,' said Mackenzie, 'I think we should put your time with us to good use, by showing you some photographs. Maybe you'll spot him again.'

32

Outside, the last light of day was almost gone: the man sat at the table and looked out of the upper-storey window, his hands clasped around a mug of coffee to disguise the fact that they were trembling. His thick brown hair was still slightly damp from the shower, but he was freshly shaved, and dressed in crisp clean clothes. When the door opened behind him, he did not turn round for one simple reason: he was afraid. He had heard the gunshots earlier: he wondered about Sewell and whether when the sun rose next morning it would reveal a freshly turned patch of earth in the garden. And he wondered whether there was a second grave waiting.

Two figures, one male, one female, walked round the table and took seats opposite him. 'Good afternoon, Mr Hassett,' said the woman. 'I am Detective Inspector Dorothy Shannon, and this is Deputy Chief Constable Bob Skinner, although I believe that you may have met already.'

'We have,' said Hassett, slowly. Some of the fear left him: these were police officers, therefore the aftermath was being handled officially. Still, there had been those gunshots.

It was as if Skinner had read his mind. 'Sewell was a hopeless case,' he said. 'I knew as soon as I saw him, earlier this afternoon, that it would have been a waste of time interrogating him. I could never have relied on anything he told us. That was his choice: he knew what it would lead to.'

'I don't believe you. You're a civilian, they wouldn't involve you in something like that.'

The Scot smiled wryly. 'Miles, if you saw the file on me that's probably lying in Sir Evelyn Grey's safe, you would realise very quickly that your assumption is way off the mark. You've been listening to the Quo for the last week, for Rudy Sewell's enlightenment rather than yours . . . I'm sure you've noticed that the music's stopped, by the way . . . but are you familiar with Dire Straits? To mis-quote their finest hour, this is a private investigation, not a public inquiry.'

Suddenly the big detective's eyes were as hard as flint, and as cold as liquid oxygen. 'We're going to do this the traditional way, like we did when you were arrested in Edinburgh, with you, me and Neil McIlhenney. This time DI Shannon's the good cop instead of Neil, but I'm still the bad cop, the very bad cop, as always. I'm going to shut up now, and let my colleague ask the questions. I don't want to have to open my mouth for the rest of this interview, otherwise I'll get annoyed. In case you thought I was an easy touch the last time, I was pretty tired then, plus I'd just killed a couple of people: associates of yours, in fact.'

Shannon sat motionless beside him, her face set. While they were waiting downstairs for Hassett to be made ready for them, Skinner had briefed her fully on what had happened at St

206

Andrews . . . or almost fully.

'Mr Hassett,' she began, 'when you were under interrogation in Edinburgh you gave an account of your involvement in the incident at St Salvator's Hall. You said that the plotters were Rudolph Sewell, of the Security Service, popularly known as MI5, a military intelligence officer, now dead, an MI6 agent, Petrit Bassam Kastrati, also known as Peter Bassam, now also deceased, and yourself. You admitted that your purpose was to change the line of succession to the throne by removing a member of the Royal Family. Do you agree with that summary?'

'Yes,' Hassett replied cautiously.

'What can you tell us about Peter Bassam?'

'That information is restricted to members of my department.'

Shannon smiled. 'Mr Hassett, you don't have a department any more. What we're looking for here is co-operation: nothing you tell us is going to become public. Please: you are in no position to prevaricate.'

'There is very little to tell,' Hassett snapped. 'Bassam was an asset of ours in the former Yugoslavia, and in Albania. When he ran out of time there we got him a German passport and brought him to Scotland.'

'Who was his handler?'

'Rudy Sewell ran him, in his time with the Secret Intelligence Service, before he was deactivated. He had been 'put to sleep', as it were, in the restaurant in Edinburgh, against the possibility that he might have been needed again.'

'That's not what Piers Frame told us.'

The man blinked. 'What do you mean?'

'This afternoon, while we were on our way here, Mr Frame instituted a search within MI6 . . . forgive me if my use of the popular name offends you . . . for the files relating to his department's relationship with Mr Bassam. The strange thing was, he couldn't find any.'

'What are you saying?'

'I'm saying that Bassam was never an asset, as you put it, of the Secret Intelligence Service. They don't know anything about him.'

'I don't believe you,' Hassett declared. 'You're trying to trick me: I'm not saying anything more.' He folded his arms across his chest and stared down at them.

'Look at me.' Skinner's voice was not much above a whisper yet it was as if an invisible hand had grasped the other man's chin and forced his head upwards until his eyes were captured by the detective's pitiless gaze. 'You're a traitor, Miles. Do you know what would have happened to you two hundred and fifty years ago? Do you know what the sentence was? This was it: 'You shall be hanged by the neck and being alive cut down, your privy members shall be cut off and your bowels taken out and burned before you, your head severed from your body and your body divided into four quarters to be disposed of at the King's pleasure.' It's said to have been devised by Edward Longshanks to discourage his enemies in Scotland and Wales, and it was so effective, and popular with the mob, that it was used for five hundred years. As cruel and

208

unusual punishments go, it was out there on its own. It makes the practices of other cultures, which we're always very quick to condemn as barbaric, seem gentle by comparison. We may not do all that any more, but we still feel the same about traitors. You're a fatal accident waiting to happen, pal, and you know it, however much you might try to kid yourself. If you look down the dark tunnel that's the rest of your life, you will see a chink of light; be in no doubt, it is indeed an oncoming train. If you want to retain any hope of a happier outcome, you will tell us everything you know and you will do it now.'

'Are you saying that if I co-operate, I might . . . '

'I'm making no promises, but arrangements could be made. You've heard of the witness protection programme, haven't you? People like you live most of your lives under aliases, so it would be a natural environment for you.'

'Can I have time to think about it?'

'No. Inspector, carry on.'

'Thank you, sir.' Shannon looked across the table, silent until she was certain that she had Hassett's attention. 'Let's go back to Bassam,' she said, when she was ready. 'We've established that he wasn't one of yours, so whose was he?'

'I don't know.'

'Where did he come from?'

'Sewell produced him: he gave me his name and address and told me to go up to Edinburgh to recruit him.'

'So this was after the plot was under way?'

'Yes.'

'How did it all begin?'

'With Sewell. He ran the Emerging Threats section within Five, and so our interests overlapped frequently. He asked me to meet him one day last June, not at Thames House or Vauxhall Cross, but on a houseboat.'

'A houseboat?'

'Yes: it's a converted barge, permanently moored in Chelsea.'

'Who owns it?'

'I've no idea of that either: at the time I assumed that the Security Service did. Maybe they do.'

'We'll check that. Did he tell you what he wanted to talk about?'

'He said that something was afoot . . . his exact words . . . and it had been suggested to him that I was a suitable person with whom to discuss it.'

'So you met Sewell there?'

'Yes.'

'What happened at the meeting?'

'Rudy went straight to the heart of it. He told me that his department had identified a most serious emerging threat to the nation, and to its security, one that if not countered would lead to the end of a thousand years of stable government. I was suitably shocked, and asked him what it was. He told me that it was the future direction of the Royal Family, a generation or two down the line. He told me that there was serious concern within circles of influence that, with the demise of the Conservative Party as an effective political force and with the absence of any meaningful parliamentary opposition, we have become a one-party state. He said that the collective view was that in such circumstances there is more need than ever for a strong Monarchy as a counterbalance to the folly of government, if the British way of life is to be preserved.'

'By 'the British way of life', he meant what, precisely?'

'He was referring to traditional British values, and the need to stop their further dilution.'

'Do you mean racial dilution?'

'There was concern about the flow of immigration, and about the inability, and indeed the unwillingness, of government to do anything about it, but I wouldn't say that the worry was primarily racial.'

'Did you share that concern when it was put to you?'

'Rudy asked me that, straight out. I told him that I did, and that many of my circle did.' He became animated, taking the inspector by surprise. 'You can't deny it,' he exclaimed. 'England is disappearing before our eyes.'

Skinner chuckled quietly. 'I know quite a few people who would consider that a bloody good thing.'

Shannon frowned at his interruption. 'Did Sewell propose a solution?' she asked.

'He did: a radical solution,' Hassett replied. 'He said that the weakness in the royal line had to be removed, and that a means of doing this had been devised, one which would be based on the use of outside operatives, who would be seen to be pursuing a monetary objective, ransom. It would achieve our objectives by removing the individual involved, and by creating an atmosphere in which the country would inevitably swing back to the Right, and in which the Monarchy would be protected, by retreating from populism and resuming its traditional role in our system of government.'

'How did you react to this?'

'At first, I didn't believe it, and I told him so. I thought it was a test of some sort, or even entrapment, but he promised me that he was being deadly serious. He said that he was the leader of a group within Five who felt that way. He told me how it would be done, and when they proposed to do it.'

'What was your role in the operation?'

'I was to handle Bassam: I was to go up to Edinburgh, recruit him and brief him.'

'What was in it for him?'

'Money, of course: what else?'

'Was he paid?'

'Oh, yes. He was given a hundred thousand up front, half for himself, and half to finance the operation as necessary.'

'And his men, the people he recruited?'

'They believed it was a kidnapping for ransom. That's what everyone was supposed to believe, after the event.'

'What would have happened to them afterwards?' Skinner asked.

'They would have been killed, immediately, on board the pick-up vessel, as their target would have been. The bodies were to have been ground to pieces in an industrial mincing machine and disposed of at sea.'

'And the men on the boat who would have picked them up?'

'Military; they were a squad assembled by an intelligence colleague.'

'No.'

'Pardon?'

'They weren't soldiers. Their fishing-boat was destroyed after they opened fire on two RAF helicopters that were sent out to intercept them. We've recovered two bodies so far; they haven't been identified, but we do know that they weren't our people. As for their vessel, it's at the bottom of the North Sea.' He looked at Shannon. 'Sorry about the interruption, Dottie. Carry on, please.'

'Yes, sir. How was the money paid to Bassam?'

'In the usual way: through a Swiss bank.'

'Where did it come from? Who funded the operation?'

'I have no idea: it was never discussed.'

'Let's go back to the meeting on the houseboat. Did you decide there and then to go along with Sewell's plan?'

Hassett nodded.

'So you were a willing participant?'

'Let's say that I saw the logic of the argument. But I saw something else at the same time: this was a very dangerous man entrusting me with a considerable confidence. I had to assume that indeed he was not alone, and that he would be prepared to plug any potential leaks before they sprang, as it were.'

213

'Are you saying that you were coerced?'

'I'm saying that having been identified, by whom I know not, as a potential participant, I didn't really feel that refusal was an option, not if I wanted to make it off that boat.'

'But you could have blown the whistle at any time.'

'Could I? I had no means of knowing who was involved and who wasn't.'

'You could have gone to the press.'

Hassett snorted. 'I'm an intelligence operative, Inspector. If I was identified as such, there are people in various parts of the world whose lives would only be worth the bullets it took to end them.'

'And also you could see England disappearing before your very eyes.'

Hassett wrung his hands together. 'Yes,' he murmured.

'So you were a willing participant from the start. Let's not fanny about: you were, weren't you?'

'If you choose to see me as such.'

'Oh, that's how you're seen, Mr Hassett, believe me.' She paused to let her words sink in. 'When did you two meet again?' she continued.

'Almost Shakespearean,' the traitor sneered. 'On a few occasions, on the houseboat, when I had feedback from Bassam: that the people had been recruited, that they were on the move and that they were in Edinburgh and ready to act.'

'When NATO intelligence reported that the Albanians had slipped their domestic surveillance, and passed a warning to London that they were heading for the UK, did you think of aborting?'

'No, Sewell was able to promote the theory within Five that they were involved in drug-smuggling, and Amanda Dennis's unit was brought in. Rudy thought that he would be able to keep them well away from our people.' He glanced around the room. 'Clearly, he was mistaken.'

'So to sum up, what you are saying is that you are not aware of the identity of any conspirators other than Sewell, and that you have no knowledge of how Bassam was recruited for the operation.'

'That's correct.'

'You are also saying that the operation was initiated by Sewell, and that you were brought in later, presumably to avoid the risk of his meeting with Bassam.'

'Yes. As a Vauxhall Cross operative, I'm unknown even to most people in the Security Service.'

'Which leaves one last question,' said Skinner. 'Since you are very much an undercover operator, who put you in the frame for the job?'

Hassett stared at him. 'Do you believe that if I knew I would keep it from you, given my present situation?'

'I do believe this,' the big Scot replied. 'The answer to that question is the most important thing in your life, at least what's left of it.'

33

'The car was there?' asked Mackenzie, as Wilding stepped into his office.

'Yes: it's a silver-grey five-door hatchback A class, a funny-looking car for a Merc.'

'I know the model. Any indications so far?'

'Give us a break, sir. It's dark, and there was no room in the garage to have any sort of look at it. It's been loaded on to a recovery vehicle, as you said, and taken up to Fettes: DI Dorward's team will look at it there. Is the mechanic fixed up?'

'Yeah, the foreman from the dealership volunteered straight away. I'm not surprised: he'll be on overtime and we're paying. He's prepared to work for as long as it takes.'

'He'll do well out of it, in that case. Arthur Dorward said that it'll be a complicated motor to take apart, for all that it's not very big.'

'That's okay. I've warned the Guardia Civil not to expect anything from us till tomorrow.'

'You've spoken to them?'

'Yes.' The DCI caught the look on Wilding's face. 'Don't worry, I've cleared that with McIlhenney. He spoke to McGuire about it and gave me the okay to run with it ourselves for now. They'll keep the SDEA informed, and call them in if it becomes necessary.'

'So, what did they say? The Spanish, that is.'

'Not a lot. I told my contact Smith's story, and

gave him the address: he's based in Madrid, but he's going to consult his people in the region to see if they have anything on the place, and to ask them to keep it under observation.'

'Don't you think they should go in there straight away? Starr's murder's been reported in the press: whoever he's associated with, they're likely to know that we'll find evidence of his drug-dealing in the course of our investigation. Won't they have passed the word to the Spanish end?'

'If they have, there'll be nobody there to keep an eye on, will there? Okay, maybe I should have spelled that out, but these people aren't amateurs, Ray, they'll get to it.'

'I suppose so,' the DS conceded. 'Have you made much progress on all those files we took from Starr's shop and from the house?' he asked.

'Not yet, but to be honest I don't expect to. I've never yet come across a drug baron who kept accounts to audit standard. I've had a look through the business books: they bear out what Eddie Charnwood and Oliver Poole have told us, that Starr was making a reasonable living, but no more. Apart from that, all I've seen is correspondence from the Inland Revenue and Scottish Power.' Mackenzie glanced at his watch. 'That's me for the day,' he announced. 'The bastard's not going to be any less dead in the morning, and one less drug-dealer's no cause for regret.'

'What's the agenda for tomorrow?'

'Depends: if Dorward has a report waiting for us when we come in, we'll need to deal with that, but if not, we'll have to interview Starr's ex-wife sooner rather than later. And then there's the autopsy report: I don't know what's keeping that fucking idle pathologist.'

The chief inspector was in the act of picking his overcoat from the stand in the corner when there was a soft knock on the door, and it opened. 'Excuse me, sir,' said a uniformed constable. Mackenzie knew that he was on the front desk, but was too new to Queen Charlotte Street to have committed the name to memory. 'This has just arrived for you, by courier.' He was carrying a bulky brown envelope, with 'Urgent' stamped on it, in red letters.

'Shit,' Mackenzie growled, replacing his coat on the hook.

'Thanks, Blackie,' said Wilding, taking the envelope. He looked at the crest on the flap and recognised the Edinburgh University coat of arms. 'Pathologist's report.'

'Not before fucking time,' the DCI snapped. 'He's had a day and a fucking half. Ah, bugger it.' He snatched at his coat once again. 'I'll see it in the morning.' He slammed the door behind him, leaving Wilding staring at it.

The sergeant shrugged his shoulders, and felt a pang of regret over the early retirement of Dan Pringle; he might have been a shade irritable from time to time, but most of that had been for show. One thing was for sure: there had been nothing erratic about him. He looked at the envelope again, then picked up a stiletto-shaped letter-opener from Mackenzie's desk and slit it open. The cover sheet confirmed that it was what

218

they had been expecting: 'Report on the post-mortem examination of the remains of Gareth Starr.' He opened it and started to read.

Professor Joe Hutchinson had never been one to sacrifice thoroughness for speed. Relatively young though he was, Wilding knew that. As always, the report was meticulously detailed, but as always it began with a summary of the examiner's findings. The sergeant went straight there and began to read.

One: Cause of death was cardiac failure brought about by massive blood loss, the consequence of both hands being severed at the wrist.

Two: Close examination of the body revealed two puncture wounds in the right upper arm, both consistent with the use of a hypodermic syringe. There was significant bruising around one of the marks, indicating that unusual force had been used. Traces of fabric from the victim's shirt were found within the flesh.

Three: The victim was drugged before death. Two agents were used. The first, sodium thiopental, would have induced rapid unconsciousness. The second, suxamethonium chloride, would have paralysed the victim. While the binding tape would have rendered him helpless, this can be regarded as precautionary, since the drug would have done that job. The level of residual traces of sodium thiopental in the body indicate that unconsciousness would have been short term.

Four: There is considerable bruising to both arms just above the elbow; this is consistent with the application of tourniquets.

Five: Both hands were severed neatly above the wrist. I have taken specialist opinion on the nature of the wounds from a consultant forensic anthropologist. She noted a ripping effect on both flesh and bone, and concludes that the amputations were performed with an ordinary kitchen knife, possibly a carving knife. I am advised that this is borne out by marks on the table.

Six: Before completing this report I visited the crime scene with Detective Inspector Dorward and studied the patterns of blood flowing from each wound. This has led me to conclude that the hands were severed with the tourniquets applied, and that these were released subsequently and gradually. The victim would have been paralysed throughout the procedure. Undoubtedly he survived the amputations, to watch himself bleed to death.

Eight: While in theory this attack could have been carried out by an individual, it is quite impossible that it could have been done by someone who had recently sustained the type of injury that was described to me in my briefing for this examination.

Seven: In all my career I cannot recall

encountering a crime of such premeditated savagery.

'Say what you mean, Professor.' As Wilding finished reading, he realised that he was shivering. He knew also that it would take a while, maybe a lifetime, for him to chase the image of Gary Starr's awful last moments from his mind. He laid the report on Mackenzie's desk. 'I hope you've had a nice big cooked breakfast when you read that . . . sir,' he muttered. 'Maybe you'll barf again.'

34

Something remarkable had happened to Maggie Rose. It was as if she had spent most of her life in a darkened room . . . a brutal childhood, an unloving mother, a nervous, fumbling attempt at marriage, and a nightmare that had ended it . . . until, totally unexpectedly, she had found herself in the right place with the right person at the right time. With that the curtains had been drawn back, and her world had been flooded with light.

It had not been an instant happening: she had known Stevie for years, as a junior officer in another division and then as a close colleague. He had been around the block too, and was beginning to acquire a reputation, of which she had been well aware, as a dangerous man with the ladies. And yet when they had fallen together, he had been revealed as the gentlest, most caring person she had ever met.

Now that they were living together, for almost the first time in her working life she found herself looking forward to the end of the duty day, and to evenings at home with him. Her career had been the one thing that had kept her going through the bleakness. A successful spell in CID had led to a stint in Bob Skinner's office, and then on to the short ladder to the top. Promotion to uniformed chief superintendent and station commander had been the acme. She knew that the doors of the Command Corridor at Fettes lay open for her. It was all the more remarkable, then, that as she leaned against him on the couch, wine goblet cupped in her hands, listening to Mark Knopfler's soundtrack for the movie *Wag the Dog*, the sort of music she had ignored for years but now loved, she found herself considering whether she would return to work at the end of her forthcoming maternity leave.

'What do you think?' she asked him.

'Do you really mean that you'd chuck the job to look after the baby?'

'Why shouldn't I? What's against it?'

'Want me to give you a list? You'd be turning your back on so much of your life. You'd be depriving the people of this region of one of the most talented police officers they have. You'd be disappointing the chief and Bob Skinner, who've got you marked out for an ACC's silver braid. You'd also be taking a hell of a chance that you wouldn't get bored with being a full-time mum.'

'I haven't heard that babies can be boring.'

'You've never been pregnant before.' He ran his hand over her abdomen. 'I've heard of this syndrome: you don't just get a big belly, you're gripped by unquenchable romanticism. Admit it, girlie: it's true.'

'It's true that I'm finding out a hell of a lot about myself, love. You know, at no point in my life have I ever thought about becoming a mother. Even when we got together, the idea of pregnancy didn't occur to me. It's as if I'd forgotten what caused it, or never knew. But now that I am, I realise what an incomplete person I was before. I don't want to be like that again. There's this too: maybe it's that I was such a good copper because I was such a blinkered character. Maybe all I could see was the job, and it blinded me to everything else that's good about life. I can see it all now, and I'm glad. That's not being romantic.'

He kissed the top of her head. 'Then here's what you should do: whatever feels right to you. But don't take any decisions now: max out your maternity leave by working as late as you can, and take the additional unpaid entitlement as well. After a year off work you'll know whether you want to go back.'

She snuggled even closer. 'What did I do for common sense before I met you?' she asked.

'God knows. When do you plan to make the big announcement in the office?'

'I'll tell people when it starts to show, and not before. At the moment, only Bob Skinner knows, and he'll keep it strictly to himself, because I asked him to.'

'Aren't you going to tell your ex?'

'No! Why should I? It's our business, ours alone. In fact when the time comes, I'll tell all the girls and you can tell all the boys. Deal?'

'Deal.' Stevie sipped his wine. 'Now that's sorted, I've got an announcement of my own. I'm being moved down to Leith.'

She sat up and stared at him. 'You are? When was this decided?'

'Over the last day or so, I gather. Neil McIlhenney rang me this afternoon to tell me.'

'Have they finally decided to separate the two of us? Put us in different offices?'

'No. I asked Neil that, and he told me that it was purely operational.'

'What do you make of it?'

'Nothing. When my boss tells me something I tend to take it at face value. What do you read into it, Ms Conspiracy Theorist?'

'I think you should take it as a compliment. You're a safe pair of hands: that's why you're going there. That Mackenzie's a bit of a loose cannon. I thought so the first time I met him, when he was still in Strathclyde. Blokes like him, when they're as flash as that, often they're compensating for something. If they start to overcompensate, they can be trouble.'

'That doesn't worry me: I'll take him as I find him. Ray Wilding's there as well now, and he's a pretty stable guy. It'll be okay.'

'When do you go?' she asked, as he rose to change the CD.

'As soon as we've caught this idiot who's stalking Alex Skinner.'

'Any leads on that?'

'Nothing solid. We're making very discreet enquiries in her workplace, but nothing's come from them yet.'

'Could it be linked to the thing her dad was involved in last week?'

'A survivor out for revenge? Or even a fringe sympathiser? Those are the unspoken fears, but I don't believe so.' He pushed the play button on his remote and Van Morrison's *Veedon Fleece* eased its way gently into the room.

225

'What do you think?' asked Maggie, as he settled down beside her. 'By the way,' she said, 'you do realise that I'm only marrying you to get access to your music collection?'

He laughed. 'My library is yours. I haven't leaped to any conclusions about the boy, and I won't. My brief is simple: catch him. I'm most likely to do that if I keep a completely open mind.'

'What happens when you do?'

'I hand him over to DCS McGuire and Detective Superintendent McIlhenney: orders from on high.'

'God help him.'

'No, God will be helping him by keeping him away from their boss.'

'The very thought of that confrontation makes me shiver. Do you know where he is, by the way? I tried to get hold of ACC Haggerty today and I was told that he was at a committee standing in for the DCC.'

'I haven't a Scooby, but the grapevine told me that he and Dottie Shannon were seen at the airport this morning checking in for a London flight.'

'Shannon?'

'The new head of Special Branch.'

'God, I never knew,' she gasped. 'See? I'm becoming detached from the job already.'

'It's all happened very . . . ' He was interrupted in mid-sentence by the ringing of the telephone. With a frown and a muttered curse, he paused Van Morrison and picked it up. 'Steele.'

'Sorry to disturb you, boss. It's Tarvil here.'

Stevie sighed: he knew that DC Singh was not one to call him off duty without thinking hard about it. 'Tell me,' he said.

'Alex has had another call.'

'Did we get a fix on it?'

'A callbox in George Street. He stayed well away from the house this time, and he's smart enough not to hang around either. We had a car in St Andrews Square when we pinned it down, but he was gone by the time it got along there.'

'Was anything said?'

'Yes. Something different this time.'

'Bring me down a tape.'

'Now?'

'I don't mean tomorrow.'

'It'd be quicker if I send it to you as an email attachment.'

'True. Do it.' He ended the call. Walked across to the bay window and switched on his computer, then logged on to the Internet. Singh's message arrived in his mailbox inside a minute.

'What is it?' Maggie asked, as he downloaded the attachment.

'Alex's latest breather call hot off the line.'

'Let's hear it.'

He grinned over his shoulder. 'Yes, ma'am.' He clicked on the play icon, and adjusted the volume upwards. In an instant, the room was filled by the sound of a ringing telephone. There was a faint click as it was answered.

'*This is Alex.*'

Silence.

'Ah, it's you again. Tell me, for I want to know this after last night, are you just an ordinary pervert or are you a peeping Tom as well? Were you looking through my window last night?'

Silence.

'You know, I really am looking forward to meeting you, and I will. I meant it, you know: my dad's on to you. If you value your nuts, you'll pack this in.'

Silence.

'Okay, I think I'm going to hang up now. I was working just now, and my time's valuable. If you want to say anything to me, you've got ten seconds to do it.'

Silence. Then, the sound of a breath, and, hoarsely, 'You hurt me, Alex, you bitch.'

There was a click, followed by the dial tone, and the sound of Alex Skinner's breathing.

35

Sir James Proud was a man of routine: he arrived at his office at quarter to nine every morning, give or take a minute, to allow his secretary, who started fifteen minutes earlier, to filter his mail and lay it on his desk. Normally the pile was not large, as Gerry was skilled in weeding out material which he need not see and directing it to the appropriate officers.

As he eased himself into his comfortable swivel chair, he noted that the filtering process had gone very well that morning: fewer than a dozen letters had survived. He decided to check the newspapers first and was reaching for his copy of the *Scotsman* when his eye was caught by the heading on the document on top of the correspondence stack: 'Scottish Secondary Teachers' Association.' He picked it up and read.

Dear Sir James

Subsequent to your recent telephone communication I instructed that a check be made of our records for material relating to Mr Claude Bothwell. I am pleased to say that my assistant was able to find material relating to his membership. As I suspected he was our representative within Edinburgh Academy for most of his time on the staff there. He appears to have been singularly unsuccessful as a recruiter, since our membership within the school fell during his incumbency from five to two. He first joined the SSTA as a newly qualified teacher on the staff of Wishaw High School, where he remained for three years before taking up a post at Jordanhill School in Glasgow. He taught there for a further four years. There was then a twelve-month lapse in his membership before he joined the staff of Edinburgh Academy. He has never resigned formally from the Association, although his subscriptions ceased forty-one years ago. I attach photocopies of the relevant material.

I hope this information is helpful to you.

Yours sincerely,

J. B. Cotter (Miss)

General Secretary

He glanced at the attachment, a single sheet of paper, which had been amended in manuscript in several places so that all three of Bothwell's schools and three postal addresses showed, although two had been crossed out. 'Good for you, Miss Cotter,' he whispered. 'Not that it takes us any further, but at least you tried.' He laid the letter down and picked up his newspaper.

He was scanning the business pages when the intercom sounded. 'Can you see DS McGurk, sir?' asked Gerry Crossley.

He glanced up at the wall clock: it showed two minutes past nine. 'Yes, of course. I'm expecting Mr Haggerty at nine fifteen, but I'm sure we'll be finished by then.'

McGurk stepped through the door at the end of the room a few seconds later. As always he was immaculately dressed, in a business suit, and his black shoes gleamed. He was carrying a slim folder in his hand. 'Morning, Jack,' the chief greeted him. 'Have you had any contact from the DCC since he went south?'

'As a matter of fact, sir, I had a phone call five minutes ago.'

'From London?'

'From a car, by the sound of it: he was checking on what was happening, that was all, passing the time, I think. I told him about the Bothwell investigation. It seemed to amuse him.'

'It would. He thinks I'm playing detectives.'

The towering sergeant grinned. 'If you are, you're pretty good at it.'

'What do you mean?'

'I had an interesting visit to New Register House yesterday afternoon. We're not looking for your lady's mother any more, at least not primarily. This is a criminal investigation.'

'What's the crime?'

'At the very least, bigamy: two counts thereof.' He laid his folder on Proud's desk. 'It's all in there. The lady you remember, Montserrat Rivera What's-her-name, was, in fact, his third wife, but there's no record of either of the first two marriages ending in either death or divorce.'

'Bloody hell! Bob suspected as much.'

McGurk fought to keep his eyebrows from rising: he had never heard the chief constable swear before. 'What do you want me to do now, sir?' he asked.

'What do you suggest?'

'As I see it you've got two choices. You can either put the lid back on this thing . . . it's forty years down the road, after all . . . and tell Mrs Friend that you can't find her mother, which wouldn't be a lie, or you can order me to trace these other women as well.'

'Would that be easy?'

'No. The truth is, the system loses track of hundreds of people every year; they could be anywhere . . . or nowhere. Remember, sir, we're talking about elderly people here.'

'What would our absent friend the DCC do, do you think?'

The two men looked at each other for a few seconds, then smiles broke out on both their faces. 'Need you ask, sir?' said McGurk.

'Let's call it a rhetorical question.'

Proud sat behind his desk and stared out of the window as he considered the options that McGurk had set out for him. As he did so it came to him that there was a third, crazy option. He thought of his career as it had been and as it was. Nobody would argue that it had not been distinguished: it had won him his knighthood and the Queen's Police Medal, the honour which he valued privately above all. Yet it rankled with him that he had achieved these things without ever deviating from the conventional, without ever kicking over the traces and taking a chance. Now it was almost at an end; he would be a long time retired . . . he hoped . . . and sure as hell he would be a long time dead.

'You know, Jack,' he said, 'I need to get out more. Thank you very much for all the work you've done in getting us this far, but my diary's clear for the next few days, and Mr Haggerty's around to deal with any emergencies, so I think I'm going to handle this stage of the investigation myself.'

The sergeant stared at him, and blinked. 'You mean you're going to pass it to the chief constable of Strathclyde, sir?'

'I'll tell him when I deem it appropriate,' Proud replied firmly. 'I mean what I say, literally: I'm a serving police officer, with a warrant card, and it appears that a crime has been committed. It's my sworn duty to look into it.' He stared up at McGurk. 'I know, son,' he said. 'You're thinking that I've gone soft in the head, and maybe I have, but there's a bit of a mystery here, and damn me, I'm going to solve it.'

36

Skinner was smiling as Amanda Dennis drove along the Hogsback, heading for Churt from a different direction than the day before because of a warning on BBC Radio of a crash further down the A3.

'What's tickling you?' she asked.

'It's nothing really, just something daft that's going on in Edinburgh. Jimmy Proud's trying to carve himself a career as an investigator before it's too late. Trouble is, it looks as if he's bitten off more than he can chew. Jimmy's been a desk pilot for all his career as a senior officer. Luckily this is a private matter, and he's got big Jack McGurk to help him, so he won't be embarrassed in front of the rest of the force.'

'I hope he isn't. I like your chief constable: he's a very nice man.'

'He's also a sucker for a sob story, which is how he's got into this thing in the first place.'

'How about your daughter's problem?'

The smile left Skinner's face. 'I spoke to Neil about that this morning: he told me they've got a lead. There was another call last night apparently, and this time the man said something. They're hoping that it'll trigger something in Alex's head that'll take them to him.'

'Let's hope so. I hate that sort of thing: it's so cowardly.'

'As the gentleman will find out when we trace him and my two Rottweilers have him in their teeth.'

'Speaking of same, have you decided how you're going to handle Rudy Sewell?'

'I thought you might like to sit in on this one.'

Dennis shook her head firmly. 'I don't want to see that man again, ever. He was responsible for the death of one of my team, remember.'

'More than that, Amanda.' She glanced at him. 'It's okay,' he said, too quietly for Shannon to overhear in the back seat. 'I know about you and Sean, but nobody else does.'

'Bob,' she murmured. 'If that man walks away from this . . . '

'That will have nothing to do with me.'

'But don't you have the power to offer amnesty in return for co-operation?'

'Yes, but I'm not giving guarantees. Sewell's very dangerous. The DG's not going to turn him loose.'

'And Hassett?'

'I'll be in a better position to take a view on that when I've spoken to Sewell. At the moment my view is Miles is a follower, not a leader. His story is that he was approached by Sewell; I want Sewell to confirm that, and I want him to tell me why Hassett was chosen. Then there's the matter of Bassam. If he didn't belong to Six, whose was he and how did Sewell come to know of his track record, and have his cover address?'

'He won't talk to you.'

'They all talk to me in the end.'

'This isn't Edinburgh, Bob, and he isn't an ordinary criminal.'

'Sure he is. He may be Oxbridge educated and he may be a member of the inner circle down here, but he's guilty of treason, conspiracy to murder, and incitement to murder in the case of Sean Green. He's a criminal, Amanda: there are no modifying adjectives that can be used with that word. They're all the same.'

'He's tough and he's trained. How are you going to break him? Are you changing your mind about physical persuasion?'

Skinner shook his head. 'It's a matter of giving him a reason to talk to me. It needn't be fear; in fact it rarely is. Most often it's guilt: people can't carry its weight. But in quite a few cases, it's arrogance. I've got Rudy marked down as a very self-satisfied person. It was the first thing that struck me about him when he came up to Edinburgh at the start of this business. If he was made of marzipan, he'd eat himself. One of the reasons why Sir Evelyn asked me to do this job is because I'm just another plod from the sticks, or at least that's what Sewell thinks. He'll be offended when he walks into the interview room and sees Dottie and me there. It'll throw him off balance. I can work on that: I'll start to demean him, attack his intellect, attack his motivation. It might take a while, but sooner or later, and I don't care which . . . I can be patient when I have to be . . . he'll be provoked. He'll start to talk, and when he does, he'll be bragging, he'll be showing me how clever he really is.'

'We're going to find out pretty soon,' said

Dennis, as she turned off the road into the approach to the safe-house. They negotiated the barrier, cleared the encircling woodland and drove up the winding road. The morning was cold and wet: they rushed from the car park at the side round to the front door, and the shelter of its porch.

Winston Chalmers was waiting for them inside. 'Hello again,' he said. 'Not such a nice day, is it?'

'No,' Skinner replied. 'And here was I thinking I might take Mr Sewell for a walk in the garden.'

'I'm sure he'd enjoy that. When do you want to see him?'

'Let me top up my caffeine level first, then we'll get on with it.'

'Do you want me to let him shower and shave, like we did yesterday with Hassett?'

'No, I want this one as uncomfortable as possible. I want him stinking, and knowing it.'

Chalmers laughed. 'Oh, he stinks, that's for sure. Where do you want to see him? In the upstairs drawing room like yesterday?'

'No, that's much too civilised. Do you have a really dark and depressing interrogation room?'

'There's one of those downstairs. I'll go get him out of his bed-sit and put him in there for you.' He turned and headed for the stair at the back of the hall, which led to the lower level of the house.

Skinner walked through to the kitchen, with the two women in his wake. He filled the kettle and switched it on, then started to search the cupboards for coffee. He had just found a jar of

Alta Rica, and three mugs, when the door crashed open. A man whom Skinner had not seen before stood there, out of breath. 'Sir,' he gasped, 'will you come with me, please?'

The detective frowned, then followed him. He took the steps two at a time, turning, at their foot, to the right, into a corridor that seemed to run the full width of the house. A few feet away, Winston Chalmers and another man stood beside an open door. They looked at the floor as Skinner appeared, and he knew at once what had happened. He had noticed in the garden, the day before, that the windows were barred, so escape was nowhere in the reckoning. He walked past the minders and looked into the place where Rudy Sewell had been confined. A powerfully stale odour swept out to meet him, but he ignored it. The room was rectangular, not much bigger than some of the prison cells that he had seen during his career. There was a bed, against the wall on the right, and no other furniture. To his left, there was a toilet and a tiny basin. A hook had been set into the wall beside the cistern and it was there that Sewell had killed himself.

'I'll bet there's no sheet on the bed, Winston, is there?' said the detective.

'No, sir, just a duvet.' Chalmers stood beside him.

'CCTV camera?'

Chalmers pointed up and to his right, towards the ceiling. 'Up there. It doesn't look into the toilet area, though, so we couldn't see what he was doing.'

Sewell had shown the true ingenuity of the determined suicide. He had ripped the sleeves from his shirt, tied them together, and had used them to form a ligature, which he had fixed tightly round his neck, securing the other end to the hook. And then he had simply knelt down, let the makeshift rope take his weight and asphyxiated himself. It was a hanging, of a kind, unorthodox, but clearly very effective.

'I'm sorry, sir,' said Chalmers, quietly.

'Why today?'

'Pardon, sir?'

'Talking to myself. I was asking, 'Why today?' He's had a week to do that, a week to work out what was going to happen to him, so why did he pick this particular morning to top himself?' He looked along the corridor and saw that Dennis and Shannon were standing at the foot of the stair. 'Hey, Amanda,' he said. 'You told me you never wanted to see him alive again. You can take a look now if you like.'

She walked towards him; he stood aside to let her look into the room, his eyes on her all the time. There was no gasp of shock or horror. Her expression changed not at all.

'Who saw him last?' Skinner asked.

The two minders each shifted from one foot to the other, their eyes still on the floor. 'Answer him!' Chalmers barked. 'Marlon, it was you, wasn't it? You took him breakfast.'

'Yes,' the man replied.

'Did you help him do that?'

Marlon seemed to recoil at the detective's question. 'No way! He was fine when I left him.'

'Did he say anything?'

'He complained that the scrambled eggs were runny and the tea was cold.'

'Did you say anything to him?'

'I told him that he had better make the best of them for he was in for a tough day. I said that a hard bastard . . . sorry, sir . . . was coming all the way from Edinburgh to have a serious talk with him.'

Skinner drew a deep breath. 'Did you normally exchange words with him?'

'No, sir.'

'No indeed,' Chalmers growled. 'No communication: it's an operational rule.'

'Okay, Winston,' said the Scot. 'Don't fry the man for a few injudicious words. Sewell was probably biding his time: looks like he didn't intend to undergo any form of interrogation, from anyone.' He frowned. 'But it's your mess; you clear it up.' He turned and walked away.

'What will they do with him?' he asked Dennis, quietly, as they reached the top of the stairs.

'They'll invent a suitable legend about an operation gone wrong. The body may turn up in a warehouse in a few days, and be blamed on organised crime.'

'Handy for your lot, in a way, Sewell killing himself.'

'Means we don't have to, you mean?'

'Exactly.'

'I'd have volunteered for the job,' she said bitterly. She looked up at him. 'You let that man off too lightly, you know.'

'What do you mean?'

'I was thinking of something Rudy said after that first meeting we had with you up in Edinburgh. You had left, and he said, out of the blue, 'Remind me never to get on the wrong side of that man. I'll bet that if he put his mind to it, he could make a rock spill its guts.' He wasn't avoiding interrogation: he was avoiding being interrogated by you.'

'Is that the impression I give?' he mused. 'Is it really?'

'What do you want to do now?' she asked him. 'Have another go at Hassett?'

'You can't.' Winston Chalmers's voice came from behind them, at the top of the stairs.

Skinner spun round. 'Why the hell not?'

'Because he isn't here, sir: he was taken away last night.'

'Who took him?'

'His own people: a man from Six called Piers Frame and another fellow. They said that now he'd been questioned, they'd deal with him.'

'On whose authority?'

'The DG's. He called me early evening and told me they were coming.'

Skinner stared at Dennis. 'Did you know anything about this?'

'Nothing, Bob,' she exclaimed. 'I swear.'

'Then I guess Sir Evelyn and I are going to have a chat. One conspirator dead, the other disappeared. Is someone trying to sabotage this investigation?'

37

It was mid-morning, and so the coffee shop in Lothian Road was at its quietest. When Alex Skinner opened the door she saw that Neil McIlhenney and Stevie Steele, seated at a corner table, were its only customers. She smiled as she approached. 'You guys do know, don't you,' she said, 'that you've got CID stamped all over you?' She took a seat and picked up the cappuccino that stood waiting for her. 'Thanks, I needed this.'

'Thanks for getting in touch,' said McIlhenney. 'We appreciate it.'

'I appreciate you meeting me here and not marching into my office. Congratulations, by the way, on your promotion. My dad told me about it on Saturday night.'

'Thanks,' the superintendent replied. 'It came as a complete surprise to me. I thought that Mario would get head of CID, and that maybe I'd go into his job, not wind up running the whole of the city.'

'God help the villains, eh?'

'That's the idea. Now, Alex, what did you want to talk to us about?'

Her eyebrows came together slightly as she sipped her coffee. 'It's about these phone calls, this stake-out thing.'

'We wanted to talk to you about that as well,' Steele replied, 'and specifically about that call last night.'

'I want you to drop it,' said Alex, abruptly.

'Drop it?'

'That's right. I want you to stop the intercept on my calls, stop listening in.'

'Why?' Steele exclaimed, astonished.

'It's too intrusive. I have a life, guys, and I'm not going to have this character interfering with it any longer. I wish I'd never let my father talk me into going along with this.'

'Alex,' McIlhenney broke in, 'what do you think your father would say if we did what you're asking before we've caught this man? He'd go nuts; he'd crucify us.'

'I'll handle him, Neil. For the avoidance of doubt, I'm not asking you to stop tapping my line, I'm telling you. If he was sat at this table, he'd be getting told the same thing.'

'Ah, but would he do it?'

'Yes, he would, as you know very well.'

'You know who the caller is, Alex, don't you?' Steele's question was quiet, contrasting with her increasingly vocal annoyance.

Instantly she was defensive. 'I didn't say that, and I didn't mean to imply it either. I want to be able to phone my friends and share confidences and the odd bit of gossip, knowing that I have the privacy to do so and that every word isn't being recorded.'

'How many of us can be sure of that?' McIlhenney murmured.

'If you really mean that, Neil,' she shot back, 'then you've been moved out of Special Branch just in time.'

243

'But you do know him, Alex,' Steele persisted. 'Don't you? You recognised him from what he said last night.'

'He said that I hurt him. Do you think I've had a tranquil love life, Stevie? Do you think I haven't hurt a few blokes in my time? There was Andy Martin for a start: everyone knows I broke his bloody heart! Will you go up to Dundee and interview him if I don't give you a list of potential candidates?'

'If I thought that was him on the tape, I wouldn't hesitate for a moment.'

'You've heard the call, obviously. Did he say, 'You hurt me, Alex, you bitch . . . and I'm going to get you for it?' No, he did not. I tell you, guys, whoever he is, he's been working up to saying that, and now he has he'll creep away, back into my past where he should have stayed.'

'You still haven't answered my question.'

'You're a good detective, Stevie,' she replied, 'and a good detective's like a good lawyer. He never asks a question unless he knows the answer already . . . or thinks he does. So let's call it quits at that. Now let me you ask one. Suppose you were right, and I do know this boy, or suspect that I do. Did it occur to you that I might feel sufficiently guilty about what happened between us to want to protect him from a meeting in a small room with Neil and Mario McGuire or, worse still, with my dad?'

'No, it didn't, but now that you've laid it on the table, I can follow that line of thinking.'

'Good, for that's as much as I have to say to you about the matter.' She glanced at her watch.

'I've got to go now,' she said. 'The phone tap stops now. If I ever find out that it hasn't, you will find something out too. However good detectives you two might be, I'm an even better lawyer.'

McIlhenney stared at the door, long after it had closed behind her. 'Jesus,' he whispered at last, 'isn't she just like her old man?'

38

'Bob,' Sir Evelyn Grey protested, 'you must realise that I am walking a tightrope. We have had a great scandal within a community which, for all the talk of openness and public accountability, still lives largely in darkness. Our natural inclination, mine included, was to bury it as deep as we can, but events precluded that. Nonetheless the facts must remain secret, for the good of the intelligence services, which do operate in the national interest, for all this spectacular lapse. My colleagues have to live with your involvement, but they are determined to protect their own interests.'

'What the hell does that mean?' Skinner demanded.

'It means that once you reported that Hassett appeared to have told us everything he knew, I was forced to hand him over to his masters at Vauxhall Cross.'

'For disposal?'

'You don't really want to know the answer to that question. To be truthful, neither do I. I'm sorry, my friend, but you know the way things are.' Grey shot him a meaningful glance. 'But, then, you've demonstrated that, haven't you? There was no autopsy on the dead intelligence officer. They didn't need one: they simply counted the bullet holes.'

'That was different.'

'No, Bob, it wasn't, and you know it. If I may say so, it even handicapped the investigation on which you are now engaged. How do you intend to proceed, by the way?'

'Carefully,' Skinner replied. 'I'm going to follow up Hassett's information as far as I can. After that, there may be nothing. I may well report that there's no evidence that the conspiracy went beyond the people we've identified already.'

'Can I give Downing Street a progress report? You can imagine how anxious the PM is about all this.'

'Are you going to tell him that you threw Hassett to the wolves?'

'Perhaps not.'

'Then don't tell him anything yet. Wait for my final report.' Skinner turned and walked out of the director general's room. Ignoring the lift, he trotted down two flights of stairs to the office that he and Shannon had been assigned. It was in Amanda Dennis's Serious Crime section, since it offered a natural cover story to explain their presence in Thames House.

'How are you doing on the houseboat?' he asked the inspector, as he walked in.

'I've eliminated most of them in that area, but I'm left with one that might fit the bill. It's a converted Dutch barge called the *Bulrush*, and it's on a pier just off Cheyne Walk, in Chelsea, as Hassett said. The mooring fees are paid by a man called Moses Archer.'

'What?'

'Moses Archer,' Shannon repeated.

'Do we know anything about him?'

'Nothing, only that name.'

Skinner picked up the phone, looked for the button with 'AD' on the nametag alongside and pressed it. 'Amanda, are you free?'

'Yes. Do you want me to come along?'

'I'll come to you. If your people see you answering my call they may start wondering. That's their job, remember: to wonder about everything.' He hung up and walked along the short corridor that led to Dennis's office.

'What do you need?' she asked.

'Everything you can get me on a man called Moses Archer: bank accounts, criminal record, family background. Start with the Port Authority: he's paying the mooring fee on the *Bulrush*; it's a barge where Hassett's meetings might have taken place. That's priority, but I also think we should look at the CCTV tapes from the safe-house.'

'Why?'

'I want to see if we can identify the man who was with Frame when he picked up Hassett.'

'Do we need to know that? He'll have been a Six operative, and they hate us snooping on their people.'

Skinner smiled. 'The DG's wrong about me in one respect: I do need to know the answers to all the questions. Don't delegate; do it yourself, and have it all ready for me when I get back.'

'Where are you going?'

'We're off to take a look at the *Bulrush*.'

39

They found it without difficulty, on a mooring in Chelsea, not quite within sight of the homes of one or two world-famous rock stars. The barge looked deserted, as Skinner had suspected it would be.

He stepped on board and took a look around: most of the accommodation appeared to be under a long wooden deck, but close to the short gangplank there was a wheelhouse, complete with steering gear. He looked inside and saw a hatchway.

'What are we going to do, sir?' Shannon asked. 'Wait here for the owner?'

'We could do that, but my gut feeling is that he's not coming back.'

'You mean we're going in? Without a warrant?'

'The outfit we're working with tend not to use those. Let's look for an alarm system.' By the clock, it was still afternoon but the light was fading: he produced a small torch and looked around for sensors, spotting one on the cockpit door. 'Gotcha,' he said. 'There's no sign of a telephone land-line, so it can't be monitored: it must be a bell-only system. So where the hell is it?'

'Here, sir,' Shannon called out, from behind the superstructure. 'There's a bell housing out of sight of the pier.'

Skinner produced an aerosol can from his coat

and tossed it to her. 'Shake that up and spray it inside the casing; get as much as you can in there. It'll set in an instant and keep the thing quiet. While you're doing that, I'll get us in there.' Amanda Dennis had provided him with a set of locksmith's tools; he took them from his back pocket and set to work on the door. 'I used to be quite good at this,' he told Shannon, 'but it's been a while. Hold on, yes, there we are.' He opened the door and waited, listening as the alarm bell let out a strangled whisper. There was a light switch just inside: he threw it, but nothing happened. He looked back on to the pier and saw a service point, with a heavy plug attached: he jumped back on shore, found a switch and turned on the power.

'When did you learn to do that, sir?' the inspector asked him.

'During my interesting and varied career,' he replied. 'We don't always open doors with sledgehammers. Come on.' He led the way into the cockpit, raised the hatchway and eased his way down the steep stairway that led below.

The accommodation was more spacious than he had expected: the headroom was adequate, although he was glad that he was no taller than six feet two. He explored and found a double bedroom and bathroom off the big living area. He looked at Shannon. 'What do you think?'

'It doesn't look lived in, sir. It's well furnished, and well looked after, but there's no personal feel to it. There are no photos, for example, no television or music system.' She stepped into the bedroom, returning after a few seconds. 'There are clothes in the wardrobe, though, men's clothes.'

'I'll take a look; you search in here.' He went through to see for himself. Sure enough, a sports jacket and blazer and three pairs of trousers hung there. He lifted a pair of jeans out and checked the size. 'Waist thirty-four, inside leg twenty-eight,' he murmured. The jackets looked as if they belonged to a much bigger man: he tried one on and found that it fitted him round the chest, although it was much too short in the sleeve. He replaced it; and searched through the storage drawers, finding socks, shirts and underwear, but nothing else. There was one pair of shoes tucked under the double bed, and a travelling alarm in the drawer of a small side-table. Leaving the bedroom, he walked into the bathroom and looked in the cabinet, finding shaving foam, razor and aftershave, but nothing else. He checked the galley kitchen, looking in the fridge: he saw five bottles of lager, and one of white wine, a carton of UHT milk and a tub of spreadable butter, which was three weeks past its best-before date. There was coffee in a cupboard and a pack of biscuits, but no other food.

He returned to Shannon in the living accommodation. 'You're right, Dottie,' he said. 'This isn't a home, it's a bolt-hole. There isn't enough of anything for anyone to have been living here. This is either a fuck-pit, pardon my French, well trendy to impress the ladies, or a place for secret meetings, or both. Have you found any mail? Any papers?'

'No, sir, none at all. What do you think? Were

Moses Archer and Rudolph Sewell one and the same?'

'If they were, Rudy must have been pretty conspicuous when he went out in those trousers: they're four inches too short for him. On the other hand, the jacket would have been pretty baggy. No, Moses was someone else.'

'D' you know who? Could he walk in on us here?'

'Oh, yes,' he said grimly. 'I know who Moses was, and I can promise you he won't be dropping in here any time soon.' He glanced at her. 'No mail at all?'

'None: I've been through all the drawers and cabinets.'

'Then let's give it a real search.' He picked up an armchair and turned it upside down, then took a clasp knife from his pocket and slashed open the webbing underneath.

They spent the next half-hour taking the place apart, probing for weaknesses in the wood panelling, stripping the bed, overturning its frame and looking under the mattress, ripping drawers from their runners and searching underneath them for anything that might have been taped there, easing the fridge from its slot and using the torch to peer behind it. 'It's clean, sir,' Shannon announced at last.

'Not quite,' Skinner told her. 'There's one place I've still to look.' He went into the bathroom, lifted the top off the toilet cistern and looked inside. 'And why the hell didn't I search here first?' He sighed. 'There was a time, after the *Godfather* movie came out, when everyone

252

did this.' He rolled up his sleeve, reached inside and drew out a package, wrapped tightly in a waterproof bag. He dried his hand on a towel, then used his knife to slash through the binding tape. He carried his find through to the kitchen and emptied it on to the work surface. It contained a pistol, which the DCC recognised as a Sig Sauer P229, a serious, special weapon, an extra clip of ammunition and a zipper-sealed clear plastic envelope, which held . . . photographs.

'What's this?' Shannon murmured.

'The gun's probably a back-up,' Skinner replied. 'These?' He opened the envelope and let the snapshots it contained spill on to the counter: as they sorted through them they saw a man in uniform, alone, and with a woman, two children, another younger woman, alone in some, but in others with a stocky smiling young man. 'This is a life, a life left behind.'

He was about to replace them when something caught his eye: a slip of paper, folded and mixed up among them. He picked it up, opened it, and read. ''This is your man,' ' he murmured. ''Peter Bassam, Turkish Delight, Elbe Street, Edinburgh. He's mine from way back; you can trust him.' It's signed 'T', that's all. So who the hell are you, T; who the hell are you?'

'Peter Bassam?' Shannon exclaimed.

'Yup.'

'What does it mean?'

'Good question. It brings us back to this: if you think of agencies with the need and the capacity to run intelligence operatives in the Balkans, and you take out our SIS, the list's a pretty short one.'

He pocketed the gun, ammunition, photographs and note. 'Come on, Dottie,' he said. 'We're out of here.'

Darkness had fallen as they stepped outside, and as Skinner secured the lock. He was about to switch off the power to the boat when he saw what was beside it, mounted on a pole. 'Shit,' he growled, 'a mailbox. How did I miss that?'

It took him less than ten seconds to open it with his lock-pick. There were two items of mail inside. He took them out and peered at them in the dim light of a nearby standard. One was junk addressed to 'The Householder'; the other bore the name 'Moses Archer'.

40

It took the chief constable very little time to learn two things that Ethel Margaret Bothwell, née Ward, and Primrose Jardine, never legally Bothwell, had in common, apart from their connection with the mysterious teacher. Records showed that they were both still alive and, like him, they had both opted out of the social-security system.

Jack McGurk's research had been thorough. He had produced background summaries on Bothwell and his 'wives', containing all the information he had gleaned from the records.

Proud read through them carefully.

Claude Bothwell, born Perth 1930, only son of Herbert John Bothwell, clerk, and Lorna Grimes or Bothwell, school teacher, both deceased. One uncle on mother's side, married, no issue, deceased; therefore Bothwell has no surviving family in Perth. He married Ethel Margaret Ward, spinster, of Thorny Grove, Wishaw, born Wishaw 1921, daughter of William Ward, industrialist, and Margaret Meek Marshall. No siblings. Mr Ward was a significant shareholder in a steel mill nationalised by the Labour government in 1951; he and Mrs Ward drowned in a boating accident in France in 1952, leaving an estate valued at

£98,000, net of estate duty, according to the will lodged in Hamilton Sheriff Court. Bothwell's marriage to Ethel Ward took place a year later in Motherwell registry office. His address at the time of the marriage was given as 34B Caledonian Drive, Wishaw. A check of the Register of Sasines showed that he was not the owner of that property, so my guess is that he was a tenant and that he moved into Thorny Grove with his wife following the marriage. The property was sold in 1956 for £21,500, a considerable sum at that time.

In 1957 Claude Bothwell married, apparently bigamously, Primrose Jardine, nurse, born 1932, of 223 Stevenson Street, Scotstoun, Glasgow, the only child of the late Hugh Jardine, welder, and the late Agnes Bell or Jardine. Mr Jardine was killed in an air raid on Clydebank in 1941; Mrs Jardine died of tuberculosis in 1954. Bothwell's address on the second marriage certificate, 14 Dundyvan Drive, Broomhill, Glasgow, matches that shown on the SSTA records. A check of the Register shows that the property was owned by Albert Ernest Pickard, who was at that time Glasgow's second biggest landlord, after the City Corporation. It was sold following Mr Pickard's death in 1964 to Mr Arnold Solomons, who still lives there.

Bothwell's third marriage to Montserrat Rivera Jiminez, daughter of Jaime Rivera and Pilar Jiminez, of Torroella de Montgri,

Gerona, Spain, took place in October 1961. Both parties listed their address as 3 Newgate Street, Kirkliston, again a rented property which passed into the ownership of the Lark Housing Association in 1962. It still belongs to them; their records show that Mr and Mrs Bothwell gave up their tenancy in 1964. Unfortunately, that is the address on the SSTA files, so we do not know where they were living at the time of their disappearance.

'Quite a trail,' Proud murmured. 'Where did Bob say he would start? At the place they were last seen, as I recall.' He scratched his chin. 'Fine, but after forty years, who's still going to be around to talk to me?' As he gazed at the notes, he frowned, then picked up his phone and dialled McGurk. 'Jack, a question: when the Ward parents' will was lodged in the Sheriff Court, who did it? Did you ask that?'

'I didn't have to: they volunteered it. I didn't include it in the summary because I didn't think it was relevant any more. It was a firm called Hill and White.'

'Thanks.'

James Proud was a latecomer to the age of information technology; he had acknowledged it grudgingly but, with Gerry Crossley as his tutor, he was learning. He switched on his computer, pulled up the website of the Law Society of Scotland and opened its directory. He entered 'Hill and White', then pressed 'search', but there was no return. He was about to give up, when he

257

saw a window headed 'Any Location'. He opened it, selected 'Wishaw', and found himself looking at a list of sixteen firms. He went through them one by one: last on the alphabetical list he spotted 'Woodburn Hill and White, 17 Church Road, Wishaw.' He looked for a website, but found none, only the names of two solicitors, neither of which was, or bore any resemblance to, Woodburn, Hill or White.

'Not promising,' he murmured, 'but it's a place to start.'

41

Alex checked her time sheet at the end of the day: it did not look good. Curle Anthony and Jarvis billed by the quarter-hour and staff below partner level were expected to charge out virtually all of their working day. Her meeting with McIlhenney and Steele had overrun and she had been caught in a traffic jam on the way to her next client appointment, with Paula Viareggio, to finalise the transformation of the family trust into a limited company. Paula had been good about it, and had even taken her to lunch, but that had dragged on too. As a result she found herself looking at an hour and three-quarters of her day that had fallen into the sort of black hole that Mitchell Laidlaw, her boss, did not like to see.

She was finalising the record when she realised that he was standing behind her looking over her shoulder. 'Sorry,' she said, lamely, glancing up at him. 'Today was a succession of disasters.'

'Alex,' he replied, 'I keep separate lists of all the days when the members of my department bill out, on one hand, less than their allocation, and on the other, more than one hundred per cent of their standard hours by working late. You're at the foot of one list and the top of another, and I won't insult you by asking you to guess which is which. You're my best fee-earner, so I'm not going to worry about that.'

'That's a relief,' she exclaimed. 'I enjoy my lifestyle.' She began to clear her desk. 'Did you want something in particular, Mitch?' she asked.

'No, no,' he insisted. 'I just called by to ask how you were doing.'

'I'm fine,' she told him. 'Why shouldn't I be?'

'No reason, no reason.' Suddenly, the firm's chairman looked unusually flustered.

'Has my dad been talking to you?'

The portly lawyer's face became slightly ruddier than usual. 'Well, yes. To be honest, he did. He told me about the unpleasantness you've been having at home, with all these phone calls.'

Alex felt her hackles rise. 'And I'll bet,' she fumed, 'that he asked you to do a workplace check.'

'Well, er, yes, in fact he did.'

'I will bloody kill him! Mitch, I'm really sorry, he had no business bringing any of that to you.'

'Of course he had. Anyone in that position can come to me, and I'll do what I can to assist. The soundings I took were as discreet as possible . . . obviously so, since this is the first you've heard of them. You'll be glad to hear they came up with nothing, no potential candidates.'

She laughed lightly. 'That's almost a disappointment. You're saying that even in a firm this size there's nobody secretly lusting after me.'

Laidlaw beamed. 'Actually,' he chortled, 'you're quite wrong. There are several, but they don't make any secret of it.'

'Thank you, sir. My self-confidence is restored. To put you in the picture, I think the thing's blown over. I've told the police to stop listening in to my calls as of now.'

'Are you sure that's wise, if they haven't caught the fellow?'

'Mitch, I'm in no danger: trust me on this.'

'If you say so.' He smiled, awkwardly. 'But you can't blame me for worrying. After all . . . '

'Don't say it! I'm your best fee-earner.'

42

'There's no such person as Moses Archer: he doesn't exist. I've run checks everywhere and that's the official verdict.' Amanda Dennis looked solemnly across her desk at Skinner, then raised an eyebrow. 'Assumed name?' she suggested.

The Scot shook his head. 'No, it's a discarded name,' he countered. 'All references have been excised from the records, everywhere.'

'What makes you so sure of that?'

He took a letter from his pocket. 'This does: it was posted last Friday, from one of the many places in the UK with an illegible postmark. The Royal Mail should have its cage rattled about that, by the way. Let me read it to you.

'Dear Moses

'I know you're a busy man and everything, but it's been a while since I heard from you. More importantly, it's been a while since your nephews heard from you. It was young Joshua's birthday yesterday. He was really disappointed not to get a card from you, or even a phone call. Mum called him, though, and sent money for me to buy him a present. She sounded well; she said she's going to visit a friend in New Jersey soon, for a break before Christmas. I hope everything's all right with you, and that you

haven't caught one of those winter bugs that laid you low when we were kids. I worry about you living on that boat. I know it's lovely and it's moored in a very posh area, but it must be bloody cold at this time of year.

'Everything's fine up here. The Dales are quiet, of course, but if we have a mild Christmas we may see more people around. I hope so, for every little helps in the bakery. Still, Elton's had a reasonable year, so I shouldn't grumble. He and I went to the Druid last weekend. The food was great as usual, and Elton said that the beer's never been better. Will we see you at Christmas? Hope so. I've got your Santa Claus suit all ready for you.

'Your loving sis
'Esther.

'The heading on the notepaper is Glebe Cottage, Stannington Drive, Bakewell. That's in Derbyshire, if you didn't know.'

Dennis gave him a reproving glance. 'Of course I knew. I see what you mean: Moses Archer doesn't exist, but he has a sister. So who the hell is he?'

'No: who the hell was he?'

'You know?'

Skinner nodded. 'If you have to leave a name behind to protect your family from possible reprisals when you join a very secret organisation, Adam Arrow isn't exactly a quantum leap from Moses Archer.' He tossed a photograph on

263

to the desk. 'That's Moses, in his teens by the look of him: it's also Adam Arrow. I'm guessing that the girl is Esther.'

'But who is Adam Arrow?'

'He was the military intelligence officer involved in the plot, the man shot dead up at St Andrews.'

'Are you certain of all this?'

'Totally. I knew Adam as well as anyone did; that's him as a kid. Half the time, when he spoke to you, he'd lapse into a very colourful Derbyshire accent; he only dropped it when he was talking serious business. The clothes on the houseboat were his size. There's no doubt. Amanda,' he sighed, 'I don't have to tell you that when you enter the world he inhabited, you have to leave everything else behind you. Major Adam Arrow lived in Dolphin Square, but I guess he was too attached to his family to allow Moses Archer to disappear completely. So he kept the *Bulrush* . . . Moses, bulrushes, there's a connection when you think about it . . . as an accommodation address. No, more than that: as a gateway back into his real life.'

'Wouldn't that have been potentially dangerous for his family?'

'Yes, it was reckless, but Adam was familiar with danger. He didn't fear it, and he could manage it.'

'And Arrow was the third plotter.'

'Yes, but I've known that all along. The thing that concerns me now is that Moses Archer was in on it as well.'

43

She had just parked her car in her space in the underground garage beneath her apartment, when her mobile sounded. The screen identified the caller: for a moment she contemplated rejecting the call, but she knew that would be postponing the inevitable.

'Yes, Pops,' she said, into the hands-free microphone.

'Alex, can you speak?'

'Yes. I'm at home, more or less.'

'What the hell is this about stopping the intercept?'

'It's what I want.'

'We haven't nailed the man yet. You can't stop it. Even if you think you know who it is, you can't stop it.'

'I can, and I have.'

'Gimme the name, then. Tell me who you think it is. I'll have someone interview him.'

'Pops, that's precisely what I'm trying to avoid.' For a few seconds the sound of her father's breathing filled the car. 'God,' she said, 'you sound just like him.'

'That's not funny!' he snapped. 'Look, give me the name and I'll go easy on him: I'll send Stevie Steele, rather than the heavy squad. He'll just talk to him, establish whether it was him and, if it was, discuss his problem with him, gently, without any threat of prosecution.'

'If I knew who it was, and I'm not saying that I do, I could do that myself. I could go to court and take out an interdict against him; if I did that, any further calls he made to me would be in contempt of court. He'd go to jail for that. If you slap a criminal charge on him the worst he'd get would be probation and a few sessions with a psychologist.'

'You've got a point there, I suppose,' Bob admitted grudgingly. 'Okay, the intercept is lifted, but put your phone on auto answer mode as a means of filtering your calls. And make damn sure your alarm's on night setting.'

'Are you trying to reassure yourself or scare me?'

'Sorry, love; the truth is I'm just scaring myself. Do it for me, though.'

'I will. But what makes you assume that I won't have a bodyguard tonight anyway?'

'Indeed? And will you?'

'Time will tell, Father, time will tell.'

44

Aileen reached across the table and took his hand. 'You're very tense,' she told him. 'And you've been glancing around the restaurant all through the meal, as if you're afraid we're being watched.' She frowned. 'We're not, are we?'

Bob shook his head. 'No, you can relax on that score. Nobody followed me from my hotel, and there's no closed-circuit camera in this restaurant.'

'Are you saying that you thought you might be followed?'

'I didn't discount the possibility. I doubled back on myself a couple of times, and stopped in a pub on the way. If there was anyone, I've shaken them off.'

'But why would anybody do that?'

'For a variety of reasons; curiosity, for example. They don't let too many outsiders into the building where I'm based. Some of the staff might have decided to find out what I'm up to. On the other hand, someone on high might have decided to give me some discreet protection, whether I want it or not.'

Anxiety crept into her eyes. 'Bob, this thing that you're doing, is it dangerous?'

'I don't think it is,' he told her. 'It's taken a couple of unexpected turns, though.'

'Can you tell me any more than you have already?'

'Your security clearance may be top level in Scotland, but not down here. There is something I might ask you to do for me, though, a piece of special help that I'd only trust you to give.'

'What's that?'

'I'll tell you if it's necessary.'

She smiled. 'Darling, I don't know if I want to sleep with someone who's as paranoid as you. Go on, give me a clue.'

'I'm sorry, Aileen,' he sighed, 'I'm being a pain. Okay, let me put it this way. I'm not absolutely certain that I can trust all the people I'm working with. If things take a certain turn, I might want to go over their heads. In that case, there's a door which only you, of all the people I know, can open for me. But you'll want to think about it: if I ask you to do this and I'm wrong, we'll both be embarrassed.'

'I can stand that. If you think it's necessary, that'll be good enough for me.'

'That's good.' He grinned at her. 'As for sleeping with paranoid men, let me tell you something. There may not be a camera in this room, but you can bet that there will be on all the accommodation floors. You'd be amazed at who can access them.'

'Now that is what I call paranoia.' She laughed.

'Maybe, my love, but it is, in fact, gospel truth. If I saw you to your room, and went inside, I could go into my temporary office tomorrow and have someone pull up the tapes of me doing so. I could even check on when I left.'

45

The phone had not rung all evening, and Alex was relieved, not because she feared another of those calls but because her time was limited. She had made it home later than she had planned, and she had to shower, change and get herself, as her friend Gina Reed would have put it, glammed up for her big night out.

His call had been the one reasonably bright spot of her day. It had come through on her mobile as she was leaving Paula Viareggio's office, taking her completely by surprise: Guy Luscomb, her occasional date from her London stint, was in town on business, and would she like to have dinner? Of course she would: so what if Guy was a little self-assured? He was pleasant and she had worked out early in their acquaintance that, as long as she did not take him as seriously as he did, he was okay.

When the entry-phone rang she was ready to go, but she invited him in for a drink, since they would be travelling by taxi that evening.

'Lexy, darling,' he greeted her, as she opened the door, 'you're looking radiant, even better on your home turf than down in the big smoke.' His insistence on calling her 'Lexy', a nickname that she had discouraged all her life, was his one really annoying habit, but she let it lie because of the compliment.

She stood back and looked him up and down:

he wore a yellow Dannimac overcoat, which hung open revealing a suit that might as well have had 'Armani' tattooed on its lapels. In that instant he reminded her of Carlos, from the Il Divo quartet; she was certain that the effect was deliberate. 'You don't look too shabby yourself, sunshine,' she said, 'considering it's December and pissing down outside.'

'It's what black cabs are for, my darling,' he told her, stepping inside and kissing her quickly on the cheek.

'That's a little formal,' she remarked, and was surprised by the awkwardness of his smile.

'It's been a while,' he pointed out.

'True,' Alex conceded. 'Last May: nice Turkish restaurant, wasn't it?'

'Your memory serves you well, and in honour of that occasion I've booked something similar tonight, a place called Nargile. I'm told it's very good.'

'It is: I've been there.' She led him into the living room. 'That'll be nice, but first, make yourself comfortable while I open some *cava*.'

When she returned with two glasses and a bowl of pretzels on a tray, he had settled into her armchair, rather than on the couch. As she set her burden on the coffee-table, she had the feeling that she was being kept at arm's length.

'Well, now,' she said, as she settled into the comfortable leather sofa, taking care not to crease her dress, 'now you've sprung your surprise, Mr Luscomb, tell me what's brought it about. Why are you in Edinburgh?'

'I've come with my corporate executioner's

outfit, actually. A dataprocessing company out on the west side of the city has hit the buffers: you may have read about it in your local business press. Bit of a story: they were New Start of the Year not so long ago, in some pretentious magazine or other; now they're calling in receivers with a view to liquidation. My firm's got the job, and as one of the insolvency partners, I'm here to get it under way.'

'I know who you mean,' Alex murmured, as she sipped her *cava*. 'We acted for them when they set up, then they left us; one of the directors has a cousin in another law firm who said he could do the job cheaper. Now their creditors are paying insolvency fees, and through the nose too, knowing what you lot charge.'

'That's business, Lexy my dear. I know I should shake my head and tut at such folly, but where would people like me be without people like them?'

'Giving positive advice rather than picking up the pieces, perhaps?'

'Ouch!'

She laughed. 'It's all right, this isn't going to be Pick-on-Guy Night. I know there's never going to be a world free of bad business decisions. I only wish they weren't so costly, in human as well as financial terms. The cousin I mentioned has been fired by his firm in the wake of all this. He's thirty-eight and his career's on the way to Seafield.'

'Pardon?'

'Sorry. That's an old Edinburgh expression.'

'Ahh, as in down the toilet, I take it.'

'You hit that flush on.'

'My, Lexy, you are in good form tonight.'

'I've been better, but never mind. Let's call a cab, and finish these while it's on the way.' She picked up the phone and pushed a single button: the taxi company number was programmed into the memory.

'How long have you been in your new place?' he asked, as they sipped the *cava*.

'About a month.'

'Is that all? You told me back in May that you'd bought it.'

'It's new, Guy: I chose it off plans in February. That gave me plenty of time to get rid of my old place.'

'How's the market here?'

'Active. It's not London, but it's pricey.' As she spoke, the buzzer sounded. She sealed the *cava* bottle with an airtight stopper, put it in the fridge, then fetched her coat from her bedroom.

Christmas was approaching and so Nargile was busy even though it was mid-week. They were shown to a table for two in the window, positioned so one diner could see the crest of Hanover Street, with its Georgian statue, and beyond, the lights of Edinburgh Castle. 'You sit there, Guy,' said Alex. 'You're the stranger in town.'

'Thank you, Lexy dear. How very thoughtful of you.'

One more time, she thought, as the name ground on her. *On the other hand, he is paying, and he's not bad looking.*

'How long will you be here?' she asked, as the

waiter brought menus.

He glanced at the wine list and ordered a bottle of Muscadet. 'Just a couple of days,' he replied. 'I got here yesterday. By Thursday the task will be mapped out; at that point I'll leave my assistant to carry on with it, and head back south.'

That's fine, she thought. 'What a pity,' she said.

'Yes, and I'm really sorry about it, but we really are busy in London. It's sad but true: third-term governments usually mean a bonanza for us insolvency practitioners.'

'I can't say I'd noticed that. Most of our corporate clients are doing really well . . . thanks to the quality of our advice, no doubt.'

'Naturally. However, if any of them do happen to have a hard time, or you hear of anyone who is, you'll keep me in mind, won't you? I'm also responsible for corporate recovery within the firm, remember.'

She looked at him across the table with a gleam in her eye, as he tasted the wine and as the waiter poured it. 'Guy,' she murmured, when he had gone, 'this isn't a new business pitch, is it? Will dinner be chargeable to the firm?'

He managed to look genuinely shocked. 'God, Lexy, you don't think that, do you?'

Too right I do. But she smiled, letting him off the hook, then raised her glass. 'If I did, sunshine, I wouldn't be settling for this when there's Moët on the list.' She took pity on his awkwardness. Okay, he was a clothes horse, and he fancied himself to death, but he was single, he wasn't that bad, and after the few days she had endured, he was there. 'Tell me something,' she said. 'When you chose this place, were you hoping for the same outcome as the last time we ate Turkish?'

He had the decency not to look her in the eye when he lied. 'Oh, Lexy, of course I wasn't.'

'How nice to hear that. You know what, Guy? There's just a chance that virtue might not be its only reward.'

46

As she lay there in the darkness, listening to his wheezing snores, she remembered what it was that had put her off Guy Luscomb. He could talk the talk all right, but that was as far as it went.

She had not slept with anyone since their last time together, such had been his effect on her. Alex thought of herself as a modern woman: she did not class herself as promiscuous, but if she met a man she liked physically and who amused her enough, she would have sex with him. It had been that way since she was eighteen, and in her first year at Glasgow University, in the light of the only piece of fatherly advice she had ever received on the subject. That had been along the lines of 'Not in your own backyard', but actually it had been unnecessary, as none of the boys she knew at school would ever have dreamed of 'trying it on' with Bob Skinner's daughter.

Even with those years of experience behind her, and her time spent living with Andy Martin when they were engaged, she did not regard herself as a sexual connoisseur. However, she knew what she liked, and she knew what she had a right to expect from a partner.

And that was a hell of a lot more than thirty seconds.

It wasn't as if the man had been drunk: they'd shared one bottle of wine in Nargile and the *cava* had stayed in the fridge when they'd got back to the flat. She had her first inkling of how it was going to be when she had gone to hang up her dress, and he had gone into the en-suite to take his turn to brush his teeth. She had turned, still in her underwear and looking to be helped out of it, to find him already in bed, grinning at her from under the slightly tented duvet.

She had tried to interest him in some foreplay, until she recalled that in Guy's mind that was a type of golf. Instead his leg had come over and he had set to work, teeth gritted. In spite of himself, he had hit the spot, and for a few seconds she had thought it was going to be all right, until his face had contorted, he had let out his patented squeal (God, the memories that come back!), she had felt the condom (hers, not his: that had been a difficult moment) twitching a little, and it had been over.

At least he hadn't asked how it had been for her. They had listened to Radio Forth for a while, until he had indicated, not in so many words, that he was ready to try again. And she had let him, more in hope than in expectation that it would be better. It had been worse: second time round he had missed the spot completely, and she had endured a full fifty-four seconds . . . she had timed him, secretly, on the bedside clock . . . of pounding before he squealed again and spent himself.

When he rolled off her, shortly afterwards, and started to snore, she had to fight off the urge to laugh hysterically as she remembered something that Gina had said on a night out a few months before. 'The saddest moments in a girl's life are, one, when her partner can't find her clitoris, and two, when he finds it.' It had been an hour before she had fallen asleep.

The radio alarm kicked into life on the stroke of seven; the bright morning voice of Spike Thomson, Andy's friend, filled the room. Guy grunted and started to waken: it took him a while, but eventually he was with her and his surroundings. 'Morning, lovey,' he mumbled. 'Sleep tight?'

'Not a lot,' she told him. 'It was a bit noisy in here for a while.'

He grinned, slightly uncertainly. 'You mean me? Ah, sorry.' A hand reached for her. She caught it before it found its mark, entwining her fingers with his. 'Fancy some morning glory?' he asked, undeterred.

'Darling, you've worn me out.'

'Ah, come on, fit young thing like you.' He raised the duvet with his free hand. 'See? I'm up for it.'

She felt her annoyance gauge approaching the red line. 'Barely,' she said. 'Anyway, I'm out of condoms. Incidentally,' she added, 'it's taken me two years to shag my way through that box.'

'I thought all you girls were on the pill these days.'

Alex propped herself on an elbow, pulling the duvet round her breasts. 'When was the last time you got laid, Guy?'

He frowned. 'What sort of a question is that?'

'It's a straight one, now answer it.'

'A couple of months ago; no, six weeks.'

'Who was the lucky lady? A steady or a one-off?'

'Someone I met at a reception: a Lithuanian girl.'

'Did you use a condom then?'

'Bareback,' he answered.

'Seen her since?'

'No.'

'Guy,' she sighed, 'are you completely unaware of sexually transmitted diseases, or are you just one of those idiots who thinks he doesn't mix with the sort of person who might have the clap, or worse?'

'Oh, come on, Lexy, don't be silly.'

She swung herself out of bed, stood and looked down on him, with a hand on her hip. 'There are a few things I hate being called. Up there at the head of the list you will find 'Lexy' and 'silly'. I'm going to take a shower now; if you want one before you go back to your hotel, use the other bathroom.'

She stayed longer than usual under the spray, taking the jet in her hand and directing it as if she was washing every trace of him from her. When she emerged back into the bedroom she was wrapped in her dressing-gown, and her hair was towelled to dampness. Guy was buttoning his shirt, his back to the en-suite. He turned at the sound of the opening door. 'Have you been washing this man right out of your hair?' he asked. The question was so near the mark that she felt a burst of guilt.

'No, not at all,' she insisted. 'This mop of mine takes a lot of looking after.' He smiled and she realised that she liked him much better with his clothes on. She knew also that it would always be that way. 'I'll go and rustle up some breakfast,' she said.

'Thanks, Alex,' he smiled as he said her name, 'but I'll get some back at the George. I'm still in yesterday's clothes and I'm due to meet the unfortunate company's anxious banker at nine thirty in his office. I'll grab a cab outside. I imagine there are plenty around at this time.'

He picked up his jacket, which he had hung carefully over the chair that faced her dressing-table, and slipped it on. She stepped up and straightened his tie, and let him kiss her lightly, on the lips.

'Fancy a return game tonight? This time I'll bring the rubbers.'

Although she had guessed it might be coming, the question still managed to take her by surprise. There was a considered and distinct pause before she replied. 'Sorry, Guy. I'm busy tonight.'

His reaction was not what she had expected. 'Ah, too bad: I won't ask what you're doing, just in case you tell me you're washing your hair.' He reached up and patted her head.

'I'm seeing my friend Gina,' she heard herself say.

He nodded. 'And I'm off to London tomorrow night. As well, I suppose: one-night stands are the best thing for swingers like us, aren't they?' He kissed her again, even more quickly, a mere brushing of the lips, then turned and headed for the living room.

She followed him as he picked up his yellow overcoat from the back of the couch, where he had left it on his determined rush towards her bedroom, and as he walked to the door she opened it, and held it for him. He grinned at her, all of his massive self-confidence back in place, then gave her bottom a firm squeeze. Her neighbour chose that moment to leave for work, trying not to look at her as he passed: his name was Griff and she fancied him more than a little, although he was married and they had exchanged barely more than introductions.

'Thank you, Lexy darling,' said Guy, in a voice that was louder than was strictly necessary. 'That was terrific. See you again some time. Call me if you like.'

As she stepped back inside her apartment, she found herself trying to work out what been happening for the twelve hours that had just elapsed. She had been vulnerable and he had been there and useful: at least that was how it had seemed to her the day before. But who had been using whom?

She drew back the living-room curtains: it was winter-morning dark, and the Water of Leith still reflected the sodium street-lamps. 'You know what, Alex?' she murmured to herself eventually. 'Someone got fucked in here . . . all one minute and twenty-four seconds of it . . . then brushed off, and I rather think it was you.'

47

Ray Wilding hung up the phone. He had been in for forty minutes, since eight thirty, but there was still no sign of Mackenzie. He had checked with the switchboard to see if a call or a message had come in from Spain; there had been nothing and so he had decided to ring Gary Starr's ex-wife, to make sure that she would be at home when he and the chief inspector visited her that morning.

Kitty Philips had been terse, but not downright rude. She had told him that she worked afternoons only in a DIY store, and had shopping to do that morning, but that she would be ready for them at ten o'clock. He glanced at his watch. The traffic could be a bitch across town; before long they would be tight for time.

When his phone rang, his first thought was that it might be the chief inspector, calling in to say that he had been delayed. He almost sighed as he answered. 'Wilding.'

'Call for you, Sergeant,' said the operator. 'A Mr Smith: James Smith.'

He had to think for a second before it clicked: Big Ming. 'Put him through.'

'Hullo.' The voice was gruff, but clearer than it had sounded across the desk in the interview room.

'Mr Smith, what can I do for you?'

'Ah've been thinkin', ye ken. Aboot that lad.

281

The one wi' the finger.'

'Or, rather, without it.'

'Whit? Oh, aye. Ah see whit ye mean. Onyway, I telt you Ah thought Ah might hae seen him: well, Ah remember where.'

Suddenly Wilding's morning was more interesting. 'Oh, yes? Where?'

'Ah dae a bit o' door work sometimes, helpin' oot a guy Ah know; bouncin' ken. There's a place Ah've been tae sometimes, an' that's where Ah've saw him.'

'What's this place called?'

'Ah cannae remember; a lot o' they clubs dinnae hae big signs outside, but Ah kin take ye there.'

'Okay. Have you seen this man in the queue?'

'Naw, naw, naw, naw, naw. He wisnae a punter; it wis his place, like, or at least he wis one o' the lads that ran it. He wisnae dressed like he wis in Evesham Street either. He wis smart, like, no' a scruff.'

'What makes you so sure it was him?'

'Ah'm no certain. Ah jist think it wis; the lad at the shop looked awfy like him.'

Wilding glanced at his watch. 'Let's check it out, then. You come here, to Queen Charlotte Street, at twelve o'clock this morning. You can show me where this place is, and we'll take it from there.'

'Twelve?'

'Are you doing anything else?'

'Naw.'

'Just as well, or you'd miss it. See you at midday; do not be one minute later.'

He rang off, and looked up to see Bandit Mackenzie approaching; he looked tired, heavy-lidded. 'Morning,' he growled. 'How's your day been so far?'

Wilding grinned, and nodded towards the phone. 'I think it just got better.'

48

'I'm sorry it's taken so long, Bob,' Amanda Dennis said, 'but I wanted to preserve security. Our internal monitoring is reviewed at regular intervals. If I had broken the sequence it would have been noticed.'

'Won't it be noticed now?'

'No, because when it was done I patched in and put a copy on to my computer. The period you want to look at is here.' She moved her mouse and clicked: within a few seconds, the entrance hall of the Surrey safe-house appeared on her monitor.

As Skinner and Shannon watched, they saw the big figure of Winston Chalmers move quickly and jerkily across the screen, greeting two men. 'Pause there,' the DCC instructed, leaning closer. One of the newcomers was instantly recognisable: Piers Frame, immaculate in a single-breasted suit that was probably Savile Row. The other presented a complete contrast: he was stocky, shorter than his companion, and he wore a three-quarter-length country coat, with a hood, pulled forward so that it was hiding his face.

'Either it's raining inside,' said Shannon, 'or he doesn't want to be recognised.'

'Indeed,' Skinner murmured, 'and I wonder why that is. He obviously knew he'd be under surveillance in there; maybe he's the guy who was going to take Hassett into the woods and put one in the back of his head, and maybe he was sensitive about it.' He felt the inspector shudder beside him. 'But maybe there's a better reason. Go on, Amanda.'

Dennis hit the play icon and the recording resumed, showing Frame and the hooded stranger waiting in the hall, until Chalmers reappeared, with a second minder, escorting Miles Hassett. 'Can you slow it here?' Skinner asked. With another click, the playback went into slow motion. As they watched, the traitor seemed to draw back, startled, as he saw Frame and his companion.

'No sound?'

'I'm afraid not,' Dennis replied. 'Not that it would have done any good. Winston told me that they didn't say anything when they met. The other fellow didn't speak at all.'

'Bugger.'

'Wait a minute, though. Let me roll on.'

She resumed playback at the normal speed. They watched as Hassett stepped forward and allowed himself to be escorted from the building. Once again, the hall was empty. And then the scene changed, to feed from another source, outside, overlooking the car park to the side of the building. The area was poorly lit, but the camera was light-enhancing, and the figures were still recognisable. As Frame opened the driver's door of the waiting car, he turned to Hassett, and spoke; to their surprise, the newly released prisoner seemed to laugh. Then he stepped into the vehicle, not into the back as a prisoner would have done, but into the front.

It was the third man who opened one of the rear doors. As he bent to slide inside, his hood seemed to slip further forward, obscuring his vision. With an irritable gesture he threw it back, giving the camera a brief, but clear view of his face. Without being asked, Dennis reversed the recording and froze on his image. He looked much older than his MI6 companions, from another generation, but from the evidence of his furtive expression, of the same world.

'Now who the hell is that?' Skinner murmured. 'He doesn't look like SIS muscle, that's for sure.'

'He isn't, Bob,' Amanda Dennis told him. 'Very far from it indeed. That's Ormond Hassett MP, Miles's daddy.'

'Jeez! What the hell is all that about?'

'That's what I've been asking myself. The best I can come up with is that the DG of Six has decided that the best thing to do with Miles is to release him into his father's care, with instructions that he disappears into the family business, to live out a long and boring life.'

'But why would Ormond be taken to pick him up? He thinks his son's a civil servant, remember.'

'Clearly, he knows different now. Could it be that Frame decided that Miles wouldn't go with him unless there was someone there that he could trust?'

'How big a surprise did he get when he saw who it was? Take another look at the playback and you'll see: about a second's worth, that was all.' He focused on Dennis. 'Who knows about this, Amanda, apart from Winston and his team and the three of us?'

'Nobody.'

'Good. Keep it that way, while I'm thinking about what all this means. Don't tell anybody, anybody at all. Can you live with that?'

She gazed back at him. 'Remember what happened to Sean, Bob? He's dead because of all this; I can live with it, no problem.'

'Of course you can,' he said quietly. He paused, then went on: 'I'm going to need everything there is on Ormond Hassett. We'd better take a look at him. While you're finding that, I need something else from you.'

'What's that?'

'A car. DI Shannon and I are going up to Derbyshire.'

49

They were passing the Commonwealth Pool when Mackenzie's mobile sounded. The chief inspector shifted in the passenger seat and reached inside his jacket. 'Yes,' he snapped testily. There had been little conversation, only a silent tension, between him and Wilding on the drive up from Leith. 'Ah, it's you, Dorward; about bloody time, too.'

As he drove, the sergeant glanced occasionally to his left, trying to read anything he could from his boss's expression. 'And that's it?' said Mackenzie at last. 'Okay, leave it with me.'

'The car, sir?'

'Yes. It took all bloody night, but they reduced the thing to its component parts.'

'Did they find drug traces?'

'Not a fucking scrap.'

'Bugger.'

'They did find something, though: the Mercedes A Class has what they call a sandwich floor construction. The mechanic got them right in there and they were able to identify very small strips of waxed paper, thick, virtually waterproof stuff, like you'd use to wrap drugs for carriage.'

'Did they match it to the packages we found in Starr's safe?'

'More or less; Dorward says it's similar.'

'Shit,' Wilding grunted. 'That's not very helpful: 'similar' is no bloody use in court.'

'It's a start.' Mackenzie took a notebook from his pocket and flicked through it, then dialled a number. 'English, please,' he said, when he was answered. 'Mr Marquez, Drugs Unit.' Beside him, the sergeant frowned. 'Antonio? It's DCI Mackenzie here in Edinburgh, about the Pamplona thing. We've completed our examination of the man Starr's car; we have found suspicious material. Do you understand? Suspicious material . . . Yes. You are clear to raid the garage and question the people there. Thanks. Please advise me when the operation is complete. You've got my number. Good luck.'

Wilding was still frowning as he cleared the complicated roundabout at the foot of Dalkeith Road and headed for Gilmerton. 'They tell me that guy Steele lives around here,' the Bandit said suddenly.

At once, the sergeant knew the reason for his strange mood. 'Gordon Terrace,' he replied, 'on the other side of the Cameron Toll shopping precinct.'

'Mmm. He's going to be our new playmate, Ray.' He tried to sound casual but failed. 'McIlhenney called me this morning; I was barely in my seat when he rang. He's moving him down from Torphichen Place. They're putting a DI in over your head, son: don't take it personally, though.'

'I won't: I've known Stevie Steele for years. He's a sound guy.'

'He must be. He lives with a chief superintendent, from what I hear.'

'That's right. I expect they've been looking for

289

an opportunity to shift him into a different office from her.'

He drove past the Royal Infirmary, and took a right turn into Humphrey Street. He drew up outside number sixteen, switched off the engine and turned to Mackenzie. 'Sir,' he said, 'about this Pamplona thing: did you brief Mr McIlhenney when you spoke to him?'

'What's that to do with you? Are you covering your arse again?'

'Actually, boss, I'm trying to cover yours. This isn't Dan Pringle's era any more: it's a new regime.'

Mackenzie laughed. 'My arse is made of asbestos, DS Wilding. Thanks for your concern, but I'll do it my way. Now come on, let's go and talk to Starr's ex.'

Kitty Philips was a small woman, but her confident stance as she opened the door sent out the message that she punched above her weight; her hair was a shade of blonde that could not possibly have been natural, she displayed more makeup than was usual for that time of the day and she wore a pale-blue catsuit, the uniform of the gym generation. Wilding wondered how she would have looked had he not called to check that she would be in.

'Yes?' she challenged.

'DCI Mackenzie and DS Wilding,' the chief inspector began.

She looked at the sergeant. 'You're the boy that phoned.'

'Yes,' he replied. 'Can we come in?'

'I'd rather that than have you stand at my door

290

for the neighbours to admire.'

The house was a semi-detached villa, built in the second half of the twentieth century. The living room was comfortably, rather than lavishly, furnished. Looking around, Mackenzie guessed that the enormous plasma television set, mounted like a mirror on a wall, was easily the most expensive item on view.

'You're late,' the former Mrs Starr said abruptly.

Mackenzie smiled at her, amused by her petulance. 'Come again?'

'It's taken you three days to get here. I'd have thought I'd have been first on your list for a visit.'

'I'm sorry to disappoint you: we had other priorities. But now we are here, I might as well ask you straight out, did you kill your former husband, Mrs Philips?'

'That's better,' she exclaimed sarcastically. 'No, I did not.'

'Where were you on Friday night?'

'At the bingo, down in Meadowbank.'

'Alone?'

'No. I was with my friends Morven and Izzy.'

'Till when?'

'Till it finished; after that we got a taxi back here and had a drink. They left after midnight. Ask them; you can have their addresses if you like.'

'What about Mr Philips?'

The woman gave a snorting laugh. 'Do you mean, did he kill Gary? He's never even met him. It'd have been some trick if he did, too. Les is a lorry driver: he was in Lisbon on Friday.'

'You were fairly quick off your mark phoning the lawyer, though, to see if you were still in the will.'

'Ollie told you that, did he? Why the hell shouldn't I? Gary was casual about these things . . . not that he'll have left much behind him. He had to remortgage to give me my share when we split up, and he only had that one poky wee betting shop.'

'How did you feel about your ex, Mrs Philips?' asked Wilding.

'I didn't feel anything about him. He was never bad to me, just never particularly good to me either.'

'How long were you married?'

'Twelve years: we were together for a year or two before that, and we just sort of drifted into it. We got divorced four years ago.'

'Why?'

'Because he was as tight as a fish's ring, if you want to know the truth. What's the point in living in a big expensive house and dressing like a tramp? I stood it for long enough; I told him how I felt but he never listened, so eventually I walked out.'

'Did you know Mr Philips at that point?'

'No. I met him a year after the divorce; like I said, he doesn't know Gary at all.'

'How much did you get out of it?'

'Two hundred and eighty thousand. My lawyer did a good job: he got me half the value of the house, the furniture and the shop, plus maintenance. The deal was so good that I worried for a while that he'd go out of business and the alimony would dry up. To tell you the truth, I don't know how he did it.'

'We do,' said Mackenzie, noting her instant curiosity.

'What do you mean?'

'Mr Starr had other business interests beside the shop.'

Kitty Philips looked incredulous. 'Who? Gary? Pull the other one, pal. Gary was a gambler, pure and simple; that's all he knew. I used to tell him that when he had a good run he should put the money into something different, like a pub, or more shops, but he wouldn't listen.'

'So all the time you were married, he never had any other source of income?'

'No, and I'm pretty sure I'd have known. He'd bring home cash occasionally and put it in the home safe. I never knew the combination, but I could see what he was putting in and it wasn't that much, a few hundred at a time, and not so often that it would ever amount to a fortune. I used to reckon that he was skimming the tax man, and I'm pretty sure I was right.'

'How about his associates? Did you know many of them?'

'You've probably met them all yourself by now, unless there are folk he's got to know since I left. Gary didn't make friends easily. In fact, Gary didn't make friends, period.'

'Who was closest to him?' asked Wilding. 'Oliver Poole?'

'I wouldn't say that. He saw Ollie only when he needed to; they might have had the odd pint, but that was all. He never came to the house, and we only ever went to his once, to a party about ten years ago. If you ask me to guess, from the people I met in and around the shop, I'd say that Eddie Charnwood was the closest thing he had to a pal.'

'Not Smith?'

Mrs Philips laughed. 'Big Ming? Gary described him as a lackey once, and that's as good a description as any. He paid him next to bugger all, I know that; minimum wage. I don't know how he survived. No, Eddie Charnwood was as close as anybody got. In fact we even got a Christmas card from him and his wife the year before I left. Her name was Sorry. I remember laughing at it; there was I feeling sorry for myself, and she was called that.'

'Takes all sorts,' Mackenzie murmured. 'You don't seem sorry for yourself now, Mrs Philips,' he went on, his voice hardening with every word. 'You were married to the guy for twelve years, and now he's dead, tied up and butchered like a veal calf.' He glanced around the room. 'Yet I don't see any signs of mourning around here. Did nobody care about the poor bastard?'

For a moment Wilding thought that Kitty Philips would live up to her name and lash out at the chief inspector like a cat, raking her claws across his face. He moved, ready to step between them, but she controlled herself, although her face was twisted with sudden anger.

'What do you know?' she shouted. 'You flash supercilious bastard, what do you know? Do you think I should be dressed in black from head to foot? No fucking chance, and do you know why not? Because if I did, Gary would be up there,' she pointed at the floor, her finger stabbing, 'or down there, more like, laughing at me. The man didn't have any love in him; he never showed it and he rejected it whenever it was shown to him. Once, just once, I said to him that I'd like to have kids. He looked at me as if I was crazy, then he said, 'And what exactly would be in that for me?'

'He wasn't inhuman, I'm not saying that, but he wasn't able to have normal relationships. There was nobody in his life that wasn't of use to him. He never gave anything willingly, he only took it. He might have left everything to his mother, but he had no time for her when he was alive. He never visited her, and when she got old he let the social-services people look after her.

'Do you know the main reason I left him? It wasn't just about money; look, if I really needed it I used to take it and that was that. No, it was because I took a look at myself one day, at the number of people I had in my life, and at the way I treated them, and I realised that he was making me like him. And I left him, before it was too late.'

She paused in her tirade to reach out and poke Mackenzie in the chest, hard enough for him to flinch. 'So, mister, don't you look down your nose at me, just because I'm not sitting in that chair crying into my hankie. It's awful that Gary died the way he did, but the fact is the world won't be a sadder place without him.' She glared at the chief inspector. 'And you know what? I look at you, and I see a bit of him in there. Now go on, the pair of you. I've got nothing more to tell you and I've got to get ready for work.'

Mackenzie might have stood his ground, but Wilding took the lead. 'Thanks, Mrs Philips,' he said. 'If there's anything else we need I'll call you.' He nodded to the chief inspector and headed for the door. 'What the hell was all that about?' he asked, as they reached the car.

'Search me. She really blew off steam, didn't she?'

'I don't mean her, sir, I mean you. Why did you rattle her cage like that?'

'Because I chose to, Sergeant. She annoyed me, so I had a pop at her, just to shake her up, just to get under her skin. And you know what, Ray? You're annoying me too. I've had just about as much of this constant questioning of my methods as I'm going to take.'

Wilding looked at him coolly. 'Very good, sir,' he said, as he opened the driver's door.

Mackenzie was fastening his seat-belt when his mobile sounded. He scowled and reached for it. 'DCI,' he snapped, then waited. 'Do you want Wilding as well?' he asked, his tone altered. 'Okay, I'll be there as soon as I can.' Pause. 'Half an hour. See you.' He glanced to his right as he replaced the phone. 'That was McIlhenney: he wants a briefing on the investigation. Get us back to Leith, and I'll take the car on up to Fettes.'

50

Much of the west of Scotland was uncharted territory to Sir James Proud, and Wishaw was included in the extensive list of places of which he was almost totally ignorant. He knew no more than that it was conjoined to Motherwell, Bob Skinner's home town, which he had visited once for an ACPOS meeting in the offices of North Lanarkshire council.

He came off the M8 at Newhouse, and headed into the former steel town, past the site that had once been home to the Ravenscraig strip mill, allowing his global positioning system to guide him to Wishaw. There was no obvious boundary between the two towns, so he was slightly taken aback when he was instructed to make a right turn, then a left and found himself stopping outside number seventeen Church Road, where a sign beside the door confirmed that he had arrived at the offices of Woodburn Hill and White.

Having checked that he was parked legally, he stepped into a dull reception area, pulling off his driving gloves and stuffing them into the pockets of his Barbour jacket. 'Can I help you, sir?' a young voice asked him. Its owner was seated behind a desk that was bound in a leather-like cream fabric, designer furniture which told him at once that this law firm was determined to present a modern image to its clients. The same could have been said of the receptionist: her hair was three different colours and she wore a top with 'FCUK' emblazoned across it. Earlier in his career, Sir James would have regarded it as grounds for arrest. A sign beside her computer keyboard told him that her name was Kylie McGrane.

'I'd like to see one of your partners,' he replied, 'but I'm not sure which one.'

'Well,' said the girl, 'there's Mr Leckie, there's Mrs Gillingham and there's Miss Ward.'

Proud's eyebrows rose slightly at the third name. 'Miss Ward, I think, if she's available. Her name doesn't feature on your website. Why is that?'

'She's only just been made a partner, sir. The site hasn't been updated yet. Who shall I tell her is calling?'

The chief constable produced a card from the breast pocket of his sports jacket and handed it to the receptionist. As she read it, her eyes widened and her mouth opened a little. 'If you'll just excuse me for a moment, sir,' she stammered. She rushed from the reception area, returning around a minute later with another woman, stocky, dark-haired, square-faced, in her early thirties, with the sort of sharp, perceptive eyes that Proud used to fear in the early days of his career, when he was required on occasion to go into the witness box.

'Sir James,' she said, extending a hand, 'I'm Ethel Ward. Is this an official visit?'

'Well, yes,' he replied, carefully, 'but a very discreet one.'

'Come through and tell me about it, then.' She led him, past a staircase, to a small room at the rear of the building; there were bars outside the window. 'I'm the junior partner,' she said, with a sudden smile that made her seem not grim at all. 'In this firm you climb the stairs through seniority.'

'How long have you been in existence?'

'As Woodburn Hill and White? Since 1969, but the Woodburn part was founded in 1931. As for Hill and White, that firm goes back to the nineteenth century, 1880, if I can remember my local history. You'll know what it's like with the older law firms; the names on the door mean nothing at all. Those three gentlemen are long dead.' She looked at him as he took the seat she offered, and the sharpness was back in her eyes. 'So, Sir James, what's brought you off your patch?'

'I'm trying to trace someone; a person who's been missing for a long time.'

'Someone from Wishaw?'

'No, but the trail's led me here. It's all got to do with a man called Claude Bothwell, a teacher of modern languages. He was once married to a lady from these parts; coincidentally, she has the same name as you.'

The solicitor stared at him, unable to hide her surprise. 'It's no coincidence,' she told him. 'That's my aunt Ethel you're talking about, the heiress, as my grandfather calls her.'

'Your grandfather?'

'Yes, Herbert Ward, Bert to his friends. He was a partner in the firm till he retired, but he's still pretty well known around here so we keep his name on our notepaper as a consultant.'

Proud was confused. 'But Herbert Ward was Ethel Ward's father.'

'Different Herbert: the one you're talking about was my grandfather's uncle. He and Aunt Ethel . . . she's not really my aunt, but that's how she's always been referred to . . . were cousins. Sir James, you'd be much better talking to him. He's got all the family history, and scandals, in his head. Aunt Ethel very definitely falls into the latter category. Hold on a minute.' She picked up her phone, dialled and waited. 'Grandpa,' she said, when an answer came, 'you're in, good. I'm sending someone down to see you. His name's Sir James Proud . . . Yes, the same one. He'll explain when he gets there.' She hung up. 'That's settled; he's expecting you. He lives in a place called Thorny Grove.'

'But that's where . . . '

'Where Aunt Ethel lived? Yes, I know, but it's different now: it's been turned into a retirement community. The big house has been converted into flats and there are some cottages in the grounds. Grandpa has one of those; it's number three. To get there,' she pointed, 'turn right at the end of Church Road, go across the Main Street, then down the hill until you come to a cul-de-sac sign. Thorny Grove's in there.'

51

Wilding glared up at the clock: it was almost fifteen minutes past midday, Big Ming was late and he was annoyed. After his most recent run-in with his new boss he was in no mood to be pissed about by a witness, especially one as gob-smackingly weird as Mr James Smith.

He retrieved his contact details from the file and dialled the number that he had been given. It rang out a dozen times before he hung up. He returned to his summary of the interview with Kitty Philips, checking for a third time to make sure that he had included all the relevant details, although in truth there had been damn few. Apart from provoking another fight with Mackenzie, the visit had added nothing to the sum total of the investigator's knowledge.

Mackenzie: there was no doubt that the man had a track record. He had proved himself in almost record time in the Drugs Squad, and before that he had been credited with some impressive arrests in Glasgow . . . among them, legend had it, his own brother. Wilding reckoned that somewhere along the line someone had told him that the end justifies the method, a dangerous principle in criminal investigation. The sergeant was a disciplined officer; he had served with Dan Pringle, Maggie Rose, Stevie Steele and other good people and had learned from them the importance of staying focused.

And here he was, working for a boss who had introduced a drugs investigation slap-bang into the middle of a homicide inquiry without calling for any specialist help, a guy who went off at irrelevant tangents during interviews yet who bollocked subordinates for showing any sort of initiative. He found himself hoping to be in the room the first time he tried that with DI Steele.

He looked at the clock again. 'Bugger,' he swore. 'Enough of this.' He walked out of the CID suite and through to the front office. 'I need a car and a driver, Mac,' he told the desk sergeant. 'I need to go up to Millend to roust out a witness.'

'You'll need a big driver, then. Mike,' the sergeant called out to a massive constable who had just walked through the front door, 'stop there, turn round and drive DS Wilding up to the Wild West.'

PC Drake sighed; clearly there were destinations to which he would rather have been ordered. The Millend scheme had earned its tag and its reputation the hard way, and guarded both proudly, prepared to defend its status as Edinburgh's hardest neighbourhood against all comers.

Wilding followed him outside to his patrol car, where his partner, PC 'Never' Wright, waited behind the wheel. He had worn the nickname so long that most people had forgotten that his given name was Johnstone. 'One of you'll be enough. We're just going to pick a bloke up.'

Mike Drake shook his head. 'No, Sarge. He

may not want to be picked up; that could lead to all sorts of problems. You got the address?'

'Seventy-seven three Pound Driveway.'

'Smashin'! Maybe we should take an armed-response team too.'

Wright drove quickly and smoothly away from the station heading westward along the Water-front. Eventually he took a left turn off a roundabout, into a street that bore no resemblance to those they had passed before. The buildings were grey concrete, ugly struc-tures that looked more like giant pigeon-holes than homes. *Give someone a house in a place like this, and you're giving him a message.* Wilding kept his thoughts to himself. He was new to the Leith office, and Drake and Wright looked as if they might be the sort of old-fashioned coppers who believed that the inhabitants of places like the Wild West were born trying to head-butt the midwife.

Pound Driveway was in the heart of the scheme, a three-storey, flat-roofed block, its walls grimy and weather-stained. Wright parked the car in front of a stairway entrance with the number 77 displayed on a wooden sign. 'Lucky,' he said. 'Most of the numbers have been ripped off to confuse the enemy, namely us.' He climbed out of the driver's seat and leaned against the vehicle. 'I'll wait by the motor, Mike. It goes best with four wheels.'

Wilding looked around; he could not see a living soul, but he knew that did not mean there was nobody there.

Big Ming's flat was on the top floor. Drake led

303

the way up the graffiti-lined stairway, past solid, unglazed doors. 'Dealer,' he said, pointing to one on the second floor. 'It's steel, with an extra big letterbox.'

'Dealing what?'

'Grass mostly. There's a lot grown around here; if we raided every house in schemes like this in Scotland we'd need to build a new jail for the folk with rooms filled with plants and sodium lights.'

Smith's door was wooden like the rest. There was no sign of extra security, only a Yale lock and a handle. Drake thumped it with his gloved fist. From somewhere down below they heard the sound of a toilet being flushed. The PC grinned. 'The dealer probably thought we'd come for him. That'll be him sending the evidence down the toilet.' He turned to Wilding. 'You sure the guy's in, Sarge?'

'He told me he'd nowhere else to go.'

Drake battered the door again, so hard that it swung open. 'What the hell? The Yale must have sprung.'

'He invited us in, didn't he, Mike?' said Wilding.

'Absolutely.'

The detective stepped inside; a door faced him at the end of a corridor. It was ajar and the sound of daytime television drifted out. 'Ming,' he called, stepping forward.

He saw the feet before he reached the doorway. They were encased in filthy carpet slippers and the toes were pointing up. 'Bloody hell!' Wilding exclaimed, as he threw the door open and stepped into the room. Big Ming was staring at the ceiling; in the middle of his forehead, there was a third, red eye, from which a thin trickle of blood ran down to the carpet.

52

Proud took time out for lunch in a small café near Wishaw Cross, then followed the directions which the solicitor had given him. In less than three minutes he found himself driving into the retirement community. He parked in an area signed 'Visitors', climbed out and looked around.

When it was a family home, Thorny Grove would have been an imposing mansion, in its surroundings, although in Edinburgh terms it was only a little above modest. Still, it looked large enough to have formed half a dozen apartments, with an attic flat above, and its gardens were large enough to have accommodated a further six small red-roofed bungalows. Number three was closest to the main building and to a block of garages; as he approached, Herbert Ward was waiting for him at the front door. He was a small, bald man, stocky like his granddaughter, and with the same inquisitive eyes.

'Sir James Proud?' His accent was gruff, and a bit like Bob Skinner's: Lanarkshire with the rough corners knocked off and polished.

'Yes, sir; it's good of you to see me.'

The old man ushered him inside, and into a small but expensively furnished living room. 'Not at all. I can't watch the racing channel all the time: bad for me. Take a seat. Can I offer you a drink?'

'No, thank you; I'm driving.'

'Of course you are. Sorry, I'm a member of the 'just the one won't hurt' generation. How about tea?'

'Really, I'm fine.'

'If you say so. Now, to what do I owe the courtesy?'

'It's a complicated story, but I'm trying to trace a seventy-year-old woman named Annabelle Gentle.'

'I can't help you, I'm afraid. I haven't had much to do with the ladies since my wife died six years ago.'

'I didn't expect you to know of her, but the connection is with a man named Claude Bothwell, to whom she was engaged to be married over forty years ago.'

'Good God!' the old lawyer exclaimed. 'So she ditched him eventually, did she?'

'You remember him?'

'I recall his existence, but little about him physically. We met on only one occasion, after he and Ethel were married when they came into the office to make joint wills. That was a joke: he had nothing, while she had the modest fortune that she'd inherited from her parents.'

'They died in a boating accident, I'm informed.'

'You could call it that. They were in Cannes for the winter and they went on a cruise on some sort of yacht: a storm got up, the thing rolled over and everyone on board was drowned.'

'And Ethel inherited.'

'She was an only child. To explain my family background, Sir James, I come from the professional side, and Ethel came from the moneyed side . . . through her mother. Uncle Bert didn't make his money, he married it. The Marshalls, Aunt Meg's family, owned the steelworks. Bert worked there and became general manager, then managing director, after they were married. Aunt Meg was a frightful snob, and Cousin Ethel took after her. I never did like the wee shrew.'

'When did Bothwell come on the scene? Had they known each other long, before they were married?'

'No, only a few months, weeks even; that was part of the scandal. He showed up in Wishaw the year after Uncle Bert and Aunt Meg died, to take a job in the High School. He was a lodger in a house in Caley Drive, hardly Ethel's social scene, but they met at a Coronation party organised by the parish church. After that they were seen together a lot: Green's Playhouse was a favourite haunt as I recall, and she had never been seen at the cinema before. She was about ten years older than him, so you can imagine the talk . . . or maybe you can't, being from the next generation.' Proud smiled: he liked to be made to feel like a youngster. 'Next thing anybody knew, they were married. Nobody was invited, not even my mother and father, her closest living relatives. We wouldn't have known about it in advance, but for a wee paragraph in the *Wishaw Press* reporting the posting of their names in the registrar's.'

'Did you see much of them after that?'

'Hardly anything; I was busy with work and my family and, like I said, I didn't like the woman anyway, so our paths never crossed.'

'How did they come to leave town?'

'Abruptly, just about sums it up. Ethel came into the office one day, about three years after their marriage, and instructed me to put Thorny Grove on the market. She told me that she and Claude had had enough of Wishaw and were selling up and moving, as she put it, 'to more acceptable surroundings'. I wished her all the best and did as she asked. The house sold for what was a hell of a lot of money at the time.'

'Did you ask her where they were going?'

Bert Ward nodded. 'That I did. She told me that Claude wanted to go somewhere he could use his French properly. The world was theirs to explore, Sir James. With the sale of the house, Ethel was worth tidily over a hundred thousand, easily more than a million in today's terms. I've often wondered what happened to them, but it's never kept me awake at night.'

'Someone must still think of her. Your granddaughter's name is Ethel, after all.'

'That's pure coincidence. She was named after her maternal grandmother.' He frowned. 'No, I suppose I've always assumed, if for no other reason than the fact that her will's still gathering dust up there in Church Road, that she's still alive, sitting in an olive grove or a vineyard in the South of France, cracking the whip over Claude. However, from what you say, if she is still cracking the whip, it's not over him. Where did he wind up?'

'Glasgow,' Proud told him, 'teaching in Jordanhill School, a year later . . . at least that's where he surfaced next.'

'She must have binned him bloody quick, then. Maybe the outside world worked wonders for her.'

'It worked wonders for him: he remarried in Glasgow in that same year.'

'He did what? But he couldn't possibly have been divorced. Not enough time would have elapsed.'

'He wasn't, not in Scotland at any rate. I suppose it's possible they went to Nevada or Mexico, or some other lax jurisdiction, but it doesn't seem likely, especially when you consider that he married for a third time in 1961, again with no evidence of divorce.'

'Good God! I'd never have thought he had it in him. So what you're saying is that he ditched her, is that it?'

As he looked out of the old man's window, Sir James Proud was visited by a dark thought, one that he had been pushing to the back of his mind, until finally he had to give it voice. 'I hope that's what I'm saying, Mr Ward. I really hope it is.'

The old man caught his meaning at once. 'You don't imagine . . .'

Proud gave him a strange smile. 'I have a deputy. His name's Bob Skinner and he's from these parts.'

'I know who you mean: Bill Skinner's son.'

'That's right. Bob and I are very different types in our approaches to police work, but the more I get caught up in this thing, the more I find myself thinking like him.'

53

For all its ugliness, Bandit Mackenzie liked the Fettes building. He had spent most of his service out in the sticks of Glasgow and North Lanarkshire; his spell at the centre of affairs in Edinburgh, in his role as head of the Drugs Squad, had been stimulating. The Leith posting reminded him of Curnbernauld, which had been by no means the highlight of his career.

He had to ask the doorkeeper for directions to McIlhenney's new office. It was three floors up in the main office wing; he climbed the stair with a frown on his face.

The detective superintendent was standing in the doorway, waiting for him. 'Hello, Bandit,' he said, as he ushered him into the room. 'That was a hell of a long half-hour.'

'Traffic,' Mackenzie grunted.

'That's always the tale in Edinburgh. Take a seat.' There was no offer of tea or coffee; the chief inspector was surprised, until he remembered that McIlhenney drank neither. 'So, David,' he began, 'what have you got to tell me? How's the Starr investigation going?'

'We've just seen his ex-wife; she's a right brassy cow, but she's well alibied for the time of death. So's her husband: he's a long-distance driver. Before that we saw Starr's current girlfriend, Mina Clarkson. Nothing there: she had the occasional bet in his shop and he gave her one equally occasionally. That's us done with interviewing family and associates.'

'Leads?'

'A few; we're following them up.'

McIlhenney leaned across his desk. 'And where exactly are you doing that? Pamplona in Spain? How about that?'

Mackenzie felt his chair shift under him, and realised that instinctively he had pushed it backwards. 'I had occasion to call the police there for assistance,' he said.

'So I gather. And in their turn, the Guardia Civil, which has jurisdiction over all drugs crime in Spain, had occasion to call the Scottish Drug Enforcement Agency and ask them what the hell you and the local plods were doing poking your nose into an operation on which the two of them have been co-operating for months. This led to the director of the SDEA calling the head of CID and asking him much the same thing, and not very politely either. Since he didn't know what the fuck he was talking about . . . well, you can imagine his reaction. Mind you, you nearly didn't have to imagine: it took all my powers of persuasion to get him to leave this to me.'

'Neil . . . '

'Shut up!' the superintendent snarled. 'How do you see me? Good old Neil, amiable guy, soft touch, string him along: is that it? Was that what you thought? Well, I've got news for you, pal. That's the face I show to my wife and kids, to colleagues I trust and to people I like, people who don't upset me. Those who do get to see the other side, like you are just now. Chief Inspector,

313

you may be pissed off about being moved to Leith, or you may be carrying some residue from the St Andrews operation. I do not know and I do not fucking care. What I do perceive is an arrogant bastard who's on a one-man mission to prove that he's better than anyone else in this department, and who's prepared to jeopardise anything in its pursuit. Well, Bandit, you may be prepared to put your own career in the crapper, but don't think that you can drag mine along with it. You don't agree with what I'm saying? You believe your own press cuttings? You want to take me on? Try it. I'll fucking bury you.'

Mackenzie looked back at him, making an attempt to summon up some belligerence, some sort of a defence against the onslaught, and then he folded. 'Neil, I'm sorry,' he said. 'I should have told you about the drugs and the money. I was out of order. It won't happen again.'

'True; not on this investigation at any rate, because you're benched.'

'You mean I'm suspended?'

'No, you're on holiday. You and Cheryl are decorating the bathroom, and you've been planning it for some time. I'll see you a week on Monday; then we'll talk about second chances.'

54

Normally, Bob Skinner preferred his dentist's chair to the passenger seat of a car. However, on the way to Bakewell he was content to leave the driving to Shannon: he had serious thinking to do.

The inspector thought that he was asleep as she turned off the M1, skirting Chesterfield as she headed for the A619 and the Derbyshire Dales: she was startled when he spoke. 'I brought my older daughter down here on holiday once,' he said, 'when she was about thirteen. Easter was late that year, and we decided to do something different. It was bloody freezing, but the pub food was terrific, and they were relaxed about letting Alex in. It's nice countryside.' He smiled at the memory. 'Maybe I'll do the same with the second lot in a few years. Jeez,' he mused, 'I'll tell you, Dottie, being a one-parent family isn't something you reckon to do once in a lifetime, but twice . . . '

The revelation took Shannon by surprise; for a moment she wondered whether she should sympathise, but decided that silence was the better option. As if he sensed her unease, the DCC moved on. 'Okay, tell me about Esther Archer.'

'She's Esther Craig now, aged thirty-six, and married to a baker called Elton Craig . . . but you knew that already from the letter. She has two sons, Aaron, who's eleven, and Joshua, who's just turned eight. The family seems to go in for Biblical names. Her parents were Joshua Archer, a soldier, and Joan Hartland, who's described as a housewife on Esther's birth certificate. The father was killed in action, serving with Two Para in the Falklands, but the mother is still alive. However, there is no record anywhere of the birth of anyone called Moses Archer.'

'There wouldn't be: Adam, and the MoD, would have made sure his tracks were covered for the family's sake. That's why I find the houseboat so hard to figure out.' He glanced at her. 'What were you able to find out about that?'

'He's been registered as owner with the Port of London Authority for the last six years. The previous owner was a Dutch registered company: Archer bought it from them for a hundred and thirty thousand pounds, paid in full by certified cheque drawn on an account in the Premier Taiwan Bank, City of London branch.'

'Who was the account holder?'

'Moses Archer.'

'Eh? Adam was a serving soldier; where the hell did he get that sort of money?'

'I wasn't able to establish that, sir, but I do know that he was getting it regularly . . . so to speak. The account was set up seven years ago with an initial deposit of two hundred thousand pounds sterling. Much of that went on the acquisition and improvement of the *Bulrush*, but since then there have been annual inward transfers, for fifty thousand at first rising to a hundred and fifty thousand this year.'

'What's it been used for?'

'Bills relating to the upkeep of the boat, mostly. There have been a few cash withdrawals over the years: the biggest of them was a hundred thousand, this summer. At the moment, the balance is standing at just over two hundred and ten thousand.'

'You couldn't trace the origin of these payments?'

'No. All I know for sure is that they weren't made over the counter.'

'What about the Premier Taiwan Bank? I can't say I've ever heard of it.'

'It's a private outfit, sir, not a high-street player: a posh people's bank.'

'Indeed? And who'd be feeding money into that?'

He was frowning as he took out his mobile, retrieved a stored number and called it. 'Merle,' Shannon heard him say, 'it's Bob Skinner. How's things in your busy world?' He chuckled. 'Look on the bright side. You're a section head now, with a staff, instead of being stuck in an outpost on your own. That's got to count for something. Listen, pal, can I ask you an idle question?' Pause. 'The Premier Taiwan Bank: does it have any special meaning for you?' Pause. 'I tripped over it, that's all; possible money-laundering.' Pause. 'I see. Tell you what: I'm having dinner with a friend tonight in the Charing Cross Hotel. There's a pub round the corner called the Clarence; full of tourists, but no players. Can you meet me there?' Pause. 'Seven will be fine. There's something else I'd like you to do for me,

317

but I'll call you later about that.'

He ended the call. 'Friend of mine,' he said. 'Her name's Merle Gower, and she's based at the US Embassy, National Security section. That bank means something to her, but she's not for telling me over the phone. We'll see her tonight.'

'We?'

'Sure. You two should meet: you could be useful to each other.' He glanced out of the window. 'Bakewell, two miles. Nearly there: do you know how to find the address?'

'I've got a map if we need it, but from memory we take the first right across the river, then we're looking for a left turn.' She paused. 'I'd have thought that the Security Service would have had satellite navigation in their cars.'

'I didn't want that.'

'Why not?'

'Just.'

Shannon's memory had served her well: she found Stannington Drive without the need for the map. They drove slowly down the leafy street until they saw Glebe Cottage, on their left. 'What was your cover story when you called her?' Skinner asked.

'I told her that you're from the Imperial War Museum and that you're doing a book on the real Falklands; I'm your research assistant. We're looking into what soldiers really thought of the war as it was being fought.'

'She bought that?'

'Hook, line and the other thing; I can be very persuasive, sir.'

'That's your way of saying you're a bloody good liar, isn't it?'

She smiled. 'If you want to put it that way, who am I to argue?' She parked in front of the house.

When Esther Craig opened the door, Skinner found himself stifling a gasp. The woman was an inch or so taller than her brother and was more slightly built, but facially she could have been his twin. 'Hello,' she greeted them breezily. 'You'll be the people from the museum, will you? Mr Skinner, is it, and Ms Shannon? Come on in.' The visitors followed her through the living room of the cottage and into a sunlit conservatory. 'Have you driven all that way up this morning?' she asked them.

'It's not that far, Mrs Craig,' Skinner replied, as he settled into the soft cushions of a bamboo-framed couch.

'This is really fascinating,' the woman said; her accent was also very similar to that of her brother, in his less formal moments. 'I've looked out some of my dad's letters. I think you'll be interested in them.'

The big Scot looked at her. 'We have an apology to make to you, I'm afraid,' he told her. 'My colleague spun you an out-and-out lie in arranging this meeting. However, she did it with the best possible motive: she didn't want you worrying unduly.' He took out his warrant card and held it up for Esther Craig to see. 'We're police officers, and we're investigating your brother, Moses.'

'Investigating him?' she gasped, as her open

319

face creased into a frown. 'Moses? Is he in trouble?'

'As of this moment, no.'

'Then what's this about, Mr Skinner?'

'Call me Bob, Esther. How much do you know about his professional life?'

'You mean what he does for a living?'

'Yes.'

'Not a great deal, because he never talked about it much. He's a policeman, like you, but he works under cover a lot. The boys, my sons, think he's a civil servant: so does my husband, for that matter.'

'He joined the army when he was young, didn't he?'

'Straight from school. After he took his A levels, he went to Sandhurst.'

'That would be about, what, twenty years ago?'

She thought for a second. 'Yes, that'd be right. He's two years older than me.'

'What age was he when your father was killed?'

'He'd have been fourteen. After that it was only ever going to be the army for him: Queen and country and all that. Our dad got a posthumous Military Cross, with a citation, and a letter to my mum from Her Majesty, thanking us all 'for Major Archer's sacrifice', as she put it. That made sure that Moses was a real monarchist . . . not that my dad wasn't, mind. God, was he ever? I remember him telling us that he wouldn't fire a shot for a politician, only for the sovereign. He believed that without the King for everybody to rally round, we'd have lost the Second World War, and we'd all be speaking German now. He never gave Churchill much credit, only King George and his generals.'

'So Moses followed him into the army.'

Esther nodded. 'Yes; but, sir, Bob, what's all this about?'

'I'll get to that, I promise, in due course. Were you surprised when he left?'

'Yes. Yes, I was. I thought he loved it; I thought that everything was going well for him. He was a first lieutenant, a company commander in Two Para just like our dad, as he'd always wanted to be, and then, what, ten years ago now, he just up and left.'

'Did he tell you why?'

'He said that he was disillusioned.'

'By what?'

'By the rules, he said. He said that it was the rules that had got our dad killed and that he wasn't having any more of them. So he told me that he was taking a job with the police in London, and that he'd be working on special things, infiltrating gangs and the like.'

'Did that worry you?'

'No. If I'd been about to worry about anyone it would have been the people he infiltrated. Moses is a lovely man, Bob, but after Dad was killed something changed in him. He's only a little chap, but he's as hard as nails.'

'Have you ever visited him in London?'

'No: he said he didn't want that. We see him when he comes back here . . . and the little sod's overdue us a visit.'

'What about your mother? Does she ever visit him?'

'No, her neither; he's been to see her in America a couple of times, though.'

'America?'

'Yes, my mum's remarried, to an American called Titus Armstead. He and Mum got married about twelve years ago, and she moved to America. Titus is retired now, and they live in Delaware; it's a lovely place, very quiet.'

'Mmm. So how did you keep in touch with Moses?'

'By letter. At first he had a post-office box number, but after a few years he bought his houseboat and I could write to him there.'

'Have you ever been there?'

'No, but he showed me pictures after he bought it. It looks lovely.'

Skinner gazed at her, knowing that the moment when he would change her life was drawing near. 'This job of his,' he asked, 'did you ever question it?'

'No, why should I? It's what he told me, and I always believe him.'

'He never left the army, Esther.'

She stared at him. 'What do you mean?'

'I mean what I say. He did go under cover, that much was true, but not in the way he told you. He was in the SAS for a while, in Ireland, and then he went into Military Intelligence, into its most secret and sensitive branch. When I think about it, I reckon that's what he meant when he talked to you about the rules. He went into a different world, one in which a new identity was created for him, to protect you and your family from the possibility of anyone ever trying to get at him through you. Moses Archer ceased to exist, and Adam Arrow was born.'

'Adam Arrow?' she whispered, incredulous.

'Yes. That's the name I knew him by.' He chose his tense deliberately and watched her as it registered.

'Knew,' she repeated quietly, lining her fingers together in her lap.

'Yes, I'm afraid so. I'm very sorry to have to tell you that he was killed on an operation a little while back.'

Esther Archer sank back into her chair and buried her face in her hands. Shannon started to rise, to comfort her, but Skinner motioned to her, staying her. 'I'm very sorry,' he repeated.

She wiped her tears, almost defiantly. 'Thank you, Bob,' she replied quietly and with dignity. 'You know, if he had to die, I'm glad it was in the same service as our dad, and for the same cause. Now can I ask you a few things?'

'Of course.'

'Why am I hearing this from you, from a policeman, rather than from a fellow soldier?'

'I was his friend, and that's the most important reason. In the aftermath of his death some things have emerged about the operation that killed him and I'm looking into them. One of them is the continued existence of Moses Archer; that wasn't supposed to happen, and I need to know who else knew about him, and knew where he was.'

'Nobody outside the family; only Mum and

me, and Elton and the boys, and Titus, I suppose.'

'You're sure of that?'

'Nobody's heard of it from me, I can promise you that.'

'Good. It's best there's no link; just as Moses' records were erased, none were ever created about Adam Arrow.'

'Is anyone telling Mum?'

'That's your job, I think.'

'Who killed him?'

He almost told her, but he bit it back. 'He was killed in a fire-fight,' was all he said.

'I see. What happened to his body?'

'Nothing yet; it's still in a mortuary.'

'Can we have him back, back here where he's from, so we can look after him?'

'I'll arrange that.'

'If it's all so secret will you be able to?'

'I know people who can. We'll give you what they call a legend, a story to explain his death, a car crash in Australia, something like that. You'll have to bury him as Moses Archer.'

She looked at him and smiled. 'What else would I do, Bob? I never knew Adam Arrow, only my lovely little brother.'

55

As McIlhenney drove inside the cordon that had been set up around the building, a plastic coffin was being slid into a dark blue mortuary wagon. The scene had been played out before in the Wild West; it never failed to draw a crowd. The superintendent looked around as he stepped out of his car, seeking out familiar faces, and seeing a few, older and more leathery, but probably no wiser for all the time that had passed since he and McGuire, in their uniform days, had forged their reputation as hard men by cracking their heads together.

'Gary Starr's board man?' he asked Wilding, as he came towards him from the stairway door.

'Yes, killed with a single shot to the head. There's no exit wound, so Arthur Dorward reckons it was probably a hollow-point bullet.'

'Initial thoughts?'

'He knew his killer, and didn't suspect him. There's not much of a lock, but there's a spy-hole in the door and a chain and a bolt on the inside. In this place, if you've got those you use them, so I reckon that Ming let the guy in.'

'Neighbours?'

'I've interviewed everybody on the stair, including the local cannabis supplier. Wise monkeys, the lot of them; saw nothing, heard nothing, couldn't tell me anything.'

'Who found the body?'

'I did, with PC Drake. We came to pick him up. He called me this morning to tell me he could identify the bloke with the missing finger.'

'Christ,' McIlhenney exclaimed. 'I wonder if he told anyone else?'

'That's been on my mind too, sir. Could the guy have found out somehow?'

'Did he tell you anything about him when he called?'

'He said that he's involved in the management of a club. He was going to take me there.' Wilding paused. 'Sir,' he asked, unable to hold back the question any longer, 'why are you here and not DCI Mackenzie?'

'Bandit's on holiday; he's taking ten days off.' The sergeant looked at the ground. 'He's on holiday, Ray,' McIlhenney repeated. 'It was booked in before he was transferred. Understand?'

'Yes, sir, I understand.'

'Let's go down to Queen Charlotte Street: I want to review where we are in this whole business.'

'Are you setting up the mobile HQ?'

'Here? We'd need to put a guard on it. We won't get anything out of this place other than any forensic traces that Arthur's lot turn up. Come on, I'll give you a lift.'

56

When Skinner and Shannon returned from Bakewell a note was waiting on the DCC's desk. *'Come and see me: AD.'*

Dennis was behind her desk when they answered her summons. 'How did you get on?' she asked.

'As well as can be expected,' Skinner replied. 'Moses told her he was a copper, but Esther had no idea what he really did. His continuing existence seems to have been kept within the family; apart from her, all the rest of them thought he was a civil servant.'

'We're not going to have a media problem, are we?'

'I don't see it, not if they get his body back for burial.'

'We can't authorise that, Bob: that's a Ministry of Defence decision.'

'Amanda, I don't care whose decision it is. It's got to happen, and that's an end of it. We'll need a cover story as well, to explain his death. If you're sensitive about it, leave it with me and I'll make arrangements.'

'If you think you can,' she said, 'but you may not find it as easy as you think. Those MoD people can get hung up on secrecy.'

'Eventually we all take orders.' As if to make his point, he continued, 'Now, what have you got for me on Ormond Hassett MP?'

'Him?' She frowned up at him. 'He's not the bumbling grain merchant that we thought. He graduated from Cambridge forty-one years ago, and won a rugby blue in the process. From there he joined the army, Royal Green Jackets; he did two tours in Ireland, then served in Germany for five years but there's no record of what he was doing. That probably means he was watching the Russians.

'Aged thirty-one, he was given a posting to the Washington Embassy as military attaché and spent two years there. That was followed by a year in Whitehall, before he resigned his commission and went into the family business. He didn't stay there long, though: he was elected to Parliament in the Conservative victory of 1979. He had a three-year spell as Parliamentary Private Secretary to the Minister of State for Defence. Towards the end of his stint he wound up back in Washington, as the leader of a back-bench group lobbying American support for the Falklands war. There's a curious coincidence here, although probably no more than that: the adjutant to that party was Major Joshua Archer, second battalion, the Parachute Regiment.'

'Coincidence is a far rarer occurrence than people think,' Skinner retorted.

'Maybe; but there could have been little future contact between them, since Archer was killed a few weeks later.'

'Did they know each other before?'

'I don't know. I'll try to find out. If I compare their service records, it might tell me something.'

'What happened to Hassett after the Falklands?'

'He resigned as PPS after the 1983 election because he wasn't given a ministerial appointment. There was some curiosity about that: received wisdom among the parliamentary lobby correspondents was that the Prime Minister of the day thought that he was too right wing.'

'Jesus, that's quite a statement.'

'Indeed! It didn't stop him getting on to the Defence Select Committee, though, or later from becoming one of the first members of the Intelligence and Security Committee. He sat on that until 1997. After that he seems to have confined himself to agricultural matters, until finally the most recent leader of Her Majesty's opposition gave him a job as a shadow spokesman.'

Skinner smiled. 'What the hell do they think we are? Hicks from the sticks, it seems. Did that man Frame really expect us to believe that a man like that wouldn't know his son was a spook? And what about the question beyond that: if he knew that, did he know what he was up to? Amanda,' he asked, 'is there any way you can access Piers Frame's service record? I'd like to see whether he's crossed Hassett's path before.'

'Only the Director General of Six could authorise that, Bob.'

'Then maybe we'll have to ask him.'

57

'I know about the drugs find, Ray,' said Neil McIlhenney, seated in the chief inspector's room in the Leith police office. The sergeant's face reddened. 'It's all right, I'm not coming after you for it: I know you better than that. DCI Mackenzie put his foot in it, but that knowledge goes no further than you, me and Mario. The SDEA want his head on a pole, but they're not having it; they're not even getting his name.'

'What about the chief, or the DCC, if they go to either of them?'

'The chief knows: he'll tell them where to go if necessary. The DCC's frying other fish just now.'

'So what happened in Pamplona?'

'The local police went crashing into the middle of a Guardia Civil stake-out; they were working with the SDEA, following up a lead that came out of Dundee six months ago. They'd been watching the place all that time. They even had photographs of your man Ming dropping off the A Class, but they didn't know who he was.'

'Couldn't they trace the car from the plates?'

'They did, but Starr wasn't stupid. They belonged on a BMW owned by an insurance broker in Hampshire.'

'Couldn't they have followed him back to Scotland?'

'They didn't appreciate what was going on then.'

'What did they find when they raided the garage?'

'Thin air. And traces of decent-quality cocaine. What did you do with the stuff you found in Starr's safe?'

'It's here, locked up in ours, along with the money.'

'Jesus! At the very least Bandit should have reported it to our own Drugs Squad, and given it into their custody.' McIlhenney looked at the sergeant. 'Ray, I know it's only been a few days, but what's it been like working with him? Off the record; nothing will get quoted to anyone.'

Wilding thought for a little, framing his answer. 'Let's say it's been a learning curve, sir. He has his methods, and they're a bit unorthodox, but that doesn't make him a bad cop.'

'If they work it might make him a good one.'

'Granted. The thing I've found difficult is his unpredictability. Just when I think we're starting to get along, he'll flare up. Like this morning: we were interviewing Starr's ex. She's forthright, but no ogre, and she was co-operating, when out of the blue, the Bandit tore into her. When I asked him why the hell he'd done that, he tore into me. Wee things seem to set him off: today I reckon it was the fact that you're moving Stevie Steele down to Leith.'

'What does your gut tell you about him, Ray?'

Wilding frowned. 'When I was a kid, I had an uncle with a drink problem, although I didn't know about it till I was a bit older. He acted just like DCI Mackenzie.'

331

'What time did he leave you at Queen Charlotte Street this morning?'

'Eleven forty.'

'He didn't get to me until twelve thirty. I didn't raise it with him, for I was too concerned with other things, but I copped a whiff of his breath when I was showing him into my office. I reckon he might have stopped off somewhere on the way. By the way, that is also just between you and me.'

'Absolutely.'

McIlhenney nodded. 'Okay,' he said, 'let's get on with business. Where are we in this chaotic investigation? By that I mean the murder of Gareth Starr, since that's where it all started out. Take me through it.'

Wilding put a hand on the case folder on the desk. 'With respect, sir, that isn't where it started. The chain of events began when we were called to Starr's betting shop, following his report of an attempted robbery, in the course of which he severed the so-called robber's finger.'

'So-called?'

'Yes. We now know that it wasn't Starr who called the police, but Big Ming, when he arrived back early from the corner shop and collided with the guy as he was running off. There was no hold-up; according to Eddie Charnwood, the clerk, the plastic gun we found belonged to Starr himself. Another thing: Starr told us he kept the bayonet in his safe, but according to Charnwood he kept it under the counter. The man faked the crime scene, sir.'

'So Starr attacked the man, not the other way round?'

The sergeant nodded. 'That's how I see it. He said that the bloke came in, pointed the fake gun at him and demanded money. We know that didn't happen. We know from Smith that the man was hanging about outside the shop when he left, as he did at eleven every morning, to go up to the corner shop. That suggests to me that the man went in there to talk to Starr, not to rob him.'

'Or to collect on a bet? Could there have been a dispute about money owed?'

'That's possible: there was money on the counter, nailed down by the bayonet. But I don't think it's as simple as that. In his statement, Starr was at pains to describe the man as drugged up to his ears, but Smith's version doesn't bear that out. There's also a big disparity in the two stories when it comes to age. Big Ming put him early twenties, much younger than his boss did, and he was quite certain about that. No, my belief is that Starr knew the man, but we'll have to find him to prove that.'

'Okay, go back to the sequence of events. An investigation into the faked robbery begins, but there's no trace of the perpetrator slash victim. It's hardly under way before Starr is found, trussed up, tortured and murdered. You and Bandit are now in charge of both investigations.'

'Yes.'

McIlhenney leaned back in his chair until it creaked. 'Why did you walk away from the idea that Nine-fingered Jack might have done it?'

'For a variety of reasons. We had medical advice that someone with such a severe wound couldn't have begun to do what was done to Starr. We considered that he might have enlisted help, but there were problems with that too. Just as Smith did, Starr appears to have admitted his killers to the house, and then to have been rendered helpless without a struggle. He wasn't a soft touch: there was another bayonet in the house, and a shotgun. If a gang had turned up, he'd have gone down fighting. On top of all that, there's the drugs that were used to subdue him. They weren't over-the-counter stuff.'

'So what's the premise of your investigation, on the basis of what you know?'

'I . . . we, DCI Mackenzie and I, believe that the murder is related to Starr's apparent drug-dealing, rather than the incident in the shop.'

'Turf wars?'

'Who knows?' Wilding replied. 'New team in town, maybe? Sending out a message?'

'If that's so, we'll hear more from them. But from what we've learned so far, Starr was the new team himself, or relatively so. I'd be more inclined to look among the old players. The trouble is, the way he was killed doesn't fit any of them, or any of the boys through in the west. They'd just have shot him and dumped the body in a field somewhere. No, Ray, I think we know who did this already; that is, I reckon he's within, or relates to, the circle you've encountered in your investigation.'

'Did we get anything out of Spain, sir?'

'Eventually. The SDEA were a bit sniffy about sharing the information, but Mario threatened to ask the Crown Office to order them to release it. They backed down at that. It's pretty clear that the garage in Pamplona was a staging point for cocaine coming into Europe through North Africa. It was owned and operated by two Egyptian brothers, Darius and Garai Goma. They were gone when the place was raided. The Guardia Civil are pretty certain that they had a warning from a contact in the local police force.'

'That doesn't take us much further.'

'On the face of it, it doesn't,' McIlhenney conceded. 'It's shut off the supply route, but that doesn't help our investigation. So come on, let's look at the cast of characters again. Starr, deceased. James Smith, alias Big Ming, deceased. Oliver Poole, solicitor? I've known Ollie Poole for years: he's respected on both sides of the court, he's a member of the Law Society council, and he's making a bloody fortune. I'll interview him again if necessary but I don't regard him as a suspect. Mrs Kitty Philips?'

'She's got a whole bingo hall for an alibi, plus she's got no motive. She took plenty from Starr in the divorce.'

'The girlfriend?'

'Can't see it: the relationship was very casual.'

'That just leaves Charnwood, the clerk. What do you know about him?'

'DCI Mackenzie dealt with him, sir. His view was that he is what he seems, an employee who was trusted because he's good at his job.'

'Any previous?'

'None at all: he's an upright citizen, family man, with a wife named Sorry, and a young son.'

McIlhenney looked up. 'What did you say the wife's name is?'

'Sorry, or so Kitty Philips told us.'

'Is that right?'

'Unusual, isn't it?'

'Mmm. Eddie Charnwood was with Bandit when he discovered the drugs and the money, wasn't he?'

'That's right. DCI Mackenzie said he nearly fainted when he saw them.'

'Indeed? Who opened the safe, Ray?'

'Charnwood did. That's why Bandit took him to the shop.'

'And how did he open it? With a key?'

'No, the boss said it had a combination lock.'

'So, Gary Starr kept a fortune in drugs and cash in his office safe, and Eddie Charnwood knew the combination.'

Wilding stared at him. 'He knew they were there? But he opened the safe for us?'

'What choice did he have? Ray, he was Starr's trusted clerk, the core of the business in a way, and there would be times when the boss was away and he had to lock up the takings. It's inconceivable that he wouldn't have known the combination.'

'But it was him who told us that the fake gun belonged to Starr.'

'Was there any way he could have known that Starr claimed it was used in the fake robbery?'

Wilding drew in a breath and let it escape in a

great sigh of realisation. 'Fuck! Starr was here for most of the afternoon after the incident. He was just leaving when I arrived to take over from Sammy Pye. I actually heard Oliver Poole say that he'd drive him home, and Starr say okay. Charnwood ran the shop all afternoon, and he never saw Starr. He wasn't a witness, so we didn't need him. Bloody hell.'

'Exactly. Now consider this. Back in the eighties, when McGuire and I were the disco kings of Edinburgh, I pulled a woman one Saturday at Buster Brown's. She was lovely, did a magnificent turn, and her name was Sorry. I ribbed her about it, and she told me it was short for Soraya. She was Egyptian.'

The superintendent stood up. 'Come on, Ray, let's go for them. We'll take armed back-up, but I have a hell of a feeling we won't need it. They're too smart to be there waiting for us.'

58

'You gentlemen seem to come in a rush,' Sylvia Thorpe exclaimed.

'I beg your pardon?' said Ray Wilding.

'I mean it: you're like buses and bills. You don't see any for a while then they arrive in twos and threes. My office has had no contact with the police for over a year, and now we hear from you and your colleague Sergeant McGurk at one and the same time.'

'It's pure coincidence,' the sergeant replied, wondering as he spoke what the DCC's office-bound assistant had been up to. 'I'm involved in a complicated investigation and the name I gave you has cropped up in it.'

'Not nearly as complicated as Sergeant McGurk's, or as interesting: I'm sure you'll hear about it in due course. As for your enquiry, it was much simpler. Soraya Goma, pharmacist, of Cairo, Egypt, and Edward Charnwood, clerk, of sixty-two Glenochil Terrace, were married in Edinburgh four years ago; their son, Edward Hosni Charnwood, was born in June the year before last. I'll fax the certificates to the number you gave me.'

Wilding noted the information on a pad. 'I'd like some family background on Eddie senior: parents, siblings, uncles, aunts, cousins. Can you do that for me?'

'No problem. Give me an hour or so.'

'Thanks, Ms Thorpe,' he said, hung up, and looked up to see McIlhenney approaching his desk. 'Guess what? Soraya Charnwood's a . . . '

The superintendent beat him to the punch. 'Pharmacist; we got word from the DSS while you were speaking to the GRO. She's employed in the dispensing department at the Western General. That means she'd have access to the drugs that were used to paralyse Starr. I've also been speaking to the SDEA, sharing our information with them; their operation with the Guardia Civil, the one that Bandit effed up, involved a butcher from Dundee called Joe Falconer. He made a trip to Pamplona as well: he was suspected of being involved in supply, so he was under round-the-clock surveillance. He dropped his car at the same garage, and picked it up a couple of days later. They went to lift him this morning and found him in his meat fridge, shot in the head. What does that sound like?'

'It sounds like Eddie and Soraya have been closing the book on anyone who could give evidence against them and her brothers.'

'Exactly. These are dangerous people: they're armed and on the run, we assume, with their kid. I only hope they know when the game's up, for his sake. Those photos we took from their place: you've had them distributed?'

'Yes, but they still may be hard to catch. They left their passports behind them at their flat; that has to mean they're travelling with forgeries. If they pick a really busy place to exit through, and change their appearance . . . '

'They can change theirs, but disguising the

wee boy will be more difficult.'

'It may be too late already. They could have been on their way out of the country by the time we found Big Ming's body. His place isn't that far from Edinburgh airport. DVLA told me that Charnwood drives a blue Escort: I've circulated the number with the photographs and I've having the airport car park checked.'

'Of course, but even if it's there it could take the best part of a day to find it.'

'True.' Wilding sighed. 'I'm sorry, boss,' he said.

'What for?'

'We should have been where we are now three days ago.'

'That's not your fault. I know you did your best to keep the inquiry on the right lines.'

'I could have come to you when I saw how it was going.'

McIlhenney smiled and shook his head. 'No, you couldn't Ray. Two or three days into a new job, with a new DCI, and you go behind his back to complain about him? I don't think so. If it's anyone's fault it's big Bob's, for sticking him down here without thinking it through.'

It was Wilding's turn to grin. 'Are you going to tell him that?'

'No, I am not, and neither is Mario. But he'd figure it out for himself if he knew what's been happening. Actually I suspect he has already: it was him that suggested I move Stevie Steele down here. Strictly within these walls, Bandit wasn't moved off the Drugs Squad as a reward for outstanding results. He was shifted because he took too high a profile in achieving them. He's a very visible copper, is Mr Mackenzie; he can't help it. Short-term, in the right situation, that can be valuable. But long-term, in a job that calls for a low profile, it's not.'

'So how's the long-term going to be in this office?'

'That, my friend, is going to be up to him.'

59

'I'm so glad you could make it tonight,' said Alex, 'even if it's only for a drink in the Traverse Bar. You've made an honest woman out of me.'

'Hey, come on,' Gina protested. 'You may not be a criminal lawyer but even you should know that an alibi doesn't count if it's fixed up after the event.'

'Maybe not but I don't like to think of myself as telling out and out porkers.'

'Speaking of which, what's he like, this guy Guy?'

'He's a Mr Smooth: he looks the part, I have to admit, even if he is carrying a bit of flab. The trouble is, he knows it.'

'That doesn't make him a bad person.'

'He isn't a bad person. It's just that he has this smugness about him that infuriates me sooner or later, but as soon as it does, and I let him know, like I did this morning, he has this way of making you feel sorry, and you wind up apologising for saying what you really think.'

'Ahem. You said 'this morning'?'

Alex smiled awkwardly and shrugged. 'Well . . . '

'Hussy.' Gina chuckled throatily.

'No! It's not as if we hadn't been there before. I slept with him a couple of times when I was in London.'

'I see. So now he gets himself a stopover in

Edinburgh, consults his palm-top, and says, 'Let's see, who's a likely bet around here? Ah, good old Alex.' That's how it was?'

'Lexy.'

'What?'

'He calls me Lexy.'

'As in Sexy Lexy? And you let him?'

'Let's say I humoured him for a while. But you're right: that's how it was, or at least that's how it turned out. If I'm being really honest, it started off the other way round. I was needing some uncomplicated male company in the flat after these bloody calls, and he was handy, so I pulled him, or let him pull me. Oh, what the fuck? It doesn't matter.'

'So how was it for you anyway, darling? Or need I ask, since you've fixed this emergency alibi to avoid seeing him again?'

Alex sniffed. 'A girl does not discuss these things. Suffice it to say that all morning I found myself thinking about the remark by a divorced lady, who said that having sex with her ex was like being fallen on by a large Victorian wardrobe with the key still in the lock.'

'So, on a scale of one to ten?'

'One and a half: he rates the extra half point because at least it didn't last long.'

'But you said it was the third time.'

'These things fade in the memory. Listen, if you doubt my rating and want to check him out for yourself, he's in the George. But be sure you take your own Durex.'

Gina looked at her, poker-faced. 'What's his room number?'

The two women dissolved into laughter. 'Thanks, pal,' said Alex, when hers had subsided. 'You've cheered me up. Guy left me feeling like a bit of a tart this morning, especially when the hunk next door saw him go.' She sipped her tomato juice. 'But,' she continued, 'I didn't want to see you just to give myself a pep-up and a veneer of honesty.'

'Or to give me a hot tip for the George?'

'Not even that. No, there's something I want to ask you. Remember that cousin of yours?'

'Which cousin? I've got ten of the buggers.'

'That particular cousin: when I was splitting up with Andy and living with you, the one I . . . found solace with.'

'Solace? Is that what you called it? Young Raymond thought all his Christmas Days had come at once. God, girl, what is this? You don't talk about your sex life much, but when you do, it all comes out. What is it? Has your disappointing experience overnight made you want to look for better? As I remember you had a pretty fine time with him too.'

'Maybe I did,' Alex admitted, 'but that's in the past. I've got no urge to rekindle anything there: I was wondering what he's doing with himself these days, that's all.'

'I'm damned if I know. Raymond is the black sheep of the Weston family; he makes me glad that I'm a Reed, not one of them. You may have thought he was a cuddly big chap, but he's not. He's been in and out of trouble for the last few years. That shouldn't surprise you either: his first bit of bother landed you in trouble with your

344

dad, when he named you as proof that he couldn't have been where the police said he was. The worst, though, was when he and a pal were arrested for making Ecstasy. Raymond wound up being a Crown witness, although he was up to his neck in it; the other lad got seven years. There was talk that his father, my uncle Nolan, fixed it with a friend of his in the Crown Office.

'Last I heard of him he had wangled himself a job as a trainee fund manager somewhere, but that he gave it up after a few months. I'm not surprised: I wouldn't let the skinny bastard anywhere near my funds, I'll tell you. So why your sudden interest in him, if you don't want to shag him?'

Alex looked at her friend. 'It's to do with these calls,' she said. 'I had one the night before last. After a while, the guy said, 'You hurt me, Alex.' Ever since then I've been thinking of men I've hurt in my time. I keep coming back to him.'

'How did you hurt him?'

'I did, Gina. I had my fling with him to get back at Andy, because I felt he was turning into my jailer, laying down the law about how I should live my life, putting pressure on me to get married and have kids before I was anything like ready.'

'Listening to you now, I have to tell you that none of that sounds like a good excuse for screwing our Raymond.'

'You're right. On top of all that, I was starting to realise that I didn't want to marry him at all. His unshakeable niceness was suffocating me; somewhere inside I knew I had to get out. I

345

suppose that Raymond was part of the process. That's the trouble, I never felt anything for him: it was a case of 'You're cute, you'll do.' I picked him up, and when it all became too much trouble, I threw him away again.'

'Let's go back to the calls. What did the voice sound like? Was it deep? Was it high-pitched?'

'It was somewhere in the middle. It sounded as if he was speaking through a hankie . . . '

'Standard procedure for perverts, I suppose.'

'Maybe, but it works. What I'm saying is that it could have been Raymond's voice, but I can't be sure.'

'I'll find out what I can about him, Alex. Maybe you're right. The words 'Raymond' and 'you've hurt me' don't sit well together in my mind, because he's a hurter. But, if you're right, that's exactly what he's doing to you. Christ, he drove you into the arms of Mr Wonderful! How hurtful is that? Leave it with me.'

60

Merle Gower had mellowed in the years since her arrival in London: she had lost a considerable amount of weight, but had gained a few grey hairs, and a little tact. When Skinner had first met her he had found her blunt to the point of rudeness, but experience seemed to have taught her that it was better to withhold her opinions until she was invited to voice them. Her job had changed also: when she had replaced Skinner's late friend Joe Doherty at the US Embassy, it had been as FBI liaison, but the growth of the perceived terrorist threat had seen her role expand and its focus change so that she reported to the President's national security adviser, and no longer to the J. Edgar Hoover Building.

The wooden-floored Clarence was quiet when she walked in, but still she almost missed the two Scots, who were seated at a table to the right of the entrance. Her broad black face creased into a smile as she turned in response to Skinner's soft whistle. 'Hey there,' she said as she joined them, 'the Big Man himself. I thought you didn't care for London.'

'It's okay,' he replied. 'It's just not my city, that's all.' He glanced to his left. 'Merle, this is DI Dorothy Shannon; she's just taken over from Neil McIlhenney as our head of Special Branch.'

'Congratulations,' said Gower, as the two

women shook hands. 'You must be good if this guy picked you.'

'Don't flatter her,' the DCC growled. 'She might believe you. What do you want to drink?'

'Gin and tonic.'

Skinner handed Shannon a ten-pound note. 'I don't pull rank very often, Dottie. Get another for yourself too.'

The American glanced around the pub as the inspector left them. 'One thing about you, Bob,' she murmured. 'You always ask interesting questions.'

'Oh, yes? That bank struck a chord, did it?'

'What made you ask about it?'

'Someone I'm investigating came into money. The Premier Taiwan Bank was where it wound up.'

'Fine, but why ask me?'

Skinner's eyes twinkled as he looked back at her. 'Instinct.'

'Why don't I quite believe that?'

'It's your job not to. These days you Yanks don't take anything at face value.'

'Do I detect a note of disapproval there?'

'You're not making yourself popular among your allies.'

'Like we give a shit,' said Gower, happily, as Shannon placed two tall glasses on the table, and handed Skinner his change.

'So, what about it?' he asked her.

'PTB's a legitimate bank,' she told him. 'But it has a pretty discreet client list. Among them you'll find several friends of the Central Intelligence Agency. It's one of their favourite channels for rewarding an asset or keeping him in working capital.'

Skinner's expression darkened.

'Did I give you bad news?'

'It could have been worse. It could have been Al Qaeda, or the Chinese.' He reached into his pocket and handed her an envelope. 'You'll find three names in there; anything you can tell me about any of them would be appreciated.'

'How soon?'

'Let's have breakfast tomorrow, Royal Horse-guards Hotel.' He pushed himself upright, leaving his pint half finished. 'I've got another meeting,' he said. 'You two get to know each other. See you in the morning, eight thirty.'

61

'You're becoming obsessive about this, Jimmy. I think it's time you stopped it, and handed it all over to Sergeant McGurk.'

The chief constable braved his wife's scolding voice, which came from the door of his study. 'In good time, dear: I've got a couple of things to check out first before I'm ready to do that.' He heard a loud 'Tch!' then a sound that stopped just short of a slam.

He turned back to his computer, and opened his mailbox. The day before, he had logged on to Friends Reunited and had found Scotstoun Primary School. Once there he had looked at the years 1943 and 1944; on one or the other Primrose Jardine would have been in her final year. Of course she might not have lived in Scotstoun as a child, but the address on the marriage certificate was the only direct lead he had to the woman. There were three pupils listed, two of them in 1944. He sent messages to all three, explaining that he was trying to contact Primrose Jardine, or anyone who might have known her. It was a very wild shot in the dark, he knew: he expected nothing from it, and so his heart jumped when he saw, waiting for him, a message from the website. He opened it and, to his delight, found a reply from one of the three.

Dear Mr Proud

Fancy you asking about wee Primrose. She and I were pals all the way through primary, and then at secondary. She left to be a nurse and I got a job in the shipyard office, but we used to see each other for a while. Her dad was killed in the war and her mum died when she was twenty-two. She was left a wee bit of money then from her mum's insurance policy and she got keeping on their council house. When she was twenty-five she married a man called Bothwell in the registry office and I was her bridesmaid. He was a teacher at Jordanhill College School and they went to live up Broomhill. The last time I saw her, in 1960 (I remember because the Olympics were on in Rome) she told me she was pregnant. When I tried to get in touch with her after that, a man told me they'd moved and that's the last I heard.

Hope this helps.
Yours sincerely,
Ina Leslie (Deans)

'It does, Mrs Leslie,' he murmured, 'it does. What's the other thing Bob says a good detective needs, Jimmy? Luck, he says, sheer bloody luck and as much as he can get.'

62

Mackenzie heard the footsteps on the gravel. He waited for the thump on the door, but instead he heard the ring of a bell, from the rear of the house. He stayed in his chair, staring at the muted television as Cheryl showed the visitor into the living room, listening to the shouts of his children, at play upstairs. 'Why did you come to the back door?' he asked.

'I wanted to count the empties,' Neil McIlhenney replied.

'That's got fuck all to do with you.'

'Wrong. When you call in sick on the second day of a murder investigation because you've had too many bevvies the night before, that has everything to do with me.'

'Hey, you've got some nerve!'

'Yes, I have, and don't protest your innocence. We both know I'm right. Are you on the hard stuff?'

Mackenzie sagged in his chair. 'I have been lately,' he admitted.

'Well, you can cut that out for a start. Try having a dry week; see whether it's easy or hard. That'll tell you a lot. I know this from bitter early experience: if you've got a grudge against the job and you look for help to forget it, you'll find it doesn't work. And you do have a grudge, we both know that too.'

'I'm beginning to think it has a grudge against

me. I don't fit into this force, Neil. Moving through from Glasgow was a mistake: I'm going to ask for a move back.'

'That would be a much bigger mistake.'

'Why?'

'You want a straight answer? You've just pissed off the commander of the SDEA, and he's a big mate of Max Allan, the Strathclyde ACC. After that they won't take you back in a hurry. If you don't believe me, put your request in and see what happens. Once that's been knocked back you'll find out how dumb you've been, because the boss won't have anyone in a key position in CID who isn't fully committed to it. You will wind up in a uniform and in an office.'

'I'd leave the force if that happened.'

'Then make sure it doesn't.'

'How?'

'First, don't breathe another word about a transfer. Then take a look at yourself, and work on your big weaknesses. You're too much of a loner, Bandit, you're too much of an extrovert and you're too illdisciplined. You're trying to be the sort of cop you find in crime novels, and we don't have room for mavericks like them. They might have been able to cope with you in a force the size of Strathclyde, but we can't, and we won't. Top to bottom, we're a team; nobody can play his own game without regard for proper methods, for rules and procedures. You want my very serious advice, beyond cutting down on the drink? Then use your time off to consider what I've said, and work out how you can be a better cop, and a better leader. When you get back you can start by apologising to Ray Wilding. He's made no complaints about you, but I'm damn sure he's had grounds.'

Mackenzie sighed. 'Okay, Neil,' he said. 'I hear what you're saying. I'll give myself a good kicking.'

'No. Remember what's happened, but don't dwell on it. Relax with your kids and come back to work rested and refreshed.' McIlhenney stood. 'I'll leave by the front door,' he said.

The two men walked together into the hall. 'How's the Starr thing going?' Mackenzie asked.

'Check the Scottish news tonight and you'll hear that we're looking for Eddie Charnwood, for the murder of Starr, Big Ming, and a dealer in Dundee.'

'Charnwood?' Bandit's face went white. 'Of course: he was too close to Starr not to have known what was going on, yet I bought his innocent act. Christ, that's how far up my arse my head must have been.'

63

'How did your big meeting go today?' Bob asked. 'What's the view on super-casinos?'

Aileen smiled ruefully. 'My opposite numbers in the Westminster parliament,' she replied, 'still have their fingers crossed that the questionable positives will outweigh the undoubted negatives. Personally, I wouldn't have had any in Scotland, but gambling isn't a devolved power, so the decision wasn't entirely in our hands. What's the police view?'

'We don't really have one. We are but poor public servants put on earth to perform the tasks wished upon us by our political masters or, in your case, mistresses. If you tell us you're going to set up bloody great gaming halls and we'll have to police them, that's what we'll do.'

'Bollocks,' she said cheerfully. 'The police have a view on everything.'

He shrugged his shoulders. 'In this case it will have to be a moral one, founded on whether or not we agree with gambling in principle. Casinos are not a policing problem, and it's most unlikely that they ever will be. My personal view is that I regard gambling as an entertainment; like everything else, how much a person spends on it should relate to what they can afford.'

'There are gambling addicts, remember.'

'And alcoholics and junkies and foodies and inconsiderate bastards in sports cars who can't help turning up their stereo systems to full volume, then driving through my home village at night with the top down. Addiction is a fact of life: self-control is impossible for some people until it's imposed upon them by poverty or death. Yes, some people bet more than they or their families can afford, but for the majority, gambling on a horse race or on who scores first in a football match is a reasonable investment, because they understand it and accept the odds. So why penalise them by banning it? You won't stop it, you'll only drive it underground, and then it will become my problem. The core task of the police service is ensuring peace and order in society: let us concentrate on preventing crime against property and the person and let everything else, wherever possible, be a matter of self-discipline, with economic rather than criminal consequences for failure.'

Aileen de Marco picked up her coffee cup. 'That, my darling, is as fine a mix of cynicism and practicality as I've heard in a while. I will make a politician of you yet, for all your protests.'

He took her free hand in both of his and looked into her eyes. 'There's something you should know about me, something I only admit to people I love.' He paused, enjoying her sudden uncertainty. 'I am a politician.'

She laughed. 'I thought you were going to tell me something serious. I know: you've got an honours degree in politics . . . more than I have if it comes to it . . . but I'm talking about practical application.'

'So am I. What's a politician's job? To work for the benefit of the people, in a variety of ways; legislation is only a small part of it, as you're well aware. What do you do with the rest of your time? You get things done, for your constituents and others. How? By considering, discovering, persuading, but only occasionally by instructing. What are your basic skills? I'd say they lie in knowing which buttons to push, knowing where the expertise lies in relation to each problem you face, and knowing who the decision-maker is in each situation. I've been doing that all my career; before I ever went to university and took the degree you mentioned . . . which also includes philosophy, in case you've forgotten . . . I learned it from my father, and I never even knew he was teaching me. I'm bloody good at it, much better than people give me credit for. They think I open doors by kicking them in.' He shot her a quick smile that seemed to wipe all the tiredness from his face. 'I suppose I do, from time to time,' he chuckled, 'but only as a very last resort.'

'We are going to be some combination,' she murmured. 'Scotland doesn't know what it's in for.'

'I'm thinking outside Scotland at the moment. And just to show you how good a politician I am, I'm going to ask you to open that door for me, the one I mentioned last night, not because of our relationship . . . I'll never do that, I promise . . . but because I reckon you owe me one.'

'I owe you more than one. What do you need?'

'I'm in a position with my investigation where

357

I need some questions answered and maybe some orders given. There's only one person who can do all that, and I need to get to see him, in total secrecy. You're my key.'

'If I can I will. Who's behind this door?'

'The Prime Minister.'

64

'How was your dinner date last night?' Merle Gower asked, as a waiter laid a full English breakfast before her.

'Fine, thanks,' Skinner replied, cutting a piece of melon. 'She had to leave for a while to make a phone call, but other than that it was a very pleasant evening.'

'She's a very attractive lady, I'm told.'

'In many ways. Were my suspicions justified?'

'Yes, they were.'

'In that case, the sooner she's out of town the better.'

Shannon looked from one to the other, puzzled by the exchange.

'We're being tailed, Dottie,' Skinner told her, 'or at least I am. Merle had a couple of her people watch over me after I left the Clarence last night. From what she's just said they spotted my followers.'

'All the way to the Charing Cross Hotel, and into the bar.'

'So now they know who I was meeting. That's no problem, for half of Scotland knows that Aileen and I are friendly. Still, I'll be happier when she isn't around here any longer.'

'If we were followed last night,' said the inspector, 'won't they know that we were meeting Merle?'

'Our watchers may not have known who she

was. But suppose they did, we're old friends too, so there's a valid reason for our meeting. On top of that, who's going to have a business meeting with a spook in a pub in the middle of bloody Whitehall?'

'I accept that, sir, but if we're being watched, won't they have seen her arrive here this morning?'

'No,' Gower replied, 'they'll have seen a woman in a white coat with a huge hood get out of a taxi. I know this because my people can talk to me, right into my ear, right now, and they report that neither of their rivals reacted when I entered.'

'Where are they, the people who are watching us?'

'One's in a car parked on the street outside; the other's at a newspaper stall.'

'And who are they?'

'Take your pick,' said Skinner. 'Five? Six? Military Intelligence? It's not Merle's lot; that's all I know for sure. Are you going to ask me why now?'

'Well, yes, I suppose so.'

'Because we're good at our job. We're being set up.'

'By whom?' Shannon asked anxiously.

'I'll know for sure before the morning's out. Merle, what have you got for us?'

The American frowned at him. 'Short answers about each of your three names. Peter Bassam is a CIA asset who was active in the Balkan republics; he was a member of Milosevic's secret service, but he was a double, until the Agency

360

made him disappear.'

'The CIA?' Shannon exclaimed. 'We were told he was one of ours.'

'We've been told lots of things, Dottie. I've rarely met anyone who was as co-operative as Miles Hassett. Go on, Merle.'

'Moses Archer, we've never heard of,' she said. 'Surprised?'

'Not yet. How about the third name I gave you?'

Her eyes narrowed. 'And where exactly did you come across it? I've been told to ask you that before I tell you anything.'

'Ask away, I'm not saying at this stage.'

'I didn't think you would; never mind, I tried. Titus Armstead is CIA from way back, but like me, he has links with national security.'

'Has? I was told that he's retired and living in Delaware.'

'The second is true, the first is not: he's still active, but he works away from the centre, out of Dover Air Force Base. That's as secure as anything in the US apart from the Strategic Air Command headquarters and the White House itself.'

'Would it be possible for him to have someone on the payroll whose identity was unknown to Langley, or to your boss?'

'In some areas of the world, it would almost be essential that an asset's identity was kept secret.'

'I don't imagine that Britain is one of those areas.'

'Of course not.'

'And yet that's what he did.'

Gower gasped. 'He ran an agent here? The third name you gave me, Moses Archer, that was him, right?'

'Right. He was Armstead's step-son, and you've met him, but not going by that name. You knew him as Adam Arrow.'

'You're crazy. You're telling me that my department has someone within British Military Intelligence as an asset?'

'For the last seven years, but not any more: he's dead.'

'I'm not surprised.'

'I don't suppose you could find out who authorised his recruitment.'

'No, I couldn't. That is so off base that nobody will ever admit to it.'

'Is it possible that nobody did, and that Armstead operated independently?'

Gower rubbed her chin as she thought. 'Seven years ago,' she murmured, 'just when terrorism was beginning to expand globally. If he had a covert budget back then, and someone like him might have . . . yes, I suppose so.' She gazed at Skinner. 'Bob, you're telling me stuff here that maybe I shouldn't know.'

'Then forget I ever did. You don't need to know it. But I'd like you to do one more thing for me.'

'I don't know if I should.'

'This is easy,' he told her, then glanced at his watch. 'I'm being picked up out front in five minutes by a car that's going to take me to a very private meeting, and I don't want anyone tailing me there. When your people see me in the doorway, I'd like them to take my watchers out of play. They don't need to be subtle about it, just effective.'

'What if I wind up fielding complaints from your Foreign Secretary?'

'You won't, I guarantee it. I'm going to meet his boss.'

65

Mr Arnold Solomons was expecting him. Before driving through from Edinburgh, Proud had taken the precaution of phoning, to make sure that the man was willing to talk to him. He was, although conversation was not what was uppermost in the chief constable's mind. More than anything, he wanted to see another place where Claude Bothwell had lived, to see if the man had left any trace of himself.

As Ina Leslie had said, Dundyvan Drive was 'up Broomhill', a left turn off a twisting road that climbed up from the Clydeside Expressway. The street was lined with leafless trees, and seemed quiet; number fourteen was a red-brick semi-detached bungalow, an unusual type of house for that part of Glasgow where most of the older dwellings are stone-built. Proud parked in front and walked up the driveway.

The man who answered the doorbell's summons would have been tall in his youth, but a spinal condition had given him a permanent, hunched stoop, so that he had to twist his neck awkwardly to look up at his visitor. 'Mr Proud?' he asked.

'Yes, Mr Solomons, and thank you for seeing me. I hope it isn't an inconvenience.'

'Not at all; if anything it's a convenience. It's given me an excuse not to go into the shop.'

'What sort of shop?'

'A jeweller's, up in Hyndland.' His eyes took on a wary look. 'You said you're a policeman, when you called. Do you have anything to prove that?'

Proud smiled at the man's caution and handed him his warrant card, watching as Solomons peered at it through thick spectacles, taking in his reaction as he read it

'It's Sir James, is it? I beg your pardon, Chief Constable. This is a very puzzling honour. Come into my parlour, and I'll get the tea organised.' He led him straight into a receiving room with a bay window that looked out on to the street, then stepped back into the hall and called out, 'Rachel, my visitor's arrived.'

Proud guessed that the organisation of the tea had just taken place. He glanced round the room, noting that practically every flat surface was occupied by painted china dogs. He looked at the old jeweller as he settled into a well-used armchair, his face relaxing as the strain was taken off his deformed spine. He tried to guess the man's age, and decided he had to be in his mid-seventies, although his disability may have had an ageing effect.

'I haven't had a policeman in this house for over twenty years,' he mused. 'Not that I had done anything myself, you understand. There was a robbery in the shop, and I was beaten up. Bastards hit me with baseball bats; that was the start of my back trouble. Anyway, the CID came here to interview me when I was recovering, to get an inventory of what was taken.'

'Did they arrest the robbers?'

Solomons' laugh was derisory. 'That lot? They couldn't have found their arses with both hands. No, they never caught them, and I never got any of my property back. I'm not at the top end of the business, Sir James. Most of the stuff probably wound up being sold on market stalls down south. My insurers coughed up, although they made me install expensive security systems, both at the shop and here.' He paused as a white-haired, bird-like woman came into the room, carrying a tea tray that looked as if it could have been silver. Proud rose to help her, but she placed it unaided on a table in front of the fireplace. 'This is my wife,' the old man said. 'Rachel, this is Sir James Proud.'

The old woman gave a tiny bow as she shook the chief constable's hand. 'Very pleased to meet you,' she whispered.

'We had our golden wedding two years ago,' Solomons told him, as she poured the tea from a pot that matched the tray.

'Congratulations,' Proud replied. 'Mine's fifteen years away; I hope I make it.'

'You look a pretty fit chap; I'm sure you will. Now, how can we help you?'

The chief constable accepted a cup of tea from Mrs Solomons, and added a little milk. 'I'm trying to find someone who lived in this house before you,' he said. 'His name was Claude Bothwell and he taught in Jordanhill School. He was a tenant here in the late fifties: I understand that you bought it in 1964.'

'Sixty-five,' the old lady corrected him. 'I'm

better with dates than Arnold.'

'She is,' her husband admitted. 'Mind, we were tenants ourselves before that. The landlord was Mr A. E. Pickard, a very famous man in Glasgow: he owned all sorts of property, flats, houses, theatres, cinemas, everything. He was a great man, Mr Pickard; famous for the jokes he played on people. My father knew him well; he told him that Rachel and I were needing a house, rather than the flat we were in, as our second child was on the way, and he offered us this place. Remember when we went to meet him, Rachel?'

The old lady smiled. 'Oh, yes. We were shown into his office to sign the tenancy, but there was no one there. So we sat down in chairs opposite this great big desk and waited for, oh, it must have been ten minutes at least, neither of us saying anything, but with Arnold getting fidgetier and fidgetier. We were both wondering where he was when all of a sudden he climbed out from the kneehole under the desk, all smiles. 'I fooled you there, didn't I?' was what he said. And, you know, he must have been about eighty-five at the time.'

'Eccentric,' Solomons declared. 'That's what he was, the last of the great eccentrics.'

'Well, maybe not the last, dear,' his wife murmured, glancing at the china dogs. 'There's still you, in your own quiet way.'

'When did you move in?' Proud asked her.

'1960; in the autumn.'

'That's right,' said the old man. 'We signed the lease, then Mr Pickard gave us the keys and

367

drove us out to see the house in his Rolls-Royce. He owned this one, the one next door and the two beyond that, but he walked us up the drive to here, and said, 'This is the best of them all; a palace fit for a prince.' I'm sure he said that to all his tenants, but who cares? He was a great man, and he made you feel good.'

'Do you recall him saying anything about the previous tenant?'

'No, I can't say that I do.'

'Yes, you can,' Rachel exclaimed. 'There was the garden shed.'

'Oh, yes; ach, my memory's shot to hell these days. After he showed us through the house, Mr Pickard took us out to the back garden. In the far corner there was a shed, a big timber thing with windows in it, so new that the maker's stickers were still on the glass. I asked him if we would be expected to pay for it, since it wasn't mentioned in the lease. He laughed and said no, that we could thank the previous tenant for it. He told us that the man had asked him if he could put a shed in the garden, and that he'd said he could. Then, less than a month later, the fellow came back to him. He told him that he and his wife were moving from Glasgow to a new job, paid him all the rent that was due and handed back the keys. 'Imagine,' he said, 'paying all that money on a new shed and then just walking away and leaving it. And here's me thinking that teachers are poorly paid.' You're right, Rachel, there was that, right enough. When I think about it, I can still hear

Mr Pickard laughing.'

'What happened to it?' asked Proud.

'What do you mean? It's still there. The thing'll outlast us.'

66

As Skinner cleared security in Thames House and moved towards the lifts, he sensed that he was being watched. He glanced to his left, quickly enough to catch the gaze of a man still upon him and to see it being averted. There was anger in those eyes, unmistakably. He pressed the call button with a feeling of satisfaction, and was still smiling as he walked into Amanda Dennis's office.

'Have you had people tailing me?' he asked her, straight out.

A slight flush came to her cheeks. 'The DG asked me to give you an escort,' she admitted, 'for your protection.'

'That was kind of him,' said Skinner, 'but it was unnecessary and even a little indiscreet. I don't really like being followed to meetings with my girlfriend.'

'Sorry, Bob. No harm done, though. I gather you slipped them the first time, and that they had another problem this morning.'

'Life's one long learning curve,' he told her. 'You'd better call them off, otherwise you'll have to give them an escort to protect them from me.'

'I've already stood them down. They wanted to know who your people were. I assume they were Special Branch.'

He grinned. 'Yes, special friends, you might say.' He sat in the one small visitor chair in the room. 'Amanda, I want to ask you something, just between you and me, if that's possible in this place.'

'It is in this room; fire away.'

'About Rudolph Sewell: when he went bad, was it a surprise to you?'

'Yes and no. He was a trusted colleague, but on the other hand, he was always a very secretive man, even by the standards of this place. I don't think anyone ever got to know him, not even Sean, and Rudy recruited him.'

'What did he know, do you think, about all this? He killed himself rather than be interrogated by me. Do you know of, or can you guess at, anything that we're not getting to?'

'You pulled that stunt, remember, to try to make Rudy think that Hassett had been executed. Perhaps he fell for it, and decided that he would go out on his own terms, not anyone else's.'

'Maybe, but perhaps there really was a big secret that he died to protect.'

'Do you really think there was, or do we know the extent of the conspiracy already?'

'Oh, I know it. I even know why Sewell died. I just need to make a few pieces fit and I'll be ready to report.'

'I have another piece for you in that case. MoD ran a check for me on the service records of Ormond Hassett and Joshua Archer: they were both in Germany for a two-year period in the mid-seventies. I still don't know where Hassett was, but Archer was stationed at Bielefeld.'

'So they could have met there?'

'Yes, but it's a long shot: we had a big army presence in Germany in the seventies.'

'The odds shorten when Archer turns up as adjutant to Hassett's Washington trip in 1982.'

'True, but what does it matter?'

'That depends who else was in Germany when they were. Thanks for that, Amanda.' He rose from the chair. 'There's something I should tell you: Dottie and I are going away on a field trip for a few days.'

'Where to?'

'I'll tell you when we get back.'

'Can I make arrangements for you?'

'No, that's all done. See you.'

Skinner walked back to his own office. He felt isolated and, unusually for him, a little excited. He had cut himself loose from Thames House, and was leaving no trail behind him.

Shannon looked up as he came into the room. 'How did it go?' she asked.

'Very well. He and I are best buddies now. Do you have Esther Craig's phone number handy?'

'Yes. Do you want me to get her for you?'

'That's okay, I'll call her myself.' He waited as she found a note on her desk and handed it to him, then picked up his phone and dialled.

'Esther, this is Bob Skinner,' he said, as she answered. 'You can start to make your funeral arrangements. Your brother's body will be delivered to your local undertaker tomorrow morning. Don't worry about the cost, that'll all be taken care of by his service.'

'Bob, thank you. I don't know what to say.'

'Don't say anything. Have you broken it to your mother?'

'Yes. She's flying over today, to be with me. My husband's picking her up at Gatwick tomorrow morning.'

'How about your step-father?' he asked casually.

'No, she's coming alone. Titus can't make the trip: he has something to do at home and he can't postpone it.'

'Mmm. Esther, there was something I meant to ask you. It's idle curiosity, really. How did they meet; your mum and step-father, I mean?'

'Titus was a friend of my dad's, originally. They met in Germany, when Dad was serving there back in the early seventies; Titus was air force then. He came to Dad's funeral service, and he kept in touch after that. He took Moses under his wing, and encouraged him when he said he wanted to join the army. Mum was against it at first, but Titus persuaded her that it was something he'd do with or without her approval, so he'd be better to have all the advantages going.'

'Do you remember someone else your father met in Germany, a man called Hassett?'

'The MP? Oh, yes; he was at the funeral too. He arranged for his old regiment to sponsor Moses' application for Sandhurst and he was one of the referees on his application form.'

'Can you remember who the other one was?'

There was a period of silence as she considered the question. 'No, I can't,' she admitted at last. 'It was someone Titus knew, but I can't recall the name.'

67

Assistant Chief Constable Max Allan looked across his desk at his distinguished visitor. 'Jimmy, are you after a bar for your Queen's Police Medal?' he asked, with a grin. 'I'm new to chief-officer rank, I know, but I've never heard of anything like this. When word of this spreads in ACPOS there will be hell to pay. What sort of a precedent have you set, running your own one-man investigation?'

'Max,' said Proud, 'if word of this spreads in ACPOS there will indeed be hell to pay, but it'll be coming in your direction, from me. I'm a private citizen laying information before you, as ACC Crime in Strathclyde, about serious offences which I believe have taken place. I expect confidentiality, and I'll bloody well have it.'

'Keep your hair on, Chief, I'm kidding, but you can imagine what the rest would say.'

'Son, at my age I don't give a monkey's what they say. I set out to do a quiet favour for a lady: in the course of my enquiries on her behalf, I've come upon something that needs looking at officially by the appropriate forces, yours and mine.'

'Bigamy.'

'That's for certain, but after forty years, and with all parties missing, I'd be inclined to shrug my shoulders at it. No, it's this Bothwell man's pattern of behaviour that concerns me. These women disappeared, Max, all four of them. It may be that Ethel Ward cashed up her fortune, chucked him out and went to live out her days in the sunshine. It may be that Montserrat Rivera Jiminez found out about his affair with Annabelle Gentle and went back to Spain, leaving them to elope to Australia on a ten-quid assisted package. But there's the pregnant Primrose Jardine, who left Broomhill, and doesn't appear to have shown up in Edinburgh. Nor was the birth of her child ever registered. She can't be explained away that easily, and nor can Arnold and Rachel Solomons' garden shed.'

'Okay, I accept all that. So what do you want me to do about it?'

Proud leaned on Allan's desk. 'I'm not after glory; I'm after anonymity in this matter, but we've got a cross-border investigation on our hands here. Since it started on my patch, it's appropriate that I take the lead. Agreed?'

'Agreed, sir.'

'In that case, Max, I'd be grateful if you'd obtain the appropriate warrant from the sheriff, and find out if there's anything under that bloody shed.'

68

'Where are we going, sir?' asked Dottie Shannon, as she and Skinner walked along Millbank, past the Tate Gallery.

'We're going to set a trap. Sorry if you're finding it a bit cold, but when you pick up a taxi from Thames House, you never know who might be listening.' He pointed to a big, modern building on the other side of the river, almost nestling against Vauxhall Bridge. 'That's where we're headed,' he said.

'But isn't that . . . '

' . . . the Secret Intelligence Service building? Spot on. Not very secret I'll grant you, but a fine piece of work by a very fine architect.'

They walked on, turning on to the bridge and crossing it, until they reached their objective. The DCC led the way inside and walked straight up to the reception desk. 'Bob Skinner and colleague to see Piers Frame,' he said, showing his warrant card and motioning to Shannon to do the same.

'Yes, sir,' the receptionist replied, picking up a phone. 'I've been advised of your visit. Mr Frame will meet you here and take you through Security.'

They waited for a few minutes, glancing around the big hallway, noting the position of the security cameras, wondering where the others were, those that could not be seen. 'Bob, DI

Shannon.' Skinner turned to see the immaculately suited deputy director approaching. 'Let's go round the gate, rather than through it,' he said, as they shook hands, nodding to the security officers, using his seniority to bypass the process. 'I've been advised of your needs,' he said. 'I can't do it all here, but I can get it under way. The first step is to take your photographs; so if you'll follow me . . . '

When they were shown into the deputy director's office ten minutes later they had posed solemnly for identification photographs, and had provided right index-finger prints and retinal images. 'Those will go to FCO,' said Frame. 'The documents will be delivered to your hotel this evening.'

Shannon could contain herself no longer. 'Excuse me, sir,' she exclaimed, 'but what documents?'

'Diplomatic passports,' Skinner told her. 'We're flying to Washington tomorrow.' He turned back to the deputy director and handed him a bulky package that he had brought from Thames House. 'I'd like that to go across in the secure bag to the embassy, to be collected by me when we get there.'

'That will be done, but may I ask why? I could make similar arrangements for you in the US.'

'Let's just say I'm sentimental.'

Frame raised an eyebrow. 'Strange sentiments. Do you want an escort in DC?'

'A pick-up from the airport would be good; from then on, definitely no.'

'I see.' For the first time since they had met,

Shannon thought that the MI6 executive looked a little apprehensive. 'You're not going to do anything that we're going to have to disown, are you?' he asked.

'Of course not.' Skinner laughed. 'I'm a police officer, remember?'

'Not like any I've ever met. Is there any other help I can give you?'

Skinner nodded. 'Two things. I'd like you to let slip our destination, very casually, to someone. But before that, I want you to tell me who it was that ordered you to spring Miles Hassett.'

69

'What's on your mind?' Louise McIlhenney asked her husband. 'You hardly said a word to the kids over dinner: Spence was just bursting to tell you about his computer test but you barely looked in his direction. You couldn't take your eyes off the television.'

'How did he get on?'

'Ask him yourself, once you've told me why you're so quiet.'

'I'm worrying about you,' he offered, more of a suggestion than a reply.

'You've got no need to: I'm fine. I see my consultant in a couple of days, but it's just routine.'

'Love, we could move your consultant into the spare room and I'll still worry about you. A first baby in your forties: I won't sleep easy until he's keeping you awake!'

She laughed. 'If I'm awake so will you be. But I'm not buying that as an excuse. I repeat: what's up?'

He gave up pretence. 'It's work stuff,' he confessed. 'If you'd been watching telly you'd have heard that I've got a double murder on my hands, and the suspect's absconded with his wife and son. It's been a full day now and no trace. I reckon he's made it out of the country.'

'That's yours? I thought you were strategic.'

'That was the idea, but I've had a small

personnel problem, so I've taken this one over. There's more than that. Alex Skinner's got a stalker, and she's giving us less help than she might in tracing him. I think she knows who it is and wants to protect him.'

'From her father?'

'From Mario and me: Bob's away just now, and he's left us in *loco parentis*, you might say.'

'Don't let Alex hear you say it. She's a very capable woman; if she says she can deal with something, I'll bet she can.'

'Maybe, but we've got a bit of extra insurance anyway.'

'What kind of insurance?'

'A good neighbour, you might call him. He's ... ' He broke off as the phone rang, reached across from his chair, and picked it up. 'The McIlhenney household,' he said.

'Boss, it's Ray Wilding. I'm going to brighten your evening. I've just had a call from the Met. Eddie and Soraya Charnwood have been arrested at Heathrow: they were booked on to a flight to Tunis under the names Edgar and Sonya Wood.'

'And the kid?'

'He was with them; they'd dyed his hair blond. It was him who gave the game away, believe it or not. The handler at the check-in desk said to him, 'And what's your name, little man?' and he replied, 'Edward Charnwood,' just like that. The name on his passport was John. The clerk pressed the panic button and the police arrived, mob-handed.'

'Brilliant. I was beginning to think that we

weren't allowed any luck. Where are they now?'

'The parents are being held in custody overnight, and the boy's in care. All three of them will be flown up to Edinburgh tomorrow morning, with an escort.'

'Am I looking forward to meeting them, or am I not? Thanks, Ray, you were right: you have made my night.'

70

Many people in the professions find that the first part of December is their busiest time of the year. Although the month is curtailed by the Christmas season, clients' needs tend to grow more urgent as the year end approaches. As Curle Anthony and Jarvis, Alex Skinner's law firm, was one of the biggest in Scotland, her workload was correspondingly heavy. It was one minute before eight p.m. when she made it home on Thursday evening. 'TGIF tomorrow,' she muttered, as she slid her key into the lock. 'Only trouble is, I'll be working bloody Saturday as well.' She stepped inside and cancelled her alarm, headed straight for the kitchen, where she switched the oven to keep her pizza takeaway warm until she was ready to eat it, then went through to her bedroom, discarding clothes on the way.

Ten minutes later, she was showered and changed into blue jeans, a sweatshirt and sheepskin slippers, when a pleasing thought occurred to her. She still had the best part of a bottle of pressure-sealed *cava* in the fridge. Soon she was seated at the dining-table, the pizza divided into eight slices to make it easier to eat with fingers, and a flute on a coaster beside it. She was halfway through both when her eye was caught by the blinking red light on her phone, advising her that she had recorded calls waiting to be reviewed.

She picked up plate and glass and moved over to the dumpy little swivel chair that she used when she was working at her desk. 'What's here, then?' she said, making a mental note to stop talking to herself. She was about to push the button when the doorbell rang. She frowned. The entry-phone from the street had a buzzer; the bell meant that there was someone inside, at the front door. She was still frowning as she walked out into the hall, glass in hand.

On any other week, she would have opened the door without thinking, but the memory of her stalker was still fresh, and so she looked through the spy-hole, to see the distorted figure of Griff, her neighbour. Intrigued, she turned the wheel of the Yale.

'Alex, hi.' He seemed a little ill at ease: he was big and fair-haired, and managed to remind her of a lumberjack she had once seen in a movie. His accent was southern hemisphere, but she found it hard to place. 'I'm not interrupting anything, am I, only . . . '

'You're not interrupting anyone, Griff. What can I do for you?'

'I hate to ask this, but Spring and I have friends in for supper, and my one and only corkscrew has just come to pieces in my hand. I wonder, do you have one I could borrow?'

'Sure, come on in while I dig it out of its hiding-place.' She led him into the living room, silently cursing because her work-shirt, complete with sweaty armpits, was still lying on the floor where she had left it. She kept her corkscrews in the top drawer of her sideboard. There was a 'waiter's friend' type and a complicated wooden affair that had once belonged to her grandfather. It had twin bars, one for twisting the screw into the cork and the other for drawing it smoothly out of the barrel. She gave Griff the waiter's friend. 'That'll do the job,' she said. 'I had a waiting job for a while when I was a student in Glasgow. We used those there: in fact, they were so good I nicked that one.'

'I won't tell anyone.'

'It's all right, I told my dad; he let me off with a caution.'

'What does he do?'

'He's the deputy chief constable.'

'Crikey, the name on the door: I should have known.' He brandished the corkscrew. 'Thanks, Alex, you're a life-saver. I'll drop it in first thing tomorrow.'

'Keep it till you get a replacement. If I'm not in, just drop it in my letterbox out front.'

'Okay, thanks.'

Pity about Spring, she thought, as she closed the door, and went back to her solitary pizza and *cava*. She had forgotten about the phone, until the red light blinked its way back into her awareness. She picked up another slice of supper and pushed the play button.

The machine told her that she had three calls waiting. The first was timed at twenty minutes to nine. 'Hi, Alex.' Her father's voice filled the room, and she felt lifted. 'I guess you'll be travelling to work right now. I haven't much time so I'll have to leave this message rather than wait till you get there. If you're looking for me over the next few days, you'll have to use the mobile number. This thing I'm on has taken a couple of turns, and I've got to head for the States. I'm not sure how long it's going to take. I'll let you know when I get back. In the meantime, if these calls continue to be a nuisance, I want you to stop your nonsense and ask Neil to reinstate the intercept. Love you.' There was a click and the sound of the dial tone for a few seconds, until the second message began; the machine told her it had been received at five thirty-five.

'Hello, lovey.'

'God,' she whispered.

'It's Guy here, ruining your evening by calling to let you know I'm safely back in London and, of course, to thank you for a wonderful night, and almost morning. Hope you've recovered your strength. You're absolutely delicious, Alexandra . . . Ha, ha. You did order me not to call you Lexy . . . and I don't know how I'm going to struggle on without you or, even worse, how you're going to struggle on without me. London would be a brighter place with you in it, you know. 'Bye, darling.'

'What the hell was that about?' she exclaimed to the walls. 'The infuriating pillock, he doesn't even know my proper name and there he is implying that I'm going to pine for him.'

She was still fuming when the dial tone ended and the next call began. The synthetic voice advised that it had been logged at seven minutes past seven. It began with silence or, rather, with the sound of breathing and traffic noise in the

386

background. She was about to push the erase button, when she heard a noise that was somewhere between a cough and a gurgle, as if breath was being drawn in. 'You really did hurt me, Alex,' the distorted voice croaked, rising as something heavy passed nearby. 'I don't take kindly to it.' Then a click; then the line was dead.

She stared at the instrument for almost a minute. 'Raymond, my boy,' she murmured evenly, when she had recovered her composure, 'if that's you, I have news for you. I'm going to hurt you again, and a hell of a lot worse this time.'

She was still glowering at the phone when it rang. She snatched it up, ignoring McIlhenney's instruction to record all incoming calls. 'Yes?' she snapped. 'What is it this time?'

'Hey, hey, hey,' Sarah exclaimed. 'Hold on a minute. Whoever it is you're steamed at, this isn't him.'

Alex sighed. 'I'm sorry. It's just . . . Something I thought was over just reared its head again.'

'Man trouble?'

'That's too kind. These are reptiles.'

'I've encountered a couple of them in my time.'

'So I've heard.' Once again there was silence on the end of a phone line. This time it was distinctly frosty. 'I'm sorry, Sarah,' said Alex at once. 'That was out of order. What can I do for you?'

'I was wondering if you knew what your dad's up to? I had the briefest of brief calls from him this morning, saying that there's no way he's getting home this weekend, like he'd hoped, and asking me to say sorry to the kids.'

'I really don't know, I'm afraid. I know where he's headed, and that's America, but that's as far as it goes. He's not saying anything about what he's doing, not even to me.'

'Mmm.' Alex could sense that her step-mother was thinking something over. 'Do you have any big plans for tonight?' Sarah asked, at last.

'Not even the tiniest.'

'In that case, you wouldn't like to come out here, would you? I know it's pushing nine, but it might be the last chance I have to talk to you, one to one, about everything that's happened. How about it?'

Alex looked at the phone: the red light had stopped blinking, but it still shone brightly. 'Why the hell not?' she replied.

71

'There's a rule, isn't there?' ACC Max Allan muttered. 'Every time there's a job to be done it has to be bloody freezing.'

Sir James Proud glanced up into the blue morning sky. 'Thank your lucky stars that we're not doing the digging.'

Screens had been set up around the Solomons' shed, dividing off a section of the garden. The Glasgow media grapevine being as effective as any in the world, a statement had been issued announcing that the police were carrying out excavations at 14 Dundyvan Drive, Broomhill, in the light of new information relating to the disappearance of a woman almost fifty years ago. It stressed that the investigation had nothing to do with the present occupants of the house. The old couple themselves seemed a little bemused by the proceedings, and by the small knot of journalists and cameramen who were gathered in the street outside.

The two senior officers braved the cold and watched as the shed was emptied, then dismantled by a team of joiners, carefully, so that it could be rebuilt later. When they were finished four burly police officers moved in, wearing steel-capped boots, Day-glo jackets and hard hats, and began to attack the base on which it had stood. They worked carefully, each sledge-hammer blow carefully placed, trying to crack rather than shatter the concrete. It took the best part of an hour before scene-of-crime officers were ready to begin to remove the pieces to see what they had uncovered.

'Is it buried treasure?'

Proud turned and saw Arnold Solomons, standing beside him inside the enclosure, his back bent and his nose bright with the cold, even though he was wrapped in a heavy Crombie overcoat, with a scarf and thick leather gloves. 'I wish it was, for your sake,' he replied. 'Now please, go back inside.'

'Will I hell: this is my garden and I want to see what's going on.'

'Sir!' The call was to Allan, from one of the SOCOs. He and Proud moved closer, with the old man shuffling behind them. 'There's a base of boulders here, but in among them . . . They're wrapped in brown paper, maybe so that anyone watching would think they were rocks too, only they're not.'

The officers stood aside, allowing the two chiefs to look into the excavation. The brown paper had been torn open in places and inside they could see white bones, some large, some finger-sized, and in the centre, a skull.

'My, oh my, oh my,' Solomons murmured. 'For all these years, I've been storing my lawnmower on top of someone's grave.'

72

'Who the fuck are you?' asked Eddie Charnwood. The eyes that looked up from the interview room chair were emotionless, and cold as ice.

'I'm Detective Superintendent Neil McIlhenney, and you are done.'

'What happened to Mackenzie?'

'He's on holiday.'

'On suspension, more like; he's a mug.'

'He's on holiday, and next time you say anything disrespectful about him I'll hit you so fucking hard you'll leave an imprint on the wall behind you.'

'Tough guy.'

'Usually I don't have to be. You can have it either way.'

'You can't touch me.'

McIlhenney turned to DS Wilding. 'Ray,' he said, 'would you step outside for a minute, please?'

'Certainly, sir: as many minutes as you like.'

Charnwood raised his manacled hands. 'Okay, okay. I get the message. Where's Ollie Poole? He should be here by now.'

'Mr Poole has declined to represent you, as is his right. You can nominate another lawyer if you like, but this interview is going ahead right now. We'll do it informally for the moment. We're going to be joined by officers from Dundee: I'll switch on the tape when they get here.'

'So get on with it.'

McIlhenney nodded. 'The first thing I have to tell you is that I wasn't kidding when I said that you're done. We've got a nice fingerprint from Big Ming's doorbell, and from the handle of Joe Falconer's fridge. We're so clever these days that we should be able to extract DNA from them, so be in no doubt, Eddie, you're looking at life imprisonment. The only question is, how long will your tariff be? Guilty pleas usually get you a few years less than if you go to trial.'

'Fuck off.'

'He's not kidding, Eddie,' said Wilding. 'That's how it works.'

'As for the drugs,' the superintendent continued, 'we're not going to bother about them. Soraya's going down for that end of it. Her brothers were the suppliers and she was the distributor, through Gary Starr, Falconer, and maybe other people we don't know about yet. You probably thought when you shot Big Ming and Joe, your own cousin, as we've discovered, that all the potential witnesses were taken care of, but we've got enough circumstantial evidence to send her to Cornton Vale till your boy leaves school . . . maybe longer if we decide to charge her as an accessory to Gary Starr's murder. Who else could have provided the drugs that were used on him, before you sawed the poor bastard's hands off and bled him to death?'

For the first time, Charnwood's arrogance cracked: fear showed in his hard blue eyes. 'I don't know what the fuck you're talking about,' he shouted.

'Sure, pull the other one. You decided to kill Gary Starr when the stunt with the bayonet went wrong. You knew it would attract our attention to his sad wee bookie's shop and that sooner rather than later we'd happen upon his other business. So you killed him in a way that you hoped would make us forget everything else and pin it on the boy with the missing digit.'

'I bloody didn't!'

'Sure you did. What I don't understand is why you left the drugs and the money in the safe for us to find. You had all Saturday to clear it out.'

'I didn't because I didn't fucking kill him.'

'Maybe you just made a mistake, and thought we wouldn't look there. I don't suppose you thought that Ming would blab about his trip to Pamplona either. You may have thought that the drugs racket would survive Starr's death. But once Ming did talk, he and Joe had to go: as the couriers, they could identify Sorry's brothers. When I think about it, we'll probably do her as an accessory there too.'

Charnwood banged his hands on the table. 'Leave her out of this! I'll do you a deal, all right. Sorry never knew what was happening. Her brothers approached me directly, not through her: I set the whole thing up with Gary and Joe. Leave her alone and I'll plead guilty to all that, and to the shootings.'

McIlhenney gazed at him. 'I might consider such an arrangement,' he said slowly. 'But what about Starr?'

'I'm telling the truth about Gary. I didn't kill him. I'd have emptied that safe as soon as I heard he was dead, but I never had a chance. You guys were all over the shop like bugs. I had to act the daft laddie when Mackenzie asked me to open it.' His eyes narrowed. 'You twigged because I knew the combination, didn't you?'

'It helped, but we'd have got you from the prints, and because you'd killed all the other contenders.'

'Not all. How many times do I have to say it? I never killed Gary.'

73

'Hey, big man, you're a star!' exclaimed Mario McGuire.

McIlhenney held the phone slightly further from his ear. 'I don't want to be a Starr: he was left with two bloody stumps where his hands used to be.'

'You can be anything you like. You're telling me that Charnwood's confessed.'

'That's right, to importing and dealing in drugs, and to the murders of Smith and Falconer. He was formally interviewed by me and by Rod Greatorix, the head of CID in Tayside; he admitted the lot on tape, and then he signed a statement, in the presence of a solicitor. He'll be up in the Sheriff Court tomorrow, for a formal remand hearing.'

'What about the wife?'

'She's been released, and her son's been returned to her. We'd have been struggling to charge her anyway, and her husband's specifically exonerated her.'

'We couldn't do her for travelling with a false passport?'

'That would be difficult: it was found in Eddie's possession, not hers, and he would probably say that she thought it was her real one.'

'Fair enough,' said McGuire. 'He might even be telling the truth; maybe she really didn't

395

know anything about it.'

'Remind me, friend,' said McIlhenney, ironically, 'is the Pope a Catholic?'

'Last time I looked. He's still refusing to admit to Starr, you say?'

'Yes, and we don't have any evidence against him, other than strong circumstantial. My theory is that he's worked out that if he does, any judge who heard what was done to him would give him a minimum thirty-year stretch.'

'He'd be right too. Bugger it, we'll settle for what we've got. It's party time in Leith and you're on the bell.'

74

'Going by the remains,' said Max Allan, 'the pathologist is saying that she was about six months pregnant when she was killed.'

'Has she made a stab at a cause of death?' Proud asked.

'She didn't have to: it was quite clear. The back of her head was smashed in. The marks on the skull indicate that he used a hammer. You're not going to believe this, Jimmy, but Mr Solomons told us that when they took over the house, Bothwell had left all his tools behind him in his brand new shed. He's still got them, and there's a hammer among them. Forensics say that it's a match: we've actually found the murder weapon.'

Mario McGuire leaned closer to the conference phone. 'Have your people made any progress on the Ethel Ward disappearance, Mr Allan?'

'Not so far. She had to be alive when they sold Thorny Grove, to sign the conveyance and lodge the money. The old lawyer told me that they moved out on completion day, and not before, but he had no idea where they were headed.'

'Do you still have records of unclaimed female bodies from that time?'

'There was only one: a woman came to the surface of the Clyde, or at least part of her did. She'd been hacked about by a ship's propeller. I had a look at the post-mortem report, but it isn't helpful. The cause of death was drowning, and the age was estimated as late twenties; that's younger than Mrs Bothwell.'

'Any chance of a visual identification from the photographs of the body?'

'Not without the head, Mario: they never found that. It was written off as a suicide and the remains were cremated. To be frank, I don't hold out any hope of tracing the poor woman, but in the light of what we found under Mr Solomons' shed we can assume that she's dead. I've advised the family accordingly.'

'Fine, Max.' Proud sighed. 'I don't imagine they'll spend too much time mourning, from what old Bert told me. How are Mr and Mrs Solomons handling it?'

A chuckle came from the speaker. 'They're loving the sudden fame. The old boy's sold his story to the *Record*. They're running it tomorrow. How about your end of the business, the Spanish wife and Miss Gentle, who thought she was his fiancée?'

'That's not easy: Adolf's been pretty good at covering his tracks. The only address we have for him in this area was out of date by the time of his disappearance.'

'Do you have any thoughts on how we should proceed?'

'Actually,' said McGuire, 'Mr Solomons' story might give us an opening. We've got photographs of Bothwell from old school year-books and the like. Let's get a specialist to work out how he might look now, and give it, and the original, to the *Record* to run with their piece, and then to all the other media immediately afterwards.'

'We'd need Crown Office permission,' his chief constable pointed out.

'No problem: they'll give it without a second thought, but we should let the press have much more than that. So far they only know about the Primrose Jardine investigation. With respect, gentlemen, has the potential magnitude of this dawned on you? We're dealing with a man who'd murdered two, probably three women . . . possibly four, since Annabelle Gentle's been missing for all that time as well . . . by the time he reached his mid-thirties, and we've lost trace of him. We're in pursuit of a serial killer here, and he's had forty bloody years to add to his tally of victims. Don't you think that it's our duty to tell the media the whole story and to ask for their help in tracing him?'

Proud picked up his letter-opener and twirled it in his hand. 'Mario,' he declared, 'I couldn't agree more. Max?'

'Absolutely.'

'Who's going to issue it?'

If it is possible to hear a smile, Mario McGuire swore later that he did at that moment. 'Jimmy,' said ACC Allan, 'there is only one man qualified and entitled to do that, and that's you. Modesty be damned, this is your finest hour as a detective. Get up there and take the credit. You'll let me see a draft of the announcement, Mario?'

'Will do, Max.'

'Speak to you later, then.'

Proud switched off the conference telephone

and swung his chair towards McGuire. 'I really am most embarrassed by all this. When I got into this I'd no idea what would come to the surface. Mario, you brief the press; I'll take a back seat.'

'Are you asking me to refuse a direct order, sir? Don't be shy about it. If I'd done what you've done I'd be up there basking in the fucking glory, but I didn't so I won't. Please, for us, and for our absent friend, you do it.'

The chief smiled and ran a hand across his brow. 'Okay, if you insist. I'd better call him before this goes public, I suppose.'

'That would be a good idea, sir,' said the head of CID. 'And someone else as well.'

'Who's that?'

'The woman who started all this: Annabelle Gentle's daughter.'

75

For several reasons, Alex was glad she had gone to Gullane for the night. It had given Sarah the opportunity to tell her, face to face, why, from her side of the situation, her marriage to Bob had failed. She had been able to have breakfast with her brothers and sister. But most of all, it had got her away from the flat, and from that damn phone. She had to admit to herself, if to nobody else, that the calls had been getting to her. The sense of being hunted was one she had never experienced before, and she did not like it. As she thought about it, sitting in the lunch-time restaurant, waiting for Gina, she felt cold, dispassionate anger welling up inside her: if she was someone's prey, then he was in for a hell of a shock when he caught up with her.

As she looked back over her week, she realised yet again how much she loved her job. It was the central pillar of her life, and she had chosen it as such, for a few more years, at least. She had been given the 'wife and mother' ultimatum when she had been engaged to Andy, and had rejected it, and him. In doing so, she had set herself a single objective: to be a partner in Curle Anthony and Jarvis by the time she was thirty. Already she was the firm's youngest associate, so she was on track: the better you were, the more you were in demand. That overriding purpose allowed her to laugh off all the blips in her social life, even Guy

Luscomb, that conceited, self-satisfied, useless prick. The dual connotation of that thought made her laugh to herself.

Or so she thought. 'Hey,' said Gina Reed. 'What's lit up your day?'

'Oh, nothing.' She laughed again. 'At least not very much. I was thinking of my flexible friend from London, that was all. How's yours been so far?'

Her friend laid a series of bags against the wall next to their table. 'Hell on earth, darling. The shops at this time of year are just unbearable, even during the week.'

Alex pointed to her haul. 'You seem to have battled through, though. I have to confess that this year I'm doing most of my Christmas shopping on the Internet.'

'Who's the big present for this year? Guy?'

'Piss off. He'll get a card if he's lucky. It'll be for my dad, I suppose, but what do you give a man who has everything?'

'A repair kit.'

'They don't make them for what's broke in his life. I had a heart-to-heart with my soon-to-be- ex-stepmother last night. She's making preparations to go back to America and concentrate on doctoring.'

Gina frowned. 'You never told me that was on the cards.'

'Sorry, but it's been a deep, dark family secret. They're still not putting it too widely about, so keep it to yourself till you hear it from someone else. There will be talk, no doubt about it: all sorts of suggestions will be made, and if any of them are made to you I'd be grateful if you'd say they're splitting up by mutual consent, no third parties involved.'

'And is that true?'

'In time it may not appear so, but it is.'

Gina rubbed her hands together. 'Ooow,' she squeaked, 'that means your dad's back in the market-place. Talk about interesting older men!'

'My dad is off limits, girlfriend, so no trying to pull him at my housewarming.'

'Bitch. In that case I'll have to make do with that new neighbour of yours. What's his name again?'

'Griff, you mean?'

'That's the man: very tasty.'

'I think Spring might have something to say about that.'

'I sincerely hope not: she's his sister.'

Alex gasped. 'His . . . How do you know that?'

'My firm did the conveyancing on his flat. I only found out about it yesterday when I mentioned to the partner involved that you had a new place. He spilled the whole tin of beans. Trust me, they're bro' and sis', house-sharing.'

'Mmm. He borrowed my corkscrew last night.'

'Hey! How phallic can you get? Was it the first move, do you think?'

'Highly unlikely, after he saw me saying goodbye to my unshaven one-night stand.'

'Yes, slut,' said Gina, cheerfully. She turned in her chair and called to a waiter: 'Any chance of a couple of menus over here? We've come for lunch, not dinner.' He scowled at her, but handed her two large plastic cards.

'You know what I like about you, pal?' Alex laughed. 'It's your subtlety.'

'Speaking of which, I had to be subtle in tracking down my wayward cousin. I called Nolan and asked him where Raymond was. I've never known my favourite uncle be short with me before but he was. All he said was 'I've no idea,' then hung up on me. I wound up having to phone round all the cousins. Eventually, one of them, Sugar . . . and before you ask, yes, that is her real name . . . came up with a mobile number for him.'

'And?'

'And so I called it. I had a pint with him last night in a pub up in Nicholson Street; bloody freezing it was, by the way. The heating had packed in. We talked about this and that, and the next thing. I asked what he was doing with himself, and he said that he had some business on the go, an investment in a nightclub, and in a new one that's opening down at the foot of Dundas Street.'

'How did he look?'

'Older than his years, but otherwise okay. Somewhere during the third pint, I finally managed to work your name into the conversation, to see how he'd react. I have to say that 'disinterested' is the best description I can come up with. I told him you were doing really well with your firm. He just shrugged and said, 'Surprise, surprise. I'll bet she's got them all by the balls.' Sorry, dear, that's a direct quote.'

'If I had they'd all be a bigger handful than his,' Alex grunted vengefully.

'Tut, tut! That's my young cousin you're speaking about. Anyway, I came out and told him that you'd been having nasty phone calls.'

'Jesus, Gina, I just wanted you to track him down for me, not confront him with it.'

'And how exactly were you planning to do that?'

Alex's reply was stalled by the surly waiter who came to take their orders. When he had gone to fetch two caprese salads, she said, 'I hadn't worked that out yet, but still . . . '

'Well, it's done. When I told him he just laughed and said, 'Tough fucking luck.' I told him it wasn't funny, and that when your dad's guys traced whoever was doing it they'd have him for breakfast, lunch and high tea, then make soup with what was left. He didn't have anything to say to that.'

'So what do you think? Could it be him?'

Gina frowned, unusually serious. 'I'd love to say 'No,' because he is my kin. I'd even like to say 'Yes,' because then it could all be sorted. But honestly, love, I just don't know.'

76

'One of the great skills of police work, Jimmy,' said Bob Skinner, his voice sounding weary on the phone, 'and probably of life, lies in knowing, instinctively, which can is the one with the worms in it. Thus forewarned, you can decide whether or not you want to open it.'

'That's as cynical as I've ever heard you, my friend,' the chief constable replied. 'What's up?'

'I'm tired, and I'm three thousand miles away from home. Most of all, I'm borne down by the knowledge that however hard guys like you and me labour to protect the innocent and bring the guilty to justice, there's another level where different rules apply, and where expediency is all that matters. I feel dirty, because I've become a part of it myself, and worse, because I've dragged a pleasant, upright young woman into it with me and let her see things that she'll have nightmares about for the rest of her life. She didn't belong in the dark, and I brought her into it.'

'That's not your fault, Bob.'

'Ah, but it is, it is. When Evelyn Grey asked me to do this investigation for him, I knew what was inside the can. Worms? Snakes, Jimmy; fucking cobras. I could have said, 'No, thank you,' but I didn't: I chose to open it.'

'Have you killed them all?'

'All but one. There's a great big king cobra at

the head of it all: I've still got to take care of him.'

'That sounds like a tall order. Do you not want to call it quits and come home?'

'Yes, but I've got to do this. I've got to finish it.'

'How are you going to kill a king cobra?'

'How else? I'm going to charm him. Then when he isn't expecting it . . . I'm going to cut his damned head off.'

As Proud listened to his friend, Kevin O'Malley's report thrust itself back into his mind. To the chief he sounded lonely, more tense and strung out than he had ever known him. 'Bob,' he said, 'your counsellor has recommended to me that you should be given time off: a six-month sabbatical, he called it, to get you out of the front line. I'm inclined to agree with him. What do you say?'

'I'm not in the front line, Jimmy; I'm somewhere behind the fucking lines and I'm not even sure who the enemy is any more. Christ, I might be the enemy myself.'

'Then maybe you should take some time to yourself and work it out.'

'We'll talk about it when I get back. But not sick leave: I will not take sick leave.'

'I'm not suggesting that: it'll be a formal sabbatical. I'll send you off to write a thesis on policing; I can arrange for Edinburgh University to publish it.'

Three thousand miles away, Skinner yawned. 'Maybe,' he said. 'Apart from anything else, it would let me spend some time with the kids when they need it, to get them used to the idea of Sarah being gone. Like I say, we'll talk about it.' He paused. 'So, this business of yours: you've spoken to the Friend woman, you said. How did she take it when you told her that you were certain her mother was dead?'

'She was disappointed, more for her daughter than for herself. She's never known her mother, and she's a strong woman, so she'll get over it. At least she's found an aunt and uncle she never knew she had.'

'And how about you? How do you feel, now that your investigation's hit the wall?'

'You don't think we're going to find him?'

'No. Mario's got you doing all the right things, but I'll be surprised if trawling other unsolved crimes gets you a result. It's a miracle that Bothwell got away with it three times: an obviously clever guy like him wouldn't push his luck.'

'But if he's a serial killer, Bob, surely he couldn't stop himself?'

'He isn't a serial killer, not as the term is commonly understood. From what you've told me, he did it for money. His first wife was wealthy and her fortune disappeared with her; you know that Primrose was left money by her mother and you know that the Spanish woman's father was in the hotel business. It's quite possible that after he'd got as much out of her as he could, he killed her and moved on. Maybe he took Annabelle with him; she didn't have a penny so she doesn't fit the pattern. Maybe she was the love of his life. Maybe,

408

somewhere, she still is.'

'You think so?'

'I don't know. I'm just airing possibilities, that's all. But that's all they will ever be, for his trail's gone cold, unless I'm wrong and your public appeal does get a response, or unless there's something you've overlooked.'

'I'm pretty sure there isn't, and if there was, someone else would have noticed it.'

'If it's in the file, that's true. I've got to go now, Jimmy. Why don't you take some time alone, and think everything through. Goodbye now, see you soon.'

Proud hung up and called his secretary. 'Gerry, ask Mr Haggerty to postpone our meeting for half an hour.'

77

McIlhenney stared across his desk at his friend. 'I know this isn't the first of April. I know this isn't Friday the thirteenth. So why the hell are you sitting in my office taking the piss out of me?'

'Would that I were; it's all too bloody true. On his QC's advice, Eddie bloody Charnwood has withdrawn his statement. He's saying that it was extracted under threats made against his wife. Now he's pleading not guilty to everything and he's going to trial. I've just had the Crown Office on the phone breaking the bad news.'

'Shit. Just when I was starting to look forward to Christmas.'

'Aye, but there's worse.'

'There can't be.'

'There is. The Crown Agent is getting nervous about the evidence. He's saying that Charnwood opened the safe of his own free will, which doesn't exactly point to guilt. He's also pointing out that Big Ming was a work colleague and Joe Falconer was a relation, so his prints could have been on their premises from perfectly innocent visits.'

'Nobody goes to the Wild West innocently, man.'

'I know that and you know that, but a gullible jury might not.'

'They're not going to let him walk, are they?'

'No, they're going to trial, but what they are saying is that, just to make sure, we need a witness.'

'We had three, but they're all dead.'

'Yes; that's why they don't count. The Crown Agent wants one who still has a pulse.'

78

The good thing about Friday was that everyone had left the office on time to prepare for the corporate department Christmas do in the Dome. The arrangements were in the hands of Pippa, one of the secretaries, who had organised for everyone to be collected by taxi; in Alex's case the pick-up time was eight fifteen.

Before letting herself into her apartment building, just after five, Alex checked her letterbox to find a bill, a credit-card statement, a Christmas card with a Tayside postmark, and her waiter's friend corkscrew, wrapped in a note of thanks from Griff and Spring. *Damn*, she thought, *I was hoping he'd return it in person!*

There were messages waiting on the red-blinking phone, but she ignored them as she opened her mail. The card was from 'Andy, Karen and Danielle Martin': she smiled at the baby's inclusion in the greeting, then realised that it was the first she had received from Andy since their split. She went straight to the Christmas list she had left lying on her desk and added the family's name.

As she finished, she glanced through the window: night had fallen, but there was enough light from the living room to let her see her narrow terrace, which stood out above the Water of Leith, fast-flowing with the recent snow-melt that flowed down from the Pentlands. In one corner she could make out a strange shape. Curious, she flicked on the weatherproof bulkhead light; involuntarily, her hand flew to her mouth as she saw that it was a sleeping black cat. *How the hell did that get there?* she asked herself.

As she opened the glass door and stepped outside, she expected the animal to stir, but it stayed motionless. She bent to touch it, and as she did the light above her head was caught and reflected by its open eyes, shining on them as if on twin pools, tiny but unfathomably deep. She had seen such eyes before, when she was fifteen and had insisted on staying with her elderly and ailing Siamese, Shorty, as the vet put him to sleep. 'It's best like this,' he had said. 'Sometimes an old cat will creep from its home and hide when it senses it's going to die. You wouldn't have liked that, Alex, because you'd never have known for sure.'

Yet this did not look like an old cat. 'You poor wee thing,' she whispered. She stroked its head, feeling no movement in return. She touched its collar; it was strange and rough on her fingertips. She frowned and tried to lift up its head, but it had stiffened in death, so instead she rolled it on to its side, and saw that it was no collar but a length of twine knotted round its neck. The animal had been garrotted.

She jumped to her feet, shivering, stifling the urge to scream. 'How the hell did it get there?' she gasped. There was no way on to the terrace other than through her apartment, or through that of Griff and Spring, with which it adjoined.

413

She backed away, into her living room, thinking as fast as she could. Could it have been theirs, her neighbours'?

She shuddered at the idea of living next door to animal torturers, until she remembered something that Spring had said in the only conversation they had had, that they were sad because they had had to leave their pets behind in Cape Town . . . That was it, they were from South Africa.

Could it have come from one of the four flats above, none of which had terraces? Maybe someone had had a bad-hair day, throttled the cat and chucked it out of the window without waiting to hear the splash as it hit the river. Hardly, but if so, what to do about it? Put a notice on the small bulletin board in the entrance hall? *'Found, on Alex's balcony, one deceased moggie. Will the owner please reclaim it.'* She stifled a slightly hysterical giggle.

What to do? Should she call the police? And have them interview everyone in the place, with all the bad feeling that could create? Hell, no. She switched off the light and stepped back outside. She took a quick look across the river to make sure that there was no one on the walkway on the other side, then stooped quickly, grabbed the animal by the scruff of the neck, picked it up, and dropped it over the railing. 'God bless you,' she whispered; in her eyes, every creature deserved a benediction.

Back inside, in the warmth, she locked the door and drew the curtains, shutting out the night. 'I reckon drink is called for,' she muttered, 'but first . . . ' She walked through to her bathroom and washed her hands as thoroughly as she ever had, then headed for the kitchen. The cava had been returned to the fridge the night before, less the glass she had poured to go with her pizza, only to pour most of it down the sink before driving to Gullane; it was past its best, but there were still a few bubbles to be seen as she filled a flute to the brim.

The red light was still blinking, insistently, annoyingly. She pushed the play button; the synthetic voice told her that the first message had been received at ten thirty-two; she started as she heard the voice.

'*Alex, this is Raymond Weston. My idiot cousin Gina sought me out last night. She told me you've been having breather calls, and without putting it in so many words, she left me feeling like I'm top of the list of suspects. So I'm calling to cross my name off: it wasn't me. I don't feel bad about you. Why should I? You're still the best shag I ever had.*'

She hit the replay button and listened to the message again, trying to read his voice, as if she could measure his sincerity level, then played it a third time before moving on.

'*Ho, ho, ho!*' the second message began, scrambling her frayed nerves for a moment. '*This is Santa, telling you that you are the lucky winner of a trip to Disney World.*' She allowed the computer-dialled, taped American voice to prattle on for a few seconds, before muttering, 'Fuck off, Santa,' and pushing the delete button.

The third call had come in at four minutes

past three. She recognised the breathing at once; she was on the point of wiping it, when he spoke. '*I hate cats too,*' he hissed. Then the line went dead.

An uncontrollable shiver ran through her. She sat in her swivel chair and hugged herself, as if she was trying to hold the warmth within her body. She stared at the red light, until her eyes misted over, and, for the first time in longer than she could remember, she gave in to tears.

She was still trying to banish them when the phone rang again. 'Hi, kid,' said her father when she answered. 'How're you doing?'

With a great effort, she stopped herself from telling him what had happened. 'I'm fine,' she replied.

'No more crap? I've been worrying about you.'

'Honest, I'm okay. Dad, hold on for a minute: there's something on the cooker and I need to turn it down.' She covered the microphone with her hand for a few seconds, until she had composed herself, then returned to the call. 'Really,' she continued, 'it's all right. Where are you?' she asked, getting off the topic of her trouble as quickly as she could.

'At the moment, we are just getting off a plane in Washington DC. That's all I can tell you right now.'

'When will you be home?'

'As soon as I can. Are you really sure you're all right?'

She made herself sound annoyed by his persistence. 'Dad, I'm fine. How are you? You sound tired.'

'Jet-lag, kid, that's all. I didn't sleep much last night, and not at all on the plane; I guess I'm not as young as I used to be.'

'Now you're worrying me. That's the first time I've ever heard you say anything like that. I wish you'd just turn around and come home now: with everything that's happening in your life, you don't need this.'

'Maybe not, but I can handle it.'

'I saw Sarah last night,' Alex blurted out.

'You did?' Bob sounded surprised.

'She invited me out for a chat. On reflection, it was a good idea: we're fine now.'

'How was she?'

'Anxious to be off, I'd say. Pops, it must be awkward for the two of you living in the same house. I was wondering, when you come back, would you like to move into my spare room?'

'I dunno. I'd like the kids to have as much time as they can with their parents together.'

'But you're not together,' she pointed out. 'You may be under the same roof, but you've separated.'

'True,' he admitted. 'I'll think about it. If I do, maybe those calls will stop.'

'Maybe.'

'So you're still having them!' he exclaimed.

She cursed herself for letting her guard slip. 'There was another,' she admitted.

'Just one?'

'Well, two.'

'Right, in that case the intercept goes back on, and no arguments.'

Suddenly, Alex felt too weary to argue. Besides, there was that bloody cat: that had been more than annoying, it had been scary. 'Okay, if you say so,' she conceded. 'I'll phone Neil.'

79

James Proud sat in his armchair and closed his eyes. In his mind he went over every step of his investigation looking for a loose end that had not been tied off. He had been thinking about it for most of the afternoon, and now, well into the evening.

As he did, a feeling grew within him, a sense that there was something he was overlooking, something glaringly obvious, that a real detective would have picked up in an instant. A real detective, sure, not a pen-pusher cop like him. He made pictures of every scene, every meeting, every phone call, but nothing stood out; he could follow Bothwell's trail to bloody Kirkliston, but no further; nobody knew where he and Montserrat had lived in Edinburgh after that. Nobody.

He sat bolt upright in his chair. 'You bloody fool, Proud!' he roared, as he sprang to his feet. 'Chrissie, I'm going out for a while,' he told his wife, as he paced out into the hall, not realising that she was in the kitchen and could not hear a word he said.

Snatching his coat from its hook he rushed out of the front door, without looking back, and stepped into his car. He knew where he was going; he knew exactly where he was going, and why the hell had it taken him so long to work it out? He swore that he would never criticise a detective officer again.

It was a long trip, across the city; the consolation was that when he arrived at his destination there were few cars parked in the narrow street, and so he was able to pull up immediately outside. He strode up the path to the front door and pressed the bell, hard. It took a while for the man inside to answer, but Proud had expected that: he was very old.

'James,' he said, as he saw him standing there. 'How good to see you again.'

'I'm glad I caught you in, Mr Goddard. I was afraid that you'd be out on your bike.'

'The road's a little too slippery for that, and anyway, I tend not to cycle after dark. You can't trust drivers these days, you know. Come on in. Will you have tea?'

The chief constable followed his one-time teacher into his comfortable old house. 'I'm in a bit of a rush, I'm afraid,' he replied. 'There's something I need to ask you about old Adolf.'

Goddard's eyebrows rose. 'Indeed! I've been reading about him in the newspapers. What a remarkable turn of events. To think that he was on my staff for all those years, and instructing children, after doing that: it's appalling. And you think he killed both his other wives as well?'

'We're certain. It's about Montserrat that I need to ask you. When we spoke last, you told me that you went to look for him after he failed to return to school.'

'Yes.'

'Can you remember where? The only address we have for him in Edinburgh is out of date.'

'That's easy. He lived in the very next street. In fact he lived in the very same house that awful man was killed in, number twenty-two Swansea Street.'

80

The ability to sleep on board aircraft had eluded Skinner all his life. He had envied Shannon as she dozed in the next seat, while he fidgeted, locked into the in-flight entertainment system as a means of passing the time, but ultimately switching off a movie that even James Andrew would have found puerile.

Nonetheless the flight had allowed him valuable thinking time, away from the distractions of the previous week. The one thing from which he could not escape was the worry over his daughter's telephone persecutor, but he took comfort in the fact that she was not too far from the ferocious protection of McGuire and McIlhenney, and also in her ability to handle herself in most situations.

He had forced her situation to one side and thought about his own. There was no mystery any more: Piers Frame's answer to his question had simply confirmed what he had known already. In London nobody was under threat, other than those who deserved to be.

In the US the situation was slightly different: people in a corner were unpredictable, often dangerously so, and especially if they saw a way out. He looked at Shannon again, and reached a decision.

The flight had touched down just before midday at Dulles International. The diplomatic passports that had exempted them from security at Heathrow worked their magic again at US Immigration. He had just finished calling Alex when they were approached by a bright-eyed young man in a Brooks Brothers suit that was pure Ivy League, made, almost certainly, in the Far East. 'My name's Ryan,' he announced. 'I'm from the embassy.'

The twenty-five-mile drive from the airport into the capital proved to be a guided tour, but Skinner was happy to let their escort do the talking, and he in turn was sufficiently experienced not to ask any questions. When they reached 3100 Massachusetts Avenue, they were handed over to another sharp suit. From the breadth of the shoulders that it enclosed, the Scot guessed that the wearer was not the cultural attaché.

'I'm Lee Ferry,' he told them, as he led them into a small office behind Reception, 'head of security for the building.'

'Has my package arrived?' asked Skinner.

'Yes.' Ferry unlocked a desk drawer, removed it, and handed it over.

The DCC ripped off the brown-paper wrapping to reveal a box. He opened it and took out the pistol that he had found on board the *Bulrush*; it had been fitted with a significant addition . . . a silencer. He ejected the magazine from the butt, checked its contents and replaced it with a satisfied nod. He was unaware that Shannon was staring at him.

'You have a destination?' the security chief asked.

'Yes, and a route. All I need is a car.'

'With diplomatic plates?'

'Preferably.'

'No problem. When do you want to leave?'

'Right now.'

'You don't have time to meet the ambassador?'

Skinner smiled. 'I doubt if he would want to meet me, Mr Ferry.'

'Maybe not,' the security chief conceded. 'Sir, I'm not asking what you're doing here, but if you wish, I'll go with you.'

'Thanks, but no. I'm going alone.' He turned to his companion. 'I'm afraid I mean that, Inspector. You've done a fine job, and I'm sorry to cut you out at the end of the road, but there are a few ways this could turn out and none of them are pretty. I need total freedom of action and don't ask what I mean. We're booked into the Jefferson Hotel; check in, do some sightseeing while there's daylight left, and I'll see you when I get back.'

She frowned. 'You do mean 'when', boss, don't you, not 'if'?'

'Of course I do. Don't read too much into the gun: it's a precaution, that's all. Lee, where's the car?'

'Out back, sir.' Ferry hesitated. 'Can I ask you one thing?'

'Sure, but I don't promise to answer.'

'Does anyone in this city have any knowledge of what you're doing here?'

'Yes. The National Security adviser has; she may have told the President, or she may not. That's her call. In her shoes, I wouldn't. Now get me on the road, please.'

424

81

Edinburgh is a city of seasons. It is most famous for its summer festivals, which span the month of August, but when Christmas approaches it takes on a special atmosphere. As night falls it seems to come alive, its centre taking on a funfair atmosphere, with its Ferris wheel, skating rink and attractions, which seem to grow in number every year.

As the CAJ party spilled out of the Dome into the brightly decorated George Street, it was caught up in the Saturday-night mêlée, and swept towards Princes Street. Pippa had appointed herself entertainments convener, and had determined that they would head for a nightclub in Market Street, on the other side of Waverley Bridge. Alex tagged along, although she had rarely felt less like celebrating: several times during the meal she had found herself staring into space, hearing that creepy voice in her head . . . 'I hate cats too' . . . or picturing herself dropping the dead animal over the terrace rail. She had spent much of the evening working out how it had got there, and had decided that it must have been thrown from the walkway on the other side of the river. There could be no other answer.

On reflection, she was glad that she had allowed her father to persuade her to reinstate the telephone tap. What had been a nuisance before had been raised to a new level. She was not afraid, as such, but deeply unsettled, and it was reassuring to know that Stevie Steele and his team were watching over her, even if it was from a distance. She had considered giving the evening out a miss, and staying locked up in the fortress of her flat, the one place she felt truly safe. When she had bought the place she had doubted whether the monitored alarm system that came with it, first year free of charge, was really necessary in an apartment block, but it had proved itself. Nonetheless she had been so freaked out earlier that she had actually phoned Guy Luscomb. With her father on his American assignment, he was the closest thing to a man in her life. She had called his London number, and had actually been pleased when he had answered.

'Hello, Alexandra, lovey,' he had gushed. 'What a surprise, and what a coincidence: I was just thinking of you. To what do I owe this sublime pleasure?'

'Oh, nothing really: I picked up your call on my answering system, and, well, I just thought I'd return it.'

'Missing me, eh?'

'You could say that,' she had lied. 'I'm feeling a bit lonely, that's all. I suppose I needed to hear a familiar voice.'

'Any time, darling. Catch a flight and you can see its owner, face to face.'

'I'm not that lonely,' she had said, and had regretted it immediately. It was unnecessary: it wasn't Guy's fault that he was a prat.

It had rolled off him, though. 'Any time you are, then.'

'Thanks. Got to go now.'

'Big night out, what? Who's the lucky chap?'

'I don't know yet. 'Bye.'

At one point during the evening, she had actually considered picking up a guy in the Dome who had given her the eye all through the meal, but that would have been the stuff of which office gossip was made, and so she had put the notion aside.

She was still thinking about him when she felt an arm link through hers, and someone move into step alongside her. 'Alex, boss,' said Pippa, 'all your colleagues, me included, have reached a conclusion. You are working too damned hard. If you don't mind me saying so, it's turning you into a really wet blanket. So here's what we're going to do about it. When we get to this club, we're going to get you rat-arsed. Are you up for that?'

She looked down at the pert face. 'You know, Pipster,' she said, 'I rather think I am.'

82

The embassy car was a blue Chevrolet Corvette, with a six-litre engine: 'In case you have to be somewhere else in a hurry,' as Lee Ferry put it. It was equipped with a DVD-driven navigation system, rendering Skinner's route map unnecessary. He switched it on, fed in his destination, and let it guide him out of the centre of the city and on to US Highway 50, heading east. He knew that the diplomatic plates made him virtually immune to speed cops, but he set the cruise control at only seventy-five, more or less the average speed on the Interstate road.

He had been travelling for just over forty-five minutes when the mighty Chesapeake Bay Bridge came into sight and with it a toll station. He cut his speed, chose a booth and rolled slowly towards it. He was almost there when a red Plymouth overtook him on the run-in and screeched to a halt. As it cut in front of him, he caught a glimpse of the driver's face in profile, the most fleeting of glimpses, but it was enough for recognition. He was astonished, but only by the odds against his seeing that one face among so many.

He watched the car as it overshot the toll booth. For a moment Skinner thought that the driver would not stop, but he reversed back and thrust a bill out of the window at the attendant, who took it, checked it carefully, then handed over change. The driver snatched at it, so hastily that a note dropped to the ground, but instead of opening the door to pick it up, he floored the throttle and roared off.

As the Scot approached, the toll collector left his booth and picked up the discarded banknote. 'Unbelievable,' he said, as he climbed back on to his perch, 'absolutely unbelievable. Guy's in so much of hurry he almost didn't pay, and then when he did he threw his money away. You can go through, buddy, he's taken care of it for you.'

'Thanks,' said Skinner, 'but let me tell you something. In this world, absolutely nothing is unbelievable: that's something of which I've just been reminded.'

For a moment he thought of gunning the Corvette and pursuing the much slower Plymouth, but he decided against it. Instead, he blended in with the traffic and drove sedately over the enormous waterway crossing.

There was no rush: he knew where the driver was headed, and he knew more than that. He knew that he was expected as he drove steadily down the Interstate, smiling as it turned into country roads winding across flatlands taking him east, with the afternoon sun shining behind him, thinking, as he closed on his destination, of nothing but his mission, and hoping that his judgement had been sound.

83

It was late in the afternoon, but the scene-of-crime team had set up floodlights. Proud, McIlhenney and DI Arthur Dorward stood in the back door of Gary Starr's villa, watching the technician as he swept the garden with a ground-penetrating radar sensor. Twice, they had produced readings that led officers to dig; the first excavation had unearthed a paint can, the second a two-pound coin. 'Our difficulty,' said Dorward, 'is that there is no sensor that'll detect bones. We have to look for metal, jewellery, belt buckles and such, or for disturbed earth, which is probably a non-runner after forty years.'

As he spoke the technician stopped and turned towards him. 'That's it, sir,' he called out. 'That's as much as I can do; I've been over the lot and there's nothing detectable here.'

Proud stepped out into the garden, with McIlhenney following, and strode across to a greenhouse that stood in the corner of the garden that was most exposed to the sun. 'You haven't covered this,' he said.

'The sensor can't penetrate concrete, sir,' the man replied.

'And this is a modern structure, Chief,' McIlhenney added. 'From the looks of it, it's only been here for a few years.'

'Perhaps, Neil, but was that concrete base used for something else before it?' He looked over his shoulder at Dorward. 'Arthur, I want this dismantled and the base broken up.'

The three senior officers retreated inside the house, watching through the kitchen window as the greenhouse was emptied of the chilli plants, which had been, apparently, its late owner's hobby, and as its sections were unbolted and laid flat on the grass. Then, just as their Strathclyde counterparts had done, the team set to work breaking up its solid floor, attacking it methodically until it was in pieces small enough for them to pick it apart with their gloved hands.

Almost all of the broken lumps had been removed, when the workers stepped back, as if at a command; one of them turned towards the house and beckoned. Again, the chief constable led the way outside. 'What is it?' he asked.

'Take a look, sir,' said the officer who had waved them over, as his colleagues backed off, clearing the area of their shadows.

Proud crouched beside the fresh earth, and saw . . . the edge of a rolled carpet protruding through it. He knelt and began to scoop out the soil until enough of the fabric had been freed for him to grab a corner and yank it away, revealing, unmistakably, the skeleton of a human foot.

84

Dover, the capital of Delaware, first state in the Union, presented a complete contrast to its English namesake, as Skinner swung the Corvette off the Dupont Highway into East Lookerman Street. There were no white cliffs in sight. The buildings were all low-rise; they were old and seemed to be built either of wood or brick. A few hundred yards down, he obeyed the navigation system and turned left, driving past the Legislative Hall, and on until he reached the long and treeshaded Duke of Melbourne Street.

The house he sought was at the end of the avenue, two-storeyed, wooden-faced, with a veranda extending across its full width. He knew it before he reached it; there was a red Plymouth parked outside.

He drew to a halt a hundred yards away, looking up and down as he stepped out into the cool December afternoon. The street was deserted; and there were no signs of any watchers behind curtains. He smiled: it was perfect, so perfect. What could spoil it? he asked himself. The answer was obvious: if the wrong man was waiting in the house, that might put a considerable damper on his day. The people he was dealing with were experienced, and demonstrably dangerous. Walking up to the front door and ringing the bell would not be the wisest thing he had ever done.

He considered his options for a few moments, then slid back inside the low-slung car, switched on the engine, and drove on, past the house, turning right into Malmsey Street, and stopping after a hundred yards. He took a small pair of binoculars from a tote bag on the passenger seat and studied the house from the rear: it stood on a big plot, enclosed by a very low perimeter fence over which he could see easily. All the windows on the upper storey were shuttered, but there was one on the ground floor that was open and uncurtained. He focused the glasses on it, making out a big oak dresser with plates displayed, but no sign of any movement within. 'Kitchen,' he murmured. 'Climbing in the window's not an option, so what else?'

He studied the building for a little longer, looking for potential entry points, until he saw, not far from the three steps that led up to the back door, a hatchway similar to that he had opened on board the *Bulrush*. 'Cellar,' he murmured. 'Let's just hope it's empty.'

He stepped out of the car once more, his bag slung over his shoulder, and walked back up the tarmac sidewalk for a few yards, before stepping over the low fence and sprinting across the open lawn to the doorway. Crouching beside it, he saw that it was secured by what appeared to be a simple mortise lock. Using Amanda Dennis's toolkit, he set to work: it was more complicated than it looked, but within a minute he heard a satisfying click.

He swung the hatch open: the cellar was in darkness, but he was well prepared. His flashlight revealed a small sloping ramp, leading down to a concrete floor. He looked into the big den and saw wineracks, tools, a lawnmower, a rowing-machine, free weights and a bench, and against the far wall, a cabinet containing two shotguns, a hunting rifle, an M4 carbine and a fifth firearm, which he recognised as the new state-of-the-art XM8 assault weapon. Beside it was a second case, containing five pistols; there was an empty space where a sixth might have been. 'Jesus,' he whispered, 'and I got in here with a toothpick. Something's not right.' He looked at the inside of the door and spotted an alarm sensor. 'Deactivated?' he asked himself. 'Or is it a silent system? Ah, bugger it!' He slid down the ramp and closed the hatch behind him.

The area in which he found himself approximated to half the floor area of the house above. He saw a door facing him and opened it to find himself in a small corridor, with another door, and with a flight of stairs rising to his left. He paused, reached into the tote bag once again and took out the silenced Sig Sauer. As he felt its weight, he thought of its owner, and of their respective fates, sealed by a shot in the dark, and suddenly he realised that his heart was pounding.

He was seized by a strong urge to get out of there, to jump back into the Corvette and leave the dust of Dover behind him. He thought of his family, the kids who needed him now more than they ever had, and he asked himself what the fuck he was doing in a stranger's cellar with a gun in his hand. But he knew the answer to that question also. Until the thing was resolved, and he had dealt with what was above, he would never be safe. He had never considered fear before; having been brought to it, he found to his great surprise that it made him angry, with himself, for lowering his guard to allow it into his presence, but most of all with those who were its cause. He secured the bag on his shoulder, shone his flashlight up the staircase, and followed its beam.

The door at the top had no lock, only a simple roller catch. He stood on a narrow landing and listened: somewhere in the house, music was playing, but not close, not immediately outside. He wrapped the fingers of his left hand round the handle, put his thumb on the door jamb and eased it open a fraction. He saw a sliver of a hallway, and beyond that a front door, slightly ajar, the curtain beside it waving in the breeze. He widened the gap a little; a long mirror came into his field of vision; framed within it he saw the back view of a man, standing, his shoulders rounded and slumped, in a bay window, looking out into the street. Loosely, in his right hand, he held a revolver.

Skinner stepped noiselessly into the hall and raised his own gun, gripping it in both hands. 'Titus,' he called out, his voice sounding above the music, 'drop your weapon, and raise . . . '

The speed of Armstead's reaction almost took him by surprise. He spun round on the ball of his right foot; his pistol coming up towards firing

435

position. It was almost there when the Scot shot him.

The bullet struck his right elbow, knocking him backwards and sending the pistol flying, clattering on to the wooden floor. Instinctively he clutched at the wound, his face twisted with pain. He stared up at the intruder, fear in his eyes. 'I was only expecting one,' he gasped. 'Who the hell are you?'

'I'm what passes for the good guy in this situation,' Skinner replied. As he spoke, he felt unexpected elation, as if a weight had been lifted from him. 'I wasn't going to shoot you, Titus . . . at least not right away.'

'What does that mean?'

'It means that if you do what I ask, I'll walk out of here, and so will you. Where is he?'

Armstead nodded towards the floor. 'In here.'

'I'll tell you what, I'm feeling ultra-cautious today, so why don't you just come over here and stand in front of me, in the line of fire, while I take a look. Maybe you two decided to surprise me by teaming up.'

'Oh, we didn't, buddy, but if it makes you happy.' He did as he had been instructed, holding his bleeding arm as he shuffled over to form a human shield as they stepped through the archway that led into the living room. There was no need for the precaution: the corpse of Miles Hassett lay in the middle of the floor, a single bullet-hole in the middle of its chest. Bizarrely, it was covered with feathers, from the devastated cushion that Armstead had used as a silencer.

Beside the body, Skinner saw a long-bladed knife.

'Do you know who sent him after you?' he asked.

'His father, I guess; my old buddy.'

'Technically, but actually it was me. But to square things between us, it was me that warned you he was coming, too, through Merle Gower in your London office.'

'Clever.' The American grimaced. 'I take him out and you come in to pick up the pieces. But what if it had gone the other way?'

'He'd still have been taken out, by somebody if not by me. But I had faith in you, Titus. An old soldier like you against a poser like him? I'll back experience every time. Now, sit down.' He took a white linen cover from a table by the window and tossed it to him. 'Here, use that to stop the bleeding.'

'Thanks.' Armstead slumped into an armchair. As Skinner stepped across to silence the radio, he rolled up his right sleeve, gingerly, and bound the cloth round the hole in his arm. 'Feels like the bone's shattered,' he said. 'Was that a lucky shot?'

'It was for you; I was aiming at your hand but I missed. If it hadn't hit you there it would have gone clean through your chest.'

'Remind me to salute you some time . . . if I can ever bend my arm again.'

'Come on, no hard feelings. Give me credit for a bit of class too; I used your own gun. I found it on board your step-son's houseboat. It's a CIA weapon of choice, with no serial number, so I assume it came from you.'

'You assume right. What do you want from me?'

'I want the truth, the whole truth, and fuck all else, as a colleague of mine named Haggerty is fond of saying. And I want it on this.' He produced a camcorder from his bag, and displayed it. 'But first,' he continued, as he produced a collapsible tripod, 'I want you to tell me why you put Adam . . . I'll call him that, because that's how I knew him . . . on your payroll.'

'Why not?' the wounded man replied. 'I have discretionary use of considerable funds, and my step-son was in the same business as me. As a matter of fact, I mentored him; I followed his career all the way through, and once he had made his reputation as a killer in the SAS, I used my contacts to get him into the intelligence world. Why shouldn't he have worked for me as well as you? We're both on the same side, and after the same people. Reviving his old identity and letting him make a little money out of the business seemed sensible to both of us.' Titus Armstead stopped, his heavy-lidded eyes narrowing. 'You knew Moses; in that case I know who you are now. He told me once about a Scotch buddy he had; a cop, tough bastard. Is that you?'

Skinner nodded.

'Yeah, I guess. He said you were the scariest fucker he ever met in his life . . . apart from me, that is, but I guess I'm getting old.'

85

'Another Saturday night.' Alex found herself singing the familiar song quietly in the back of the cab as it cruised through Comely Bank just after ten o'clock. When she had awakened, uncomfortably, on Pippa's couch, she had felt better in her life, but despite her mild headache, the night out had done her good, and the crisp clear winter morning was lifting her spirits with every moment. It was her habit on Saturdays to go out to Gullane to see the kids, but this one was going to be different: this, she was determined, was the day when her trouble was going to end. She would lock herself in her flat, she would wait for the phone to ring, and she would trust the police to nail her perpetrator, good and hard.

Despite Raymond Weston's denial, she still harboured a nagging suspicion that he was her stalker, more by default than anything else, for she had no other suspects. He was cocky, he was arrogant, and thinking back to their brief relationship, she had suspected then that there was a dark vein of cruelty running through him. Good luck to him: she thought of him in a small room with Mario McGuire and Neil McIlhenney and wondered how self-assured he would be then.

She told the taxi driver to drop her at a convenience store close to her apartment, where she bought a copy of *The Times*, a bottle of Lucozade and a Mars bar, to serve as breakfast. Walking home, she stopped, on impulse, on the bridge on Deanhaugh Street and looked along the river. Yes, she reckoned, there was room to swing a cat on the footpath, and it would not have required superhuman strength to launch it on to her balcony. As she stood there, her neighbour's patio door opened and Griff stepped outside. He glanced up towards the bridge, saw her and waved: she returned his greeting and moved on, feeling guilty and embarrassed. *God, she thought, the other day he saw me seeing off my gentleman caller, now I'm getting in well past daylight in my party clothes. The man will think I'm a call-girl.*

When Edinburgh enjoys a night out, it takes time to recover: Leith Water Lane was deserted as she approached the building. She let herself in, then, happy that she had encountered nobody in the hallway, unlocked her flat and cancelled the alarm. As she did she noticed that she had mistakenly put it on night setting when she had gone out. 'Silly girl,' she muttered, 'but no harm done, the living-room sensor was still active.'

She laid the paper and the bag containing her makeshift breakfast on her desk and slipped out of her coat. She was on the point of heading for the shower when the phone rang. The red light was unblinking: no calls were waiting. She was on the point of letting the machine answer when she remembered that her watchers were back in place. She picked it up. 'Alex.'

Silence.

'Ah,' she said wearily, 'it's you again. Your timing's immaculate: I've just this minute walked in the door.'

Silence.

'Be that way if you want, but since you're on the line, let me give you a piece of my mind. That thing with the cat: how could you do something like that? You're not just a pervert, you know. You're a fucking sadist. I reckon when my friends catch up with you they'll have to send for the men in white coats.'

Silence.

'That's right: I reckon you're mental, friend. You know, until yesterday, you had me feeling just a wee bit guilty, in spite of myself. Not any more. Now I'm just one hundred per cent angry, you ba . . . '

The cord came over her head in an instant, knocking the phone out of her hand. She had no time to react before it was tight round her neck, choking her, cutting off her breath with a man's strength. It felt cold and soft, as if she was being throttled with a silken rope. Her defence mechanism and her martial-arts training kicked in at the same moment. She sagged back into the figure behind her, twisting and throwing her right elbow into his gut, and at the same time lifting a foot and slamming it down, hoping against hope that her high heel would find his instep, hearing a crunch and a gasp of pain as it did. The ligature slackened, only for a moment, but long enough for her to grasp it with her left hand, slipping her fingers under it, scratching herself but not caring. She pulled as hard as she could against it, but her attacker used her own momentum against her, turning her and forcing her down on to the floor. She felt his knee in the small of her back, she felt the pressure grow, she felt herself weaken, she heard a crashing sound, and as red spots swam before her eyes, she wondered if she would ever hear anything again.

And then the pressure was gone, and the weight was lifted from her. She lay there, her face pressed into the carpet, gasping for breath. Something was happening in the room: she heard snarling, the sound of flesh on flesh, and finally a crash, but she was too shocked and too dazed to be concerned by it. Her only interest at that moment lay in sucking air into her lungs. She lay there until the hammering of her heart subsided and its beat came back to something approaching normal.

She felt a hand on her shoulder. Instinctively, she turned away, then sprang lithely to her feet, kicking off her shoes to give her greater freedom of movement, holding her hands like blades before her, ready to kill, if she could.

Griff stood facing her, hands up, palms facing outwards. 'Whoa there, Alex,' he exclaimed. 'I'm the cavalry.' And then she saw the man on the floor behind him, unconscious on his back. Suddenly, her legs seemed no longer able to support her; she felt herself sag, but he grabbed her forearms, and held her steady. When she was ready, she shook herself free of his grip and stepped past him, to look down at the bloody face of Guy Luscomb.

'I don't understand any of this,' she

murmured, in a strange, weak voice that seemed to belong to someone else. 'How did he . . . How did you know what was happening?'

'DI Steele called me, and told me to get in here on the double.'

'Stevie Steele?'

'I'm a police officer, Alex: detective constable. I was in the force in Cape Town, until I applied for a transfer over here. I was asked to keep an eye on you when this whole thing began. You've hardly been out of my sight; I shadowed you last night till you went back to your friend's place.'

She looked at him, bewildered. 'But still, how did Stevie know he was here? There was the phone call.'

'He called you from inside the flat, on a mobile. They can pinpoint these things to within a few feet.' As he spoke, Alex heard a noise; she turned to see two uniformed officers as they came into the room. Behind them, through the entrance hall she saw her front door lying open, its frame shattered.

'I think I'd better give you a spare key,' she said, 'just in case you ever have to do this again.'

86

'You should have told us about that dead cat right away,' said Mario McGuire.

'I know,' Alex replied hoarsely, 'but when I agreed to let my dad put the phone tap back in place, I thought that was enough. I thought that the cat was just an ugly, perverted stunt.'

'No, it was a marker: it meant 'You're next.' If Neil or I had known about it we'd have moved you right out of there and put an officer in your place.'

'Who? Griff in a wig?' She began to laugh, but stopped abruptly, wincing from the pain in her throat.

'We might have been a bit more subtle than that. All kidding aside, the fact that DC Montell just happens to live next door to you was an enormous stroke of luck. We'd never have known either, if he hadn't happened to mention it to Stevie Steele. He noticed your name on the letterbox and, like any good copper, wondered if there was any link to the DCC.'

She smiled. 'The sod played his part well. He acted all surprised when I told him who my father is.'

'Good for him,' said Neil McIlhenney. 'When we set up the surveillance Stevie took him off normal duties and told him to stay at home for a few days, keeping an eye on you. We guessed you'd have thrown a moody if we'd told you that you had a bodyguard, so we kept it to ourselves.'

'If you'd told me it was that particular bodyguard,' Alex croaked, 'I might not have minded.' She pulled herself up against the pillows, and reached for the glass by the side of her bed. When she had been examined after the attack, the police doctor had insisted on hospitalisation: McIlhenney had arranged for her to be admitted to the very discreet Murrayfield Hospital rather than the Royal Infirmary, where the media would have been able to identify her without difficulty. He had been doubly careful: as extra insurance of privacy, she had been admitted as 'Mrs Louise McIlhenney'. She had spent most of the previous twenty-four hours asleep, and still felt woollen-headed from the sedative that the admitting doctor had insisted on giving her.

'Suppose you had moved me out,' she asked, 'what would you have got him for? Nuisance calls and housebreaking, that's all. The way it worked out, you've got him for attempted murder, and for hitting Griff's knuckles with his head, if you want to throw that in as well.'

'Actually,' McGuire told her, 'we think we've got him for a hell of a lot more than that. However, we don't need to go into it now. This is an unofficial visit from two friends: the formal stuff can wait until tomorrow, or even later, when you're rested and ready for it.'

'I'm ready for it now,' she insisted. 'I'd rather know than wonder about it.'

The detective looked at Sarah, who was standing by the window of the small room.

'What do you reckon, Doc?'

'I reckon she's okay,' she replied. 'When you arrived we were debating whether she should stay here for another night or come home to Gullane with me.'

'Well, if you're sure, Alex . . . '

'I'm sure, Mario: get bloody well on with it! What else has he done?'

'Relax, then, and try to stay calm as I'm telling you. Once we had him charged and locked up at Fettes, we ran a check with the National Criminal Intelligence Service: it's automatic now in a case like this. We discovered that there are three unsolved murders down south, two in London and one in Birmingham, each bearing striking similarities to the attack on you. The victims were all women in their twenties. They were all murdered in their homes, and in each case they had been receiving nuisance phone calls, although only one of them had reported the fact to the police. The investigating officers found out about the others from their friends. There were also a couple of incidents where dead animals were found near the victim's home.' McGuire paused. 'Do you want me to stop?'

'No; carry on.'

'Very well. In each case, the police are looking for a man who was in the victim's life but has disappeared. The names he used are Barry Richards, William Dell and Bernd Schmidt, but we know from DNA that they're all the same man. All three identities were borrowed for the purpose, from real and wholly innocent people, just as your attacker borrowed Guy Luscomb's name and professional background. When you were attacked, the real Mr Luscomb was at home in Suffolk with his wife and two children. The man we're holding is called Willis Gannett; a series of comparisons are being done even as we speak, but we've no doubt that what we have from Gannett will be a match for the other three cases.'

As the reality of what had happened to her hit her for the first time, Alex stared straight ahead, looking in the direction of the picture on the wall opposite, then at Sarah, but not focusing on either.

'Are you sure you're okay?' McIlhenney asked anxiously.

She nodded uncomfortably. 'Why me?' she whispered.

'You seem to fit the physical and social type he goes after,' he told her. 'Attractive, young, single, white, professional and successful: two of the other victims were solicitors and the third was a doctor.'

'Has he confessed?'

'We haven't put the other cases to him yet. That won't happen until we've got the DNA match, and when it does it'll be done by the investigators in each case. But he's told us everything about the attack on you.'

'Did you give him any option?'

'We offered him the choice of being interviewed by your dad when he gets back. He didn't fancy that. In fact it made his memory crystal clear. He didn't chuck the cat across the river, Alex; he planted it on your balcony. When you invited him to your flat, he watched you set the alarm as you left, and cancel it when you got back. Next morning when you were in the shower, he stole your spare keys . . . for future reference, hide them, don't leave them somewhere obvious . . . had them copied, and put them back. He made all the calls from Edinburgh, and when you and Gina were in together last weekend, he was watching you from the other side of the river.'

'But he went back to London. I phoned him there.'

'No, he didn't. Your call was diverted automatically on to his mobile. He moved out of the George, that was all, and into Jury's Inn, where he registered under his own name.'

'So he had access to my place all that time?'

'Yup. First to return the keys, then to plant the cat. He really doesn't like cats, by the way; that seems to be part of his ritual.'

She shuddered. 'I'm going to look a real idiot in court, when all this comes out in evidence.'

'It may not get to court,' said McGuire. 'The English murder charges will take priority; he'll get three life terms, probably with a full life tariff. The Lord Advocate may well decide to let your case remain open . . . unless you insist on prosecution, that is.'

'I'll have to think about that. My dad may insist on it, though. Does he know yet?'

'He knows there's been an arrest,' McIlhenney replied. 'I called him on his mobile. But I didn't give him any of the detail, or any of the other stuff. That can wait till he gets back, by which time I hope to hell we'll have turned Mr Gannett over to the people from Scotland Yard, and he's well out of his reach.'

'Forgive me, Neil, but the way I feel, I'd like my father to have some time with him.' Her face twisted into an unattractive grin. 'About thirty seconds would be enough: that's all he's good for.'

87

He had thought that there would be elation, but as the weekend had played itself out, he had found that the opposite was true. As in many of life's facets, the thrill was in the chase, not in its sad, squalid conclusion. For all his colleagues' congratulations, ultimately, he asked himself, what had he done? He had discovered three unknown, decades-old crimes, and in the process he had disturbed two graves. But that was all: he was no closer to the perpetrator than he had been when he started on his silly, selfish quest.

'Supercop my arse,' he whispered, as he gazed out of his window on to the frost-covered sports field outside.

The ringing telephone broke into his thoughts with the insistent sharpness of a dentist's drill. He picked it up. 'ACC Allan, Strathclyde, sir,' Crossley advised him. 'And Detective Superintendent McIlhenney's on his way up.'

'Put Max through, then send Neil in when I'm finished.' He waited for a few seconds.

'Jimmy? How goes it? Anything new on your skeleton?'

'I'm just waiting for word. I'll let you know when I get it.'

'Thanks, but in the meantime, I've got something to tell you. One of my very thorough detective officers may have found Ethel Ward, or Bothwell.'

'Have you, indeed? Where?'

'Bristol.'

'Eh? How the hell did she get there?'

'By train. Fifty years ago, about six weeks after the last sighting of Mrs Bothwell, the remains of a naked woman, cut into pieces and wrapped in sacking, were found in a pile of coal, which had just been unloaded at a depot down there. It was part of a consignment that started from Lanarkshire and picked up more trucks in South Yorkshire. They couldn't be certain where the body originated; details were passed to the old county constabulary up here, and to Leeds. There were press appeals, but the head was too badly crushed for an artist's impression, never mind photograph, so she was never identified. After a while, the police buried her in a local cemetery. She's still there, waiting to be dug up. Your friend Bert Ward is going to give us a DNA sample for comparison. If it's close, it's her.'

'Good for you, Max, and well done to your officer. Keep me informed.'

'Will do. Cheers, Jimmy.'

He replaced the phone in its cradle, with the strange, flat feeling inside him intensified rather than dissipated. *This has been pure self-indulgence for me*, he thought, *but for these poor women it was pure tragedy*.

There was a quiet knock on his door. 'Come,' he called out, and McIlhenney stepped into the room. He was carrying a bound folder in his right hand.

'Is that it, Neil?' Proud asked urgently.

'Yes, sir. The pathologist and his team finished

an hour ago; the ink's barely dry.'

'What are the findings? Have they established a cause of death?'

'They're saying multiple stab wounds, Chief. They're also saying that there is no doubt that the remains are around forty years old, and that the victim was aged over thirty.'

'And Annabelle Gentle was only twenty-nine. So Bothwell killed Montserrat and ran off with her.' Proud sighed. 'Damn it, I was hoping that Trudi Friend would be spared that. I'd rather we'd dug up her mother's body than find that she's a murderer.'

A strange smile spread over McIlhenney's face. 'Well, sir, that's the question. What the hell is she?'

'What do you mean?'

'I mean that the autopsy has established that the remains in the garden are those of a man. It looks as if we've found Claude Bothwell after all.'

88

'You had always been close to your step-son, hadn't you?'

Titus Armstead looked straight at the camera, unblinking. As he watched the monitor screen, listening to himself ask the question, Skinner was reminded of a television series called *Northern Exposure*, and an actor who played a retired astronaut. 'From the time his father was killed. Josh Archer and I met in Germany when we were both involved in NATO intelligence, and we became friends.'

'That would have been the early seventies?'

'Yes. Towards the end of the Nixon era.'

'You met Ormond Hassett there around the same time, didn't you?'

'We were in the same theatre of operations, yes.'

'Close colleagues?'

'Yes.'

'Would you say the three of you were ideologically compatible?'

'Hell, yes: we were all soldiers in the front line against Communism, spies in uniform. There were no liberals in our outfit.'

'After Germany, where did you go?'

'Ormond and I headed in the same direction. I was hauled back to Langley, to CIA headquarters, and he was posted to the embassy in Washington.'

'And Archer?'

'He stayed on in Germany for a while, but we kept in pretty close touch.'

'How close?'

'Very. Josh was a good source of information.'

'Are you saying that he was on your payroll?'

Armstead nodded at the camera. 'Yes.'

'Explain this to our viewers,' Skinner continued, 'and remember that I've got the gun. Why would a CIA operative want to recruit British intelligence officers as agents?'

'Simple. Back then we couldn't always rely on our allies to share and share alike. We were in the business of knowing everything, so we took steps to make sure that we did.'

'That'll go down well in London; scare the shit out of a few people too, I imagine. But let's move on a few years, to 1982. Hassett's an MP, an aide to the defence secretary, and he and Archer show up in Washington to make sure that your team are on-side over the Falklands operation.'

'Yeah, and Josh told me he was going to fight. I told him he was crazy, that there would be a load of casualties down there. Ormond could have gotten him a desk to ride, but he was set on action; dead set, the way it turned out. He knew what he was getting into, though: last time I saw him, he asked me to keep an eye on his family, if things did go the other way.'

'And you did?'

'I kept my word, yes. Whenever I was in England I went to see them up in Bakewell, just to make sure they were all right. After a few years, once the kids were grown and on their way in life, I asked Joan to marry me and she agreed.'

'You kept an eye on your step-son's career too.'

'I made sure he was all right, but I needn't have worried. He was a better soldier than his pop ever was, a real little terror. When he moved into intelligence and assumed a new identity, I knew about it and I took him under my wing even more. A few times we took care of things for each other.'

'So you weren't surprised when he approached you with a proposition?'

Armstead's eyes widened in surprise. 'Ah, no, you got that wrong. Moses didn't approach me. Ormond Hassett did. He came over here to this very house. He sat in that chair where you're sitting and he told me that there were people in London who were scared shitless about the future of their country. They saw it heading into a federal Europe, a super-grouping in which the role and purpose of the British Monarchy would become irrelevant, until it ceased to exist and Britain became, as he put it, the sort of mongrel state we're seeing in France, Spain, and even the United States. He said that the thing that scared them most was the fact that those standing in succession to the throne appeared to be in favour of the idea.'

'And his solution?'

'To take one of them out.'

'How?'

'That was what Ormond asked me. After I told him he was crazy, I told him that the most vulnerable point of attack was the student prince, but that anything that happened to him had to be seen very clearly to have happened from outside. That's where Pete Bassam's Albanian gang came into the picture. Kidnapping's national sport with these guys; the idea was, they grab him from his university, they hold him for ransom, but somewhere along the line he gets killed.'

'What did Hassett say to that?'

'That I was a fucking genius. He said that it was so simple it was beautiful. The way he saw it, not only would it take one of the problems . . . maybe the main problem . . . out of the equation, but in the scandal that followed the British government would be thrown out of office and replaced by a right-wing, anti-European, Conservative administration, with a commitment to withdraw from the EU and rescind the commitment to the Treaty of Rome.'

'With Ormond Hassett as one of its leading lights?'

'He didn't say that, but that's what he meant.'

'You know what, Titus?' Skinner heard himself chuckle. 'I think he'd have been right.'

Armstead said nothing: he simply looked at the camera and smiled.

'So when did Adam Arrow, Moses, come into it?' his interrogator continued.

'When I brought him in. Ormond didn't recruit him, I did. I visited him on the boat in London and I told him about our discussion. If he had told me I was a mad old man even to consider such a thing I'd have forgotten all about

456

it, but he didn't. He said that he shared Ormond's fears, and came on board. I knew we needed him, you see. I knew we needed extra insurance on the inside, within the British military, and someone to run the mercenary pick-up team at sea. With his okay, I told Ormond we were green for go, then I gave Moses Bassam's location and young Hassett was sent to activate him. The operation was under way.'

'Why did you give him the gun?'

'To take out young Hassett after the game; Moses thought he was a weakling, and that we couldn't trust him.'

'So where did Rudolph Sewell fit in?'

For the first time, Armstead's eyes left the camera lens and moved to the man beside it. 'Who the fuck is Rudolph Sewell?' he asked.

Skinner reached across and switched off the DVD player. 'Imagine that,' he said to Sir Evelyn Grey. 'As serious a player in the spooking game as Titus Armstead is, yet he's never heard of your head of counter-terrorism. But that's not all he didn't know: Moses and the Hassetts never told him about the fall-back plan, to try to wriggle out by blaming it all on Sewell if things went wrong. No wonder Miles was sent to kill him; too bad Moses was right and he wasn't up to the job, eh?'

'Indeed,' the director general agreed. 'Nevertheless, the warning you sent to Armstead through Ms Gower was a shrewd move: of some assistance to him.'

'Yes, but still, taking on a tough old bastard

like that with a knife was a pretty stupid thing to do.'

'How would you have handled it?'

The DCC scratched his chin. 'I'd probably have hidden in his garage and blown his head off when he came in to get his car.'

Grey smiled thinly. 'How glad we must be that you're on our side.'

Skinner was out of his chair like a flash, reaching across the table to slap him, back-handed, across the face, with such force that it sent him flying sideways out of his seat. 'I've never been on your side, you bastard, and I never will be. You're a traitor, the worst this country has ever seen. You've run this whole operation, from the very start, through your stooge, Ormond Hassett, and his son.'

He glared at Grey as he picked himself up. 'Sewell was never involved; he was a victim. We were led to believe that he had directed Amanda's team towards the theory that the Albanians were drugdealers, away from their real objective, but the truth was that he was following your orders. You had your fall-back story planned out, all four of you, and it involved setting up poor old Rudy, then throwing him to the wolves. After Adam Arrow was shot, he named him as the leader of the conspiracy, to protect you. I fell for it, bought the story and reported it to you when you debriefed me in Edinburgh after the attack. Christ, I've just called Sewell a mug. What does that make me?'

He glanced to his side, where Shannon and Amanda Dennis sat, then picked up a document

458

and thrust it towards the director general. 'Winston Chalmers isn't nearly as tough as he looks, Evelyn. This is his statement, witnessed by Dottie; I had the whole story out of him in about two and a half seconds. He admitted to me that he strangled Sewell, on your orders, before I had a chance to interrogate him. He throttled him and then fixed it to look like suicide. If I'd chosen to see Sewell first, he'd have done it the day before. He also released Miles Hassett, again on your orders, into Piers Frame's custody. As for Frame, he was astonished when you told him to pick up Hassett, but he didn't question it, not until I did, not until I told him the truth. When you ordered Chalmers to release Hassett to Frame, we were meant to assume that he had asked you to turn him over to M16. But that's not how it was, Evelyn, was it?' He glared at Grey. 'Was it?' he repeated.

'As you know, it was not,' the DG replied, wiping a trickle of blood from the corner of his mouth. 'I told Piers to go and get him, and to take Ormond with him so that Miles would know he was safe, that he wasn't going to be driven off to a convenient hole in the ground somewhere. Piers thought he was being released into his father's custody; given Ormond's intelligence background that was entirely reasonable.'

'Sure, but actually, he was just being released, to take care of the Titus Armstead problem, because by that time, you knew I would link him to his step-son, and through him, to you.'

Skinner looked around the room, the big

upstairs apartment in the Surrey safe-house, the same one in which he and Shannon had interrogated Miles Hassett a few days earlier. 'What do you think of your new accommodation, Evelyn? I hope you like it, because you're going to be here for a bloody long time.'

Anger seemed to ooze from the Scot's pores. 'I haven't hated many people in this life, but you're high up in the group. Why? For many reasons, but chief among them is the fact that you played me, man, and you did it by using my weakest point, my inflated bloody ego. Why the hell should you have invited me to run this inquiry? Logically, I should have been a witness not an investigator, but no, you said you had to have me, and that the Prime Minister himself had backed your choice. I was hardly even flattered at the time; I believed you, took it as my due, until doubt crept in, and I went to see the Prime Minister, to discover that he had no knowledge of my involvement.'

His eyes blazed. 'In fact, he had no knowledge of the conspiracy at all: he had been fed the official version, that it was a kidnap attempt, foiled at the last minute by his gallant forces. But once he knew what was happening, he opened all the doors for me, and he gave me access to the information I really needed, your own service record.

'Evelyn, you've been hovering behind these guys for the last thirty years: when Josh Archer and Ormond Hassett were getting to know each other in Germany, you were their boss, the senior NATO intelligence officer out there.

That's when the three of you got together. When young Moses Archer needed referees on his Sandhurst application, who did it? You and Ormond, that's who. Titus Armstead asked you both to do it, and you did. Anything for an old comrade's son, and to oblige a CIA buddy as well . . . and, who knows, the boy might prove useful in the future. You and Titus met in Germany too. All I have to do is run that tape some more and you'll hear him admit that, and the rest. You and he have been pursuing your own agenda ever since.'

Skinner resumed his seat, facing the prisoner. 'I knew all that before I went to America, and I had Piers Frame let you in on my plans. So you sent Miles to kill Titus . . . but I warned him through Merle Gower that he would be coming. From the moment I left the PM's room in the House of Commons you've all been under surveillance. Once I left Armstead with his video confession in the bag, I made a phone call and you were pulled in. The Americans are taking care of Titus, by the way: they set a team from the Dover air base on my signal and took him, and Miles Hassett's body, away in a black van.'

He leaned across the table again, until the spymaster flinched. 'You chose me to run your so-called investigation, Evelyn, because you thought you could control me. A soldier died in your plot after all, and you had Defence Intelligence to placate, so within your own community you had to be seen to do something. You planned to silence Sewell, and have Miles implicate him and name him as Bassam's

461

controller. Everything would have been closed off, and I'd have written a classic whitewash report for you to show to MoD and to take to the PM when you chose, to cover your arse.'

He looked at Shannon. 'That's what it was all about, Dottie, except for the part I've missed out: if Hassett had killed Armstead, he'd have been waiting for me to arrive, probably armed with part of the small arsenal that Titus kept in his cellar. That's why I had to leave you in Washington.' He gave a small involuntary shudder.

'The irony of it all, Inspector, is that it wouldn't have come to that, the whole thing would have worked, if only Miles hadn't embroidered his carefully planned story by saying that he met Sewell on the *Bulrush*. Rudy was never there: it was Arrow he met, Arrow who gave him Bassam's location, courtesy of his step-father. I'd never have gone looking for a houseboat but for that slip. If I hadn't, I'd never have found out who Moses Archer was, and I'd never have been led to Armstead, Ormond Hassett, and ultimately to the arch-traitor across the table there.'

'And to what conclusion?' Grey asked quietly. 'As you said of Sewell and Miles at the beginning of all this, they can hardly try Ormond and me for all this, and we're too important simply to disappear.'

'Wrong,' said Amanda Dennis, as she took a small-calibre pistol from the pocket of her grey jacket and shot him between the eyes.

89

Alex was at her desk, thinking about heading back to Gullane, when the phone rang. She had spent Sunday night there, and still did not feel quite ready to return to her flat. She had spent the morning giving Mario and Sammy Pye a formal statement, describing every stage and detail of her relationship with Willis Gannett. She had found parts of it embarrassing, but there had been the consolation that she was speaking to people she knew and could trust. Once she was finished, she had covered her bruises from the dressing-gown sash with cosmetic and had gone back to the office, blaming her brief absence on a sore throat, with the voice to back it up. No one related it to the stories in every Scottish newspaper about the arrest in Edinburgh of a suspected serial killer; only Mitch Laidlaw knew the truth and his discretion was absolute.

Work was the best therapy she knew. She was aware that it would not keep the horror at bay for ever, but the longer it did, the better she would be prepared to handle it. The worst thing for her was her father's absence. He had always been there for her; she had never experienced missing him, and she found it a strange and disturbing experience.

She picked up the phone, and gave her standard office answer. 'Hello, this is Alex.'

'Hi.' She recognised the voice at once: it was only a few days since she had heard it, recorded, on the phone. 'It's Raymond. I was wondering how you are?'

'I'm fine, thanks. What can I do for you?'

'I'd like to see you. Not for long, just a quick drink.'

'When?'

'Now, if you like: I'm downstairs in Saltire Court.'

As she thought about it, she realised that she was feeling a little guilty. She had suspected Raymond Weston; more than that, she had been ready to believe his guilt without question, something of which she was ashamed, personally and professionally. 'Okay,' she said. 'I'm finishing a couple of things here: go across to the Shakespeare and I'll join you in ten minutes.'

She took some time over her makeup and her hair; it had been a few years since she had seen him and it was important to her that she made the right impression. She did not want to appear vulnerable; she did not want to appear weak; she did not want to appear a victim.

The bar was quiet when she stepped inside; she spotted him at once, sitting at a table facing the door, with a second chair pulled up, and a pint of lager and a tall glass of what looked like orange juice waiting. He stood as she approached, offering her a smile, but no handshake. She was shocked when she saw him, and hoped that it did not show on her face. Raymond was at least four years younger than her: when she had met him, and enjoyed their brief fling, he had been a teenager. The man she was looking at could have passed for thirty: he was pale, gaunt, and there were dark circles under his eyes. He was well dressed and well groomed, but still he looked to her like someone who had packed too many heartbeats into too short a time.

'Hello,' she said, as she sat, then pointed to the tall glass. 'Is this for me?'

'Yes. I thought you'd probably be driving so I got you an OJ. You can have something stronger if you like.'

'No, that's fine. A perfect choice in fact. So, how are you?'

'I'm okay, thanks, and you're wondering why I've turned up like this.'

'True.'

'Well, first, I want to apologise for that message I left on your phone on Friday. It was inconsiderate, it was crude, and it was unforgivable. I'm sorry.'

'Apology accepted. In turn, please accept mine for suspecting you in the first place.' She raised an eyebrow. 'So what you said about me wasn't true?'

A flash of the younger Raymond shone in his eyes as he grinned. 'Oh, that's still true,' he exclaimed. 'It shouldn't have been told to an answering-machine; that was all.'

'Well, thank you, sir. We're not going back there, but for the record you were more than adequate yourself.'

'I'll cherish the compliment. The other thing I wanted to ask is, are you all right?'

There was something in the way he put his question that made her hand go to the scarf around her neck to check that it was covering the marks: they had darkened, and foundation cream no longer did the job. 'I'm fine,' she replied. 'Why shouldn't I be?'

'I went to see you on Saturday morning, Alex. I was going to drop by and apologise then. I admit I was pissed off at first that you should suspect me, but when I thought longer about it, I could see why you might have. I could see as well what sort of an effect calls like that can have on a person. So I thought I'd just turn up at your place with a box of chocolates and make amends. I was nearly there when this police car went crashing past, blues and twos, pulled up at your door, then hit the buzzer to get inside. I stood there for a while at the end of the street, watching, until they brought this bloke out, in handcuffs and with his face all bloody, chucked him in the back and drove him away. Then more cars arrived, and all I could think of was you and those fucking phone calls. Finally you came out with another guy, not looking your best, I have to say, and he drove you away. I did my head in all day, wondering, and then I read in yesterday's *Express* about the guy they've arrested, the serial killer from England.' His eyes widened a little. 'Was that him?'

She looked at him, then removed her scarf.

'God!' he whispered.

'Have you told anyone about this?' she asked.

'No.'

'Then do me a favour and keep it that way: the

press don't know about my involvement, and I don't want them to find out.'

'Not even Gina?'

'Not even her. I'll tell her myself if I feel the need.'

'Okay, I promise. I'm glad you are all right; you didn't look it on Saturday, that's for sure.'

'I didn't feel it either.'

'I'll bet.' He watched her as she drank, noting the tiny pain lines from her still swollen throat that suddenly appeared on her face. 'Take care of yourself, Alex,' he murmured. 'Having to be strong all the time can get you down.'

She replaced the scarf before anyone else in the pub noticed her. 'You too, Raymond. Gina tells me you've been making a mess of your life lately.'

'That's what the family believe, but it hasn't been all bad; my business side has been okay. Still, I admit that I've spent the last few years being a general fuck-up, hurting people without giving a damn about it. I'm going to change, though, I swear: I have to, or it'll be terminal.'

'If there's anything I can do to help you, I will.' She sipped some more orange juice. 'You've got my number, so keep in touch. Now, I've got to go: I promised my young brothers I'd let them annihilate me at some video game or other.'

She rose from the table. 'Before I do, though, there's something I just have to ask you. Why the hell are you wearing that mitten on your right hand?'

90

'I'm looking forward to spending Christmas in Italy with your mum,' said Paula Viareggio. 'Not just because I enjoy it there, but because it means she's accepted the way things are between you and me. I know she liked Maggie: she blamed me for the break-up for a while.'

'You're imagining that,' Mario protested. 'Mum's always had a soft spot for you.'

'It didn't stop her from giving me a few frosty looks when it all happened.'

'Babe, that's nothing to what she gave me at first. We can both thank Maggie for going to see her and telling her that our marriage had run its course, on both sides. She even told her that I'll never be one of nature's husbands, and that you and I are carved from the same stone.'

'How is Maggie?'

'Happier than I ever thought she'd be. I'm dead chuffed for her.' He headed the discussion in another direction. 'What do you want to do tonight? Movies?'

'Sure, there's a new Hugh Grant film on along at Ocean Terminal.'

'Will it be much different from any other Hugh Grant movie?'

'Probably not, but they're funny, as a rule.'

'Okay, let's try it. Pizza first?'

She laughed. 'You and your bloody pizzas; you don't have to prove to me that you're Italian.'

'I have to prove myself to you every day.'

She slid herself along the couch and pressed herself against him. 'Forget about the days,' she murmured. 'Concentrate on the nights.'

He grinned. 'I do . . . as hard as I can.' He kissed her softly, tenderly, feeling her flick his teeth with her tongue.

'Beats old Hugh any day,' she whispered, as they broke off. 'Maybe we'll just watch a DVD.'

'That's not a bad . . . ' The phone rang, insistently. 'Fuck!' he swore, as Paula picked it up. 'That is one of nature's bloody laws.'

'And another,' she said, holding it out, 'is that it's always for you. It's Neil.'

'Hi,' Mario grunted into the mouthpiece.

'Bad time?'

'Almost.'

'Sorry, but it's important.'

'Everything's important these days.'

'This is interesting too. I've just had a call from Alex Skinner: she wants to meet the two of us tonight, soon as possible, in a police office.'

'Why?'

'She didn't go into detail, but she said that it has a bearing on a live investigation.'

'I thought we'd sorted all her problems.'

'So did I, but this didn't sound like one of them. She told me that she was calling as a solicitor, not a pal. I've told her to be at Fettes in half an hour. Can you make it?'

'I'm afraid so. See you there.' He made his

best 'sorry' face for Paula, as he handed the phone back.

'Don't worry,' she told him, 'it'll keep. Bring in the pizzas when you get back.'

91

They were waiting in the head of CID's office when Alex arrived, just after seven thirty. She was not alone: the man with her was young, somewhere in the first half of his twenties, if a little careworn. He was taller than either McGuire or McIlhenney, but slightly built. He was well groomed, well dressed and, from his expression, very, very nervous.

'Thank you for seeing us so swiftly,' Alex began. McGuire looked at her and saw that this was not the boss's daughter; this was the razorsharp young lawyer he knew from his business dealings with what had just become Viareggio plc.

'This is Raymond Weston,' she said. 'He's here to make a voluntary statement, and I'm here as his solicitor. I know it's not my specialist field, but I've cleared my temporary involvement with my firm, since Raymond would only agree to come here if I accompanied him. Earlier this evening, in the course of what had begun as a social meeting, he told me something that put me in a difficult position as a lawyer, as an officer of the court and, not least, as my father's daughter. I've persuaded him that he must share it with you, but before we go any further, I'd like you to give me an undertaking.'

'What's that?' McIlhenney asked.

'Raymond is here as a witness, and also,

technically, as a complainant. However, what he's going to tell you will also incriminate him. I want you to promise me that he'll walk out of here tonight without charge, and with immunity from prosecution.'

'That's a big promise,' said McGuire.

'I know, but I'm confident you'll be able to make it.'

'If you're that confident, I'll agree in principle, subject to what Mr Weston has to tell us.'

Alex looked at her client. 'Raymond, I'm happy with that.'

'Are you sure? They might still renege.'

'They won't. They don't know it yet, but they need you. Take off your glove.'

Neither detective had noticed that he was wearing a mitten: it was hidden by his long-sleeved raincoat. He removed it and held up his right hand: it was heavily bandaged and the index finger was missing.

'I'm the man you were looking for,' he said, 'the man Gary Starr attacked. There never was a robbery.'

'We know that now,' said McIlhenney.

'I couldn't come forward at first; I thought I'd be charged with a hold-up.'

'I can see that, but there was another reason for staying in the long grass, Mr Weston, wasn't there?'

The tall young man nodded. 'I'm part-owner of a club in the West End called Secreto. About eighteen months ago, I was approached by a man named Edward Charnwood. He made me a proposition; he said that he had a supply of good-quality cocaine and that he was looking for distributors in nightclubs. He offered me a fifteen per cent cut of everything I sold to my customers.'

'Why did he approach you?'

'I have a history. I was arrested a few years ago and charged with involvement in the manufacture of Ecstasy. My father intervened on my behalf, I made a statement and the charges against me were dropped.'

'You were a Crown witness in the case?'

'It never made court; the other guy pleaded guilty.'

'So you accepted Charnwood's proposition?' asked McGuire

'I did. The arrangement was that I'd call in at Gary Starr's betting shop at eleven sharp every Friday morning, to pick up a supply and to hand over my takings. Starr was Charnwood's partner in the dealing. They staked me to the first week's supply and it went on from there. I had to account for all of it, to give them their eighty-five per cent and to show them what I had left if I hadn't sold out, although most weeks I did.'

'What prompted Starr to attack you?'

'Charnwood put his wife into the club one night to check up on me. I didn't know who she was, so I sold her a bag like any punter. She analysed it and discovered I'd been cutting the stuff, enough to skim an extra fifteen per cent. Next time I went into the shop, Starr was waiting for me. When I put the money on the counter, he grabbed my hand.' Weston's face

473

twisted at the memory. 'He stabbed me with an enormous knife, and he said, 'You cut us, we'll fucking cut you.' I screamed the place down but there was nobody there to hear me. Starr told me that I was getting off light. Charnwood had been planning to follow me home from the club one night and shoot me. He was still holding my hand: I went mad with the pain and hit him with the other one. He let me go and I ran for it. On the way out I bumped into the guy who worked there: I always had to wait for him to go before I went in. That day I was early, so I was waiting outside when he left. I recognised him: he does the door occasionally at the club.' He looked at McGuire and McIlhenney, from one to the other. 'That's my story. Do I have a deal?'

The head of CID looked at Alex. 'Your client, Miss Skinner, is the luckiest bastard in Edinburgh. One, Gary Starr saved his life: if Eddie Charnwood said he was going to shoot him, he'd have done it. Two, you're right: we need him in the witness box, not the dock.' He turned back to Weston. 'I'd like to be able to do Soraya Charnwood too. Did anyone see you sell her the baggie?'

'My partner, Double D.'

'He knew about the coke?'

'Yes.'

'Then he gets the same deal, if he identifies her. If he refuses, he's in the slammer. Jesus, you guys: I won't kid you, Weston, I'd really love to be locking you up. Your club's going to be closed down; you know that, don't you?'

'I'd guessed as much.'

'Do you appreciate the favour Alex has done you here?'

'Yes.'

'Well, do her one in return. Don't ever tell anybody of her involvement in this, and don't ever go near her again. She doesn't need her career, or her life, sullied by you. There's a bit of the deal I'm not going for, but you'll live with it, for I'm not in the mood to take any chances with you. I'm holding you here overnight: in the morning, you'll be taken to Leith police station where you'll make a formal statement to Detective Superintendent McIlhenney. After that, you'll be released on bail. Don't try and do a runner on us, for you'll never get far enough away.'

'I won't.' When Raymond Weston looked up he had tears in his eyes. 'Believe it or not, I do want to clean my life up.'

'I'm glad to hear it; just hold that thought overnight. Tell us where we can find your partner.'

'He'll be at the club in a couple of hours; his full name's Denis Diamond.'

'Okay,' said McGuire. 'You sit here while I call a custody officer. Neil, show Alex out, will you?'

'Sure.'

Alex stood, and patted Weston on the shoulder. 'The bit about not seeing me again, Raymond, that's not just from him. It comes from me too. I'd appreciate it.'

He nodded. 'I promise; and thanks. I do know what you've done for me here.'

She had stepped into the corridor when McIlhenney turned in the doorway. 'One more thing, Raymond: who treated your hand?'

The young man looked round at him. 'My father. He's a surgeon. Didn't you know?'

92

Nolan Weston made no attempt to hide his irritation. 'This is very inconvenient, Chief Superintendent,' he snapped, as McGuire was shown into his room. 'I was due in theatre at this precise moment, ten o'clock. I've had to reschedule and there will be a knock-on effect right through the day. They're not in-growing toe-nails either: all of my patients have cancer.'

McGuire looked at him; even though he was seated behind his desk he could tell that the man was as tall as his son. 'I'm sorry about that, Professor,' he said, 'but if I'd had you brought down to my office in Fettes, you'd have been even more inconvenienced.'

'What the hell do you mean by that?'

'Last night a colleague and I interviewed your son, Raymond. He was brought to see us by a solicitor. He no longer lives with you, I guess.'

'Why do you guess that?'

'Because you'd probably have noticed his absence. He was held in custody overnight. This morning he's making a formal statement at the Queen Charlotte Street statement in which he'll admit his involvement in the distribution of cocaine in his nightclub. I believe that you intervened on his behalf last time he was involved in a drugs situation. I'm here to warn you not to upset the apple-cart by trying that again. I've made enquiries; I know that you were at school with the Crown Agent and talked him into cutting Raymond a deal. I tell you, the Mafia could learn a lot from Edinburgh Academy when it comes to old-boy networking. Do you understand what I'm saying to you, sir?'

'Yes, I think I do. But if you think that you can bully me out of using everything at my disposal to help my son, you're underestimating me.'

'That's the last thing I'll do, Professor. You don't need to pull strings this time anyway. Raymond's agreed to be a Crown witness in the trial of his supplier, Edward Charnwood. His partner in the club has also agreed to co-operate. As a result neither of them can be prosecuted. So you stay out of this, sir, please.' Suddenly, McGuire grinned. 'If you do decide to stick your oar in, be warned: I've advised my chief constable of the circumstances of the case and the earlier one. I believe that he was head boy at the school when you were in first year. I think you'll find that he still has the power to give you lines, or worse.'

The ceiling light reflected for a moment on Weston's bald head as he leaned forward, staring frostily back at the detective. 'If you assure me that Raymond is in no jeopardy, I will stay my hand.'

McGuire's good humour vanished as quickly as it had come. 'Who or what do you think you are, Professor?' he snapped. 'Your son's the luckiest boy in town. Gary Starr may have maimed him but Eddie Charnwood was planning to put a bullet in his fucking head. And why? Because he couldn't be content with the money he was making feeding the habits of his club members; no, he had to wring out even more by adulterating the supply he was given. He's a criminal, and if he wasn't of use to me at this moment he'd be going away for seven years minimum, and neither you nor any of your pals could prevent it.'

'Do you have any children, Chief Superintendent?' Weston shot back.

'No.'

'Well, if you had, perhaps you wouldn't be so judgemental. If you think I would stand by and let him be victimised by the police or brutalised by a thug . . . ' He stopped, abruptly.

'He isn't a victim, he's a fucking predator. He preys on impressionable kids and turns them into addicts. You know, last night he was crying in my office, promising to go straight from now on. I'd love to believe him, but I've heard too many people say that to take it at face value. If you want to help him, be more involved with him, help him point his life in the right direction.'

He paused. 'But you've helped him already in this one, haven't you? You operated on him after Starr cut off his finger, you closed the stump off properly, and you dressed it, and you kept him hidden in your home, while we were looking all over bloody Edinburgh for him.'

'And what would you have done, in my shoes?'

'Given your skills,' McGuire replied, 'probably the same thing. But I'll tell you what I wouldn't have done. I wouldn't have operated on Gary Starr as well.'

'I have no idea what you mean.'

'Raymond told you what had happened; he admitted that last night. He said that he told you why Starr had done it too. And he said that you went absolutely crazy.'

'And wouldn't you?' Weston shouted. 'That boy is my flesh, my blood, my bone, and I love him whatever he does. To see him hurt, violated in that way by a pitiless animal like that little creep . . . What would you have done?'

'I'll tell you, man to man. I'd have gone to see him and I'd have beaten the living shit out of him, beaten him to within a centimetre of his life. But what I wouldn't have done is drugged him, tied him to his kitchen table, cut off his hands before his eyes with the carving knife that's missing from the set in his kitchen, then let the poor bastard watch his own death flow out of his veins. What sort of a pitiless animal does that? And how the hell, Professor,' McGuire's voice rose, 'did you know that Starr was a little man?'

The surgeon thrust himself to his feet, towering over the still-seated detective. 'Chief Superintendent,' he hissed, 'if you had a shred of evidence to back up that allegation, you would not have come here alone. We both know that. This interview is over.' He strode from the room, slamming the door behind him.

93

Bob Skinner stood against the boundary wall of the small churchyard, listening as the priest intoned the words of committal, watching as the oaken coffin was lowered into the grave. There were few mourners; most were people in their thirties dressed in traditional black. No one present wore any other type of uniform. As they dispersed, they filed respectfully past the bereaved family, shaking hands with the weeping mother, and with the sister, brother-in-law and two young nephews.

He waited until they were gone, and until Esther Craig caught his eye. She said a few words to her husband; he glanced in the Scot's direction, but did not follow as she walked towards him.

'Hello, Bob,' she said. 'Thank you for coming, and for helping us do this for Moses.'

'Please give my condolences to your family,' he replied. 'Whether you tell them what I have to say to you now, well, that's your choice to make.'

She looked at him, and saw his hesitancy. 'What is it?' she asked him quietly.

'There's something I held back from you when I saw you last, something you have a right to know. I told you that Moses died on an operation, in a fire-fight.'

'Yes.'

'That was true, but there were facts I left out, important facts. The situation, the thing that happened, well, through his beliefs, Moses found himself on what most people would regard as the wrong side.'

'Was Titus involved?'

The question took him by surprise. 'Yes, but why do you ask that?'

'Because my step-father is a very mysterious man, and because he and Moses were thick as thieves. Where Titus led, he would follow.'

'In this case, I'm not sure who followed whom; in truth I think they were both manipulated by someone else. But the most important thing I have to tell you is that I was involved in that operation, on the other side.'

'But you're a policeman, not a soldier?'

'Nonetheless, I was.' As he spoke he saw something in her eyes, and he knew that she was remembering the sensational news coverage from a time not long past, and details that he would rather had been kept secret.

'That thing,' she whispered. 'Your name; I remember now.'

'That thing,' he repeated.

'What happened?'

'Lots of things happened, and very fast. It was dark and we couldn't see the faces of the people we were shooting at, but we knew that we had to. When it was all over, I found that I'd shot my friend Adam, your brother Moses.'

She looked at him for moments that seemed to stretch out, as if a scream, a denunciation was building up within her. But when it broke, it was quiet, a question. 'Are you saying it was a mistake?'

'Friendly fire? No, not in the sense you mean. Your brother made a choice he believed to be right for his country. Unfortunately, it brought him into conflict with me. I will live the rest of my life regretting that it happened, but it did. The way I rationalise it is that I believe, as he did, that it was something I had to do.'

'I understand that,' the woman told him. 'I sense the same strength in you that was in Moses, although you're very different men. But there's one more thing I have to know, Bob. Why have you chosen to tell me this, when you didn't have to? I think I realise that it's not the sort of thing that's ever going to be made public. So why have you come?'

He shrugged his shoulders, then straightened them, as if he had thought the gesture might convey indifference. 'Because it would have been cowardly not to,' he replied, 'and also because, if things had been the other way round, it's what my friend would have found a way to do.'

94

'I'm sorry to call you up here again, James,' said Russell Goddard.

'Rector,' Proud replied sincerely, 'I wish I'd come up here more often over the years. What can I do for you?'

'You can ease my conscience, James.'

'About Claude Bothwell? You don't have any need to reproach yourself there. You were the key to finding him.'

'No, it's not about Adolf, damn the swine. This is something else; it has to do with the murder of that awful man Starr.'

'I beg your pardon.' Proud gazed at him, taken completely aback.

'There's something I should have told you before, but I couldn't believe that it was relevant. I was sure that there must be some explanation other than the most terrible one. Also, I was expecting to be asked about it by one of your people, but none of them ever called on me.' The chief constable thought that he detected a note of criticism.

'I'm an old man, James,' Mr Goddard continued, 'but I've retained most of my faculties. My vision is sharp, with glasses, and I'm remarkably fit for a man of my age. One of the ways I've achieved that is by remaining active. I go out on my bike during the day and sometimes I'll even go out for a walk at night, when the television starts to bore me. I did so on the night of Starr's death, at around ten thirty. I put on my coat and hat and I went out of the back door, for convenience. It's easier to lock and unlock and not so heavy. I was just stepping into the lane when I saw a man. He was opening the door to Starr's back garden. He didn't see me at all, but I got a good look at him, and in the moonlight, I recognised him. I knew him because we were reacquainted at a school reunion last Easter . . . one that you missed, incidentally.' The rector smiled.

'Who was it?' Proud asked, as eager as a schoolboy.

'It was young Nolan Weston, the surgeon.'

95

For once, the *Scotsman*, the *Herald* and the red-tops were united in their view on what was the lead story of the day. Their headlines trumpeted the appointment of Aileen de Marco, newly elected leader of the Labour Party in Scotland, as the country's First Minister, the youngest person to hold the office, and the first woman. Their reporters reviewed her meteoric career, praising her skill and her courage; the few who referred to her private life reached the conclusion that it was exactly that. Their leader writers decreed, again with unprecedented unanimity, that her accession signalled the start of a new era for the country, in which the old stagnant political attitudes and structures would be swept aside.

Sir James Proud studied them all, his satisfaction growing with each favourable finding. He ended with the *Herald*, and was about to set it aside when a headline leaped at him from the foot of page one: '*MI5 Chief and MP Die in Chopper Crash.*' Beneath it, there was a subhead: '*Tories Face By-election Test.*' He folded the newspaper and read.

Downing Street confirmed last night that Sir Evelyn Grey, the director general of MI5, was one of three victims of a helicopter crash in Salisbury Plain. Ormond

Hassett MP, the Conservative frontbench agriculture spokesman, also died when the craft went down and exploded on a flight from Surrey.

Sir Evelyn (64) had been head of the Security Service since 1989. He was regarded as one of the government's most influential advisers, and as the most powerful figure in the British intelligence community.

Announcing his death, the Prime Minister's Official Spokesman said, 'The gap left by Evelyn Grey's loss will be extremely hard to fill. The contribution which he has made to the national security cannot be over-estimated.'

Mr Hassett (63) had been MP for the Spindrift constituency since 1979. A grain merchant, he spent most of his career on the back benches, until his appointment to the agriculture team in 2003. It is understood that he and Sir Evelyn had been attending adjacent seminars in Surrey and that the intelligence chief had offered him a lift home. The pilot of the aircraft, Mr Winston Chalmers (37), was also killed.

'Now there's a tragedy,' the chief constable said aloud, sighing as he laid down the newspaper and turned to his in-tray.

Twenty minutes later, it was almost empty, when there was a knock on the door. 'Come,' he called out. It opened and his deputy entered. Proud beamed with pleasure as he rose from his chair. 'Bob, welcome back. I wasn't really expecting to see you again this year.' He picked up the *Scotsman*. 'I've just been reading about poor Evelyn Grey. Has that put your investigation on hold?'

Skinner stared at him blankly. 'Sorry?' he said.

'The helicopter crash: he was killed yesterday, along with a Tory MP. Didn't you know about it?'

The DCC recovered from his surprise, but not too quickly, he hoped. He replied with the literal truth: 'No. Nobody told me. A helicopter?'

'Yes.'

'Did they say how Hassett came to be on board?' The words were still echoing, when he realised that the chief had not named the dead parliamentarian.

It was a monumental gaffe: Proud knew that just as well as Skinner did. And then another possibility struck him. Had the slip been deliberate, even if only subconsciously? If so, it would make no difference, for the subject would never be raised by either of them again.

'You look tired, my friend,' said Proud Jimmy, as Skinner settled into the chair that faced across his desk. Then he corrected himself: 'No, you look exhausted.'

'I am. And, sweet Jesus, am I glad to be back.'

'You're finished in London?'

'Yes, it's all signed off: I've spent the last few days debriefing people, and being debriefed myself by some Americans.'

'Americans?'

'Yes, it went transatlantic. It was a very messy

488

business, Jimmy: it showed me that I'd never really understood treachery before. I found out a lot about myself, too, and a lot about other people that I hadn't really appreciated. As an example, I thought I knew Adam Arrow, but I didn't, not at all. I saw this ultra-hard, ultra-efficient wee soldier, but really I was looking at a guy who had spent his life trying to live up to his dad, until it made him into someone else's puppet. As another, I've always seen myself as a tough guy, but a moral one, yet Amanda Dennis was able to believe that another hard man would kill himself rather than face interrogation by me. That's not what happened, but knowing me, she still accepted it without question. There's one plus point, though. I found out that I can't shoot someone dead in cold blood, not any more at any rate. The Americans gave me the okay to do that when I'd completed my mission in Delaware, but when it came to it, I declined. Maybe that was only because I actually liked the bastard I was suppose to terminate, but I hope not.'

Proud looked at him. 'Is all this self-discovery going to change you, do you think?'

'I'd like to believe that it's going to make me a humbler, gentler, wiser and more considerate man. Yes, I'd like to believe that . . . but I don't know whether I'm actually capable of change.'

Proud thought of the report that still lay in his desk. 'O'Malley's worried that you might be approaching your breaking point,' he said.

Skinner stared at him, and then he laughed bitterly. 'That's ironic, Jimmy, because I'm worried that I don't have one. Will I tell you the conclusion that I've reached?' He carried on without waiting for an answer.

'I'm never going to do anything like this again. From now on, if someone says to me that I'm the only man for a really tough job, I'm going to ask him whether there's any part of 'Fuck off!' that he doesn't understand.

'I'm no longer interested in exploring my outer limits. My priorities are my family, which in time will come to include Aileen, and doing my job to the best of my ability, which means being a conventional police officer, not a fucking action man looking for every opportunity to stick his thick fucking head above the fucking parapet!'

'Does that mean you're ready to step into my chair?' the chief constable asked quietly.

'Only if I believe myself worthy of it, and I'm not sure that I am.'

'As someone who's sat in it for more years than most, I'm damn sure you are.'

'Thanks, but I've got to convince myself.'

'Then have some time off. That sabbatical that O'Malley recommended: six months; take it.'

'That's way too long, man.'

'Three, then.'

Skinner sighed. 'Okay, I will, but I'll go off at the end of January, to give me time to let the smoke clear and to let the new people settle into their new jobs. How's McGuire been so far?'

'Commanding. That post has been waiting for someone like him since you stepped up.'

'McIlhenney?'

'He's making his presence felt already; and not just felt but respected.'

'And Willie Haggerty? How's his situation?'

'He's going. The Dumfries and Galloway board met yesterday; he'll be their new chief constable.'

'Are you ready to confirm Brian Mackie as his successor?'

'Once Haggerty's appointment is announced officially, I will.'

'Christ, that means the wee Glaswegian will outrank me.'

Proud laughed. 'The solution to that lies with you. Go off on your leave and get your head sorted out.'

'Okay, I will. Now, let's change the subject to continuing investigations. Before I came in here I read that pile of papers on my desk. What have you done, in the light of your old rector's evidence?' Skinner asked.

'I took Mr Goddard to see McIlhenney, of course, as senior investigating officer, and he made a formal statement. What else would I have done?'

'Nothing. Absolutely nothing at all. What's happened since then?'

'Weston's been arrested and charged with murder. When his house was searched they found ampoules, virtually empty, but still bearing traces of the drugs that were used to subdue the man Starr.'

'The murder weapon?'

'That hasn't been found,' said Proud. 'However, they have obtained a set of knives that match those in the victim's kitchen and they've had a specialist look at the missing one. She's prepared to say, under oath, that the amputations were performed with an identical blade.'

'How will the old man stand up in the witness box?'

'Bob, there's every chance that he'll have taught the fathers of both prosecuting and defence counsel, not to mention the judge himself. He'll cow them with a glance.'

'Nice one.' Skinner chuckled. 'But, Jimmy, you keep saying 'they'. It's not: it's 'we'. It's your force, a team, and you're at its head. Man, while I've been away you've been leading from the front, all the way through.'

'Even if I was a little self-indulgent over Trudi Friend's mother?'

'What was self-indulgent about that? If I'd been here I'd probably have farmed it out to a detective constable down in Peebles and we'd have heard no more of it. You did it your way and you uncovered a mass murderer, or what was left of him. Congratulations, Chief.'

'I'd be grateful if you'd say all that to Chrissie: she still thinks I'm an old showboater who fell for a pretty face and went out of my way to impress her. As for your congratulations, I'm not sure I deserve them. I never did find Annabelle Gentle, and now, I never will.'

'Oh, no? What did you find?'

'Claude Bothwell, dead, and that was that: no trace of the women, no more leads, case closed.'

'What did you expect to find under that shed? One dead woman, or maybe two. If that had been the case it really would have been all over. But you didn't. You had a triangle, but not the way you expected.'

'I'm sorry,' said Proud. 'I'm old and tired. Walk me through this.'

'Rubbish,' Skinner retorted. 'You're an out-standing police officer, you can work it out for yourself. Jimmy, a few days ago I found myself telling a guy in the States that nothing in this world is unbelievable. Now I'm being shown the truth of that yet again. I think I know these women.'

96

'They come here every day that the weather permits,' the captain told him, as they walked at a leisurely pace up the narrow street. 'Except for Mondays, of course, when it is market day and very busy.' They passed cafés, a pâtisserie, boutiques and a shop offering leatherwear, before stepping out into a sun-bathed square. 'This is it, the Plaça de la Vila, the town place, you would say in English, and this is where they will be, at a table outside the Bar Isidre.'

'Thank you,' said Proud. 'And you're sure they have no idea I've been asking about them?'

'I haven't spoken to them, nor to anyone else. I have handled this thing myself.'

'Good.'

'I think it's best I leave you to wait for them. They won't be hard to recognise. They are still very beautiful.' The policeman gave a brief salute, then turned and walked out of the square, not by the way they had come but up another street that wound its way up towards the old church.

Proud settled into one of the plastic chairs outside Bar Isidre, his favourite spot in Torroella de Montgri. There were people around, but in January they were few, retired, mostly, from northern Europe, escaping dark winters; his ear caught German voices at the next table, English at another. He ordered a coffee and a croissant from the beaming proprietor, and settled in to wait. He knew the square well, and he loved its quirks. There was the big painted sundial on the south-facing aspect, three centuries old, set to Greenwich Mean Time, and ten minutes fast, whenever the sun shone. Opposite stood the restored building that was a care centre for the elderly, north-facing to keep it as naturally cool as possible in the summer months. Across the square there was the old exhibition hall with its spindly clock tower, topped by bells that rang the hour, then did it again two minutes later, in case anyone had missed them, or miscounted.

He dunked his croissant in his coffee, listening and counting as they rang twelve times. And then he saw them, two figures walking up the hill towards him, each slim, each elegant, each with silver hair piled on the top of her head.

They were chatting as they approached, the smaller of the two laughed at something, calling out a few words of Catalan: Proud could see her daughter in her face. He beckoned to the proprietor, whose name, printed on the sugar packets, was Josep. 'Would you ask the ladies,' he said quietly, 'if they would care to have coffee with me?'

He studied their faces as his invitation was conveyed, taking in their surprise, returning their glances with a smile and a nod, rising to his feet as they came to join him. 'Good morning,' he greeted them. 'I'm very pleased you can join me.'

'You're Scottish,' the taller woman observed.

'I am, from Edinburgh, as it happens.' He stood until they had taken seats, then resumed his own as Josep, unbidden, returned with two *cortados*, strong coffee with milk, served in small glasses. He smiled. 'My name is James Proud,' he began. 'Forty-two years ago, I was a reasonably good athlete. I won a trophy at my school sports, and you, Señora, presented it to me. I've never forgotten you; I think I'd have recognised you anywhere.'

Montserrat Rivera gasped; her mouth opened slightly and her face seemed to pale very slightly under her tan.

'What do you do in Edinburgh, Mr Proud?' Annabelle Gentle asked; her tone was more suspicious than curious.

'Actually, it's Sir James,' he said, almost shyly. 'I'm the chief constable.' Their eyes narrowed slightly. 'I can't tell you how pleased I am to have found you. I promised someone that I would.'

'And who is that?'

'Your daughter, Miss Gentle.'

'My . . . '

'Her name is Trudi Friend. She wants to find you because your granddaughter is getting married, and also, I believe, although she hasn't said as much, because she thinks it's time. She's waiting in L'Escala, at my friend's house, with my wife.'

Montserrat Rivera gazed at him coolly. 'If you've found us,' she murmured, 'you've found Bothwell. It was I. I killed him, not Annabelle. It was what he planned to do to me, I know it.'

'So do I,' Proud told her. 'He'd already killed two wives.'

Her eyes creased as she winced. 'Why does

that not surprise me? He was an evil man. Charming and handsome on the outside, but when you saw what was within him you knew that it was rotten. He beat me.'

'I know.'

'He stole from me; all the money my father gave me when we married.'

'I guessed that.'

'He seduced Annabelle. He told her I was a monster and that he was leaving me, after the school year was over. And then Annabelle and I met. She sought me out, because she wanted to see for herself how wicked I was. She bumped into me, as if by accident, in Patrick Thomson's, the department store. We got to talking; we met again, and eventually she told me the truth. I was no fool. He had bought a new hut for the garden.' Her eyebrows rose. 'Imagine!' She snorted. 'A man is leaving, yet he does that, and buys cement to make concrete to stand it on. I saw him dig in the garden, and I feared what he was digging. So when he tried to kill me, in the kitchen, with a hammer, I was ready for him, and I killed him.'

'No.' Proud was startled by Annabelle's forceful whisper. 'That's not what happened. We both killed him. I came to the house and we confronted him. He went berserk, flew into the most horrible rage I've ever seen, and he attacked us both with the hammer. I grabbed his arm and Montsy stabbed him. That's how it was. When it was dark we rolled him in a rug, we buried him in the hole he had made, and then, next day, Montsy mixed the concrete and covered him. When it was hard, we moved the shed on to it. When we were finished we left, made a run for it in his car and came here, to Spain, where there was no extradition.'

'You've lived here ever since?'

'Yes,' Montserrat replied. 'We went to work in my father's hotel, and when he retired, we took it over. We sold it five years ago; we're retired now.'

'What about Bothwell's money?'

'I found a bank-book for an account in the Channel Islands. I took back what was mine and left the rest. I still have the book.' She looked at him. 'So . . . Sir James . . . what happens now? You will have us arrested here, I suppose, and taken back to Scotland. There is extradition now.'

'And what the hell would I do that for, Señora?' Proud replied, with a chuckle. 'I'd be a laughing stock, prosecuting two lovely senior citizens for defending themselves from a double murderer. Even the very worst advocate in the country would be sure to get you acquitted, and your defence would be handled by the best.

'You know,' he continued, 'there have been times lately when my memory has let me down. In fact, it's happened again; blow me, but I've forgotten every word you two have just said to me. Apart from 'What happens now?' The answer to that is that, with your agreement, I will take both of you to L'Escala in my Hertz car, and Annabelle will be reunited with her daughter. How does that sound?'

As he looked at Annabelle Gentle, he saw her eyes fill, and overflow, not contradicting the smile on her face, but somehow enhancing it. 'It sounds,' she said, 'like something I should have done fifty years ago.'

'Good,' Proud declared. 'Let's get on with it.' He placed a ten-euro note on the table and waved to Josep. As he rose from his seat, he realised that, throughout a long career, he had never felt as good about anything he had done as he did at that moment.

As they turned to leave the sun-washed *plaça*, Montserrat Rivera linked her arm through his. 'You know,' she said, 'you really are a most remarkable detective.'

97

With her head on his shoulder, she gazed up at the bedroom's corniced ceiling, dimly lit by the lights of St Colme Street. 'Do you think the official residence is meant to be used for love trysts?' she murmured.

'This one's entirely legitimate . . . by twenty-first-century Western standards, at least.'

'I suppose so. It's a new year, you're divorced, and you're on your own with the kids and the nanny.'

'Yes, First Minister,' he replied, 'all of that is the case. And on Saturday, as agreed, you're coming to meet them.'

'God, maybe I should find that frightening. Until now we've only been contemplating a relationship; now we've got to make it work.'

He laid his hand on the flatness of her firm belly, feeling her warmth, feeling the velvet smoothness of her skin. 'We've made a pretty good start,' he said. 'You survived dinner with Alex this evening. How did you find her?'

'Terrifying at first, until we broke the ice; I'm glad she's a lawyer, not a politician.'

'She takes after her dad, so don't be so sure of that.'

'I'm sure of you, and that's enough.'

'You could still walk away, you know.'

'If I did, would it make your life easier?'

'Far from it: it would make me wish that I was

back in Titus Armstead's cellar in Dover, Delaware, and that Miles Hassett was waiting for me upstairs, with an assault rifle.'

She propped herself up on both elbows, staring at him. 'You mean that you'd want to be dead?'

'Hell, no; I mean that I'd want an excuse to take it out on some fucker, in a big way.'

She laughed wickedly. 'Now that's the Bob Skinner I've come to know and love.'

'You and everybody else. I had a call from your friend in Downing Street this afternoon, on my secure line. He offered me a job.'

Aileen sat bolt upright, twisting, staring down at him. 'He did what?' she exclaimed.

'He offered me a job,' Bob repeated. 'He asked me to become director general of MI5.'

'And what did you say?' she asked.

'There was a moment when he almost got the answer I told Jimmy Proud that I'd give in such circumstances.' He reached up and drew her back down beside him. 'But when I'd thought about it, I contented myself with thanking him, then telling him there are things I have to do in Scotland which are much more important that that.'

We do hope that you have enjoyed reading this large print book.

Did you know that all of our titles are available for purchase?

We publish a wide range of high quality large print books including:

Romances, Mysteries, Classics
General Fiction
Non Fiction and Westerns

Special interest titles available in large print are:

The Little Oxford Dictionary
Music Book
Song Book
Hymn Book
Service Book

Also available from us courtesy of Oxford University Press:

Young Readers' Dictionary
(large print edition)
Young Readers' Thesaurus
(large print edition)

For further information or a free brochure, please contact us at:
Ulverscroft Large Print Books Ltd.,
The Green, Bradgate Road, Anstey,
Leicester, LE7 7FU, England.
Tel: (00 44) 0116 236 4325
Fax: (00 44) 0116 234 0205

Other titles published by
The House of Ulverscroft:

FOR THE DEATH OF ME

Quintin Jardine

It's summertime in Monaco and Oz Blackstone, now an international film star, is
relaxing on the verandah of his opulent
mansion — one of three homes. Life doesn't
get much better than this. But somebody
knows where he lives . . . A struggling actor
talks him into buying the movie rights to his
novel for $50,000 — and a shocking trap is
laid . . . The demons of the past creep up on
Oz's life: blackmail and murder lurk in the
shadows. Oz travels to Singapore to find the
owner of some incriminating photographs,
but he's in grave danger of over-exposure.
And as organised crime muscles in on the
picture, Oz is getting perilously close to
losing a lot more than his wealth and
reputation . . .

LETHAL INTENT

Quintin Jardine

Somewhere in Scotland the unthinkable is about to happen, and for Deputy Chief Constable Bob Skinner, deadlines are looming. Four Albanian gangsters have infiltrated Edinburgh's underworld and MI5 are all over it, believing that they are moving into the city's drug scene. But do the criminals have a bigger objective? The son of a police officer is found dead in the shadow of Edinburgh Castle. Could it be a foretaste of things to come? Meanwhile, Scotland's First Minister plans to take over the police force . . . As the crimes begin to collide, fragments of truth are revealed. Skinner races against time to piece them together — but will it all come down to a shot in the dark?